I0636049

WEB OF LIES

BLOOD BOUND SERIES BOOK THREE

J.L. MYERS

A NEW ADULT PARANORMAL ROMANCE

BECOME A VIP AND GET A FREE BOOK!

J.L. Myers is giving away a free short prequel to the Blood Bound Series.
Use this link to get the your free copy.

http://bit.ly/JLFreePrequel

CHAPTER 1

Desperation lit like fire in my bones, threatening to ignite my world and shatter it to hell. Again. The spilled combination of blood that had filled once-living vampires and the damned choked up my throat. But my tears were reserved for the fast-fading life bleeding out before me. Lying in a growing pool of his own blood, Ty clenched his teeth, molars grinding. A seizure rode his body and his arms flung up, unable to stop the shakes. Unable to cover the leaking slice in his chest. Fear and longing drenched his golden irises as they met mine, cut off as his lids slammed shut. Horror seeped through my chest.

Time wasn't on our side.

Not now. Not then.

Because this wasn't the first reenactment and it sure as hell wouldn't be the last. The broken bodies and black and red smeared hall with all its shattered glass proved that. I couldn't stop the events from playing out any more than I could change the outcome. And I couldn't save my breaking heart from shattering all over again.

The second the seizure released, I tore into my wrist and pressed the bleeding punctures to Ty's lips. Vampire blood to heal a lycan, like our long-ago ancestors used to do before the two races became enemies. My blood pooled, mixing with his own until his mouth was so full that it overflowed. A vibrant torrent ran down either side of his face and I fought back tears. "Ty, *please.* You have to swallow."

Ty's pinched expression released, lids flinging open only to have his eyes roll back. His trembling body began convulsing. All the blood in his mouth streamed out like a river breaking its banks. My free arm clung tighter to him, willing his body to become still.

And then it did.

Every muscle that had been so taut and rapt with spasm released. My breath caught. Not in relief, but in fear. I knew what was next and I couldn't stop it. My arm shook as I extended my bleeding wrist.

"No. It's t-too late."

Despair drowned me as Ty faded into that dark tunnel. He was slipping away again, right before my very eyes. "No. You can't mean that. You're not dead. There's still time."

Ty's rough and warm hand shook as he pressed it against my cheek. Death mirrored across his face and wet breath rasped from his throat. It became shallower as tremors flooded back through his body. Yet his hand remained glued to my jaw, muscles bunching with dying strain up his arm. His thumb grazed my bottom lip. Resolve of the inevitable stole the sad longing from his stare. His mouth parted with the shadow of a smile. "I-I...l-love you, Amelia. I w-will always...l-love you."

"Ty, no!" I screamed, that same helplessness flooring my heart like a tidal wave. I clutched his shoulders and shook him. "Don't say that. Don't say goodbye."

In my violently shaking hands Ty's entire body turned limp. His eyes rolled back to the whites and the breath released from his lungs. Without warning, his body felt as if it weighed more than a freight train. He slipped from my grasp and his skull cracked against the marble.

I threw a leg over his hips. "Don't leave me!"

With the heel of my palm, I began compressions. But it wasn't enough. I needed voltage. The spark from my own hands like a defibrillator to jump-start his heart.

But there was nothing.

A rib cracked under my palms as my compressions became desperate. "Wake up!"

There was speaking and hands trying to pull me away. Faces I refused to register. Then screams. My own as I fought to stay with him. "Let me fucking go!"

The tunnel grew longer and Ty's lifeless body became smaller. "You're not dead. Move. Speak. *Do* something, Ty!"

All of a sudden, everything went quiet. All the talking and faces that had surrounded me were gone. Only the shattered windows remained, the bodies and the blood. Quiet peaceful carnage after the battle had run its course.

But this wasn't normal. This extension of time after his death. Something had changed. But I wasn't about to complain. Time was time. Even if it wasn't the way you wanted it.

Lost in the silence, I ran my hand down Ty's handsome face. A face that would never smile at me again. At those perfect lips that would never press against mine with unrestrained passion. I sniffed back tears, refusing to lose this clear view of him as my fingers stilled across his cheek.

Then the surroundings flickered, slow like a faulty bulb at first, then faster. No. Too soon. Not yet. The flashes strobed until there was nothing but light.

The surroundings were gone. Only Ty's body straddled beneath me remained.

Color and definition crept in: three dark walls, a curtain-covered doorway, and a daybed beneath me. Ty's skin was no longer shredded and soaked by black and red patches. Blood no longer painted his chin and neck. His old scars remained, but the hole in his chest was gone. Despite the lack of sound from a beating heart, his pale face held clear muscle control. He looked peaceful. Sleeping rather than dead.

Oh, God. *"Ty?"*

Ty's eyelids flung open and his crimson pupils drilled straight into my soul. In a flash, he arched up on the bed, ice-cold lips capturing mine. I kissed him back, consumed by the taste of him. A wish come true. Even in a warped dream. I let myself get lost in the moment. Lost in the fact that this was Ty and he was kissing me. That when I couldn't control my dreams, this could be the last physical connection beyond replaying his death.

Suddenly his cold, hard hands shot to my waist and flipped me onto my back. Now straddling me in nothing but jeans, Ty smiled, long fangs peeking through his pale lips. "Hello, beautiful."

I SHOT UP RAMROD STRAIGHT, forehead blistering hot and my entire body shivering as if submerged in an ice bath. I would have screamed, and in fact did during the first few times of waking from this nightmare. But now this was at least a twice a week occurrence. I blinked and saw his slack face. Then those red eyes opened behind my lids and I cringed. The memory of Ty haunted me, just as crippling now as it had been six months ago when he'd died in my arms.

The pain of his memory still struck my chest any time I let myself remember. And even when I didn't.

I blinked my vision clear in this dark expansive room while my stomach started its vocal demands. The surroundings were a mash of shadows created by dwindling sunlight. Gentle beams peeked around the closed drapes covering every window and the balcony terrace doors. So I'd slept in again. The wrought iron, wall-mounted lights were off and I didn't dare turn them on. I liked this space better in the dark, better when I could pretend I didn't know who this royal suite at the Armaya had belonged to. Caius. My traitorous, evil father. My attempted murderer.

And Ty's killer.

In the dark, I fought the impulse to cringe. After the damned invasion and mountain of deaths, the RVC—aka Royal Vampire Council—forced my move here. Their prized Oracle needed to be kept safe—at all times.

At least I hadn't had to move here alone. Kendrick had returned with me. And being an unexpected orphan, Dorian had decided to make the move too, now residing in a house outside the castle's walls in the surrounding vampire community. My relationship with Mom was a sore point and one I wasn't about to dwell on now.

"Stand aside."

Right on cue. The physical and mental, soul-deep bond I shared with Kendrick was on lockdown from my end, control mastered after hours, days, and months of practice. But the channel to Kendrick's thoughts and emotions was wide open, letting his worry for me stream through. If my dreams were clockwork, then so was Kendrick's reaction. He never failed to come to my aid after each waking nightmare.

"As you wish, my Lord," the two guards on rotation outside the main door to the Bathory suite answered in unison.

The door clicked open and the thick cut of hardwood swung inward with a long creak. From the bed, I couldn't see the entry, but light filtered in through the foyer and stole the shadows from the bedroom. Stone walls and expensively clothed and wooden furnishings filled the space. The almost empty bottles on my bedside glinted as if taunting me. Then the wrought iron lights beamed on as the door swung shut.

A shadow cast as Kendrick plowed through into my bedroom. Although he'd already been awake for hours, his eyes were bloodshot. The concern across his face was riddled with anguish, morphing into something else at the sight of my flimsy white tank.

I blushed as I swung my legs over the side of the bed and pulled my robe on. "You know I prefer the lights off." And not just because his leaked desire was getting to me.

Kendrick locked his emotions down without apology and met the side of my bed. His gaze flicked to the red-rimmed bottles then back to me. "You just don't want me to see you." He knelt and cupped my face, running a thumb down my cheek. "You're pale. Worse than yesterday. Worse than the day before. The week before that."

Here we go again. I pulled away and got up as my gut churned with a vengeance. My stride to the terrace doors—feet padding over stone then plush rug—made my head swim. I reached inside the robe's pocket, palming a wrapped chocolate. Though there was no point eating it. Chocolate used to be my remedy to take the edge off, to calm my nerves, or curb my depression. Too bad it no longer worked. A few weeks ago the taste had gone from rich, velvet heaven, to cardboard. As had every other kind of food. All vampires' need and want for food eventually declined, while their need for blood replaced it. I just hadn't expected it to happen to me so soon.

With my back turned I opened my jaw, closed it, then swallowed, trying to force my growing hunger as well as my fangs to recede. "Have you forgotten we're vampires?" I threw open the drapes and pushed the double doors open, stepping out onto the balcony. "Pale comes with the territory."

"Amelia, stop joking about it." Kendrick came over to stand behind me in the doorway. Though I wasn't facing him, I knew he was past leaning against the frame to reason with me. Instead, he stared at the back of my head, wishing I'd turn around, his fists clenched in frustration. "You've lost more weight, too. And those dark blue veins up and down your arms and legs aren't decoration. You're hungry. All the time. You know bottled human blood isn't cutting it. You need something more potent."

Yeah. Like pure vampire blood. I'd learned when I'd last lived here that royals did bottle and drink other Pure Blood's blood, aging it like you would with wine. It was a luxury. Not a staple diet.

Not normal.

Like anything about me was.

Still I couldn't take the leap and make the dietary change. Not yet. It was too close to breaking my promise to Ty. And besides, the hunger had been slowly building over the past six months. Another few weeks wouldn't kill me…

I gazed past the royal gardens and over the town at the snaking cobblestone paths, then at the winged angel fountain. Shop owners appeared to welcome customers with the growing shadows of fading twilight. Now that is was early August, the nights were beginning to grow longer, but twilight still lingered long past sunset each evening, bathing the Alaskan landscape with a gentle glow. The Victorian street lamps began to illuminate in a sparkling sequence. I considered jumping the balustrade, pajamas, robe, and bare feet, but I knew he'd just follow me. So our new and recurring ritual would continue. The pleading. The argument. The resulting stalemate that got neither of us what we wanted. So here we go. "Kendrick, I made Ty a promise and I'm not breaking it. Drinking live blood is not an option. Not until I find—"

The shatter of glass made me flinch and a familiar scent swelled from behind me. Fresh. Pure. Blood. I spun, fangs throbbing and saliva pooling. In one hand Kendrick clutched the neck of a jagged bottle. On the mirror side... Kendrick's shirt was slashed down the sleeve and a long cut marked the inside of his forearm. Blood gushed down to his fingertips, dripping onto the glass fragments at his feet with a hypnotic *pat, pat, pat.* Eyes frozen, I licked my bottom lip, my fangs grazing the top of my tongue. I took a step forward. Then another.

Sate your thirst. The unspoken words were desperate and full of hopeful regret. *Take the edge off.*

I paused and knelt, reaching out to touch his bloody hand. Tingles fired beneath my skin, but I didn't let any surface. Since being struck by lightning and absorbing the power into myself, I'd learned to master control over its volatile currents in most circumstances. Like right now.

In a trance, my tongue forked out, sliding over my bottom lip. The aroma was intoxicating. The color so vibrant, so pure. So free-pouring. Just like... I blinked and saw Ty, the pool of red and black streaming from his mouth and down his face as he lay across my lap. *"It's t-too late."*

I screamed a tortured cry and shot up, shoving Kendrick back over the threshold and into my suite. The static I now kept contained beneath my skin surged, and an escaping volt added momentum to the shove. He tripped back and landed on his butt as two guards stormed in. My raised hand halted the armed protection in their tracks—even the female guard I could see through the opening at the door who'd been about to pull the manual alarm. I jerked my chin at them. "Leave us. Now."

Reluctant but unable to refuse with the lack of threat, they each nodded and backed out of my suite, closing the door behind them.

I leveled a glare down at the guy who was supposed to be my best friend. My soul's mate. "How dare you. You have no right to—"

"To stop you from killing yourself?" Kendrick swiped his healing arm across his pants and reared off the stone. Anger boiled beneath his skin, adding color to his cheeks. "We've been searching for months, Amelia. Months. We've found squat." His broad hands clenched so hard his joints cracked. His next words were a hiss. "Because there is nothing to find. The mark Vanessa gave Ty after the cruise made it impossible for any damned blood to mix with poison from a bite. He can't come back. You know it. I know it. We're searching for a ghost. Risking our lives—"

"Get out." The words from my mouth were barely a whisper. My entire body trembled with rage. Eternal hope and promises were all I had left at this point. And no one was taking them away from me. No one. With a step forward, glass cracked under my foot and sliced in deep. The pain didn't register. Sparks swarmed across my skin, gathering with my bursting emotions. I was pushing one of the last people I had left away, but I couldn't stop. I couldn't give up. "I said, get the hell out!"

Kendrick set his jaw and turned away with a shake of his head. "Have it your way. *As always.*"

As I watched him leave without a backward glance, my heart broke all over again.

I sighed deep and long and took a step back into my bedroom. "Ouch!" Lancing spears shot from my foot up my leg, the embedded glass registering as my rage subsided. The grinding returned to my

9

gut too, feeling like rocks on spin cycle. Reality had come crashing through and I couldn't shut it out.

More than that, I didn't want to. My brain had started spinning and it wasn't about to stop. Before Kendrick's arrival I'd seen a change, and I needed to understand what it meant. Only when I tried to piece it together now, the details refused to gel. Starvation had turned my mind to soup.

Half delirious, I hobbled from stone to rug then stone again through the bedroom to the lounge room, opened the bar fridge and cradled three bottles to my chest. Returning to the balcony, I plonked down onto the cold stone with the glow of the waking city and twinkling stars. One, two, then three bottles were drained, stealing the grinding but not the hunger.

Same as usual.

I began picking the glass from my foot, scraping the closed and healing skin open to get to deeper shards. Each removed piece hurt as it slid free, and weeping blood coated my fingers. The smell of it mixed with what Kendrick had spilled mere feet away from where I sat. But I refused to think about him now. As the delirium lifted, the only thing on my mind was Ty.

That everyday feel of breathing underwater returned. Of drowning just a little more for every day Ty was out there. For every second his heart no longer beat with life.

Kendrick was wrong. There were signs that Ty was alive.

My recurring vision/nightmare was always backed up by hunger. This time had been no different. The hunger alone proved it was a vision. Or at least I hoped it did. But to what extent? The first part was a re-run of Ty's death. The same nightmare I'd been having for the last six months. A glimpse into the horrible past. The rest was new. Those piercing eyes. That kiss. My body tingled all over at the memory, while intruding uncertainty warred with the replaying images. What I'd dreamed didn't mean the rest was still to come. Didn't prove it was more than just my heartbreaking hopes manifesting in a recurring nightmare. A tease that would never come true. But I couldn't let myself believe that. Until there was undeniable proof, I had to believe that what I'd seen would play out. That I would find Ty in the state of being…alive. It was all I could cling to. All that could keep me here in the world of the living and breathing. And I wouldn't give up. Not now. Not ever. I'd find Ty and I'd save him, somehow.

I sighed and stood up, testing to see if I'd removed all the glass by putting weight on my foot. All good. As the light of a rising full moon cut through the growing darkness, I went to go back inside. Then something in my peripheral vision stopped me dead. My head whipped around and my eyes scanned—past the royal gardens below my balcony, through the winding roads and close-knit houses. As my senses heightened, I heard the gentle-flowing water from the angel fountain and the breeze rustling grass and trees in the distant field beyond.

There.

Cloaked in shadow beneath a billowing tree from the hue of nautical twilight was a dark figure. Strong, broad, tall, and totally familiar in what I swear was a black *Skillet* T-shirt. His red eyes shone like rubies and were leveled right on me. A target locked on its prey. Even from this distance, I was struck by the desire and smug calculation in that stare.

I tugged my robe closed, hugging my arms around my body. A war began between my head and my heart that raced as if I were running for my life. And maybe I should have been. But only one thing registered past the elation and panic.

Impossible.

The Armaya was impenetrable, heavily guarded and marked with wards that triggered a community-wide alarm.

For a moment I wondered if I was going deaf. But there was no panic and screaming in the streets. Residents casually made their way to opening shops and cafés. So the alternative? I was losing my ever-loving mind. And this wasn't the first time. The first imagined glimpse. I blinked hard and rubbed at my eyes. When I opened them, the shadow and its burning eyes were gone.

Just like every other time.

CHAPTER 2

I stood my ground, body weight slightly forward, knees bent in brace, and my sparking hand holding my ready whip. Exhaustion radiated like cancer through my body, daring me to give in.

Like that was an option.

Not with the formidable threat before me. Not with the reason that drove me here in the first place.

The body-fitting Under Armour gear I wore was damp, with more than sweat, and full of holes. Slash marks created by my opponent. An opponent who didn't look like he'd even considered giving in while I heaved for air.

Mr. Malau towered over my five and a half feet, built and ready to inflict pain. That I'd already experienced. Was far from free of.

The alpha's clawed hand swung, cutting into my arms. His other raked down my calf as I cartwheeled away. I hissed at the sting and lashed out my whip as I spun. My body cried out at the demand of speed and I faltered. Missed.

But he didn't.

Claws plunged into my back and my feet left the ground as I hurtled across the unlit expanse of this dusty barn. Instant bruises flared as I hit dirt, unable to land on my feet. Mr. Malau launched across the straw-littered dirt floor, razor-sharp teeth bared in anticipation.

At the last second, I managed to flick the butt of my silver whip up into his nose. With a crack and spurt of blood the alpha recoiled. Aching all over and woozy, I somehow caught the butt. I sent the spiked length on assault, the last few inches punching holes in his cheek.

The backlash didn't interrupt his driven intent as he unsheathed a long slice of metal from his back.

Oh shit.

Sunlight filtered through the web-laced window and caught on the silver machete in his hand. He growled, razored teeth lengthening as the holes in his cheek closed over. The flow of blood down his face stopped. "Good aim, but my neck would have been better."

Compliment *and* an insult. As usual. The thought of waving my hands like a white flag was tempting. But I wouldn't give in. "I won't miss next time."

I kinked my wrist back, rolling out my whip. Tapping energy stores I lunged, sending the silver length sailing through dust motes. The inch-long spikes jutted out, ready to claim his chest and curl down his muscled body.

But they never caught their target.

Instead, Mr. Malau shot straight up into the air and out of its path. He landed in front of me and cracked me in the jaw.

I stumbled, dazed, but corrected my balance, sending an electric fist into his gut.

With a snarl, he raised the machete as I cranked my whip back. It snaked around his ankle, pinging as it hit bone. He didn't even flinch, smashing the butt of the machete into my lip. Blood spurted across my face and eyes, and stars danced in my vision. I dropped like a stone.

Don't black out. Don't you dare black out.

I fought against unconsciousness and strung a foot of whip between my hands with the spikes pointed out. Then, blinded by blood, I shot up—

The cold slice of metal pierced my waist, coming clean out the other side. I gasped and staggered, the metal gliding free.

But I wouldn't fall.

Legs on fire, I forced them to hold my weight. Instant electricity fired across my body as my side leaked. Blue streamed for my palms and then it was all over.

Sawdust puffed up around my opponent as he fell and the machete went sailing. He coughed and winced, twitching as he levered up on his elbows.

Numbing warmth flared from the gash in my side, sending relief to my pain receptors. I glanced down as the gash slowly began to close. Given how blood deprived I was the fast healing wasn't possible. But the rules of reality didn't apply in a dreamscape; an alternate dreamlike reality a lycan could create while the person of interest was asleep. "Guess I misjudged your aim."

"We all make mistakes." Mr. Malau's hand appeared through the dust and I took hold, hauling him up. "Two straight hours of combat will do that to anyone. Even a damned would have been losing stamina by now. And that voltage? Good surprise. Didn't think you had it in you after the gutting."

I strolled over to the dusty window and did my best not to groan as I lowered onto a bale of hay. I watched as the many bruises and slash marks faded from my arms and legs. Still, the bone-deep exhaustion plaguing my body had my muscles cramping.

Even without vamp training at the Armaya earlier today—which Kendrick had conveniently skipped—the exhaustion was always there. And this real/not-real sparring wasn't helping. But I wasn't about to give it up. Our recurring training sessions, which Mr. Malau had been teaching for the past six months, were hidden away on an old acreage property in Wasilla, Alaska. Which he'd physically moved to soon after our alliance.

Beyond the window were thick trees that bordered the entire property and kept the noise of his lycan training from traveling to surrounding properties. Not that that was a concern with our dream-scape meetings. "How's Harper doing?" I asked absently.

Mr. Malau had started humming a tune—one he hummed often —but stalled at my question. "Still at boarding school in New Hampton."

There was a shift of crates followed by a slice of his machete being retrieved, but I kept my back turned. If Mr. Malau wanted to kill me, he'd have done it twenty times over by now.

Watching the wind-waving trees, I remembered his words the first time I'd asked. *"He's far away from all this mess. I've already lost one son and my wife. He's all I have left."* I sighed and recited the last words he'd said to me that first time. "Until we find Ty."

A scent similar to Ty's swelled behind me and I turned back around as the machete was sheathed. Mr. Malau looked down at me with thinly restrained hope. He handed over a folded piece of paper. "Troy's uncovered a nest in the town over. Palmer. No reported deaths there yet, but it's only about an hour's drive for them to make a trip to Anchorage."

Troy had been the beta in Ty's pack, but with Ty gone, he now held the acting alpha role, second only to Mr. Malau's instruction. I took the address, ignoring the ache in my bicep and forearm as I looked it over and handed it back. "So it's all a go for tomorrow, then?"

Mr. Malau nodded. "Troy's ready to go and has a few of my old pack to pick up any slack. Your cover will arrive after three a.m."

Old enemies or not, Mr. Malau and I were on the same team. At least until I found Ty alive…or dead.

A flash of Ty lifeless and decomposing struck my mind. I squeezed my eyes shut and cringed, my whole body twitching. A shuddering breath did little to shake off the cruel memory. "Great. We'll be there." I opened my eyes, dreading the broken, fitful sleep that awaited me. I stood up to recoil my whip— "Wait. If there haven't been deaths in Palmer, then how did Troy find the location?"

Mr. Malau smiled as if impressed. "There have been reports of animal attacks on livestock. A farmer who ran to check the commotion of his cows claimed an animal attacked him. Not a wolf or bear, but something else."

"*Ty,*" I breathed, my heart suddenly skipping with the possibility. It had to be. The damned didn't hunt animals, and even preferred vampire blood to human blood. After months of leads and raids, this was the first sign that Ty could still be out there somewhere. "If he's there, I'll find him. I'll bring him back. You have my word."

Mr. Malau nodded, no hint to his now closed emotions leaking through. "I know I do."

I SPENT the long daylight hours sleeping fitfully until I just couldn't stand to flip-flop in bed anymore. When six p.m. rolled around, my body and mind were on overdrive. The confusion over my Ty sighting refused to leave, while the next damned lead filled me with anticipation. Still, through it all, I couldn't forget my fight with Kendrick who'd now steered clear of me for the past twenty-four hours. The regret swimming in my chest grew by the second. And I couldn't stand it. I had to make things right. Before I took off.

Escaping my suite, I went to find Kendrick, a male and female guard tailing instantly without word. I needed to make up for our fight—even though I was still pissed at him for trying to force his blood on me. It was a jerk move. Totally out of line. But I understood why he'd done it. He needed to protect and look out for me. Regardless of how it affected our friendship. And regardless of how it endangered his life. Now with another venture to take me off castle grounds and far away, I needed to give him the choice. One I gave him every time the opportunity came up...because even though I knew he'd decide to come with, I needed him to know our friendship wouldn't suffer if he bowed out.

Almost an hour later I was still touring the labyrinth of gloomy castle corridors with no sign of him. A bone-deep ache had taken up residence in my legs and refused to budge. I reached out through the bond again and got nothing. Nada.

Heading toward the west end, a clatter from behind reminded me of the two guards that followed. Forever armed with swords at their backs, at least they were trailing behind with their hunger-inducing veins of blood. Being next in line for the Bathory throne came with unwanted inclusions and restrictions. Like not being able to leave the Armaya without guarded permission.

Too bad I didn't bend well to rules.

I blinked when I realized I was leaving the main hall again and going up the corridor that led straight past Caius's old office. It had been left to me after his imprisonment and proof of my lineage. But I'd never stepped foot inside since then. And as I shuddered at my closeness, I knew I wasn't about to now.

I picked up the pace, heading for the curved stone stairwell ending the corridor—and almost slammed straight into Kendrick as he shot out of Marcus's office. My heart jumped along with Kendrick's, and the male guard went to unsheathe his sword before relaxing at the familiar face. I tried to control my breathing and took a step back as his scent clouded my mind. "Kendrick, I ah, I've been looking for you." Now that I'd found him, my tongue felt tied over the apology I'd wanted to make. With his face shadowed between wall-mounted lanterns, I couldn't read his expression. I glanced at the closed door that was only a few yards from Caius's. "Been hanging out with Marcus?" Well duh.

Kendrick shrugged, his thoughts and emotions barred from me. "We were sourcing more weapons for the training rooms. The number of interested community members keeps going up."

Not surprising after what happened in Portsmouth. The Royal Vampire Council had responded quickly, setting up training rooms for royals inside the castle, and ones around the town for turned vamps too. Training wasn't compulsory, unless you were a close direct descendant to one of the seven crowned royals. Which put Kendrick and me both on the list. But none of that mattered right now. "Oh, that's good."

Heavy silence hung between us, stretching out in painful seconds. Kendrick broke the rising tension. "I'm gonna go get some breakfast. I'll see ya..." He began walking back toward the main hall and I picked up an unusual smell on him. Old, musky, and... something else.

My own stomach got vocal at the thought of food, and I dismissed the smell. That was the last thing on my mind now. "Wait!" Our friendship had been through the wringer. Still, I couldn't let him go.

Kendrick turned back around, and flickering lantern light flared

19

across his face. His expression was wary, but more so, it was tired and edged with thinly masked worry. As if my blood deprivation was sucking the life out of him, too. Yesterday's fight fast-forwarded through my head, ending with his words, *Have it your way. As always.*

I sighed deep and long, the anger I'd held onto for him fading. "I don't want to keep fighting with you. I hate it." I continued speaking through the bond. *But I can't break my word, not when there's a chance he's still out there.*

Kendrick's broad hand met my waist while his other drew my hair back over my shoulder. I held my breath as he stared down at me, seeing into my very soul. "I know," he said with a sigh, releasing my waist to take my hand. We walked on in silence, reaching the main arcing stairs that glistened with gilt rails and white marble steps.

Bright chandeliers lit our way as we climbed the stairs. Kendrick glanced sideways at me and spoke without moving his lips. *New lead?* I nodded, stomach knotting as my lips parted to tell him he didn't have to come. Kendrick spoke first. *You don't have to keep asking if I'm staying behind. Where you go, I go. That's it.* He paused at the landing that spanned either way down a luxurious, looping corridor to the royal suites. The guards waited further down the stairs. *I'll organize Dorian and Vanessa.* Which was easy now that Dorian lived in town and Vanessa visited frequently. *Meet time today?*

I hesitated, still wanting to talk him out of risking his life for me, again. *Three-thirty a.m., give or take.*

We'll be there. Kendrick leaned in close and pressed his lips to my cheek. "You know I can't change my mind. I'll be with you until the end. As always."

I VENTURED out of the Armaya's formidable castle doors and down the cobblestone steps, eyes heavy but wide open. Following the path that separated the castle from the gardens, I entered the graveyard, full of hidden anticipation. Holding my Vans in one hand, my bare feet skipped over pavers surrounded by white gravel. Red's song *Glass House* played from my iPod's loudspeaker while I weaved in and around tombs to my destination. In this labyrinth of stone, cement, and marble, I could almost pretend my entourage of two wasn't my constant and near-following shadow.

When I reached the graveyard's center, the path opened out to twelve massive tombs made of chiseled concrete and ivory columns. Each one had their family's name in stone above the doors, and housed the remains of deceased rulers and heirs.

I passed the first four and stopped at the fifth, mounting the marble stairs. The name marking this tomb was Ruthaven—one of the royal families The Council believed to be extinct. But I knew better. In this tomb lay the remains of the royal who'd been burned at the stake for loving a lycan. Ty's biological grandfather, and the vampire who impregnated the lycan who bore Ty's mother.

I grasped and lifted the bulky latch, then glanced over my shoulder at the guards. Now standing just below the steps on either side of the tomb, they clasped their hands in front of them and turned their backs. None of the rotating guards knew why I visited this tomb, and none had ever asked. It wasn't their place. In fact, no one bar Kendrick knew about Ty's heritage, and alive or not, it was going to stay that way.

With a deep breath, I pushed through the doors, stepped inside, and shut them behind me. My iPod was out of my pocket and now loudly playing *Alarm the Alarm* by Write This Down.

Although it was pitch black inside, I knew what surrounded me. Three walls with concrete blocks that covered the stacked remains of the old deceased. A few urns on heavy stands, and a large concrete coffin that centered the space. I knelt before the concrete box and caught the amulet Ty had given me in my palm. The one that had belonged to his mother before her death. *My heart in stone against yours.* I sighed deeply, then I said the same words I'd said during every visit here for the last six months. "If you're out there, I'll find you."

A hot hand struck out in the darkness, clutching my wrist. No sound accompanied the swift connection, but I knew that hard yet feminine grip. I stood slowly, drawing my shoulders back with a smile. A click of my iPod turned on the screen and lent dull light to the surrounding tomb. "With that alchemist mark blocking your scent," I whispered, "I almost thought you hadn't shown up. Couldn't even hear your heart beating with the music going."

"That was the plan," an equally quiet voice responded.

I met Marika's glowing golden eyes and began taking off my jeans and tank top. The rustle of her removing her own clothes was lost to the music. I re-dressed in my stashed Under Armour gear—in all black—and hid her not-so-concealing club-style clothes. Marika had been all-in from the start in our task of locating Ty. Which I could never even attempt to do while trapped inside the Armaya's walls.

The Council knew without doubt that I had been involved with Ty, a lycan, and our race's sworn enemy. It wasn't just taboo, it was illegal, punishable by death...at least in centuries past. If Caius had still held his royal throne and wasn't toiling away down in the royal cells, the old punishment may have been passed. With him not calling the shots and planting ideas in the reigning seven council members' ears, I'd been given leeway. Five of The Seven weren't happy about relaxing their harsh rules, but Uriel Aswind wouldn't have me burned or condemned. Not when I held the power to see their future and warn them of the dangers to come. And Marcus, the guy who'd come to my rescue more than once, and who was now the crowned Lord Vladimir, wouldn't let them entertain the idea of a harsh punishment. I was the only living descendant of the monster formerly known as Lord Caius Bathory. So in the end I'd gotten off easy.

But not without consequence.

Reside at the Armaya permanently and be guarded at all times… for my own safety, of course. Yes it was customary for ruling royals to have their shadows, but I knew there was more to mine. They were my 24/7 jailers without the bars.

Too bad for them I'm as stubborn as I am determined. And a promise is a promise.

Which is why my beautiful Ducati was stashed outside the perimeter under the seclusion of an old horse shelter, waiting to be brought to life and pushed to her limits. And why I was now pulling my blond hair up into a high ponytail and plaiting the end. With the length, it was a nuisance while fighting and moving at speed.

Fully re-dressed, my right hand clasped Marika's forearm, drawing any stray currents back into my chest. "Here we go again."

"We all have a role to play," Marika said, flashing her canines. "Plus I have a good feeling about this one." Her face scrunched up, eyes squeezing shut as her grip on my arm became strangling. Then her whole body shuddered, rippling in waves as her form morphed from tan skin and wavy black hair to my own chalky white complexion and straight blond tresses. The iPod screen blacked out, but I didn't need to light the kerosene torches between concrete blocks on the walls to know that the metamorphosis was impeccable. A perfect mirror image. After seeing the results in the past and getting away with this every week or so since being imprisoned inside the castle's walls, I knew it was flawless. A carbon copy. An imprint that only a born werewolf could create. Even her voice was a perfect match.

I handed over my Vans and Marika tipped one up, letting a small, velvet bag slide free. "There are five vials in each. Enough to stock up a bit."

Getting onto the Armaya's grounds wasn't an easy feat. A razor wire topped fence marked the first border that ran around the national-park-sized grounds. Then through a thick cover of forestry, a stone barrier surrounded the entire community. The gated entry was manned with armed guards at all times, and intermittent alchemist marks kept any non-vamps from crossing the threshold without setting off the alarm. But we had a way around that. Pure vampire blood. With just a small amount in her system, all Marika had to do was scale the walls and get to this tomb without being caught.

So far so good.

"It pains me to say that I'm getting used to your taste." Marika sighed and picked up my iPod as I shrank behind the door. "Good luck," she said. The sincerity in her voice and the hopeful gleam in her eyes was short lived. "Oh, and don't get yourself killed. If I get stuck here I'm personally blaming you." With a raised brow, she cut off the music and pushed through the doors. The dim glow of nautical twilight invaded the tomb as she strode out to my entourage. "I'm up for an afternoon of pampering in the spa with a night of pool in the bar. Who reckons they can drink me under the table?"

CHAPTER 3

*H*ope and jittery anticipation distracted me from what I'd convinced myself was travel fatigue. After two hours on my Ducati we'd finally reached our destination. "That's the place, then?"

I stood with my mismatched group on a hill in Palmer, still surprised at how far we'd come together. And at the lack of fights we'd had along the way. It was early morning, the glaring sun making an appearance over the horizon and forcing me to squint. Down below, a decrepit weatherboard shack ended a dirt road. Overgrown grass and weeds marked the front yard, and a metal chimney flue came up one exterior corner of the shack. No smoke came from the flue. With the beings that resided inside, it probably hadn't been used in a very long time. At least since humans lived there. Who'd probably been slaughtered in their sleep by the damned that now called this rundown place their home. Behind the house, thin leafless trees that trembled in a chilly breeze led on to thicker forestry. A secluded location where screams would be swallowed by the surrounding wilderness.

"Not much blood-sucker action during daylight," Troy sneered as he slid his second stake into the loop on his belt. A dagger was strapped to his thigh, and a silver machete—not unlike the one that had run me through yesterday—lay strapped against his back. "But after dark is a different story."

I wore a similar array of weapons, except that my specialty item was my silver, spiked whip. Kendrick's standout was a gun, not to be used in battle, but in the case of interrogation. He holstered it and sent me a determined smile. The look in his eyes said everything he kept inside. That he'd do anything to help me save Ty, and he hated that doing exactly that could end the romantic hope he still clung to for us.

I glanced away as Dorian flung out his crossbow and attached the CO_2 cartridge and a canister of silver bolts. "What are we waiting for?" He curled an arm around Vanessa's waist and kissed her with open passion. He hadn't missed a single mission to back me up—out of loyalty, and because he loved the action. "Let's go already."

Vanessa blushed, then dropped stomach-down to the ground, propping her sniper rifle on its stand before peering up at Troy. Since her grandfather's passing a few months back, she'd taken to joining in on our missions—rather than being just our reliable supplier of all that was sharp and deadly. "On your command."

Kendrick bristled as Troy glanced down to the two older lycans. Fully transformed, they weaved through the long grass, scoping out the property's exterior. He still wasn't used to letting Troy call the shots as our acting alpha. And he sure as shit didn't trust him for a second. Still, after months of following Troy's lead, I'd come to accept that we were protected under his command. As long as the operative was to find and rescue Ty, Troy would do anything to keep us safe—and had. For the time being, I trusted him with my life.

Troy, who watched the two lycans intently, nodded as if they'd just sent him a signal. "We're good to go."

In black stealth mode we left Vanessa and scaled down the hill like creeping shadows. Tapping his elemental ability, Dorian stirred up moisture from the grass, turning it into thick fog around us and the shack. Troy and Kendrick took the front door and Dorian and I headed to the back. The two lycans remained on opposite sides of the house, just in case any damned crashed out through the boarded-up windows. Which, despite the sun burning the damned on contact, had happened on a few past occasions. I shuddered at the memory. Compared to instant incineration, watching them die in a ball of flames while hearing their tortured screams was something I wish I'd never had to witness. Instant death was much less cruel.

Which is where Vanessa came in.

A tense moment passed, the only sound coming from chirping crickets and wind-whooshing trees. Dorian peered around the side of the house, waiting for Kendrick's signal from Troy. Then the nod came and we all sprang into action. I kicked the back door in and rushed inside. Down the hallway, Troy crashed through the front door at the same time. With Dorian right behind me and aiming the crossbow over my shoulder, I kicked open doors to check rooms. Empty. Next. Empty... Being a shack, this place was small. Only a few rooms marked the left and right of the hall. As I reached the center of the house, we were met by Troy and Kendrick. Troy clenched his jaw and shook his head. They hadn't found any lurking damned, either.

"Maybe they didn't come back here last night," I whispered.

"Or they didn't make it on time and fried on the way home," Kendrick said, leading us back down the hallway.

We stood in the front of the house that was the living/kitchen area. Soiled mattresses lined the floor to one side and the kitchenette was falling apart, most of the cabinet doors missing or hanging from one bracket.

Dorian went to the dinged-up fridge and cracked the door open. "Looks like we've got the wrong place." He shifted, exposing the contents of the fridge. A few loaves of bread had been shoved into the bottom of the shelfless fridge, and there was a carton of long-life milk. "Junkie squatters probably crash here."

"That's not for squatters." Troy paced around the living space, stomping over the thin mattresses. "It's for their captives. I saw them bring one back here the night before."

"Wait. What?" Piecing things together, I couldn't believe Troy's total disregard for life. "You saw them bring a victim back to feed on and you did *nothing*?"

Troy turned on me, gold eyes dangerous. "Rescuing that guy would have ruined our chances of finding Ty and likely gotten me killed, too. Then where would you all be?"

I glared up at him, clenching my fists. "Waiting didn't do us any favors, either. And now there's another life on our hands."

"Not our hands." Troy's lips curled over lengthening canines. "Theirs—"

My hand shot up, cutting off his spat words. "Shh." I held up my other hand so the amethyst pendant tied around my wrist was at his eye level. The same one Madam Rosalie had gifted me that warned of approaching threat. The purple stone was hot, sizzling against my wrist. We weren't alone.

Troy's eyes darted and he unsheathed his machete as I grabbed my dagger. Dorian and Kendrick spun their backs to us, ready for the approaching threat and palming their stakes. Seconds passed with all of us standing statue-still. My ears buzzed, hearing nothing but the old house creaking and branches scratching against the outside of the boarded-up windows. Without the amethyst still blazing against my skin, I would have called a false alarm. But we weren't alone. No way. My skin was crawling—

A crack of wood splintered from below and a trapdoor swung open. Troy went sailing as the mattress he'd been standing on became airborne. Eight damned streamed from the hole, fangs deadly and gazes starving.

Cornered back into the kitchen, I slashed out with my dagger as two rushed my way.

Kendrick's eyes clouded and he dove out of the hallway as sudden gale-force wind swept through the house.

The two damned coming after him got caught in the force and catapulted out the back door. Two almost undetectable whizzing sounds sliced through the air and cut off their screams as sunlight turned them into human-shaped fire torches. Vanessa and her rifle had taken out their voice boxes while the sun finished the job.

The two lycans ran in, one taking off down the trapdoor and the other backing up Troy and Dorian, who fought with everything they had.

I sent a bolt of lightning into one of my attacker's chest. In the same instant, I swung my dagger and slashed the other's throat. The gash sizzled from the silver but didn't slow his attack. And my voltage didn't stop the first damned from shooting back at me.

His claws sliced for my stomach as I retreated back. My Under Armour tank took the brunt of the damage—and I head-butted the top kitchen cabinet. Stars danced in my vision and my head became airy.

Bad move.

The two damned prowled forward, fangs ready to devour me— when they both let out a blood-curdling scream. Instant incineration took hold and they collapsed into a smoldering pile on the cracked linoleum.

Kendrick stood in their absence, a stake in each hand and ash across his face.

I couldn't hide my relief at his safety and my narrow escape. But there wasn't time for thanks.

In the living space, two damned still fought on. Dorian had abandoned his crossbow and was in hand-to-hand combat with a dagger and a stake. The first lycan joined his assault. The other damned had Troy pinned to a mattress, claws embedded in his neck and fangs closing in.

"Go back to hell," Troy snarled. His own canines bared as his arm between their bodies jerked, driving his stake into the damned's heart.

As ash exploded all over him, the second lycan sprang up from the trapdoor and clamped its jaw over the last damned's neck.

Panic cleared my mind and I rushed over. "Don't kill it!" This was the last damned, and Ty hadn't been here. I dared to touch the lycan's shoulder. "We need answers."

The damned seethed and bucked, trying to break free of those tough lycan jaws.

"Hold it still."

Troy and Dorian helped pin the damned down and Kendrick unholstered his gun. Two shots were plugged into each of the damned's arms and legs.

The damned's thrashing against Troy and Dorian instantly stopped, arms and legs no longer able to move in any way because of the alchemist marks etched into each of the silver bullets.

The lycan released the damned and, with a bark at Kendrick, moved aside. Troy hauled him to his jelly-like feet and twisted his dead arms behind his back.

Vanessa appeared through the door then, her own gun cocked. The ready tension fell from her face at seeing the controlled scene. "What now?"

Troy spat ash and smeared the remains across his face. He jerked his chin at one of the lycans then shifted his gaze to the trapdoor. "Any more down there?"

The lycan who'd done the investigating shook its head side to side then let out a whimper.

"No more damned," Troy said. "But there's something down there."

"Ty!" Without forethought, I vaulted down into the darkness below and adjusted my vampire night vision. The passageway was a tunnel made of dirty, cracked concrete.

The tunnels were created during a past human war, Kendrick spoke through the bond, even though he was following right behind me. *Most have been caved in for human safety, but I guess they missed this one.*

The tunnel opened onto a square, concrete area and I froze. Total and earth-shattering disappointment struck me first. A lantern on a card table highlighted everything in yellow-stained light. Ty wasn't here. Just a few wooden chairs, more mattresses, another tunnel that the lycan wouldn't have missed checking...

I gulped. And a small pile of dead bodies. The 'something' Troy had mentioned. These ones were fresh, judging from the mild smell of decay rising off them.

I wheeled around as the others entered, including Troy who carted along the immobile damned. A sudden flashback replayed every other useless lead we'd taken down. The damned. Their victims. Rage at not finding Ty, and for the murder of those poor humans, bubbled up my throat.

I shot forward and yanked the damned from Troy's grasp, swung him around, and slammed him into a chair. My fangs extended as I clutched his cheeks, letting my nails stab into the tough skin. Black blood welled around my fingertips and ran down my hand. "Where's the lycan? Where's Ty?"

With his face leaking, the damned glanced over my shoulder. "The lycans came with you, bitch."

"That's not what I mean, and you know it. But if you want to play hard…" Releasing his face, I took out my silver dagger and carved a gouge through his T-shirt from his sternum to his belly button.

The damned seethed as more black seeped out, the smell marrying with the decay in the air. He stared at me with hatred. "Heard we dropped one back in Portsmouth."

Troy growled over my shoulder. "And where is he now?"

The damned chuckled. "Worm meat. Six-feet under. Your guess is as good a mine."

"You disgusting excuse for—"

Kendrick pulled me back before I could drive the dagger through the damned's heart and aimed the gun there instead. *We need him alive, for now.* To the damned he said, "You're full of shit. Spill your guts or we'll spill them for you."

The damned laughed then sneered up at Kendrick. "Go on then, hero. Make a few more holes. Won't make me spill shit."

"We'll see about that." Kendrick removed the magazine and replaced it with a different one. Then he cocked and fired a single shot into the damned's chest.

The damned's smug expression pinched with agony and he wailed before clamping his teeth over his bottom lip. Even without the sound, his scrunching face showed just how much pain that single bullet was inflicting.

Kendrick shrugged. "Liquid silver. Explodes on impact." He

glanced at Vanessa with a grin. "Thanks to Vanessa. And now it's spreading through your insides like an oil leak. Feel like spilling now? Or do you need more encouraging?"

The damned hissed up in defiance as Kendrick re-cocked the gun and pressed the muzzle over his heart.

"Fine!" the damned shouted. "You want to know? Then here it is. We had our orders and we kept to them. The lycan was dragged from that hall and he wasn't wasted. Every drop was drained." He smiled as the leaking from my nail punctures on his face stopped. "Every last drop. The lycan's dead, bitch. I watched his dry body burn."

I stood in morbid disbelief as my held-back exhaustion resurfaced. Shocked out of words, Dorian and Kendrick took over, questioning the damned on the commander's identity and location. Kendrick even encouraged a response with a few more bullets. But all he got back was oily spit on his DCs and a flash of fangs. "If I open my mouth, I'm worse than dead," I barely heard the damned grate.

When Kendrick's gentle hand found mine, I shook myself free of the shock. The others kept up with the questions as he drew me away into the tunnel. *Don't believe what he said. This isn't the proof you've been waiting for.*

I frowned at him. *Why are you giving me hope? I know you want every time we do this to be the last. Why—*

Because I know you, Amelia. The strength and turmoil across his face had tears forming in my eyes. *I know you're not ready to give up. And accepting that damned's claim will only leave you wondering. Until there's no doubt, we go on. Okay?*

I squeezed his hand hard. I was running on borrowed hope and I wondered how much longer it would keep me going. "Okay."

Kendrick turned me back toward the concrete shell. "Now, it's time. Before Troy and Dorian kill the bastard with silver."

Seeing Troy with a dagger pointed at the damned's heart—that with a stab and twist could end its sorry life and reduce it to ash—I spoke up quick. "Back off, Troy."

His glare was akin to a stuck-up middle finger. He snarled and then lightly shoved Vanessa. "Let's start the cleanup. I hate watching this freak show."

Vanessa spared a glance for Dorian who nodded her off. Then he smiled down at the damned. "You're gonna wish you'd talked."

Before the damned could question why, Dorian lifted his trembling hand. At first the damned gagged, and then blood leaked from his eyes and mouth. I moved quick, collecting all the voltage that existed within my body and redirecting it to my palms. The damned hissed and I cupped his face and let the surface sparks go. This was going to hurt all three of us, but trial and error was the only option we had to test my ability to restore the damned. And so far each different attempt had failed.

Kendrick slipped back out the tunnel without a word. He never stayed to watch. And he'd never told me why, despite my questioning. Which left me guessing it had to do with watching me expend my already-deteriorating health and strength.

With him now gone, I let the full force of my voltage go. The instant drain on my body and mind was punishing, but I kept sending my power out. In my hands, the damned shook like he was strapped to an electric chair, the wood supporting his weight creaking in threat of giving way. His bleeding red eyes began to stream black. And the many bullet holes in his chest, arms, and legs poured out the glossy oil, too.

My hearing sharpened, waiting for that *thud-thud* I needed to hear. But it never came. Instead, the damned cried out as silver followed the leaking black from its chest. There was a distinct sizzle, like a piece of wood catching flame. Then his heart ignited—I could see it through his gray skin—and his entire body burst into hot coals.

Now alone in the empty tunnel, my legs trembled as I leaned against the cold, hard surface. The fatigue that imprisoned my body seeped deep down into my marrow. It poured like hot acid through my head and threatened to put my racing thoughts on standby. I should be so lucky.

Failed. Again.

At restoring. At finding Ty—who, if what the damned had claimed was true, was dead and gone. Guilt sat like a red-hot fire poker in my heart. Pain I deserved a thousand times over.

Sliding down the wall to the dirty ground, smoke carried on a faint breeze down through the trapdoor. The others were out back, burning the human victims' remains and clearing out all the damned ash from inside the shack. Covering our tracks was a step we never skipped. Like we needed to deal with human suspicion on top of everything else.

With a groan, I shoved myself upright and walked into the open concrete space. The disappointment of another dead end felt like a suffocating bag trapped over my head. After the animal attack reports, my hope had soared. Now it was shattered to oblivion.

I reached for the lantern and twisted the knob to cut off the kerosene. Just before the dark ate up the light completely, the pendant at my wrist blazed. A shadow moved in my peripheral vision.

The outline of a person.

I twisted the knob back and dying light lent some visibility to the dark as I spun.

There, in the tunnel that continued out of this space to who knows where, was a set of red eyes. And was that jeans and hunting boots? The guy inched forward, smiling with extended fangs as his face caught the fading light.

My fried heart back-flipped beneath my ribs and tingles inundated my body. Pulse surging, my breath caught. *"Ty?"* I took a slow step forward. The guy's hair was black and his shadowed features revealed the face of my dreams and my nightmares. But that flesh was pale and ghastly. And that deadly stare filled with cruel intent made me shudder. "Is it really you?"

Ty lunged and I tripped over my Vans, smashing back into the card table. With a chorus of noise, I caught myself in a crouch that made my knees creak as I freed a stake from my belt.

Not fast enough.

Not even close, thanks to my dead-blood diet.

He caught my wrists and hauled me up, smashing my hands into the wall hard enough to splinter bone. As I dropped the stake, his face lowered before mine, red eyes tunneling into my own.

I gasped at the face before me, getting a lungful of a smoky staleness off his clothes. A total stranger stared back at me. The hair was brown, not black, the face structure narrow, not angled, and lips thin, not full and irresistible. A stark contrast to Ty. My mind was playing tricks on me.

Sudden fight bubbled inside of me, throwing off my fatigue. I thrashed against the stranger as his jaw cracked open and his fangs neared my neck.

Sudden noise echoed down into the concrete shell from the shack. Kendrick was rushing our way at breakneck speed.

"I'll come back for you," the damned said as I struggled to get free. "But first—" His smile was sinister. Then he gouged his claws into my stomach, cutting deep and fast. "Getaway distraction."

My eyes squeezed shut at the pain, and the hold on my wrists released. I fell, hearing a rush of air as the damned fled and I curled in on myself.

Kendrick shot in through the other tunnel then and rushed to my side. Panic struck his face at the gush of blood pouring from my abdomen. He invaded my mind, replaying the scene I'd just escaped from. The need to chase down the damned warred with his need to help me. My well-being won out a second later and he bit into his wrist. "Take it. Quick."

"No," I croaked, shoving his arm aside. Pain swamped out from the gouges to every one of my pain receptors and I was losing blood fast. My shredded tank was drenched and glued to my lacerated skin with all the sticky wetness. But even though my mouth watered and my gut spasmed with hunger, I wasn't breaking my promise. Not again. "No...live blood."

"Dammit, Amelia. There's stubborn and there's just plain stupid."

Dorian and Troy raced in and I faked stability, nodding down the other tunnel. "It went that way."

Troy wavered for a nanosecond then took off after the damned.

Dorian remained and knelt beside me to place his hands over my open wounds. Worry creased his forehead, but the rest of his expression was resigned. "Won't take blood, then?"

As always, he knew me too well. I bit my lip and shook my head. Fleeting or not, as long as there was a chance Ty was still out there, I wasn't taking anyone's vein, human, vampire, nobody. "It's —" I gasped as pain lanced through me. Part of it was the regeneration process trying to kick in; the other part was more to do with the extensive injury. "It's not going to kill me." I coughed and

37

blood sprayed from my mouth across their faces. "Probably not going to."

Kendrick swore and Dorian called out, "Vanessa!" Then his hands lifted a fraction, trembling as he stared intently down at them. The pool of blood, my blood, that I now sat in began to recede, drawing back up and into the gaping gouges across my stomach.

When most of it had returned, Vanessa appeared through the tunnel from the shack. She rolled her eyes and handed me a bottle of blood. "Good thing Kendrick forces me to bring supplies. Every. Single. Time."

I drank the full bottle and winced as the seriously slow healing process kicked in. Under normal circumstances my lacerations would be stretching back together over my exposed insides. But with my deteriorating health and constant fatigue? It was like watching a fast-forwarded documentary on serious slow-mo.

Dorian kept his hold though, the quaking in his hands vibrating up his arms. Vanessa forced three more bottles on me then supported Dorian's shoulders as the whites in his eyes turned bloodshot.

The wound was halfway closed, but still bloody and ugly. I reached out to still Dorian's hands. "I'm okay. You can stop—"

Dorian scowled down at me as if to say, *shut up and let me finish.* And I knew better than to argue. Blood related or not, I was his sister and he'd always do right by me—even if it hurt him in the process. As red-tainted tears collected in the corners of his eyes, the last laceration knitted back together.

Dorian released his hold on my blood and rolled back onto his butt. "You're welcome."

"Thanks." I didn't know what else to say.

Vanessa helped Dorian up and they both nodded, and then jogged down the tunnel after Troy.

I glanced up at Kendrick, who was clearly pissed that I'd refused his blood. "I'm sorry. You know it's not about you."

"No. It's about Ty."

Of course it was about Ty. That was the reason we were all here. In a flash I saw his face as I'd turned the lantern off. Beyond any and all doubt, I'd believed it was him. *I'm losing my mind.* I had to be. Since Ty's death, I'd seen him over and over again. Most of the time in random places, including at the Armaya like yesterday, and also at past raids. But every time I'd been wrong. Imagining things. Seeing a ghost. A memory I couldn't grasp onto. "I thought...I mean, I was so sure this time."

Kendrick leaned back on his haunches, face stony. "Your mind is playing tricks on you." *Because you're not functioning on the bottled shit,* the afterthought leaked through the bond. "You're not crazy."

The leaked thought affected me more than his spoken words. When had he become my caretaker? My existence was my own, not his. Irritated, I got to my feet with a groan and dusted off my Under Armour leggings. I would never agree to stop seeking out Ty's existence, and I would never stop believing he could be out there.

Dorian resurfaced from the other tunnel then with Vanessa. "The tunnel splits further along."

Troy appeared behind him and flipped a dagger with one hand. "Blood sucker got away."

CHAPTER 4

The next day I paced in my suite, waiting for Kendrick to retrieve me for the big event of Caius's trial as two a.m. approached. Vampire early afternoon at the Armaya, and the time these things usually took place. My legs ached like someone had mistaken them for punching bags. The aftermath of yesterday's shack invasion and, if I was being totally honest, a result of refusing live blood.

But none of that was on my mind right now. Because the day I'd been waiting for was finally here. Caius would now be held accountable for plotting against the Royal Vampire Council and commanding the slaughter of his own kind. Sickening trepidation at having to see Ty's murderer kept my legs moving across the stone in my suite's foyer. Circling the table that centered the hoop-shaped space while my long, black gown swished, my hate for my own father soared and I could barely stand that his blood ran in my veins.

A double knock had me springing the main door inward. "Thank God you're—" But it wasn't Kendrick. "Mom?"

Dressed for the formal occasion in floor-length silk, she was poised perfection. But her guarded expression told another story. Her arms bent before her and tight-clasped hands confirmed it.

Since being relocated to the Armaya the day after Ty's funeral, I hadn't spoken a word to her. I hadn't let her explain anything before leaving, either. Back then I'd been too pissed off. Because her decisions and involvement with Caius had made me the target for that monster's experiments. It had changed who and what I was. It had taken my twin brother's belief in who he was and where he'd come from and ripped his world apart. And inadvertently, all of this was linked to Caius killing Ty.

"What are you doing here?"

Mom swallowed, looking so unsure and maybe even scared. "I needed to be here," she said in a shaky voice. "I needed to hear the evidence and charges against Caius. And I wanted to talk to you about…everything."

Amelia, you've got time, Kendrick spoke without preamble through the bond, his own distant relationship with his mom encouraging his words. *At least see what she has to say.*

"I don't understand why he did what he did," Mom went on when I didn't respond. "What your father's justification could be—"

"He is *not* my father." I yanked her in and slammed the door, my jaw clenching. Enough was going on today with the trial, but I'd put this encounter off for too long. It was time to hear her version of events. But first… "You are never, *never* to call that monster my father."

Mom shook her head and glanced down with glistening eyes at her tied hands. "You don't know your fath—" She cleared her throat as I glared. "I mean Caius, like I do. What happened at your Oracle ceremony…you and your brother have blindly accepted the Royal Vampire Council's viewpoint. You haven't even considered—"

"Dorian's not yours. He never was."

Mom recoiled with a gasp as though I'd slapped her. Her mouth opened, then it closed with a deep breath. Her eyes became distant, her head shaking back and forth. "He is my son. Every memory I have of the both of you includes him. Blood or not, I will always see him as mine. I raised him. I love him."

"And when we were first born..." I strode past her into the sitting room and, minding the skirt of my gown that I so badly wanted to shred to relieve some tension, I lowered onto the couch. "The son Caius tore from your body, that was Dorian?"

With a gulp, Mom walked on shaky legs to sit on a patterned wing chair opposite me. She folded her hands in her lap. "You saw it in a vision?" I nodded. "Then you know that I was human until then." Another nod. "My memory of that night and the first few weeks of your lives is foggy at best. I remember two blood-covered babies, a boy and a girl. My next clear memory is of the both of you about a week or two later."

Mom's memory troubles probably had more to do with Caius compelling her to forget things he didn't want her to see. But I didn't need to point that out. From the look in Mom's teary eyes, she suspected the same thing. Still, there was something else I'd witnessed in my vision. "If you had nothing to do with Caius's plans, then why did you force him to infect us?"

Mom swallowed as though she were trying to clear a brick from her throat. "I want to start from the beginning. You have a right to know everything." She laced her folded hands together, fingers squeezing tight enough that her bones showed through her pale skin. "I met Caius eighteen years ago when I was twenty-five. He was older, though I didn't know by quite how much—not until he revealed what he was to me." She glanced out the window and into the night-cloaked sky where a fat moon slowly sank. "I guess I should have thought about my future then. But I was so in love. Vampire, human. It didn't matter to me. Even having to give up college and leave my family to move to the Alaskan wilderness didn't. Nothing did. Not until I became pregnant. All of a sudden my life changed. The decisions I made no longer affected me alone. They would affect the lives growing inside of me. I wasn't known to the RVC. I wouldn't have been accepted into the Armaya as anything but a donor. But children born heirs to the throne?" Mom's gaze lifted as she came around the glossy-white coffee table and perched on the edge. She stared down at my hands as if she wanted to hold them but knew the touch would be unwelcome. "If they found out Caius was hiding his own children, they'd force you into their world. Decide your futures and take away your rights to become whatever you eventually chose to be. I'd already locked myself away from the outside world, but I didn't want an imprisoned life to be pushed onto either of you."

"So Caius devised a plan to make us appear human."

"Eventually, yes." Mom nodded. "He had been working on his experiments and thought he could create a serum that would keep you from developing vampire characteristics. But it was my badgering that forced him into the idea. Caius tried to talk me out of it, tried to convince me that living as vampire royalty wouldn't be so bad. He wanted to be with me, he wanted to be a father and to finally have family of his own. But I wouldn't have it. My need to protect you from their world was too strong, even if it meant giving up my relationship with Caius."

I sat for a long moment, letting everything Mom had said sink into understanding. "I'm glad you told me your version of events. I am. But you're wrong about one thing. And you're in the dark about so much more." At least, I hoped she was. "Caius never wanted to be a father. He never loved me, and Dorian was just a decoy."

"I don't believe that, Amelia. Yes, Caius has grown harder over the years. I blame myself for that. I took the option to be a father away from him. But I saw how he was, especially with you. You were his pride and joy, his one and only daughter. As a father he loved—"

"I told you not to call him that!" Fresh rage at her total blindness maddened me and I couldn't hold back the word-vomit. "Blood or not, he doesn't get to have that title. A father doesn't poison his own child. A father doesn't compel her into a comatose state so he can drink her blood to test its readiness. A father doesn't drag her down to those disgusting catacombs to kill her so he can steal the purpose he engineered her for. He doesn't send damned vampires after her and her friends and brother with the intent of killing them. And a father sure as shit doesn't stage a massacre as a last attempt to kidnap his own daughter."

Mom slipped from the curved edge of the coffee table to the floor, knocking a glass dish off the top. It shattered as it bounced off the rug and hit the stone ground. "Your…" She shook her head, face turning ghost-white as instant tears trailed down her cheeks. "He *did* all of that?"

I narrowed my gaze at her. Did I really think my mom could have known about any of this? "So you weren't involved?"

"Oh, God. Amelia." She scrambled forward, her gown making a tearing sound from the shattered glass, and mine creasing as she caught and pressed our hands into my knees. "No. Sweetheart, no. I love you *and* Dorian. You're my children. The most important things in my life. Why…why would he do all those things?"

That I knew the answer to. Blood was thicker than water. But whose blood had more pull? A daughter who'd been taken from you, and who you couldn't raise as your own and bond with like a normal parent? Or a mother who'd raised her son and devoted her life to saving her lost daughters before losing the battle, becoming the one that needed saving herself? "I'm Caius's key to restoring the damned. His mother Erzsebet is one of them. She's still alive."

A knock at the door stalled Mom's stunned reply and halted her sob. Kendrick came in and poked his head through the archway. "The trial's about to begin. We need to take our places."

I rose and smoothed down my long black gown, then glanced at my mom. Her silent tears made me want to hug her. But I couldn't get past this. Not yet. "Goodbye, Mom." I took Kendrick's arm and began walking—out to my destiny and a future I couldn't escape from.

A CACOPHONY of blurred speech filled the air around me as we descended the central marble steps siding the main hall. My earlier trepidation resumed and I fought the impulse to run. The thought of seeing Caius unnerved me, and had the static beneath my skin screaming to break free. The impulse to light up my voltage in readiness of Caius's appearance was intoxicating. To let it all loose to stream into that monster, frying him from the inside out. But I couldn't. There were rules here that I couldn't openly break. No matter how much I wanted to.

Plus the entire hall was packed, filled to the brim with vampires —royals and turned alike. They even piled out through the soaring, iron-braced main doors, standing on toes to get a glimpse of the stage. And beyond the tall, speared windows where the not quite pitch-black of night meant the equivalent of human daytime, more vampires filled the surrounding grounds. It seemed almost every vampire in existence was here to watch justice prevail.

"You'll be okay," Kendrick said, releasing my arm and kissing my cheek as we reached his reserved seat in the first line of pews before the stage. His fierce protection and total belief in my strength reached me through the bond. "I'll be here the whole time."

Unable to breathe properly, I tugged up the bodice of the gown I'd been required to wear. No one knew my purple-laced Vans were hidden underneath. Well, except for Kendrick. I curled my arms around his waist and didn't want to let go.

"You look stunning." I twisted to see Marcus on the stage steps with a welcoming yet somber smile. The unexplained connection I felt toward him put me at instant ease as he held out his elbow. I squeezed Kendrick one last time then looped my arm through Marcus's. "Don't worry, Baldassare," he said with a dangerous glint in his eyes. "If the traitor tries anything, I'll cut him down a notch."

Kendrick's lips curved in a genuine smile. Since moving back to the Armaya with me, his friendship with Marcus had returned to normal. And his little jealous outbursts had stopped, too. He knew there was nothing romantic between Marcus and me. "I know you will."

With that, Kendrick took his seat and Marcus whispered in my ear. "Time for justice to prevail."

I gulped as we mounted the steps, seeing the other crowned royals already seated in their thrones. The hilt of a mounted sword poked above each tall backrest. A new norm since the PVC—Portsmouth Vampire Council—attack. There were seven thrones in total: one for each of the remaining royal bloodlines. As Caius hadn't been sentenced, I hadn't been sworn in as yet—but I'd been summoned to sit on my family's throne for the trial. Among the five others was Uriel Aswind, her turquoise gown iridescent and her features determined. Next to her sat Serafina Baldassare, all dressed in crimson and black with her hard stare trained on me. Being Kendrick's mom hadn't affected her feelings for me, not when she'd been—and perhaps was still—one of Caius's supporters. The last three were Lord Paole; a thin, middle-aged man, Lord Strigon; a thirty-something-looking man with paled-out olive skin, and Lady Rasputin; who had gray-streaked black hair. Except for Marcus and maybe Uriel, none of them seemed to like me.

I threw a quick glance over my shoulder at Kendrick who smiled at me from the first row. Behind him, extended royals decked out in formal attire gossiped their thoughts on the trial, all of them eager for the proceedings to begin. Kendrick's voice spoke in my mind, his eyes catching mine. *You'll be fine.*

My thoughts shut down as I took my seat alongside Marcus and the crowd hushed. Among their faces, I caught sight of my mom. I couldn't bear to look at her, couldn't bear to see the upset she felt for a man she now knew had tried to kill me.

Uriel spoke out. "We bring to order the trial of Lord Caius Bathory." Her commanding gaze shot to the guards armed with swords at an arched door to the left of the stage. "Bring forth the accused."

The guards opened the door and stood aside. Chains rattled as a man in dirty ragged Armani that once shone with gold stitching was forced through the opening. Caius. He stumbled, the short chain joining his ankles tripping him up. The same cuffs tied his wrists, and a long chain connected his hands to his feet. Like an inmate on death row. One whose fate would be decided by others. The guards righted his balance, their hands clenched around his arms tightening. Caius went to shake them off with a snarl, but they held tight and forced him around the stage and into the dock stationed before the audience rows. As he was forced to his knees his dull eyes flicked up—right at me. Sudden and deep sorrow struck his tired face, freezing my world.

"Lord Caius Bathory," Uriel Aswind said, interrupting my stare and bringing me back down to earth. "Your witnessed actions prove you are in league with the damned and command their will. You stand accused of the assassination of all but one of the Vladimir line, the organized genocide of your own people, and treason against the Royal Vampire Council. How do you plead?"

Caius glared up at her. "Not guilty."

The entire hall broke out in an uproar, some people getting up to come at Caius. Countless guards swarmed in from the sidelines to shove the people back.

"Order!" Serafina called over the din. "Advance on the accused again, and be prepared to spend the night in our cells." Her hard eyes raked over the entire audience and then settled on Caius. The hardness marking her face softened, a look almost of regret betraying her true feelings. "As is custom, have you anything to say in your defense, Lord Caius Bathory?"

Caius clutched the dock, his chains rattling as he shakily got up. From the look of him, they'd been limiting his intake of blood. Keeping him alive, but far from thriving and strong. "The invasion at the Portsmouth Council was not meant to result in a bloodbath. It was merely a diversion to take possession of my daughter, Miss Amelia Lamont."

"That is Lady Bathory to you and all others," Marcus snapped from his throne beside me.

Caius's lip curled, his eyes gleaming up at Marcus. "How the young forget their place."

"What was your intention in taking your daughter?" Uriel interrupted, slight emotion showing how much she wanted him to pay for his crimes as much as the whispering audience.

"She is mine, my heir. She belongs to me. The intricacies of why do not matter." His sharp gaze shifted to me, his silver-gray eyes tunneling into me with…sadness. "Had I known then what I know

49

now, I may have chosen differently. I thought it was the only way. Now it seems that I was wrong. Yet I cannot take back my fatal error. Words will never make this up to you, but perhaps one day my actions will. I am sorry, my dear daughter. I truly am—for everything."

Marcus demanded an explanation while my mind and heart raced. Caius was talking cryptically, keeping the who, why, and how of his plea silent. I knew he was talking about the ability he'd given me, the one he'd tried to kill me to steal, and that he believed could somehow be used to save his damned mother. What I couldn't figure out was why he was keeping the details to himself. Did he still believe he could escape and achieve his goal?

"So you refuse to answer any questions in relation to your daughter?" Uriel demanded.

"Correct." Caius raised his voice to fill the hall. "I never intended for there to be a mass slaughter. The damned were merely meant to keep everyone inside occupied until I could get Amelia away. That was the command that I gave. I am sure you do not believe that I alone commanded such an army of damned."

"You admit someone else is now controlling them?" Marcus looked surprised.

Caius slid his gaze from him to Uriel, hatred flaring from his tightening expression. "Was controlling the damned then, too. Or so it would seem. I had no input into the assassination of the Vladimir line. The news of their extermination was as much a shock to me as it was to any of you."

"You actually claim not to have taken any part in their murders?" The look on Uriel's face said *liar!* "That another was then—and is now—controlling the damned solely?"

The smug smile on Caius's face was a glaring confirmation.

"If what you say is true, and you are innocent of these crimes," Marcus said, "then you'll have no issue spilling their name."

Caius smiled at Marcus, then at the remaining council members, including Serafina, and then at me. "That I cannot divulge. But I will say this." He turned toward the crowd and I caught sight of alchemist marks below a slash in his once-white shirt. One stood out above the rest, a mark to block use of his earth ability. "The damned commander will not stop until they achieve their ultimate goal. The extinguishing of all royals in existence to take rule over all vampires, living and dead."

The audience exploded in uproar and Caius spoke over them. "Heed my warning or perish at their fangs."

Uriel called order back to the trial as the guards kept control over the people. "The Royal Vampire Council will adjourn momentarily to pass judgment." She and each of the other royals—excluding myself, as I wasn't sworn in—exited stage right to enter the board-room just down the corridor. Hearing the doors shut, I sat anxiously, trying to ignore the weight of Caius's eyes tunneling into me and the countless comments being thrown about by the audience on what Caius had claimed. Each second felt like forever, but when the royals returned, it hadn't even been ten minutes.

Now back on their thrones, Uriel was the one to speak. "Lord Caius Bathory, regardless of your alleged accomplice and their supposed actions, you are hereby found guilty of unleashing geno-cide on our people and for plotting against the Royal Vampire Coun-cil. Your crown and position are now and forever more relinquished. In twenty-eight days—the last day of August—the sentence for your crimes will be carried out. The punishment is death."

As the guards moved to remove Caius, my mom's heartbreaking sob cut through the cheering crowd.

TWO HOURS LATER, I stared down at the note in my hands. *I wish to come clean.* Glued to a wing chair in the sitting room, I studied the messy handwriting, trying to hold my shaking hands still. Even with the tremors, I couldn't miss the dirty fingerprints left by the person who'd written it. Caius. The vampire whose seed had spawned me. The man who'd earlier today been found guilty and was now on death row. Though unlike human executions where the guilty was injected and fell into a permanent sleep, Caius would lose his head. The execution would be public, and I'd be required to watch.

I cringed at the thought. Deserved or not, it was a gruesome way to go. And I hated to admit it, but I felt robbed. All my life I'd believed my father was dead, had died protecting my mom and his unborn children. John Athobry had been a hero. The kind of father I wished I'd had as a role model growing up. But the reality? My father was a traitor, a murderer. A vile excuse for a man. Knowing his blood ran in my veins, that his genes played a part in who and what I was, and what I would become, sickened me. Almost made me want to tear my own veins out, too.

I would *never* be like him.

Never let his part of my genetic makeup seep through to stain the pages of my life. Like my life since discovering I was far from human, I would fight to become the person I wanted to be. Someone with honor, pride, and above all, integrity.

As a kid I'd wanted a dad like all the other *normal* kids; now I wished I'd never had one at all. That the hero I'd been told so little about had been real and just as dead as the fake memory.

Now prison guards were escorting my pathetic excuse for a father to my suite at my request. The option to visit his cell was mine, but I couldn't bring myself to go down there. It was too close to the catacombs; the place where he'd drained the life from my veins.

A gentle creak sounded as the main door in the foyer opened and shut. Footsteps neared before a quiet click turned the lamp on beside my wing chair and spread a dim glow over the furnished space.

I didn't flinch or look up from the note. I was glad he was here.

Kendrick slid onto the armrest knowing exactly what was about to arrive at my suite. Total support reached me through our bond and his broad hand rubbed circles over my back. A distant sound of rattling grew closer, and then there was a knock at the main door that had every one of my muscles straining. "You can change your mind, you know. I'll tell them to take him back."

After my mom ambushing me, followed by the trial that put Caius's life on a deadline, I wanted to hear what he had to say. Whether he spilled truth or lies—probably lies—I needed to hear him out...my father.

"No. I need to do this." I stood up from the patterned wing chair and Kendrick's hand curved around my shoulders as he rose with me. "You may enter."

As the door swung open, my chest cavity ratcheted tighter. My heart jumped as the prison guards dragged Caius around the foyer table and into the sitting room by his arms. The two guards stationed outside my suite also entered to stand watch in the foyer. The same shackles encircled Caius's wrists and ankles, which I noticed were connected by alchemist-engraved chains, probably to prevent escape and to weaken their prisoner. His dull eyes were already on me as the prison guards shoved him to his knees. The five-foot gap between us was way too small, and his stare—filled with unexpected hope and purpose—unnerved me.

I scanned over his ratty clothes and disheveled features. Kendrick had been guessing in the past when he told me Caius was over five hundred. And he'd been wrong. Although he looked closer to six hundred, he was only in the fours. I wondered if self-inflicted experiments had tacked on the years, taken what should have been middle-aged features and smacked them with the look of time.

While I watched him, unable to look away, Caius did a scan of the suite, seeing the changes I'd made to his former home. Replacing his antique touch was a collection of modern wooden furnishings and cloth seating. Framed motorbike posters now covered some of the exposed stone walls, and the marble fireplace was free of his possessions. "I like what you've done with the place."

His casual tone pissed me off, as if we were more than enemies and having a nice social gathering. "Shut up."

Caius chuckled. "There's the defiant daughter I know and love. I see so much of myself in you," he said, eyes sparkling with pride. "Your determination, your drive, your strength."

His misplaced pride and reference to our blood-connection boiled my own. "I am *nothing* like you. You disgust me."

"Oh? So you don't allow your friends to risk their lives for your selfish cause?" He smiled like a devious Cheshire cat. His words muted any response I could make—because how the hell could he know about my excursions to find Ty, or that I even thought he was alive? "You are like me, child. In many more ways than you know. I am simply more direct in my actions."

Kendrick stalked forward and booted Caius in the chest. "She said shut the hell up!"

Caius toppled over, and a tearing of his tattered clothes sounded as he connected with the hard stone ground. The guards didn't move to help, and Kendrick returned to my side as Caius righted himself back into a kneeling position. He struggled to his feet, chains rattling as he rose. The guards took hold of his shackled wrists, making sure he couldn't take a single step. Caius's eyebrows rose at me, waiting.

"You want to come clean? Fine. This'll be your only chance."

"I loved your mother," Caius said, not waiting a second. "I still do. Since the first moment I saw her, this feeling I had never experienced before, wrecked my heart. And I accepted it. Accepted her as a human. Allowed her to remain one and kept her from my world—as she wished. It killed me not to turn her, to know I would only have seventy-odd years with her before she would wither and die. Though I guess that is love. We make sacrifices, concessions..."

Reminded of his warning the first time I'd been forced to the Armaya on how devastating it can be to lose love prematurely, I almost believed the sincerity of his words.

A look of distant joy crossed his face. "When she became pregnant I was overjoyed. But of course she would never want her child to be a vampire or to live among them. She was going to be a mother. That protective instinct is as sudden as it is severe. There was no talking her out of it. So I found a way to nullify your vampire genetics, make you as close to human as possible. The process was severe; Lamayli would pay for your normal future with her own life. But she could not leave you without a mother. And I could not lose her. In the end the only concession I asked for was that Lamayli would agree to let me turn her to save her life."

"What a hero." Kendrick clapped his hands together once in mock applause.

Caius laughed, the throat vibration bringing on a coughing bout. "Hardly. I am a vampire, one of The Seven. It is custom to create an heir, someone worthy to take my place when the time comes. I was angered that I would lose those initial years to mold you into my successor. But I knew I would eventually have the chance. The elixir was never meant to be a permanent fix; in time it would wear off. I gave you and your mother your childhood, free from obligation, free from our world."

Remembering the grisly death he'd almost led me to, I shuddered. "But you never intended to let me live past being a teenager."

"Actually, I did. It was never my intent to kill you at all. But as I got to know you after your move here, I realized how you would react when you discovered your power. You would never be satisfied with saving Erzsebet." Caius paused, reading my lack of surprise at the mention of his mother as knowledge. "You would want to save them all. In the end, you would bring about your own painful and drawn-out death. Restoring life has a cost, and in the end you would pay it…for the greater good. I could not stand to watch your slow demise, my dear. So I decided to take your power. To make your death quick, rather than letting it drag on."

Caius's disgusting honesty shocked me silent. Dying as he'd drained my blood had been the most excruciating pain I had ever experienced. Second only to seeing this asshole kill Ty. And that was a kindness? "So I should thank you for killing me quickly rather than taking your time. You fucking—"

"You cold heartless bastard," Kendrick cut me off. His fists clenched and he barely held himself back from using Caius's face as a punching bag.

A look almost like regret pained Caius's weathered features. "I made a mistake."

"A *mistake*." My cheeks turned fire-hot and steam exploded from my ears. "You tried to fucking kill me. Not just once. Over and over. And you came after my friends. My brother. You set the damned on the Portsmouth Council and everyone inside."

"I admit I took your vein and drained you, my dear. But those other things were not my doing."

"Liar! You sent those vacations with intent. You sent damned to kill my best friend and brother and…" Ty's name hung in the air unsaid, too heart-wrenching to say out loud.

"Dorian is not now nor has he ever been your brother. Your one and only twin perished at birth. Regardless, it was not my actions that sent you all away."

My glare intensified, wondering absently if my twin was really gone.

"I will not pretend I did not know about it," Caius tacked on. "And I admit I did nothing to prevent the aftermath. But all I wanted out of it was you, my daughter. The rest was out of my hands."

I screamed and backed up past the wing chair before I gave in and lunged for the asshole. "Guards, take him—"

"You think I would have let your mother be present if I knew the damned were going to attack?" Caius raised his voice as the guards began hauling him back.

Curiosity forced my lips to move. "Wait."

The guards stopped hauling and Caius spoke quickly, like he knew I was past the point of hearing much more. "I would never put Lamayli in danger like that." At my snort he said, "You do not believe me? Then consider this. If I had total control of the damned, would it have been necessary for me to hide your mother below the dais once they attacked?"

"You are so full of it," Kendrick spoke while my mind ticked over the details and possibilities. "The damned didn't even touch you. If you weren't commanding them, you'd have been fair game like the rest of us."

"The damned know me. I was protected."

I finally found my voice as I braced myself against the back of the wing chair. "So you're not the evil asshole you've made yourself out to be." I laughed, the sound fueled by disgust while I screamed inside my head, *freaking liar*! I saw again all the times we were attacked, ambushed and surviving only through luck and determination. Then I saw Caius's sword driving through Ty's chest and sliding free with a smear of red. Kendrick's arm slung around my waist, knowing I was about to collapse. "Then why the fuck did you kill *him*?"

"You will never believe me, my dear, but I killed that boy with full knowledge of what was intended for him. What he would become. I did it to remove a bargaining chip from the table that may force your hand. To protect you."

"You fucking liar!"

Caius jogged his wrists, making the chains rattle as I lunged, only to be held back by Kendrick. "I have said all I need now. Guards, escort me to my cell."

CHAPTER 5

J sat cross-legged in the Armaya's gymnasium the next day. After forty-five minutes of training, I was so exhausted I could barely see straight. The hangry grumble of my stomach intensified. The gut-grinding made me want to puke up the three bottles of human blood I'd chugged before arriving. Those blue veins that were a dead giveaway of my constant starvation were turning darker by the minute. And my purple-and-black leggings and tank were saturated with sweat. The movement and clatter of vampires warring with deadly weapons around me made my head spin. Midday mandatory training—really midnight—happened every day. But it was still a helluva lot better than the upcoming event of being crowned as Caius's heir.

Uriel Aswind strolled through the glass doors then and caught my eye. A tattered book tied closed with a leather strap was held tight against her chest—as if the thought of sparring vamps knocking it from her grasp frightened her. She smiled as she made her way over and knelt in her gown on the yoga mat in front of me.

She kept one hand holding the book and brushed her red hair back over her shoulders with the other. "Amelia, I see you've expended yourself training, though I had hoped to attempt something less physical and more mental." She tapped her temple. "I want to train you to bring on a vision."

In my spare time over the past six months, I'd tried over and over to bring one on, hoping to see something, anything related to Ty. Every time I'd failed. And now this royal had the bright idea to simply 'help' me?

I tugged my plaited hair over my shoulder and toyed with the end as the angry in my hangry took control. "I thought there was only one Oracle at a time. So if I'm the only vamp with The Sight, how can *you* teach me how to control something you can't even begin to understand?"

If it had been any other crowned royal, there would have been backlash for my disrespect. But Uriel simply smiled, patting the book she still held tight. "This here is a journal. One that belonged to my father, Lord Dimitri Aswind. The last known Oracle, who perished some centuries ago—shortly after he learned to bring on visions at will. Some of his processes are recorded here."

I sat quietly for a moment, thinking morbid thoughts at her use of words. "He was killed because of his visions?"

"Partly." Though Uriel's reply was light, something deeper showed through in the set of her jaw and shift of her downward glance to the old journal. "Had he mastered control of The Sight sooner, he may have seen and been able to change his fate. Though many more factors were at play, in his case."

Without warning, Kendrick thumped onto the mat beside me and I jerked. He back-flipped up, flashing me a quick smile. *Have a go, Amelia. What could it hurt?*

He jogged back over to Marcus who nodded my way as if in

encouragement. "Two-to-Five," he said to Kendrick. "Your point."

"Ahem," Uriel cleared her throat, stealing my focus from the guys sparring across the gym. "Now, shall we begin?" At my reluctant nod she said, "Close your eyes and clear your mind. Imagine you are in an empty void with no surroundings. No interferences."

My lids slid shut, cutting out the sight and non-stop movement as I attempted to rid all thoughts from my mind. The noise of hand-to-hand combat along with clanging weapons filled my ears. I squeezed my eyes shut even tighter and scrunched my lips together. The noise around me grew lighter, fading until all that remained was a gentle vibration. My stomach clenched, my previous hunger verging on starvation. With its demand my sense of smell soared, highlighting different scents in the air: plastic from gym mats, sweat from those sparing, and the blood that filled their veins. My mouth watered and my fangs slid free. My devious inner voice reared its head. *You can't do it. You'll never be able to do it.*

Yes you can, Kendrick rebutted instantly. Across the gym, even in a headlock, he was with me the whole way. He knew how hard I'd struggled with this and he wasn't going to let me give up so easily. *Believe and you'll get there. Maybe not today, but eventually you will.*

Raw determination fired through me at his total and unyielding belief in me. I clenched my teeth together, forcing my fangs to recede. Then I shut down everything external, even the interrupting grumble from my stomach. Every sound and smell was stripped from my consciousness, replaced by a black void that surrounded me, so thick and empty that getting stuck like this would mean eternal nothingness. "Now what?"

My spoken words floated on an invisible wave around me as an answer returned, not really heard or seen, but somehow *felt*. "Reach into the darkness. Take hold of something tangible."

My hand lifted, fingertips disappearing into the surrounding black. I fought the need to shudder at the touch of something wet and slimy. It was almost like reaching into a mystery box filled with unknown dangers. More slimy things grazed over my hand, feeling like it was submerged in a pond filled with eels. Then I took hold, pinching the tail of one. I began to pull, drawing the slime into my hand and feeling that same heat swamp my body that always did when a vision was about to come on. The heat turned into power inside me that collected and—

"Amelia, stop!"

My eyes flung open and reality crashed back into place. A grunt erupted as power streamed from my body into Kendrick, whose grip tore from my shoulders to send him flying across the room.

Around him, others were floored, too.

I bolted upright, seeing through blurred vision blue streaks continually shooting from my body and all around the gym. The voltage struck at the remaining, horrified royals, flattening those who didn't leap fast enough. New waves grew and split free—

A set of arms flung suddenly around me from behind. Like flames underwater, my voltage died, the person holding me absorbing the volatile power.

"Oh, shit." I staggered free to realize Marcus was the one who'd disarmed me. Just like he'd done when revealing my vision to The Council in Portsmouth. But I couldn't think about that now. Not when everyone I had shocked was slowly getting to their feet with looks of fear. Except for Uriel who instead of looking fearful, looked determined.

Kendrick rushed over and tripped on his feet, still jittery from the static shorting out through his body. "They'll—be okay," he said, forcing his body to stop shaking as he righted his balance. "The power was shared rather than being concentrated into one source."

Swaying on my feet, I absently noticed the now darker spider-webbed veins tracking up my arms. I shook my head, pretending I hadn't seen them, even though I felt Kendrick's growing concern through our bond. "And now I'm the freak who's a live wire."

"They knew you had the power beforehand," Marcus said. "They just hadn't seen it in action since the Portsmouth attack."

"They also know that your power forced the damned to flee when you struck Caius during the battle," Uriel added as she picked up her prized journal. Then she nodded to Marcus and Kendrick. "Please excuse us." She took my arm and drew me to the exit, showing no fear at the possibility of being shocked again. Right outside the glass barrier, where recovering vamps continued to struggle to their feet, she faced me, corridor lanterns lighting her soft expression. "I know this all seems like a curse. Something too big for any one person to have to deal with. But I know you will learn to control your electric ability as well as your visions. You were close to bringing on a vision today."

Perceptive of her—or a guess in hopes of forcing me not to give up. "And you know that how?"

Uriel smiled, broad and encouraging. "Because I've seen this reaction before. When my father first attempted to control his visions." She handed me the journal. "Have a look inside?"

I frowned and opened the leather covering to a satin bookmark. The words inside were written with the tip of a feather in flowing cursive, and described a fateful event that had life-changing consequences. The scene I'd witnessed in a blackout-vision in Vanessa's basement before acting it out myself. "Your father was the man struck by lightning."

"You saw him in a vision," Uriel stated, rather than questioning. "You saw him beacon the source of power into himself."

I nodded. "It's what led me to seek out the lightning myself.

63

AFTER SHOWERING off the dried training sweat and struggling into my gown, I found myself in the corridor outside Marcus's office. My crowning was closing in, and the dark-purple bodice suffocated me. But my mind wasn't on the impending and inescapable event. Wasn't on the male and female guards that stood like shadows down either end of the torch-lit corridor, or Marcus's that were living statues guarding his door. Wasn't even on my non-shifting hunger, the four bottles of blood I'd drunk, or the indigo veins covering my exposed arms.

Because all I could think about in this moment was Marcus and how he'd absorbed my power. The same power that rendered every other being a living floor rug. I thought back to that feeling I'd had when we first met. My soul had recognized him. And the fact was, two babies had been pulled from my mother's womb. One was me, and the other hadn't been Dorian. Caius said my twin had died at birth. But after this reminder of the unexplained connection I shared with Marcus, I wouldn't believe that without proof.

I went to look at the photo in my hand again.

"Amelia?" The office door swung in without a sound and Marcus smiled at the sight of me. In a pristine suit and shiny black shoes, he was clearly ready for my crowning, too. "Thought you were out here. Are you okay? Nervous?"

Instead of answering his questions, I blurted, "Don't you ever wonder about that? Our connection, I mean."

Marcus frowned, gaze sliding left and right to the guards, then back to me. "Want to come in and talk about it?"

I entered as he stood aside before closing the guards out. Inside, the office was dark, a twinkling night sky visible beyond the open drapes. A tidy marble-topped desk faced out from the window with a single candle that reflected flickering light into the many mirrors that patterned one wall. I took a seat on the Chesterfield sofa against the opposite wall, legs rejoicing at the break. Then I held out the photo. The same one of Caius holding two light-haired infants.

"You think you have no side effects from Caius's experiments, but I think you're wrong." I let sparks dance down my arm, electric blue compared to the blood-deprived dark veins. "Today in training you absorbed my power, and it's not the first time."

Marcus lowered himself down beside me, leather creaking in response. "What are you getting at?"

I let my index finger touch his hand and watched as a stray spark absorbed into his skin. "I think this photo was a keepsake. I think you could be my twin."

"Amelia, no." Marcus stood and paced to the black desk, perching on its edge. The candlelight emphasized his high cheek-bones and sharp jawline. The look on his face was troubled. "I don't know if Kendrick ever mentioned this, but Caius raised me, well mostly."

"So you are—"

"No. I'm not." Marcus swung his legs over the desk to stand behind it and opened the top drawer. A thick but small sheet of paper was pulled free. A deep and sorrowful sigh lifted and dropped his chest as he stared down at the photo he held with gentle care. "I'm a Vladimir. My mother died during my birth. My father..." He glanced away and closed his eyes as if trying to hold back tears. "He blamed me. Could barely stand to look at me back then. And then he didn't have to. He moved to Russia and built his manor while setting up a council there. Caius took over raising me, among the castle staff. He treated me like a son, I suppose. But he's not my father."

I got up and met his side, my hand going to his shoulder. "That doesn't mean he's not. There could still be some way—" I froze as I caught a glimpse of the photo in Marcus's now trembling hands. A beautiful woman with dark blond hair lay in a bed, her face slack, pallor gray, and eyes unfocused. She was dead. There was no doubt. Tucked into one arm was a newborn, naked and smeared with the proof of birth. Marcus. The son she'd died to give life to. "Oh, Marcus. I'm so sorry." I clutched his arm with both hands. "I just thought…"

"I wish you were my blood," Marcus said quietly, turning to crack a smile despite the sorrow in his teal-flecked eyes. "Then at least I'd have someone."

This was the most vulnerable I'd seen Marcus since his family's funeral. And I hated that I'd been the one to cause this pain in him. I hugged my arms around his waist and laid my head against his chest. "Blood or not, you've got me. I promise you that."

KENDRICK KEPT his arm looped through mine as we headed from my suite down the lavish, portrait-lined corridor toward the main hall. I wouldn't admit it, but we both knew the physical support was keeping me vertical. After drinking more bottled human blood following my talk with Marcus, my bone-deep fatigue hadn't improved. I kept the growing aches that swam through my body locked away from our shared bond. Still, I wasn't fooling Kendrick. I knew that much as his hold on my arm and fingers laced through mine tightened. His drowning concern over my ever-decreasing vitality was wearing on him, but for right now he kept the peace. Swallowed his worry and locked it down. A war of words before the ceremony wasn't going to get him anywhere, and he knew it.

A split-second image of him swinging me up into his strong

arms leaked through, but that too was shot down. Though not before heat scoured my cheeks.

On top of my hunger-induced weakness and friendship complications, the nerves inside my chest were almost as debilitating. My long, dark-purple gown, made solely for this occasion, swished as we walked as if announcing my approaching arrival to everyone that waited. It was heavy as hell, too. The tight, beaded bodice was even more suffocating than earlier, and static battled around beneath my ribcage, desperate to break free. I clutched the heart-shaped amulet —the only thing I had of Ty's—and gritted my teeth. Forcing the static to remain trapped so my flesh and limbs would remain electricity-free took energy I didn't have. But I'd already scared enough people with my power today. Hurt some of them, too.

In minutes, the ceremony would begin that would see me crowned as the reigning Bathory, and there was nothing I wanted less. Already being the Oracle meant I was bound to deliver my warning visions while remaining imprisoned in this castle for as long as I lived. Nine hundred and eighty-three years, or thereabouts. Barring the times when I snuck away, leaving Marika to fill my place to avoid suspicion. Though with our missions turning up no leads or proof that Ty was alive, I wondered how much longer it would go on for. And once there was no reason to have Marika cover for me, I'd have no way to escape the grounds.

We reached the landing to the central stairs and I let the bloodstone drop below the cover of my bodice. All eyes turned on me, a mixture of acceptance and uncertainty in them. Having had my birthday before Caius's trial, I was now seventeen. The minimum age required to take a seat on the Royal Vampire Council.

I looked to Marcus, already seated with the other royals on stage. His formal attire matched the other crowned males, and a royal cape was draped over his shoulders. He smiled in encouragement. Having turned seventeen before me, he'd been crowned straight away.

Two thrones remaining empty would have shown weakness.

And as we were in the middle of a war between vampires and the damned, the last thing the RVC wanted to portray was weakness. My crowning had only been put off this long because of Caius's trial. Formal charges and sentencing had to be passed down before a successor could take his position.

I returned a tight-lipped smile to Marcus as Kendrick led me down to the main hall, directing me through the center aisle between pews. Heads turned and whispers rose, commenting and even criticizing everything about me: my age, attire, reputation, Oracle ability, electric power, and being Caius's daughter. So many of them thought I was a fraud. Those who'd accepted my heritage either thought of me as the disgraced daughter of a traitor, or as being in league with the traitor.

As we reached the steps leading up to the stage where the empty Bathory throne waited beside the others, Kendrick turned to face me. His lips brushed my ear. "I'll be right here. As always."

I squeezed his hand then nodded, demanding my legs hold my weight without his support. Lifting the heavy hem of my gown—though not enough to flash my hidden Vans underneath—I mounted the stairs. With a few shaky steps, I made it onto the stage.

Uriel rose from her throne and walked toward me, her stunning green gown as vibrant as her braided red hair. A wink and her smile did little shift my angst. "Lady Amelia Bathory, you are summoned here today to stand before the Royal Vampire Council, not solely as our Oracle, but to be recognized as one of The Seven. Have you come here of your own free will, ready to take your place as the living heir to Lord Caius Bathory?"

I swallowed, and it felt like I'd just tried to stomach a brick. Like

I really had a choice. My heart drummed, but I didn't let my internal panic show on my face. Instead, I dipped my head, curtseying in respect. It took all my remaining strength not to fall at the awkward angle. "Yes, Lady Uriel Aswind." The words Marcus had taught and practiced with me tasted like poison in my mouth, daring me to swallow them back down rather than spit them out. "Of my own free will, and ready to take my rightful place imposed by my blood."

I rose, quaking legs thankfully hidden by my gown's long skirt.

Uriel glided past me to a table covered in crimson silk. She took hold of a silver, wavy-edged sword with a serrated tip. The same one she'd handled at the PVC battle. Then she grasped the same jewel-encrusted, gold ceremonial chalice that had been used during the Oracle ceremony.

I stiffened at the memory of that night. The contents of that chalice fed to Marika in my place, had been one step in the path to the damned battle and Ty's death. If she hadn't been found out, we may have all escaped before the damned broke in. Then my never-easing guilt would have been over the deaths of countless vampires, rather than the death of my lycan boyfriend. Neither were forget-table consequences, and even if given the choice again now, I wasn't sure I'd change the course of that night.

"Ahem," Uriel cleared her throat, now standing right before me.

The smell of blood registered. My eyes widened as my fangs throbbed, aching to slide free. Lost in those memories I hadn't even noticed her return, or the process of her slicing each crowned royal's wrist so they could add their blood to the chalice. Uriel had donated her blood too; a red smear and scar line all that was left of the act. Now it was almost all I could think about.

Except...

I frowned at that line as I held out my arm, palm up. Ritual was part of life as a royal vampire. Blood offering came with many of those rituals. Uriel sliced the blade along my wrist. The cut she made was wide and angled to keep the blood flowing before my vampire healing could kick in. The thick slice alone caused a sting rather than the silver—because unlike most vamps, I was immune to the metal. Blood swelled as I tilted my wrist, letting the red cascade fall and blend with the existing blood that filled the chalice. I was tempted to strike out and snatch the chalice so I could gulp down the contents, but I kept my desperate hunger in check by biting the inside of my cheek. When the bleeding stopped and I turned my wrist up, a scar was left. The same type of scar I'd seen in my vision of the guy who'd commanded the damned and led the Vladimir assassination.

Uriel handed me the full chalice. "Kneel before your people and repeat the sacred oath."

Mouth watering, I turned to face the crowd and knelt, my long gown pooling around me and my legs rejoicing at no longer having to hold my weight up. I lifted the chalice and froze as a strange sensation weighed down on me.

The feel of eyes on me. And not just anyone's.

Ty's.

My gaze skittered around, seeing the waiting faces of the royals on stage then everyone in the crowd. Beyond the uncovered Gothic windows, nothing but a post two a.m. glow was visible. The feeling vanished and my shoulders slouched. He wasn't here. As usual, I was imagining things. Wanting to see him so badly that I created these delusions.

Returning my attention to the raised chalice that was making my arms ache with its weight, I let my voice carry over everyone who watched. "I vow to uphold the laws of the Royal Vampire Council. To be honest and true in all my actions. To seek justice and mercy for all that come under our laws. As long as I live, I vow this all."

I lowered the cool edge to my lips, and although desperate hunger screamed at me to drink, I paused. My heart skipped a beat. This was the closest I'd come to live blood since Ty's death. It wasn't from the vein straight to my mouth, but it wasn't bottled human, either. Unfortunately, I didn't have a say in the source. Without drinking from all the crowned royals, the ritual wasn't considered complete. Without options and starving, I let the cooling blood fill my mouth and went to swallow—

I gagged on the blood, barely a drop making it down my throat as my eyes rolled back in my head. My bones turned to jelly, hands dropping the chalice that clanged against the stage as I tipped. My head struck the wood and everything vanished.

Catapulted back to life, I was suddenly upright. My surroundings blinked into sharp focus. Standing in the center of an opulent room with a swaying crystal chandelier, something was off. The velvet and cherry-wood furnishings and many antique decorations were stained by red splatters. I glanced down and my heart stopped. Dead bodies littered the ground all around me, vampire fangs visible from some of their gaping mouths. My own mouth opened to scream and the view split and changed. Now a kitchen surrounded me, marble benches and stainless steel appliances painted red. A family of five lay sprawled across the polished concrete floor, chalky-white skin visible between a coating of splattered blood. Before I could register the carnage, I found myself in another scene, this time a grand foyer. Another large group lay slaughtered, bodies broken and dumped up the double arcing stairs. Then I saw a couple dead in their bed, as twisted and crumpled as the shredded silk sheets.

As the sight of their bodies faded like a light being dimmed, I knew two things for sure. Every victim had been vampire, and the damned had killed them all.

CHAPTER 6

I awoke with a start, gasping at the surprise of being out of it. Panic tightened my chest and fog clouded my mind. The hunger roiling my gut was epic. Where was I, and how the hell had I gotten here? Softness surrounded me, and I patted with my hands, finding a mattress, pillows, and plush, welcoming sheets. My blurry eyes slitted open. Yep, I was in my own four-poster bed, surrounded by live performance posters of Above Only and Red, crisp-white furniture, and...I wasn't alone. Movement in the cheval mirror's reflection across the room caught my eye. Someone was right beside me. My head whipped sideways and I went to scramble away.

"Shh, it's alright," Kendrick's voice soothed as I registered his familiar face. Tainted relief swamped through the bond as he smiled, the dark circles under his eyes bulging. "You're finally awake."

"Finally?"

My senses caught up, scenting his rich blood. My mouth watered as I glanced to the open drapes on my other side. Beyond the open balcony doors it was dark, night to all humans, but daytime to all vamps who lived at the Armaya. Where had I been before? I vaguely remembered taking the chalice and tasting the first drop of the crowned royals' blood. Then…

A gentle breeze carried through the balcony doors and into the room, the chill prickling my skin. I glanced down…and—"Shit!"—rushed to gather the sheets up around me. Apart from the amulet dangling between my small cleavage, I was wearing nothing but my underwear. Black, lace, and as see-through as glass. "Why the hell am I practically freaking naked?"

Rather than being embarrassed or defensive, Kendrick sighed, a deeper worry taking place of any possible attraction. "You blacked out on stage after repeating the sworn oath."

The foggy memory began to return as I groped for the dressing gown across the foot of the bed and tugged it on in a rush. I closed my eyes, securing one length of the silk over the other with a tied knot as I tried to force the pieces of my memory together.

Like seeing a scene through thick bars while moving at speed, I caught a few snapshot glimpses. I'd lost consciousness on stage. A vision had taken control.

Well that explained the dry starvation crawling up my throat, I thought as Kendrick's steady pulse registered. But before I could recall what I'd seen, another swirl of cool wind reminded me that I'd almost been naked. "You still haven't told me how I got back here—and undressed." I refrained from placing my hand over his. After the full frontal in black lace, the thought of touching him felt like an intimate step. "What happened?"

"When you fell, I jumped onto the stage and caught you. I held you there and waited, wondering what you were seeing. Minutes passed and still you didn't come to." Kendrick frowned and deep worry lines scored his face as he looked into my eyes.

I saw in a flash of images in my mind what Kendrick had witnessed. In his arms I had been limp, lifeless bar the slow, almost invisible breaths that made my chest rise and fall beneath my bodice. Uriel took control, directing the audience who'd come to watch my crowning to disperse from the hall. As the last exited, Kendrick shook me a little, terror striking through his soul. Seeing me like this was too close to his memory of the time Caius had almost killed me. When Caius had convinced him through compulsion to think he'd been the one to take my life out of jealousy. *Wake up,* he sent through the bond. No reply came back, not even any feeling that proved our link was still in check.

Wrecked by worry, Kendrick had lifted me into his arms and carried me up to my suite. Then he'd sat down on my bed and leaned my dead weight against his chest. With gentle fingers he untied the lace down the back of my bodice, all the while wishing that undressing me like this was for romantic reasons rather than in this terrifying situation. For all he knew, I may never wake up. He laid me back down against the pillows and closed his eyes. With blind hands, he minded where he touched as he removed the bodice. Then he gripped both sides of the dress and worked it down over my legs. Lastly he removed my Vans and pulled a comforter from my feet up to my neck. He sighed deeply and let his eyelids slide open. *Wake up, sleeping beauty.*

The memory faded and I blinked my vision clear. Any initial embarrassment at Kendrick undressing me vanished. His actions had been carried out with total respect. Even though I wasn't mad, fear still lingered from him through our bond. Though it had nothing to do with Kendrick undressing me, and everything to do with me passing out. He knew I was still refusing live blood, and believed passing out after my last vision was proof of my body being deprived. But I wasn't about to get into that argument again. At least not now. And definitely not when I'd just caught myself searching for that throbbing vein up his neck.

Still, I needed to know what had happened before. "So you brought me up here, undressed me, and then I woke up?"

Kendrick shook his head, jaw clenching so tight his teeth ground together. "I removed your gown so no one else would...then I waited."

Suspicion had me gripping his hand with tight fingers. "For how long?"

"Your crowning was yesterday. You've been unconscious for over twenty-four hours."

Before that revelation could hit me like a ton of bricks, the memory of my vision rushed back. The blood, the bodies, all those lives taken by deadly and malicious force. "Oh my God."

I jumped up from the bed and staggered, legs tangling in the sheets as Kendrick ran through my vision's details. I caught myself on the bed's edge, tearing myself free as Kendrick's wide eyes met mine.

"I'll call an urgent meeting with The Seven." He raced toward the foyer, eyes meeting mine even though my bra was on show. "Get dressed and meet me at the boardroom." Rose colored his cheeks as he turned to duck out through the foyer. "And drink some blood. I know you're starving."

The door opened and shut and I muttered, *"Shit."* In reliving my vision he'd picked up on my hungry desire from moments ago. But there wasn't time to dwell on that. Instead, I did as told, got dressed, drained a few bottles, and forced my putty-like legs to take me from my suite and downstairs.

Outside the double doors to the boardroom, I clasped and unclasped my hands. Fear that my blacking out had resulted in others' deaths sat like poison in my stomach. "What's taking so long?"

"Half the RVC's off-grounds. Uriel and my mother are trying to contact the others." Kendrick ran a hand up and down my arm, nerves shooting out like live grenades through our bond. He was worried this vision's warning would come too late, and that my unconsciousness would be the cause. He feared what that grief would do to me, but there was something else. Something barricaded behind those worries that he was holding back.

I began to hyperventilate, and my already-weak legs twitched at the strain of having to hold my body weight up. "What aren't you telling me?"

Before he could utter a word, the doors cracked open. Marcus stuck his head out, expression grave as he took my hand and squeezed. "Thought you were here." His kind eyes said, *everything'll be fine,* but the tight set of his jaw told a different story. "Ready?"

No! I screamed internally, but there was no time to waste. Lives were at stake…at least I hoped they still were. "Absolutely."

I let Marcus pull me through the doors and into the boardroom, leaving Kendrick outside. The room was large, with a soaring, peaked ceiling of stone, and Gothic windows glimpsing out onto the boundary of the extensive gardens that surrounded the castle. A slab of polished marble made up a round table with seven thrones spaced evenly around the outside.

Lady Serafina and Lady Uriel sat on opposing sides, with crystal glasses and a decanter filled with vibrant blood centered between them. My mouth watered and my stomach gurgled. I ignored the resulting stab of pain. Right now, my hunger could take a distant second seat to what I had to reveal. As could my casual jeans, Vans, and tank that were less formal than Marcus's black pants, sports jacket and squared dress shoes. And totally subpar compared to the gowns Uriel and Serafina wore.

"Amelia, please sit down," Uriel spoke with urgency, rising from her throne and turning to view me over the tall back of the carved wood.

Marcus led me to Uriel's left, before taking his place to her right. I squeezed around the hard wooden armrest, rushing to sit on the patch of crimson velvet. The wooden backrest towered over my head, making me feel tiny, rather than in a position of power.

"We hear you have some dire news, Amelia." Serafina eyed me with clear scrutiny. "Tell us what you saw in your vision."

I clasped my sweating hands and took a deep breath. "Four different locations all with the same scene played out. Vampires left dead with their throats torn out..." I went into rushed detail on the locations and how many were killed at each, getting the words out as fast as possible. When I'd finished relaying everything, I was out of breath.

"My dear God." Uriel put her hand to her mouth. "Every one of those locations is the main residence to our extended families."

"Excluding mine," Serafina said. "All I have left is Kendrick." Her eyes met mine with the most heartfelt and real emotion I'd ever seen in her face: fear. "Did you see my son, too?"

I shook my head, struggling to speak past the knot of dread clogging up my throat for all those families. "No."

"We must get warning to them," Marcus spoke up as Serafina muttered, "Thank God."

They each picked up their phones from the round table and began dialing. Minutes passed like centuries as I waited for their calls to end. With only one side of three conversations audible, I couldn't be sure what was going on. When Marcus and Serafina hung up, Uriel stood and began pacing before the windows.

"Lord Strigon and his family are untouched," Marcus said with sheer and total relief.

"As are the Paoles," Serafina added.

Uriel's hand holding her phone dropped. Her eyes were glassy and her vision unfocused as she stood at the back of her throne. "Lady Rasputin was able to contact her family in Canada. A relative of hers on the council there had noted my brother absent. They traveled with guard to his home and discovered the...*scene*." Uriel choked on a sob. "He was slaughtered...along with his wife and children."

I sat in shock, my stomach threatening to release a volcano of dead blood. I saw that family of five again, those poor children twisted and broken in their own blood. If being unconscious after my vision had resulted in their deaths, I would never forgive myself.

Serafina came quickly around the table to support Uriel, whose legs shook violently. "When did this happen?"

"Over a day ago." Uriel glanced at me, silent tears rolling down her face. "Hours before your vision. It couldn't have been stopped."

Unwarranted relief swept through me. *Their deaths weren't my fault*, the thought repeated over and over in my head. The vision had been a warning to get the rest out alive.

"They cannot stay where they are," Marcus said suddenly. "Compromised yet or not, the threat still stands. We must prepare our private jets now and relocate them all here to reside within our walls."

Serafina kept a firm hold around Uriel. "Force them?"

"We must," Uriel whispered, her voice hoarse and expression vacant. "Had we not given the option after the Portsmouth attack, my blood would still be alive."

"Then we bring this to a vote," Marcus said. "I vote yes. All in favor?"

The others chimed out "yes" and after a minute, Marcus had approval from the rest of the absent Seven. Then three sets of silver-blue eyes leveled on me. The last thing I wanted to do was take away anyone's right to choose how and where they lived. But even if I said no, I was outnumbered. There was no point going against the grain, and in this situation, moving their families was in their best interest. "I agree."

AFTER URIEL HAD EXCUSED herself to see to her dead family's needs —refusing assistance or company—Serafina spoke up. "Now that we have settled the safety of our families, we must cover a flow-on issue regarding you, Amelia." She eyed me in a way that made ice tingles crawl up my spine. Like whatever she had to say in my regard displeased her greatly. "An issue that has needed to be dealt with for quite some time now."

It suddenly felt like I was on trial and all the vampire portraits strung around the room were staring at me with ready judgment. "Regarding me?" I looked from her to Marcus, who remained quiet as he reached for the decanter and filled three glasses. He handed one out to Serafina and himself. Then he slid one past Uriel's empty throne to me, eyes not leaving the glass to meet my questioning gaze.

"After fainting on stage yesterday with your vision, something that needs urgent intervention has come to our attention." Serafina took a sip from her glass. "Our stocked human, bottled blood is not providing you enough sustenance."

My traitorous stomach grumbled as if announcing its agreement. I glanced down at my arms, the blue spiderweb veins standing out in stark contrast to my pale skin. The same marks covered my legs beneath the jeans I wore and even snaked up my stomach and chest. I could see the proof above the low neckline of my Under Armour tank. I couldn't lie my way out of the facts. Instead, I looked to the full glass in front of me. The blood was there for the taking, but I didn't pick it up. Despite the saliva pooling in my mouth, I knew the blood on offer was human. Just like before this meeting. One glass wouldn't even lighten the veins running up my neck. Drinking it would only prove it wasn't cutting it.

I leaned back in my throne, shuddering at the flash of Uriel's murdered family that flooded my mind. Even if my vision had been delivered on time, it still wouldn't have saved their lives. And I knew something needed to change after my blackout, but I'd already given my life and future to live here and deliver my visions. I wouldn't let them force me to break my promise, too. "I won't drink live human blood. From the vein is not an option."

"Refusing live blood is clearly taking a toll on you." Serafina motioned to my chest and neck. "Do you wish to explain why you refuse it?" she said as if she already knew.

The explanation was simple. As long as there was a possibility that Ty was alive, I wouldn't break my promise to him by drinking from anyone's vein. But I couldn't tell her that. She already knew I'd been involved with a lycan and that he'd died during the Portsmouth invasion. The fact that he'd fought alongside our race had fared well with the RVC's judgment of me. So had me being their Oracle and one of their future rulers. It had been swept under the rug. Left only to rumors and speculation among the general public. But none of The Seven—not even Marcus—knew that I thought Ty was still alive. And that I was sneaking out on a regular basis and risking my life—which now belonged to our people—to try to find and save him.

I glanced down at the glass of blood before me. "I made a promise that I will not break of my own free will."

"So you will let yourself slowly die because of that lycan?"

My neck craned to Serafina's sharp voice. So she did know the reason, or had at least guessed it. Back when Ty had been imprisoned at the PVC, she'd been the one to piece together that we'd been involved. "He died protecting our race. The least I can do is keep my word."

"Amelia, you know you can't go on like this," Marcus said with reason. At my glare he grimaced but kept on talking. "I'm on your side. I am. But she's right. You're not just a royal. You're our Oracle. Bottled human blood will never be enough."

The same thing he'd told me before my Oracle ceremony.

Serafina lifted her own glass and swallowed the contents. "Neither will human blood from the vein." She slid her throne back and rose. "What you need to sustain your body, mind, and abilities is much stronger than that."

Even though I wanted to argue, I knew they were right. Bottled wasn't cutting it. And what was stronger? I sighed and nodded. To make sure there wasn't a repeat of yesterday's blackout, and to protect lives, I could do this. And I could still keep my promise, too. "Vampire blood," I said in a rush. "I'll start drinking bottled vampire blood. If we can just arrange—"

"The decision is no longer yours to make, Amelia," Serafina cut me off. She glided to the carved, wooden doors and I twisted in my throne to track her. When she turned back to me, a tight smile pulled at her lips. "Since you have proven you cannot be trusted to care for yourself sufficiently, we have made a decision for your own good. You will take a Pure Blood donor. We have made an allowance so that you only have one supplier at present. The donor has already been informed and has volunteered to be at your disposal for as long as you live, if necessary."

As I went to argue, she swung the double doors open and Kendrick stepped into the room.

What the hell! I spat at him through the bond, but it didn't get through. And now that I thought about it, he'd been vacant from my mind since I'd entered this boardroom. "You knew about this? Why didn't you warn me?"

Kendrick averted his gaze to stare down at his DCs. His mind remained shut off as he refused to meet my glare. "I'm sorry. I was going to..." The deep regret in his unfinished words revealed everything he was hiding.

"*You?* You did this. You went to them?" And now they wanted me to drink from him? To take the act that had always been highly sexual with Ty, and do it with him? Hell no! His feelings for me alone made this beyond wrong. And the betrayal— "No. I won't agree to this."

Marcus leaned over Uriel's throne to cup my clenched hand. "I'm sorry, Amelia. The discussion was already voted on while you were unconscious. The motion was passed."

Marcus stood reluctantly and walked out to the corridor. Serafina cleared her throat. "I will leave you two to some privacy." Then she was gone, closing the thick cuts of wood behind her.

I spun around to face Kendrick and shoved him back with a pinch of voltage. "How dare you!" He said nothing, shoulders slouched as he nudged between thrones to get to the table. With his back to me I let the insults fly. "When you went to them you knew what would happen. Knew they'd force me into this. And you put your freaking hand up. How could you do this to me? You know what my promise—"

I flat-out stopped speaking as the scent of fresh blood poisoned the air. My mouth watered and my fangs broke free.

"What are you doing?"

"You couldn't keep going on the way you were. I tried to reason with you, but you gave me no choice. And I knew you'd never agree to this. After you blacked out, the RVC wouldn't let up on the subject, either. Your well-being matters. To them. To our race. To me. If you die there will only be six. So I went to them and offered to be your donor."

Kendrick faced me and I gasped at what he was doing. Two fang punctures marked his wrist that bled steadily into a crystal glass. My gut churned and my fangs ached. A little voice in my head whispered, *screw the glass. Take the vein. Take it all.* But I ground my teeth together and remained still.

"It won't do as much, but it'll still be heaps better than bottled human." Kendrick held out the glass, staring at it rather than up at me. "I won't force you to take my vein. And I won't tell them you didn't. So long as you drink my blood like this whenever you need it."

Regardless of his explanation, the same words kept repeating over and over in my head. *You betrayed me for them.* It was irrational thought, deep down I knew that, but the words wouldn't stop, just kept boiling my blood while rushing in my head. I swiped the glass from his hands and chugged it dry. Then I slammed it down on the marble slab. Crystal splinters sprayed out from the impact. "*Happy now?*" Seeing red, I spun and stormed from the room.

CHAPTER 7

I tossed and turned in bed, unable to get comfortable. It was now the equivalent of vampire early morning, with the sun not due to set for over four hours when ten-thirty p.m. rolled around. Which wouldn't deliver darkness even then. Being early August, civil twilight would linger for another hour or so after that.

Sunlight blared through my windows now. Which was doing shit-all to help me sleep. I would have gotten up to close them, but I knew my insomnia wasn't caused by daylight. All afternoon and evening, my head had been racing, spewing unending voiceless words. I was still so pissed with Kendrick. But I was also pissed with myself. He'd gone behind my back to the RVC and made promises that took away my right to choose. He'd conspired with them to force me to drink his blood. At the time, part of me had thought it was a way to bring us closer, to force me to drink from him. Except I knew that wasn't true. He'd already decided to supply his blood from a glass well before seeing my livid reaction. That fact I'd plucked from his mind since storming away from him.

Which brought me back to the second person I was angry with.

Me.

I knew I'd do anything to protect anyone I loved and cared about. I'd walk through fire, take a bullet...or a stake. And if I saw one of them self-destructing, fading away like I had been? Nothing would have stopped me from doing everything in my power to save them. *Dammit!* That's all Kendrick had done. And he'd done it knowing his actions could end our friendship. Well, I wasn't about to let that happen.

I lurched upright and tugged on my robe. The lack of blue veins up my arms was noted the instant before the cover-up. So was the missing bone-deep exhaustion and any sign of a dizzy spell at the sudden vertical shift. The *I told you so* went without saying. Padding barefoot past my weapon crates along the wall, through the foyer and around the central table, I reached the door.

Knock, knock.

I paused, my hand an inch from the handle. I was about to ask, *who is it?* But then an open sensation washed over me. Kendrick. He was on the other side, separated by a few measly inches of solid wood. Regret poured from him through our bond like a dam breaking its banks.

I swung the door open and Kendrick's lifted hand froze then dropped. In his other hand he held a full box set of The Vampire Diaries and a purple Under Armour tank—my favorite color and workout brand. Unedited images traveled through the bond, revealing what he'd been going through over the last months. Watching me grow slowly thinner, weaker, and gaunt while being powerless to help. It had emotionally killed him. "I'm so sorry."

Drawing my robe a little tighter over my flimsy satin shorts and tank, I redirected any stray currents away from my skin. With a step forward, I wrapped my arms around his waist. My head turned sideways, resting on his chest. "Me too."

Kendrick put up a sudden block, but the split second of his attraction at holding me snuck through. A similar yet vastly different attraction seared through me, making my mouth water. Since taking Kendrick's blood yesterday, I hadn't had a single drop, of his or of bottled human. Yet despite the hunger, I felt revived, stronger. I shut down the need and bolted shut our mental ties. Without being too abrupt, I released him and took hold of the box set. "TVD marathon?"

Kendrick smiled. "That was the idea."

We set up in the lounge room, situated off the foyer between the open walkways from the bedroom and sitting room. From the mini fridge and full-wall cabinet below the wall-mounted TV, Kendrick took out a bag of potato chips, some bottles of blood, and a full bottle of vodka. At the same time, I shut the drapes, put on disc one, and pushed play as I settled cross-legged on the sectional couch. The new couch that had replaced Caius's musky, floral-patterned antique one.

Kendrick reclined on the adjoined chaise and placed the open bag of chips between us. As the first episode started, I shoved some of the salt and vinegar chips into my mouth. They used to be my favorite. Now they tasted like ash. The vodka-spiked human blood wasn't helping, either. Watching the season where Elena struggled with her own hunger, being a new vampire herself, seemed like a cruel taunt. She couldn't stomach animal blood, and only human blood fed her hunger. In my case, only vampire blood seemed to take the edge off. It was like after taking Kendrick's blood yesterday, a switch had been flicked. Now my body knew what it needed, what it wanted, and anything else was a poor substitute.

Regardless, I kept shoveling chips and drink in as the episodes went by. Each mouthful or gulp did nothing to put a dent in my growing hunger. Kendrick ate and drank too, oblivious with my bond-block in check. When we reached the last episode, my hands began to shake. I downed the rest of my glass, throat swallowing past what felt like sandpaper. I couldn't take it any longer. Yet I still hesitated. Wanting Kendrick's blood so bad tightened my chest with guilt. Because of Ty. And because of Kendrick's feelings for me. The last thing I wanted was for this to affect our friendship. But I couldn't escape this. The RVC wouldn't allow it, and with tremors now spreading up my arms, I knew my body wouldn't either. I pursed my lips and swallowed my doubt, letting the blocks between us fall.

Kendrick, who had been almost asleep, half drunk, and leaning my way, jerked upright with a cough. "Bloody hell, Amelia. Have you been suffering like this for the past few hours?"

I bit my lip and shrugged. "It wasn't that bad. Not like I'm not used to the hunger."

Kendrick cursed and grabbed my now empty glass and bit into his wrist. He shook his head as he completed the bloodletting act before holding the glass out to me. "Take it."

I hesitated with the glass in my hand, that peppery smell from his vein making my head spin. But the shakes were getting worse—like a coming-down junkie—and I met the cool edge with my lips before the contents could cover my robe. The blood slid down like pure, slightly heated velvet. Energy and power refueled every cell in my body. At the same time, the vodka I'd drunk seemed to finally catch up to me. Or maybe it was Kendrick's blood-alcohol levels that boosted the effects. Warmth coated my body like an invisible, humming blanket, and I leaned into Kendrick. My eyes were suddenly so heavy I could barely keep them open. "Thank you," I whispered and ran my hand down his arm to lace my fingers through his. "You always look out for me. You always do what's best."

There was a long pause in return as Kendrick's chest rose and fell with deep breaths. Head on his arm, I heard the increasing speed of his heartbeat. "Not always," he muttered, then pushed me back on the couch and brought his lips down on mine.

I gasped, my eyes flinging open as Kendrick's hands curled around me. His lips moved against mine, full, soft...and needing. Sparks brewed at his touch and I went to push him away—because this was Kendrick, and it was wrong.

But then I stopped.

I needed this...this intimacy, this closeness. I needed to feel something other than heartbreaking despair. I needed to feel love. Even for just a few fleeting seconds.

I gathered the swarming electricity back into the center of my chest. My hands came up and cupped his neck, holding him close as our lips parted. My heart hammered as I licked over his tongue. He tasted like...home.

"Ahem."

I shot away from Kendrick like he was on fire. Heat blazed across my face and down my neck. Marcus stood at the entry from the foyer, amused speculation across his face. And I had just been... *What the hell is wrong with me?*

Frozen as if I might just lunge across the couch and belt him, Kendrick said nothing.

Marcus finally broke the silence. "I didn't mean to interrupt any—"

"You didn't," I cut in. I was angry at Kendrick for instigating what had happened, but I was angrier with myself for letting it go on. For *wanting* it to go on. Ty was out there somewhere, and I'd just been making out with my best friend. *Cheater!* my mind screamed. "It-it was nothing."

"Didn't seem like nothing."

"She's right," Kendrick said, hiding how much my denial gutted him. "Too much vodka. Did you, ah, want something?"

"Thought we could practice abilities in my office." Marcus smiled at me. "You too, Kendrick…if you want."

"I'll pass," Kendrick said quickly, getting to his feet and rearranging his Burton T-shirt like he was suddenly obsessed with wrinkles. He frowned as he looked down at me. Knowing I was still recovering with my new diet, he considered telling me not to go. Then he changed his mind. After what had just happened, he knew I needed a distraction. "But you should go."

"Uh, sure." Face scorching and hating myself, I nodded at Marcus. "I'll be there soon."

Marcus left my suite, and Kendrick walked backward to the foyer. "I'm sorry, Amelia. It was my fault. I should never have kissed you. I mean, I wanted to, I just… It shouldn't have happened. Don't blame yourself."

With a solemn last look he turned and I heard the door open and shut behind him. I lifted a hand to my still-throbbing lips. *"Shit."* Whether Kendrick had started it or not didn't matter. The blame for what had happened sat with me. The crushing guilt that churned the chips and blood in my stomach was just part of the punishment and proof. Because I had kissed my best friend back…and I had liked it.

"I DIDN'T WANT to vote against you," Marcus said, closing the drapes behind his desk to block out the setting sun. We were alone, our guards stationed right outside the closed door. "But I'm not blind, Amelia. I couldn't continue to stand by and watch you waste away." He walked by the stone fireplace across the room to perch on the armchair, instead of joining me on the Chesterfield sofa. With elbows on knees and hands joined with tense fingers, his gaze slowly rolled up to mine. "Can you ever forgive me?"

I sighed as I glanced around the office, unable to hold his pleading stare. Black candles topped the fireplace's mantle, the few glass side tables around the room, and the coffee table that separated us. The remaining wall space on either side of the fireplace was filled with different sized mirrors. Mirrors that showed just how much of a difference taking Kendrick's blood was making. Mirrors that also spotlighted over and over the rosy color still across my cheeks…from the memory of that kiss.

I groaned and went horizontal, knees propped up as I stared up at the ornate ceiling. I forced my thoughts back to Marcus. He'd come to check on me while I was out cold and Kendrick had confided in him. Together they'd brought their concerns for me up with the RVC. That I had only just found out. And I wasn't mad. Not really. I was more concerned about his opinion of me after what he'd walked in on. Not that he would really judge. He didn't even know Ty might be alive. "It's okay. I get it."

"Oh, good. I'm glad." Marcus inched back in the armchair, the leather creaking in response. "Shall we start on practice, then?"

I twisted sideways to look at him. In the darkness of his office, with only one lit candle on the glass coffee table, his teal-flecked eyes showed relief, but there was something else. Anticipation. He hadn't called me here just to hang out or to confess. He wanted to help me bring on a vision. The last time I'd tried I had electrocuted everyone in the gymnasium. "I don't know if this is a good idea. I don't want to hurt you."

Marcus came around the coffee table and perched on its edge.

He held out his hand and waited. I sat up and reached out, blue sparks that I didn't try to hold back running down to my fingertips. Then I threaded my fingers through his. Rather than convulsing at being shocked, the sparks absorbed into his skin. "You can't hurt me, Amelia."

I'd seen this happen before moving to the Armaya. Neither of us understood why, and even with the proof, I still felt unsure. "That doesn't mean a full-on expulsion won't hurt you." *When I haven't already zapped a dozen or so other people first*, I thought.

"I'll take my chances." Marcus smiled as I let go, holding his hand out with his fingers splayed. Instantly every candle lit up, their flames adding flickering warmth to the room and reflecting off the wall of mirrors. The feel of the room was suddenly inviting, myste- rious and...*romantic*. "Use the sound of the burning wicks to concentrate."

His voice was deep and smooth, and I watched him as he moved back around to the armchair. He was devastatingly attractive, those seductive eyes, sharp jawline, prominent cheekbones, and spiked blond hair adding to his perfectly toned physique. Beneath a plain white T-shirt, each contour of his chest and abs was visible. Yet all the eye candy and the feeling of being so inexplicably connected to him did nothing to attract me in that way. Anything between us was and always would be platonic.

I reclined on my back, the glow of candles remaining behind my closed lids as I focused on the only sound in the room. Hearing that slight crackle that surrounded me from every angle, I pushed the light away until all that surrounded me was darkness. The black void was endless—no below, no above, no far, no near. Just...nothing. Only the sound of the crackling flames remained as the shadows crept in and I took hold of one.

The flames grew louder with swift intensity. No longer the

gentle crackle of countless candles, but a raging inferno. Red and orange light exploded around me and my eyes flung open. Fire. It was everywhere. Glass exploded out on a café front and screams filled the air. Vampires scurried in panic all around me. Not from the flames. Not from the explosion. Dark figures tracked them, taking them down before they could escape. The damned. They were inside the Armaya's walls—

I jacked upright with a start, raging fire replaced by gentle candlelight. Screams replaced by a rush of movement as Marcus came around to kneel before me. My whole body glowed blue, a thick volt splitting from my hand right as Marcus's palm caught mine. Instantly the blue died off and the sparks sizzled away. But I wasn't okay. Body swaying and head light, my eyes rolled back in my head— "Oh, shit."

Kendrick burst through the door and slammed it on Marcus's and my guards just outside. He got to my side, sheer panic hijacking his features as he tore a bottle from the backpack at his shoulder. Short of snapping the glass neck open, he removed the cap and forced it to my lips. "I was bringing supplies to your suite when I felt you—*oh God*—don't pass out again."

The blood, his blood, slid down like a dream. The cottony tingles that threatened to take my consciousness receded. My lids blinked open, my sight going from blurred to sharp as Kendrick lowered the empty bottle.

Marcus raised an eyebrow at my best friend who clasped my hand. "You're not supplying her from your vein?"

"As long as it's not necessary...no. That okay with you?"

Marcus lifted himself onto the edge of the coffee table with a shrug. "Sure, but what did you see, Amelia?"

Before I could reply, the images of my disturbing vision faded while tiny sparks pinched Kendrick's hand and absorbed into

Marcus's. Marcus's hand fell away while Kendrick continued to hold on, feeling the panic I'd felt at what I'd seen replaced by confusion. He frowned down at me and I felt the familiar tingle of him prodding over my brain. "You're blocking me? What did you see?"

My mouth opened, lips ready to speak. But nothing came out. Kendrick couldn't access my vision, and now that I tried—

I winced as sharp stabbing pain speared through my frontal lobe. A black smudge was left in place of the memory. "I'm not blocking you. The vision, whatever I saw…it's gone."

CHAPTER 8

I sat on my throne on stage the next day, beside the other crowned royals. All of us were decked out in white, black, and gold gowns and suits for the occasion. Five open-lidded, black coffins were lined up in front of the raised level, with relocated royals mourning over the murdered Aswinds. With the castle's private jet, those five bodies had been delivered home and prepared for the funeral. And I could barely stomach it to look at them, so quiet and still. Those poor defenseless children with their hands folded in front of them—God, they were young. Imagining the way they'd died was unconscionable.

The memories it stirred up had my hand covering Marcus's on the throne beside me. The terrified girl's eyes I'd seen through all those months ago had warned me of the threat to the Vladimirs. And failed to save them. Marcus's whole family had perished at the hands of the damned. I blinked back tears as I glanced to him. "Are you okay?"

With a gulp, his jaw tightened. His hand turned up and his

fingers threaded through mine. He nodded stiffly, but kept his focus glued to the mourners who wept as they paid their respects. "So long as I have you."

Around the hall, the number of guards had increased, with the extra ready to be assigned to every royal in line to a throne. But someone was missing. And when Kendrick found out about the guard assignment? I gulped at the thought. After stocking my bar fridge yesterday, he'd been blocking me, too. Still was now.

As the heated memory of our shared kiss stole my breath, Kendrick rushed in from the back corridor. I shut the memory down. Taking a seat in the front row, he didn't meet my eyes, even though I knew he could feel me watching him.

Where have you been?

His face was flushed as his gaze slid to mine. With his thoughts still on lockdown, he shrugged. *My room. I forgot what time it was.* His focus settled on the lined-up coffins and stayed there. Subject closed.

I frowned but followed his stare. After his stolen-but-returned kiss, he was probably just trying to normalize things between us. Keep the lines clear even though he was now supplying his blood to me. Which was good. It was.

Uriel Aswind, having already delivered a eulogy of sorts, watched with grave features as the last royals moved from the first coffin down to the last. My heart ached for her, unable to imagine losing everyone I loved and still being able to go on. But she remained a pillar of community strength as the mourners moved back to their seats. Though her eyes were red, she hadn't shed a single tear in public.

Marcus released my hand then and crossed to the podium, reaching out to touch Uriel's shoulder. "Are you ready to say goodbye?"

Uriel nodded and glanced to the cloth-draped table across the stage, her face vacant with held-back grief. Her wavy-edged sword lay there beside the chalice. "I want to give a blood offering to safeguard their souls."

Marcus nodded and retrieved the chalice and sword, which he then handed to Uriel.

"Would you join me in blessing my dead?" Holding the sword by its gold hilt, she stared down the silver length.

"It would be my honor." Marcus unbuttoned his sleeve and held out his arm. He didn't flinch as she ran the serrated edge across his wrist. The blood trickled into the sparkling chalice held below as he met Uriel's gaze. "With my blood, may your lost find eternal peace."

Uriel continued the ritual with the other crowned royals who all participated. When she reached me I held up my arm before she could ask. "With my blood, may your lost find eternal peace."

As Uriel cut a channel across my wrist, the sound of collective whispers changed, the surrounding noise becoming crisper. I blinked hard and Uriel frowned at me before gliding back to the podium and repeating the ritual on herself. The hall with its lit torches began to flicker. I could still see Uriel at the front of the stage, slowly moving to drip blood from the chalice onto her murdered family. But that wasn't all I could see.

In the flicker, a large area lit by wind-dancing candle flames replaced reality. Two workbenches—similar to the ones in Vanessa's basement—housed ancient small and large glass bottles that caught and reflected the orange flames. But this wasn't a room I'd seen before. The walls were made of stone, as was the ground, and a Gothic frame made up a glassless opening in the wall with a view of a plunging hillside at night.

A man sat behind one workbench, his puffy white sleeve rolled up to his shoulder as he stared away from me and out at the black sky. There was something so familiar yet unplaceable about him. "How many have failed thus far?"

Next to him was a woman—I did a double take. I'd seen her before. Long blond hair, piercing silver-blue eyes, wearing a gown made up of ruffled skirts and a choking neckline.

Erzsebet's stare on the man was raw determination personified. "This time it will work." She used a dagger to slice through his exposed forearm. The wound began to pull back together and she quickly grabbed a small glass bottle and spilled the contents onto the cut.

The man hissed and tensed, oil-black veins growing all the way up his arm, neck, and across his face. His head twisted, teeth gritted and eyes shining for a second in vibrant red.

I gasped as the vision melted, Erzsebet and her guinea pig fading from sight. I'd seen his face before, too. The man I now knew had been Uriel's father, Lord Aswind.

With another blink the scenery fully reverted to the hall. What I'd seen and how conscious I'd remained had my curiosity peaking. And I wasn't the only one. No longer across the stage, Uriel was staring at me, curious expectation across her sad face. Still holding tight to her sword she said under her breath, "You had a vision."

Around us the entire hall was a mash of blurred noise as royals consoled each other over the loss of the Aswinds.

I tried to talk, but my fangs punched free with desperate throbbing. Roaring hunger struck my stomach with drowning need. I zoned in on the blue veins inside her wrist. Hiking up the hefty weight of my long gown, I was one second away from becoming a vampire-turned-ripper. My mouth parted—

Kendrick appeared on the stage then with a swift leap. He'd been helping with the coffins, but shot over upon feeling my sudden hunger and seeing the replay of my vision. He knew I needed blood, but he wasn't about to force his vein on me or reveal our alternative. Instead he said, "Maybe I should take you somewhere private for a moment to cull your hunger."

Kendrick began to help me up, but Uriel caught my wrist. "Please, I must know what you saw."

I forced my body back onto my throne, and gripped the solid armrest to keep my fangs from doing the walking. God, it was hard to talk. "I saw...your father and Erzsebet Bathory," I spoke around my teeth enhancements, trying to ignore the milling vamps and the collective smell of blood in the air. "Together." I really didn't know Uriel that well, bar the fact that she'd seemed intent on winning the jewelry box at the auction, and that her father had been electric, too. I had no idea what her motives had been back then. And I was no closer to knowing them now. I wasn't about to give too much away without something in return. "Were they involved?"

"Of course," Uriel answered, eyes shifting to her sword then back to me. "They were crowned royals at the same time."

"And that was all they were?" Kendrick questioned.

"Why do you ask?"

I shrugged, my hold on the armrest creaking the wood. If she wasn't going to play along, then neither was I. "They just seemed close."

"Well this is very interesting." Uriel held out her sword before me. At my frown, she smiled. "My father mastered an ability connected to The Sight before his death. He could bring on a vision related to the owner of a certain object."

Although my mind was hazy with thirst, I thought back. I hadn't even considered why that particular vision had come to me at that exact moment. But Uriel had just sliced my wrist with her sword when my senses began picking up things that weren't real in that moment. This was huge. Through the touch of an object, which meant... "That sword belonged to your father."

"Yes, it did."

A feral squeal escaped my stomach and a fresh strike of hunger had my arm clamping over my gut.

"Let's get some blood into you—before you pass out."

Kendrick looped his arm around my waist and nodded to Uriel, who resumed her throne. Then he helped me off the stage and down the corridor to the boardroom doors. By the time he carted me in and closed us inside, I was barely holding back from tearing into his neck. The smell of his blood and the thrum of his heart were like a drug and well within my reach. I shoved out of his hold.

"Would be easier if you just took my vein," he muttered, reaching toward the decanter on the table and snatching a crystal glass. The secret wish that I'd actually do just that wasn't missed.

Despite the temptation and the fact that I was staring at his neck, I croaked, "Not happening." The memory of our stolen kiss returned, and I locked all thoughts down. I forced myself to look out the tall windows to the empty path outside. No funeral procession yet, and I knew why. My hand went to the hidden pocket in my gown, flicking my iPhone's silence button off and on, off and...

Kendrick bit into his wrist and filled the glass. "Here," he said, forcing it into my hands. "Hurry up before someone comes. The funeral march—"

An outburst of noise penetrated the almost soundproof door as I chugged the blood, my sanity and restraint returning in a crystal-clear rush.

Kendrick frowned at the door then moved to the first window, scanning up and down the empty path. "Why aren't they marching?" When I didn't reply, the confusion across his face became suspicion as he turned back to me. "You're blocking me. And you know what's going on out there. Just tell me, already."

After my vision practice yesterday, Marcus and I had attended an RVC meeting. New concerns were brought to attention and motions were passed. Not in my favor.

Knowing the argument telling Kendrick would start, and with him blocking me out, I'd kept the details to myself. But I was out of time now. "At the meeting yester—"

The boardroom door suddenly swung inward. I shoved the empty glass I was still clinging to behind my back as a single guard entered. He bowed at Kendrick. "My Lord."

Kendrick returned to my side and tilted my chin up so I'd look at him. "What's going on, Amelia?"

"A guard's been assigned to every royal in line to a throne." I gulped in horrid anticipation. "The whole community's on lock-down. No royals are allowed to leave."

As the vocal disputes continued beyond the open door, Kendrick unleashed a string of internal arguments and curses. Hurt at my deception had his fists clenching as hard as his jaw. Rules or not, I still had a way to sneak out while remaining on site, but he didn't. And Kendrick knew that when the next lead came, I wasn't letting anything hold me back from seeking Ty out.

"Wait outside," Kendrick hissed at his guard through gritted teeth. The guard quickly complied and he swung the door shut, arm tightening with the need to slam it instead. "I'm not letting you go anywhere without me," he said as he caught my wrist.

I pulled away, irritation growing at his unwarranted protective-ness. Right now his worry was for nothing. Without another lead, I had no plans to leave. "They're just scared. They'll ease off with the lockdown—"

My iPhone in the hidden pocket of my gown belted out the first few seconds to Red's song *Lie to me*. Heart now thumping, I pulled it out. The text was from Marika. *'Tomorrow night 7PM. Could be the motherload.'*

Shit! I shoved the phone back into my pocket, absently wondering why a Mr. Malau dreamscape hadn't been used to deliver the message. The lead I'd been waiting for was finally here, and according to Marika, this one was huge. I'd been worried by the long silence from the wolves—but now, having just this one lead... made me feel like I could breathe again. If Ty was anywhere, there was a good chance he'd be there. And Marika would be on her way to cover my ass tomorrow night.

"No way in hell," Kendrick spat at the same time I said, "I can't not go."

"The hell you can't." Those fists cranked tighter while anger-laced fear marked his face. "I'm not letting you go without me."

I stared him down, trying to hold on to my irritation. But it paled to the total fear pulsing off him. Fear I understood all too well. If I died when he wasn't there to protect me, he'd never forgive himself...just like I could never forgive myself if we didn't find and somehow save Ty. "Then we need an alternative." I tugged out my phone again and dialed Dorian.

"Hey, sis—I mean, Amelia. What's doing?"

"Blood or not..."

"I know. I know. You're still my sister. So what's up?"

"We're taking off tomorrow, but I need your help. Is there any way you can get Vanessa to your place with her marking gear?"

There was a slight pause before Dorian replied. "Well, actually, she's already here. With her gear. Marcus brought her in to help the castle alchemist. She'll be here for a few days."

"Perfect." My sigh of relief was tame compared to the instant released strain from Kendrick's muscles. "We'll be 'round at seven p.m."

I hung up and texted Marika. *'Meet at Dorian's.'*

ANTICIPATION of our plan fueled my steps, along with the possibility of finally finding Ty as I crossed the street with Kendrick the following evening. Though as we neared Dorian's house, uncertainty weighed me down. I still hadn't succeeded in restoring any damned. Had killed all the ones I'd tried to cure.

Shouldering the strap of his Burton backpack—which was stacked with a thermos of blood, changes of clothes fit for fighting and blending, and weapons—Kendrick nudged me. *If we find him, we'll catch as many damned as it takes to figure that out. He won't die at your hands from a failed attempt.*

I smiled, knowing he hid his words because of our new constant of three heavily armed guards. My two flanked from either side, while Kendrick's one tailed behind. Being not quite seven p.m., it was at least three hours till sunset and four until civil dusk, but as they were all of royal blood, cover from sunlight wasn't a must.

I mounted the front step and knocked on the blue door. Already knowing their orders, the three guards fanned out, one to the front external corner of the weatherboard house, another down to the back corner, and the last down the uncovered side.

The door creaked open, releasing a stream of dance music into the atmosphere. Dorian bounced on the balls of his feet. "Finally. Let's get this party started." It was a good cover, but I knew his excitement was real. Despite the serious task of locating Ty, he reveled in the action and adventure of taking down more damned.

Like it gave him purpose after learning he didn't really belong anywhere.

We went inside and Kendrick shut the door and followed us into the living room. Vanessa sat cross-legged on the dark carpet with a thick book in her lap.

"Hey, Vanessa," I said with a wave.

"How's the gig in the lion's den panning out?" Kendrick tacked on.

Vanessa shrugged, her loose-knit sweater falling off one shoulder. "With all the royals and guards from other councils being relocated here, Marcus commissioned me to lend a hand." She flicked her wavy red hair over her shoulder. "Which gave me the perfect opportunity to get inside the gates and visit your brother," she said, not bothering to correct the fact that Dorian wasn't really my brother.

Dorian sat down on a worn, cloth sofa, pulling Vanessa up onto his lap and planting a kiss on her neck. "Can't say I'm complaining."

The dance music kept blaring from an iPod plugged into a dock on a battered side table as I glanced around the room. Had we arrived too soon? I kept my voice low so the words would be muffled by the constant music. "Marika's late?" That would be a first.

"No," Dorian said, nodding toward the ceiling.

The manhole slid aside and a girl in all black slipped out. Marika landed on her feet in the center of the room and shrugged. "Thought I'd lay low in case your guards decided to routine check the place or something." Alchemist tattoos patterned her skin from her wrist all the way up to the sleeve of her tight T-shirt. Each did something different, from blocking her scent to giving her strength and stealth. And each would be hidden below her imprinted cover once she took my form. The vials of blood I'd given her last time gave her a way to pass through the wards without setting them off. She frowned at me. "So what's with the change of address and audience?"

Now our plan was finally going to be put into action. "Kendrick's been assigned a guard and can't set foot off grounds. So we need you, Vanessa, to mark him to boost his compulsion. We need the guards to think that when they see my double that they're also seeing him."

Vanessa shook her head and squeezed the book onto the side table. "Won't work. I just spent the last day giving all new guards anti-compulsion marks. A boosted mark won't override it."

Kendrick shifted so close to me I could feel the instant angst radiating off him. "Amelia, you're not leaving here without me."

So far he'd come with me to every damned location. He'd risked his own life over and over to keep me safe and watch my back. And until now, there hadn't been an issue with him meeting up with me outside the Armaya's walls. But after my vision and the attack on the Aswind line, that had changed. Still, I couldn't let this lead go with the possibility of missing the one place we could find Ty at.

"There's nothing I can do." I stepped back, feeling suffocated by his overwhelming urge to protect. "And I have to see this through. You know I can't stop until I know—"

A knock at the front door cut off my argument. Kendrick shot there first and cracked the blue barrier. "You were ordered—"

The door swung in, knocking Kendrick back. Marcus strode inside, flinging the door shut on his two guards standing across the street under a canopy of trees. He eyed Kendrick then me, hurt-laced anger painting his features as he cleared the hallway. "Having a party without me?"

I blocked his way before he could enter the living room. "Marcus, what are you doing here?"

"Don't bother hiding," he said, voice edged with challenge but quiet like he didn't want the guards outside to hear. "I know you're in there." He stared down at me. "You're planning to leave the compound."

"What makes you think that?"

Marcus pushed past me into the living room. Kendrick and I were right behind him, able to see that Marika had remained unhidden. "Why else would you have a lycan sneak over the walls?"

"You saw that?" Marika glared at Marcus, body frozen like she was ready to bolt or attack.

No longer sitting relaxed on Dorian's lap, but on her feet, Vanessa's eyes were wide as she rubbed her knee like she'd knocked it on the side table. And it was no wonder. Marcus had gotten her this job inside the walls and now he'd found her hiding out with a lycan.

Now standing beside Vanessa, Dorian took her hand, but in a reassuring, nothing-shocks-me-too-much kind of way.

"You weren't that stealthy, lycan." Marcus smiled at me. "I know you've been slipping away these past months. Your personality and turn of phrase were a dead giveaway." The look he gave me said our unexplained connection was the nail in the coffin. Imprinted or not, there's no way Marika could replicate that. "And I can only assume it has to do with the lycan."

There was no point lying. And really? I didn't want to. "We think he's alive...damned."

"So, why are you here?" Kendrick crossed his arms over his chest. "To talk us out of taking off?"

"I'm here because the guard assignment and new marks will stop you from going along with Amelia. And I couldn't live with myself if anything happened." Marcus met my eyes with deep sincerity. "So, I'm here to help. With this..." He tugged a slip of paper from the inside pocket of his pea coat and flashed an intricate symbol of swirls and lines that made up what resembled a series of eyes. "If my father's book was right, this can break through even anti-compulsion marks."

Vanessa came up close and studied the picture. "I haven't seen this one before, but from the detail, I think it could work."

"Great." Marcus gave Vanessa the paper and clapped his hands together. "Marika, it's time to take Amelia's place. Vanessa, take me to your marking gear." Before I could question why he was getting marked, he added, "If the compulsion needs re-establishing, or if rotations are changed, I'll be here to do it."

The next twenty minutes passed in slow-mo. After pushing Marika from the living room into Dorian's bedroom so she could imprint me and take my clothes, I re-dressed in Under Armour black gear and my zip-up hoodie. The noisy tattoo gun kept drumming away from the bathroom where Vanessa was inking Marcus. Finally the sound cut off, and they returned from down the hallway.

When we were all back in the living room, Marcus instructed Marika to leave and take my guards with her. When all that remained was Kendrick's guard and his two, Marcus waved goodbye and backed up to the front door. Then he was gone, leaving the rest of us standing inside.

Vanessa turned off the music and we all listened in complete silence. I crept to the front window and peeked through the curtains.

"You have safely delivered Kendrick Baldassare back to his room," he stated, hands on Kendrick's guard's shoulder and gaze locked on his. "Remain stationed outside and do not let anyone in, except for Lady Bathory. Leave now."

Without argument or even a sound, Kendrick's guard marched in the opposite direction back to the castle. Marcus eyed his own guards who looked confused but remained sheltered by the lined-up trees. Their confusion melted with his next compelled words. "You didn't see that." Then he winked over his shoulder and strolled down the cobblestone street, his guards right behind him.

I veered my Ducati onto a dirt road in Wasilla, minding the uneven ground with old and new water trenches and potholes. Which would have been a helluva lot easier if the sun hadn't already dipped past the tall overhanging trees that lined the way. The old home and barn were just up ahead, past the curved road and down an even bumpier dirt driveway that vibrated my body. And I could barely stand to slow down for the sake of my bike. This was our drive-by stop before taking off with the wolves to the damned location, and hope-fully...to Ty.

But then my focus shifted. Hard up against my back, Kendrick's thighs rubbed against mine with all the bumpy driving. His broad hands around my hips tightened for a split second. Watching over my shoulder, he hissed in his breath as his romantic desire leaked through the closed bond; a prelude to what could be a seriously hot situation. On my bike we were so close, his thin T-shirt and jeans along with my fitted gear doing almost nothing to establish a barrier. Something unwanted stirred within me as our freaking kiss replayed in my mind. I slammed the replay down hard.

I was a total piece of shit.

How could I be thinking of anything but Ty when we were here to set off on another potential rescue mission?

The earthy forest scents mingled with an overload of lycan blood then. Apprehension joined Kendrick's desire through our bond as I pulled up before a crowd of male and female werewolves.

"What's with the audience?"

Feeling suddenly hot and claustrophobic, I dismounted so fast I almost kicked Kendrick in the face. I shucked off my zip-up hoodie and, with uneven breath, I scanned them over. Most were in human form, but a few rocked their furry alternative. Then my heart stopped dead at a flash of red eyes. Was that...?

"What is it?" Kendrick asked, getting off the bike.

I froze, doubling back to the guy standing on the edge of the pack. I shook my head and looked away. The traits were the same: black hair, scarred tan skin, determined gold—not red—stare, and hunting boots with jeans. It wasn't him. A few inches taller, it was Troy. My eyes were playing tricks on me, again. I killed the engine. "Nothing."

Dorian pulled up behind us on the old bike he'd borrowed from Vanessa—since with her job she'd stayed behind and didn't need it. Which saved his M5 from the dust and possible stone chips that driving on this road could inflict. "What's up with the heat?"

Mr. Malau stood out in the center, a towering hulk even among his own race. "You made good time." He stepped forward and his arm around my shoulder caught the length of my long plait. "Come with me. We have matters to discuss."

Kendrick stiffened, ready to remove the alpha in any way possible. Dorian stepped before us, blocking the way.

"It's fine, guys. Really."

They stood down reluctantly and Mr. Malau dropped his arm, indicating for me to head down the dirt path around to the back of the house. Standing in yellow porch light at the back steps, Mr. Malau handed me the address, which I took with eager hands. Holding what could potentially deliver me to Ty, I frowned at the piece of paper. "This is in the old industrial area in Anchorage."

"According to Troy, it's the busiest location we've uncovered. The abandoned warehouse could very well be the main nest. My wolves will infiltrate and take down every damned they cross, bar one. Your order is to locate Ty and restrain him long enough for Troy to tranq him."

A shiver took flight in my neck and ran down to my toes. "So Ty's there?" Desperation edged my words because my recurring dream of Ty's death had stopped a week ago when the ending had changed. Was it a sign that we were already too late?

Golden emotion rippled across the alpha's irises. "If he's alive, he'll be there. If not..." Mr. Malau disappeared up the steps and through the creaky, hole-filled screen door. A few heartbeats later he reappeared. He sighed, deep and slow, reservation all over his face. "The leads are drying up. It's been over six months and we've infiltrated location after location and put down how many damned?"

I'd stopped counting after killing twenty, but collectively it had been getting up there. "At least two hundred."

"And each time you've interrogated at least one damned. Have they resulted in any leads? Any information at all that would indicate that a lycan now exists among them?"

"No, but—"

"Eventually rescue missions become recovery missions," he spoke over me, stairs creaking as he leaned back into the doorjamb. He looked totally defeated and worn down. "But even without a body, we must accept that there is an end to this hopeful searching. We must move on and do what is best for our races. Tomorrow will be your last mission under my command."

"No." Disbelief and panic that this could be the end made my insides feel like they wanted to crawl up my throat. "I don't accept this. You can't just give up. I can't—"

"I am not giving up, Amelia, but what you do after tomorrow is your choice. Continue fighting, or accept you are the vampire Oracle and one of their rulers. Whatever you decide, I will not be pulling the strings." Mr. Malau held out his hand, an inscribed silver stake resting across his massive palm. "I want you to have this."

My heart clenched as if trapped in a vice and about to explode. The moment I'd jumped onto Ty's coffin and ripped the lid open replayed in my subconscious. This stake had belonged to Ty. It was the very same one that had been placed in his empty deathbed. I tried to speak as I took the stake, but tears choked up my throat.

"For your allegiance, my promise to you is that our temporary truce still stands. As long as you and your friends live, you will not be our enemy. But…if you ever find yourself needing backup where the damned are concerned, I'd like to repay the favor."

CHAPTER 9

When the sun had set and darkness was growing like a plague, we arrived at the abandoned warehouse in the industrial outskirts of Anchorage. The pendant around my wrist flared with unrelenting heat. There were damned inside, all right. Heaps of them. My hand caught the amulet around my neck in a tight fist. Everything before now had come to this. And my last hope, which hung by a thread, was soaring. Ty had to be here. He just had to.

The bristling wolf pack snapped at each other as they led the way, fully transformed and ready to kill with their canines. All bar Troy. He remained in human form with Kendrick, Dorian, and me, just as decked out as we were. Silver stakes decorated our belts, four each. Kendrick and Troy had holstered daggers, too, while Dorian shouldered his crossbow and I held my silver whip.

The warehouse was huge, three levels high with a splash of six sixteen-paned windows across the front. Some were cracked or missing, but every single one was boarded up, preventing light from filtering inside. Which made no difference now in the growing night's darkness. All our previous raids had been in the early morning hours, with the sun's light to aid us. But this location, although abandoned, wouldn't be free of passersby during broad daylight hours. Only night accomplished that. And even then, it wouldn't be pitch black.

Troy pushed through the crowding wolves and held up a pair of wire cutters. Raw determination laced with unspoken vulnerability scored his features as he glanced at me. This was the end of the line and he knew it. He refocused on the pack. "Stick to the plan. Bark for backup." He cut across and down on the chain wire and bent it back like a door. "No damned leaves here alive, bar Ty. Howl when you find him."

The wolves padded through the opening, making no sound as they surrounded the building. Kendrick remained glued to my side, sticking with the wolves up front. He'd established where he belonged, and no amount of ordering from Troy could change that. *As always,* the words streamed from his mind to mine, the *I'll be right here* not needing to be said.

Dorian followed Troy and the remaining wolves around back, his never-dying support and trust in my fighting ability portrayed in the stiff nod he sent my way.

I unraveled my whip and faced the door.

For a moment of heart-stopping silence, I waited, my pulse thudding in my ears. Then the thump of a steel back door being kicked in rang out.

I kicked the front door in and screamed, "Get in!"

Inside it was dark, the light of lingering twilight outside cutting off as I slammed the door shut. My vampire night vision came alive. Debris littered the open shell: old machinery, packing crates, and waste metal. The gentle glow beyond the machinery from the back door cut off too. The stink of decomposing flesh poisoned the stale air and choked up my throat. Glowing red eyes filled the darkness between the waste, ready and waiting.

I scanned them in a flash, desperate for that one face to stand out above the rest.

No luck.

Then it was game on.

The wolves pelted at the damned, jaws wide and canines ready. Kendrick and I ran after them in shadow. But the damned were prepared for our attack. And we were matched in numbers.

In the background, I heard the second group of wolves. They were fighting their own battle behind a shield of old machinery. It sounded like they were making ground, wolves barking out after they tore the throats from their opponents. The call needed for one of us to finish the job permanently with a stab of silver through the heart.

I caught a quick glimpse of Dorian, cutting down a group of damned like they were easy pickings. Either he'd gotten a super mark from Vanessa, or those damned were already wolf bitten. But I didn't have time to find out.

On our side, it wasn't such easy sailing.

I shadowed the wolves to one side of the warehouse while Kendrick took the other side. His eyes clouded as he conjured wind to send a crate flying at the wall. As it shattered, fragmented timber pieces speared through the air, impaling damned and slowing them down for the wolves to catch.

At the same time, I lashed out my whip, using the spiked length to cut flesh, solid handle to crack noses, and twisting it like a silver choker around damned necks. Electricity batted around beneath my ribs, desperate to break free.

But I held it back.

For every damned who came at me and for every one I tracked to kill, I registered their face…hoping like hell it would be Ty. The power I reserved was for him and him alone.

The battle went on and on, the enemy not tiring and us not giving up. For every damned we injured, the wolves pounced and shredded their throats. But there were still so many left. For as many damned that perished, a wolf fell. The damned were relentless, tearing into the wolves with nails and fangs like tiny daggers.

Scrapes, cuts, and bruises patterned Kendrick's body as well as mine. Blood dampened our slashed clothes. Kendrick's power ebbed from overuse and my legs felt like heavy stumps.

Dorian's team appeared around the machinery then, injured but fighting fit. He bolted off with Troy and a few wolves, taking the railed stairs leading up the back wall. The remaining wolves, fur tacky with blood, joined our assault.

With the extra numbers, we began to make a comeback. Now Kendrick and I could get to the second part of Troy's command.

While the wolves took down the still-encroaching damned, we holstered our weapons. Throatless damned littered the concrete floor and we unsheathed stakes. All with various injuries, some lay still as death. Others twitched all over. Kendrick dropped beside the first and drove his stake home. With a cry, the writhing damned turned into a body-shaped pillar of live coals. Then it imploded with a puff of ash.

I followed suit, using a random stake and keeping Ty's inscribed one looped in my belt. That silver point would only be used on him. To make his dead heart beat again.

A loud commotion sounded upstairs. How many more were up there? Did Dorian and Troy need backup?

I hoped like hell they were okay, but I couldn't leave to find out. Killing these half-dead damned was my priority. Even though they were werewolf bitten, there was no guarantee they wouldn't regenerate enough to come after us. The only way to truly kill a damned? Silver to the heart or decapitation.

Even as panic for Dorian's safety filled my heart with dread, I kept eliminating the damned.

When the sounds around us dwindled, so did the ruckus upstairs.

I turned from the puff of coal-turned-ash beneath me and shot to my feet. Stake holstered in the loop of my belt, I rubbed ash from my sore eyes.

The wolves had stopped fighting behind me. Kendrick was on his butt, breathing heavy with black smudges all over his pale skin. My breathing was heavy, too, though I'd only just noticed it now that I'd stopped.

Around us, the damned were no more. All that remained were piles of black ash, and puddles and splashes of black and red blood. Among the ashen piles were bodies, lycans that had died and turned back into human form. Just like Ty had.

And it was clear in the quiet carnage that he wasn't here.

A creak of metal filled the now deathly quiet warehouse. The depression that threatened to swallow me went on standby as Dorian and Troy trudged down the stairs.

They weren't alone.

Being dragged on what at first looked like a leash, was a damned. The silver chain Troy held over his shoulder was curled tight around the damned's neck, continuing down his body to restrain its arms. The sizzling of its burning flesh grew louder as they descended, as did its hiss. Black blood gurgled from countless holes across its chest and the gashes marking its face.

It wasn't Ty.

But the damned didn't struggle against the restraint. Didn't retaliate even though wolves snapped at its heels.

"You're okay?" I scanned my brother over.

Dorian nodded, tight-lipped as Troy tugged on the chain. The damned stumbled forward, and Troy kicked the back of its knees, forcing it to kneel. "Repeat what you told me, leech."

The damned looked up at me and I sucked in my breath. Terror stained his eyes, his glowing *red* eyes. I'd never seen a damned look anything but evil, defiant, and starving. "What's wrong with him?"

"Newly turned by about six months," Dorian said. "Or so he swears."

"The insanity builds slowly with each full-consumption kill," Kendrick added, moving to stand beside me. "Looks like he still has breaks of clarity…regret."

"I do." Wounds across his body where the chains weren't touching began to pull together. "I'm not like—"

"Answer my question." Troy pointed the tip of a silver dagger at the damned's temple. "Or find out what this feels like." With a sizzle, black blood bubbled from the puncture like it was boiling on contact.

"I—I know the l-lycan you're looking for," the damned stammered, red eyes wide with fear. "The one they took from Portsmouth."

"You *know* him?" My heart galloped, alive with hope. Ty wasn't here, but this wasn't the end. "You know where he is?"

The damned lifted its face to the exposed-beam ceiling, shutting his eyes. "I was at the PVC. They sent us from the Armaya to see *you*." His red eyes leveled on me, still scared but with a look of awe. "Our Oracle." He blinked and looked down at his stomach, hand trying to reach there but the chains stopping him. "I died that day, in that hall. Then I woke up here. The lycan was here, too. I transitioned with him in the basement. The steel door's hidden below the crates back there. But, the lycan…he didn't make it. He's dead."

118

I fell to my knees, tears glazing my sight. My need to attempt a restore on this damned paled at his confession. Wet drops slid down my cheeks and over my lip. They tasted like salt in my mouth. It couldn't be true. I couldn't have come all this way, risked our lives over and over, and failed.

There was a sound across the warehouse like large items being tipped and thrown, but I took no notice. This was different to the last damned's claim that Ty was worm meat. He wasn't seething and driven by hunger and the need to kill. He was tortured, too. Affected by the scene he'd described and been part of. Looking at him through tear-blurred vision, I believed his words. "You're not lying."

The wolves behind me shifted uncomfortably. Before I could gather myself or voice another word, Troy swiped the dagger from the damned's temple. He nailed it through a gap in the chains into the damned's chest. With a sideways twist, the damned's face froze, mouth gaping as he turned black all over. Then he collapsed into ash, the chains clattering into a pile on the concrete.

Shocked, I wiped the tears from my eyes. Despite hearing Ty was dead—if it were even true—anger scorched my veins. That damned had been one of us. A vampire who'd died at the Portsmouth Battle. He wasn't completely one of them. He hadn't deserved to die like that. And what if I could have...*saved him.* "What the hell did you do that for? I could have tried restoring—"

"And what would be the point? Ty's dead. All this fucking time and he's dead." Troy stalked forward and sneered down at me. "A good damned is a dead damned. And you're just one step—"

Kendrick shoved the acting alpha back, fangs bared as he reached for his dagger.

"Cool it, Troy!" Dorian sprinted over from a steel door in the ground where crates had been stacked. "We're not the enemy here."

The basement. I hadn't even seen him leave. Now that he was

119

back, too-late fear for his safety churned up my stomach. I clambered to my feet. "Why didn't you say something? There could have been more damned—"

"Amelia," he cut me off. "There's something you need to see. I'm not sure if it proves anything, but…" He grabbed my hand and hauled me along. "Just come. See for yourself."

Feeling numb, like my body was going through the routine breathe in, breathe out, and my legs were moving only because I was being pulled forward, I followed Dorian downstairs. As we got closer to the basement level, the smell of rotting flesh grew stronger with each downward step. Warmth also increased in the air, making the smell soar. I covered my nose while dread swam in my stomach. *Oh God, don't be what I think.*

I'm right here. Kendrick followed close behind, dagger in hand and ready for anything.

As we stepped off the landing, Dorian released my hand and red light from across the space sent a glowing ambiance over the concrete room. Compared to upstairs, the area was relatively clean. No crates or scrap metal. But it wasn't empty. Now I knew where the heat had come from. And the light. A giant furnace sat to one side, the massive door closed over vibrant flames behind the glass. In front of the furnace was the source of the smell. A line of dumpster bins on wheels—stacked full with bodies.

My legs gave out again, but this time Kendrick caught me, his arms keeping me upright and off the ground. "What is all this?"

Troy inspected the bins, his expression grave as he moved from one to the other. "Human victims, mostly. Looks like a few leeches, too."

Dorian took my hand again and led me to the last bin. "I wish you didn't have to see this. I think it's their failed attempts to turn vamps, too."

I dared to peer inside the bin, a shiver sliding down my back. Dorian was right. Among the tangle of decomposing bodies, one trait was clear. Of the few skulls I could see, vampire teeth still remained. My focus skipped from one face to the next. Then I noticed something shiny amongst the gruesome mix. Locking down my gag reflex, I weeded through the decay and pulled...

Links of silver chain came free, matching the ones I now noticed hanging from the back wall—

My consciousness shifted, stomach heaving as though I'd fallen through the ground. But I hadn't even moved. Still standing in the basement, the surroundings remained the same. But the company didn't. Sitting up against and chained to the wall was the damned Troy had just killed. Expression strained, the boy looked scared shit-less. The silver trapping one ankle made his flesh sizzle.

Next to him and also chained was... *Ty*.

"You'll b-be alright," Ty said to the boy, face sweating as if he had a fever. His teeth ground as his jaw clenched, eyes pinching shut before reopening. Black veins snaked out like hairline fractures across his skin. He was in transition and starving. Hadn't yet taken life to complete the process. The ugly rent in his chest was still there. But it was smaller than it had been, and no longer free-pour-ing. "I'm not g-going anywhere. And I have p-people that will find us. Just. Hold. On."

The boy slammed sideways then, face twisting and body convulsing. His eyes squeezed shut along with his mouth, and his teeth screeched. Ty reached over and rolled him onto his side, holding him down until the convulsions eased. After seconds that stretched into minutes, the boy lurched up, weak and jittery. Then his eyes opened.

Red.

Booted footsteps neared, but I couldn't see the source in the darkness behind me. All I could hear as the steps stopped was sobbing. Then a girl was thrown forward to land before Ty and the boy. "Had this Pure Blood snatched from her home." The voice that spoke was horrible and cold and familiar. It belonged to the damned commander. "I brought her especially for you, wolf. To ensure your hybrid blood joins my army."

"I'd rather die than take her life," Ty snapped with a growl. The other boy crept forward on the concrete and reached out as if in a trance, but Ty caught his hand. "We don't want her." His long fangs slid from his gums in protest, but the steel in his stare was unwavering. "Let. Her. Go."

The unseen commander laughed with amusement. "You can't save her. If you die first—and you will if you don't feed soon—your transitioning friend will take her. If he refuses, I'll take her myself." The girl sobbed louder. "No point in wasting that delicious blood."

Ty's mouth opened with a snarl. "Just wait until Amelia—" Suddenly choking, his eyes rolled and he tipped. The boy scooted back into the wall, staring in horror at Ty's convulsing body. While the girl shrieked, the sound of those boots faded as the commander mounted the stairs. On his back and still shaking, his chains rattling, Ty's lids remained open, his limbs stiff and held at awkward angles. Red oozed from the slice in his chest, gluggy and congealed.

I screamed for the boy to do something, but like all my visions, nothing came out. Then froth bubbled up from Ty's mouth. The convulsing stopped then, and all the tension released from his body. His face became slack and his dead eyes bled from gold to red.

Frozen in horror, I watched as the boy grabbed Ty's shoulders. He began shaking. "Wake up. Don't leave me here with them."

I saw it all again. The Portsmouth battle. Caius's sword striking through Ty's chest. Ty dying in my arms. I'd failed. Then and every moment since then. There was no more hope for that boy than there had been for me back at Portsmouth. Only fifty percent of vampires lived through damned infection. And that was only if they killed through full consumption. And Ty had made his choice. I could see the writing on the wall in the vacantness of his slack face and body. The way his head hung and swayed with the boy's shaking. The way his red eyes stared lifelessly.

Now he was at peace.

I blinked and the view of Ty's body faded. Back in the basement, here and now, the others stood around me in a circle. Behind them, the wolves shifted uneasily. I stared down at the chain in my hands, endless tears falling from my cheeks onto the silver links. I'd just watched the love of my life die for the second time. "I saw it happen. The transition…"

My voice failed with a sob, and Kendrick made quick work of reliving the scene through our linked minds. He wrapped his arm around my waist as my legs gave out. "Ty didn't make it."

CHAPTER 10

I came out of my trance with a numb awakening. Held up by Kendrick, I saw that everyone else was gone: the wolves, Dorian, the bodies. The smell of burnt flesh hung thick on the heated air. A tidal wave of rage bubbled up inside of me. One that I couldn't and didn't want to contain. Warped grief became all I could see and all that encompassed my reasoning. Denial had been my sanity over the past months, but that scene I'd witnessed had smashed all my hope to smithereens.

Feeling like I'd die if I kept still, I commanded my legs to support my weight and shoved free of Kendrick's hold. Despite starvation and a whole-body ache, I leaped upstairs to the ground level. No light peeked through the boarded-up windows across the front of the warehouse. It was still night outside. In that basement with the dead and their fiery erasing, I'd remained in Kendrick's arms, in a conscious trance but not really there. Now I was wide awake. The crippling agony of losing Ty so brutally tore my insides apart all over again. I needed to let it out: the pain, the regret…the anger.

With a tortured cry, I lashed out, throwing crates around before tearing them to pieces. When every crate resembled kindling and my palms and fingers were pierced with splinters, I turned my rage onto the old machinery. Hands cut and bloody, I drove my fists into the rusted metal, over and over. Red was left splattered across the dented and cracked surfaces as the sharp edges cut fresh slices in my hands. The physical pain was like a drug, deflecting my internal agony. When my bones splintered and cracked, I drove my fists in even harder.

The taste of blood registered in my mouth from my screamed-out throat, and my eyes felt like someone had rubbed sand in them from all the salty tears I'd shed. My lips were cracked from the breath that sawed in and out of my lungs. When my hands became numb, no longer feeling the repetitive impact, I unleashed my built-up electricity. Every boarded-up window and glass pane was shot out on both the ground and upper levels. But it didn't help. Didn't even begin to release the never-ending stream of torrid energy that rushed through me like poison.

I shot back down to the basement and skidded to a stop. The now empty dumpsters made me cringe. Had Ty's body been among the ones burned before the others left? Was this his lost life I could smell in the heated dank air?

Without conscious movement, I found myself standing before the hanging silver chains that swayed from my sudden entrance. This is where Ty had refused to become a monster. And if my vision was the end...then it was also where he'd died. Again.

I collapsed to my knees in an old bloodstain, frozen in the horrific replay. In that moment, I almost wished for death. But I deserved the returning pain, every little bit of it. Death would be an out, a kindness. It was too good for me. Ty had trusted and put his faith in me. He'd believed I would come and rescue him. And I'd let him down in the worst way possible. I'd cost him his life. The only penance I could offer now was my eternal suffering. And for every breath that passed my lips while Ty's no longer could, I hoped it never let up.

Feeling helpless, the anger in me rebuilt. My last few tears escaped my eyes and trickled ever so slowly down my cheeks, as if they wanted to remain with me in my grief but couldn't escape gravity's inexorable pull. I jumped up, streaming more voltage to my hands.

"Amelia, stop!" Kendrick caught me around the arms from behind. The block he'd held in place during my rampage came crashing down. Pure agony choked him up at seeing me in this state. His total desperation at needing to be strong for me kept him in control. "Tearing this whole place down won't bring him back."

I fought against him, trying to break free, needing to unleash the rage still burning inside me. The scent of his blood tempted and turned my stomach at the same time. But it wasn't enough to stop the internal torment I was battling with. Kendrick didn't let up though, able to hold me back after all the energy I'd expelled. As time passed, fatigue filled my bones and my drive to fight slowed. My mind took over the battle with irrational argument. My vision wasn't definitive. It wasn't absolute proof. It contradicted my earlier vision/dream of seeing Ty come alive with piercing red eyes. Experiments were at play here, and the outcome wasn't always as expected. Ty could have lived through that part of the transition to feed. The other vampire could have done something to bring him back. Or the damned commander could have. He'd wanted Ty for his army. Needed him. "Ty could still be out there. We can't give up. We'll find him and I'll save him. There's a way. We know there is. I'll give my own life if I have to."

I was bargaining with everything I had. And Kendrick wasn't

going to lend me false hope. He spun me in his arms but didn't let go. Sorrow for my loss shone in his eyes. "Even though Ty made it to that point in your vision, he couldn't have turned damned even if he had wanted to. Being a hybrid, his odds would be almost non-existent. Plus you know he was marked to prevent damned blood and venom from mixing. What you saw was only a matter of time. We've been chasing a lost cause from the start."

I clenched my fists and batted into his chest while he held me. "No. You're wrong. The commander was there. He expected Ty to turn." When fresh blood added to the black and red on Kendrick's shirt and my fists throbbed with pain, the hits died off. Letting Kendrick hold me up, I sobbed. "Why? If you thought searching for Ty was hopeless all along, why'd you keep helping me?"

"Because I knew you weren't ready to give him up. Because less damned in existence meant safety for our race. Mostly, I hoped vengeance would give you some peace. And as long as I was there to keep you safe, I let it go on. But *this* can't go on. Not now that we're on our own without the wolves. The next raid could be the death of you. And I won't have it. Ty is dead, but you don't have to be, too. You've suffered long enough, Amelia. You need to forgive yourself. You need to give yourself permission to live again. To move on."

Unable to consider the possibility of ever moving past losing Ty, pain lanced through my heart. I stared at the bloodstain below the dangling chains. "I—I can't accept this," I whispered, throat choking shut with emotion. "As long as there's doubt in my mind..."

"What if there wasn't?" Kendrick pulled his iPhone from his torn, bloodied pants and swiped and tapped the screen. He turned it over for me to see a Boston address along with a familiar name. "Good or bad, Madam Rosalie will know the truth."

A MASH OF TREPIDATION, unwarranted hope, and fear constricted my chest as I snuck off the main street and down a side alley. After two flights, it was the following evening in Boston—after shop hours, but still daylight for another ninety minutes. Standing at the back door to a glass-fronted hippie bookshop, this was my last stop for the truth. And good or bad, I wasn't sure I was ready to find out.

Kendrick slid past me and cranked down on the back door's handle until it creaked and let out a ping. Breaking and entering had been my idea. But he was with me all the way. Wouldn't say it, but I knew he hoped our visit would give me closure and acceptance rather than false hope.

"After you..." With his backpack over one shoulder, which had thankfully had a change of clothes to get us through airport security, he nudged the door—

A chime sounded with the flicking of a mounted bell and we both froze. After a second of wide-eyed silence, I shrugged and went in with Kendrick right behind me. I paused at the curtain ending a narrow hallway and peeked through. Books lined the side walls from floor to ceiling. The smell of new and old books hung in the air, mixing with pungent incense that assaulted my nose. The rest of the shop was filled with small table displays, varying from tarot cards, jewelry, scarfs, and unlimited crystals and stones.

The plan was to fry the alarm with my voltage, then search for Madam Rosalie's home address. But as I raised my blue-streaked hand, something stopped me. The 'armed' light on the alarm panel by all that glass frontage wasn't illuminated. And that wasn't all. I could hear a heartbeat. Slightly elevated but clear as day. *Someone's in here.*

Kendrick had heard it too and was equipped to compel us out of here if needed. *Let's find out who.*

Striding through the curtain with Kendrick, past the hippie clothing and hemp bags hanging from stands, I followed that consistent beat. A few steps led up to another level that was cloaked by a velvet curtain. Printed on the star-embossed cover was *Madam Rosalie, Fortune Telling Extraordinaire.*

Before I got the chance to fling the curtain aside, a woman's crackly voice called through the barrier. "Come in. I've been expecting you."

I exchanged a look with Kendrick then pushed my way through. The small, dusty room was painted black and lit by dozens of candles. They were all different colors and heights, most bleeding wax over the table or shelf they sat on. Behind a round table draped in silver cloth, sat Madam Rosalie. Her hair was the same wiry gray color but hung loosely in wild waves. Her hands were curled around a crystal ball in the table's center, her rings clinking against it as she tapped her bony fingers.

"You knew we were here?"

Madam Rosalie glanced up from her crystal ball while waving her hand over the top. "I felt your aura just now." The candlelight to one side of the table caught on the round, glossy surface as she moved her hands. Light refracted and shone through the ball and onto the walls. In the light, a symbol stood out. "And this has been announcing your arrival for hours."

"That's alchemy," Kendrick said, accusation in his tone as his eyes narrowed.

At the same time, the pendant at my wrist flared. I lifted the amethyst and one of the candle flames backlit the stone. Almost invisible was the same mark somehow inside.

The old woman smiled at Kendrick as I looked up. "In my line of work, you discover things normal people would not. From the moment you sought my help last year, I have known what you were...vampire."

Kendrick tensed, as if ready to silence the woman in case she decided to scream out in danger.

Wait up. I stepped forward, placing my hands on the back of a cane chair.

Back at the Arts and Psychic fair, Kendrick had paid the old woman to deter me from Ty, claiming he would alter my life. Paid off or not, that part had been true. The rest had been, too. Her prediction of my imminent death had been real. *Beware the blood that runs in your veins,* she had warned back then. After discovering Caius was my father, I knew she had been right. His blood ran in my veins, and he'd been the one to try to take my life. This woman had the ability to see into people's futures, and I trusted her word.

Kendrick had never told her what we were, though. But the old woman had proven she knew things beyond the realm of normalcy. And she showed no fear as I hovered before her. "You're not afraid of us." Though I thought it was absurd, as I could tell my own, I asked anyway. "Are you a vampire?"

"No, I am not a vampire, nor am I gifted by your elements. I am simply human, a descendant of a long line of psychics. Touch is my main channel of power and insight." With a chin tilt, Madam Rosalie motioned for us to sit. With two cane chairs available—guess she had expected the both of us—we sat. "And no. I am not afraid. Much like the first time I met you, girl, I can sense your aura. Your pure intentions. His are pure, too." She glanced to Kendrick. "Though not so *transparent*."

I glanced sideways to my best friend and felt heat in my cheeks. Images of his hands around me, his lips pressed to mine, and my encouraging hold around his neck penetrated me through the bond.

Kendrick locked them down. But it was too late. I knew he still wanted me. Always would. Whether I wanted to admit it or not. My feelings had shifted, too, on that day. And since then, too. Fresh guilt tore me apart and I glanced away.

"Your friendship has many complications. But that is not why you came." Madam Rosalie held out her hands around either side of the crystal ball. "You seek answers on the boy. The one who holds your heart."

I gulped and took her bony hovering hands, holding the voltage back inside my ribcage. Even still, a tiny current fired at our touch. With eyes closed, her eyeballs moved behind thin, papery eyelids. And now that the time had come, I had to know. Even if it would break me. Even if it would kill me. "Is...is he alive?"

Madam Rosalie frowned, her grip tightening. Then she gasped and her lids sprang open. Certainty and empathy were clear in her beady eyes as she glanced from Kendrick to me. "Alive? No."

Being that the damned weren't technically alive, that wasn't a definitive answer. Something jumped to the forefront of my mind. "You must accept the light. It's the only way to save him," I recited her final warning from back at the fair. "You meant this light?" I said, holding up one sparking hand. "And when you said him, you meant Ty."

Madam Rosalie nodded, eyes still as she watched me.

"Then he is out there. I can still save him."

Madam Rosalie shook her head slightly back and forth. "Fortunes are not concrete, only the past is unchangeable." She blinked slowly as if rehearsing the words she was about to say. "The boy you love...he no longer exists."

CHAPTER 11

*I*t had been days since Madam Rosalie delivered the unthinkable news. Days that felt like years and minutes that felt like an eternity. Ty was no more. The scene of his first death in my arms flashed across my vision again. The second scene—where he'd decided to die with honor—snapped my heart in two and left it bleeding out on the floor. I blinked hard through the tears, but they wouldn't melt away. Music blasted from the dock at my bedside on never-ending shuffle, and every song I related to Ty. Every word was torture: monster, disease, sinner, gone. The never-ending torment I deserved? I didn't want it anymore. Couldn't stand it for another second.

On the edge of my bed, I reached into my bedside drawer. Ty's cold, smooth stake came free. With overcast early morning light beyond the windows siding the posts of my bed, lamplight glinted across the inscription. The Greek words shone. *Deliver back unto hell.*

All in good time, but first...

I grabbed my iPhone from the open drawer. There was one last call I had to make. Dialing a number I knew well, my fingers squeezed around the cool length of silver. My bleeding heart drummed.

"Amelia?"

That voice, so strong and powerful, and so much like Ty's. Except for the unmaskable agony of loss. "Mr. Malau…I…he's… I failed you. Failed…" My voice cracked. "…Ty. I'm sorry."

As I sobbed down the line, past putting up a front, and past pretending I was strong, Mr. Malau hushed me. "We did all we could. You did." He let out a long sigh that caught before he spoke again. "I forgive you. I don't blame you."

I could barely believe his words. Their kindness. Their acceptance. But I hadn't called to seek his forgiveness. Because with or without it, I couldn't forgive myself. "I—I just needed you to know." Still holding Ty's stake, I ran the tip from my collarbone down over my chest. "Despite our differences, I'm glad I knew you, too…"

"Amelia, what are you—"

"Time to go." I hung up and turned my phone off. My free hand caught the amulet around my neck. Soon my heart would be stone cold like this bloodstone in my palm. Like Ty's heart already was. And I wouldn't be interrupted.

On returning to the Armaya, Kendrick had informed and relieved Marika who'd been beyond devastated. But I hadn't spoken to anyone. Had remained holed up in my suite with the bond link secured like Fort Knox. I'd screamed for Kendrick to leave me the fuck alone. I'd refused daily training. Refused to attend RVC meetings. Not even starvation had gotten a look in. And I was starving. Blue veins covered every inch of my skin, now hidden below my long cotton PJs—because the sight of them pissed me off. Reminded me of how Ty had fed me. How he'd protected me. How he'd died for me. Plus I didn't want to drink anything…or anyone. I wanted the physical pain to stay, to amplify my emotional agony. Why should I feel any kind of okay when Ty was dead?

That recurring bout of rage built back up, that feeling of being powerless, of drowning and having no surface to swim to. The only break I got from the suffocating depression. And the drive I needed to go through with my last-stop plan.

I lined up the sharp, silver tip and shifted, dropping the amulet to curl my other hand over the one clutching the stake. My lids slid slowly shut as I reclined on the bed—then opened when purple light penetrated the corner of my eye. Releasing the stake's downward pressure, a drop of blood bloomed as I sat up. Shifting clouds beyond the windows had released a stream of light into my bedroom. Beams highlighted the amethyst stones on the jewelry box on my bedside as if heaven-sent. The jewelry box that had belonged to Erzsebet and that Kendrick had restored after I'd twisted it into trash.

I dropped the stake to my side. With shaky hands, my heart shattered as I reached out and lifted the lid. I knew exactly what lay inside its satin-padded walls. Oh, God. The photo shook like a leaf caught in a breeze as I drew it free. The memory cut like a blade through my every nerve ending. Ty, smiling with his arms around me, and a *welcome aboard* sign behind us. The photo had been taken moments before we boarded the cruise. I remembered the passion we'd created while I was hard up against him, my fangs deep in his neck. On our shared bed. In the busy club. Beneath the waterfall. I remembered Ty's strength and determination to save me from the damned. And the way he'd almost died there.

All this after I'd acted like a monster and tried to kill that quarterback. After I'd repeated the trend by attacking him and even Troy.

He'd fought alongside his enemies for me and he'd died protecting not just me but them. He'd died with honor. And he'd given everything he'd had until the very end.

"What the hell am I doing?"

Like being plunged into an ice bath and resurfacing, I finally woke up from the deep depression I'd been wallowing away in.

I was being weak. Unworthy of the sacrifices Ty had made to save me and his enemies. The damned were still out there, even if Ty wasn't. Still murdering the innocent and threatening the vampire race.

With my bedhead and days-old PJs, I looked like a joke compared to the heir I was meant to be. And for what? To waste away the days feeling sorry for myself. To end it because I was too weak to go on without *him*. No. I wouldn't give in. I wouldn't be a waste of flesh. In Ty's memory and to honor his sacrifice, I would pick myself up and forge on. It had never been in my nature to give up. Stubborn should have been my middle name. And I wasn't about to have a permanent personality transplant now.

New leads from the wolves or not, the damned were still running rampant. Still vying for vampire destruction. Someone was controlling them, even now. And I knew just who could give me the right information to track them all down.

Hands no longer shaking but firm with resolve, I placed the photo up against the base of the lamp. A reminder of why I had to go on. Of why I couldn't give up. The pain of losing Ty would never leave me, and I was okay with that. I never wanted to lose that sting that would forever keep him in my heart.

Shifting the small key inside the jewelry box aside, I retrieved a folded piece of paper. Marcus had found this note in Caius's office and handed it over before Kendrick and I had escaped after my attempted murder. And I'd held on to it all this time. Unfolding it, I read the single line: *'The damned are evolving and I fear we may lose control.'*

In less than five minutes, I stripped, showered, and dressed in clean jeans and a tank. And downed four bottles of Kendrick's blood from my mini bar. I left my suite, two guards my instant shadows as I ventured down the back stairs. Without a word, I followed the weaving corridors to the back section of the castle, getting lost at a few dead ends before finding my bearings. With the metal across my guards' backs, it sounded like a small armed force tailed me. Despite them being my constant babysitters, their company was almost comforting. My last trip down to the catacombs had been when Caius carried my unconscious body down the spiral staircase from his office to kill me. But I wasn't heading to his office or setting off toward that dingy cell that reminded me of hell. I was heading to the main gate of the in-use cells. The two guards at the entrance unlocked the marked chains from the metal gate and cleared the way. Chiseled stone that had been carved into blocks made up the stairs leading down below the castle. More wall-mounted lanterns lit the narrow path, creating moving shadows as we descended, and when we reached the bottom, another chained gate was unlocked for us to pass. A round, gloomy stone-walled room opened up with a succession of evenly placed solid steel doors. Each had a slider at eye level for peeking inside, but I wasn't in the mood to play seek and find.

I turned on my guards. "Where's Caius's cell?"

One of the two nodded over my shoulder while the other said, "Door centered behind you, Lady Bathory."

Every step in my Vans echoed as I strode to the door. Each beat felt like a nail to my pounding heart. "Open it."

One of the prison guards moved without question to unlock the steel slab. Without opening the way, the guard dipped his head and resumed his post.

I narrowed a stare at my entourage of two. "You will wait out here." I pushed my way inside and closed the steel behind me.

The cell was gloomy and depressing, dark stone making up the floor, walls, and ceiling. There were no windows, for obvious reasons, and unlike the old chambers and cells, this one didn't stink of death and decay. Instead, it reeked of lung-squeezing bleach. The bareness of the cell surprised me. No cot. No bars to see anything beyond this space. A seat-less steel toilet. Along the floor was a grate that ran from one wall straight to the other.

"It is a drain," Caius offered from a dark corner where a single bulb's light didn't reach. "Prisoners and their surroundings are hosed off routinely with bleach."

Neck pinching as I cringed, I followed the voice.

Caius stepped forward into the light, wall-bolted chains rattling as he slid down the wall. He propped his knees up and his dull silvery eyes locked on me. Perception of my hidden pain danced in them. "Hello, daughter. Is everything—?"

"Don't you dare call me that." My fangs shot free in warning.

Caius chuckled. "What would you prefer, *my dear?*"

My skin crawled at the loving name he used to call me. "I am nothing to you, and you are nothing to me."

His stare dropped to his hands on his knees, frowning as if studying them. After a deep breath in and out, his head nodded almost imperceptibly, then he looked up. "As you wish. Though I assume you have not come here solely to argue about formalities."

I held out the note clutched in my hand and unfolded it. "The damned are evolving and I fear we may lose control," I recited. "Who sent you the note? Who warned you about the damned?"

Caius frowned. "Where did you get that?" When I remained

quiet, his lips parted. "Ah, I see. Well, you should know, my dear, that note was not sent *to* me. It was written *by* me. *I* made the warning. *I* wanted to change the plan."

"With the person you've left in charge. The one who's commanding the damned while you await your death sentence."

Caius's stare locked on me and his eyes drilled into my sockets. "I left no one in charge. I never had control over the damned."

I stepped forward, judging how close I could get by the pooling chains at Caius's side. "Then tell me who does. If this commander has gone against you, left you here to rot, you should have no issue telling me their name."

Caius's mouth parted like he was about to speak, but nothing came out. Then it shut and his stare dropped. "That I cannot tell you, my dear." He clasped his hands on top of his knees, blue veins vibrant and poking out of his thin flesh. They were still keeping him weak through blood deprivation. "Are we done then?"

My tongue burned to argue. To demand he speak their name. But there was no point. Caius wouldn't tell me anything he didn't want to, and I had no real power to force him to. But there was still so much I didn't know. "How were you going to save the damned?"

With a grunt, Caius used his hands to push himself back up. He swayed, the chains rattling as he leaned against the stone wall. "Not the damned, well not anymore. The price to save them all collectively is too great." Regret transformed his wrinkled, veiny face, and his dull gaze turned glassy. His Adam's apple went up and down with an exaggerated swallow. "Though I wish I had discovered that fact before I did the unspeakable to you, my daughter."

I flinched at the name and my heart sped up in response to his emotional words. I gritted my teeth, fangs still extended. It was all an act. "If you're not trying to save the damned," I said, surprised by the steadiness of my voice, "then why did you keep coming after me?"

"I thought if I could get you away, explain, then perhaps maybe you'd help me...save my family. My mother. My Sisters. Not that I deserved such a favor after what I did to you."

I shot down the true emotion he showed. I would never feel sorry for a man who'd tried to kill me. But I needed to know... "What price needs to be paid?"

Caius slid down the wall back into his crouched position. A hint of fear broke through his still-lingering sorrow. "To pay the price, light and dark must first be joined. You are but a piece in this puzzle, my dear, and I am sorry I put you in such a position. Though I will try to amend my deceit with this warning. Only life can restore death. Do not join light with dark. It will be your end."

I LEFT Caius's cell with a chill swamping out from my spine, but before I could dwell on his cryptic words, a gate screeching open brought my head up. Kendrick was exiting a tunnel I hadn't noticed before.

The second he saw me he froze.

The wall-mounted lanterns cast flicking firelight across his surprised face. "Amelia! What are you doing down here?" He glanced back down the tunnel as he swung the two-inch-thick bars shut and bolted them.

The guard blocking the way who'd been waiting by the door bowed slightly to Kendrick. He was Kendrick's current guard—who'd waited up here while Kendrick was...

Wet shoe prints marked his path as he entered the circular space. "Are you...okay?"

No. Never would be again. But suspicion stole my focus. I came closer and detected an unusual scent coming off Kendrick's polo shirt and cargo pants. One I'd picked up on him before. "Where does that lead?"

"The old abandoned catacombs," Kendrick said, running a hand from his shoulder and across his neck...like he was nervous. Although his thoughts were on no-access to me, through the bond he added, *Where the cell Caius took you is located.*

Fire at the memory of it all set my veins alight and I stepped back as though I'd been pushed. My heart started drumming at the memory of being drained alive. The location explained his nerves in being caught out. But not the reasoning. "Why? Why would you go down there?"

"I...I just wanted to make sure we hadn't missed anything. And we hadn't. I didn't tell you because I didn't want to upset you. The last few days have been hard enough for you without having to relive that nightmare, too."

That scent coming off his clothes seemed stronger, but I still couldn't place it. There was a hint of that old dank cell, but there was something else, too.

"Why are *you* down here?" When I remained silent, Kendrick noticed my clenched fist. He stepped closer to me, paying no attention to the guards as his fingers grazed my hand. His eyes found mine and he spoke through the bond. *What's in your hand?*

Although his touch was as soft as his reasoning voice, instant defensiveness washed over me and I jerked away. My hand squeezed tighter around the note in my palm. Not because I wanted to keep my reason of being down here from him, but because I knew how he'd react. "I visited Caius." At the instant tight snapping of every one of his muscles, I dropped enough mental bricks to show almost how low I'd been and the purpose I'd found to fight on for. I held up the note. "I needed to know who wrote this. I needed to know who's controlling the damned. Where I can find them."

Even with what I hid, Kendrick knew he'd come close to losing me. Blamed himself for leaving me to myself. It ate at his insides like he'd chugged battery acid. But the relief that I'd found a new purpose had him rushing to wrap me in his arms. Every fear he'd pegged down came flooding to the surface. "I was so scared. But I knew better than to ever stand in your way."

Fresh fear at my commitment had his heart pounding against my ear. At the same time, hope tunneled its way in. A quick fast-forward of our lives to come passed from his subconscious to mine. Us fighting side by side together. And us together in my suite—in bed and between the sheets.

Kendrick's hands splayed over my back with a sharp inhale, then released as he backed up, his face shadowed with the closest lantern behind his head. The leaked fantasies faded away. "I, ah… It's good to have the fight in you back." Brow scrunching without looking at me, he nudged my arm. "But now we need to decode what Caius said."

I LAY ON THE GRASS, knees propped up and hands behind my head, soaking up the early morning sun. Flowing water traveled across the field from the angel fountain at the city center, which was otherwise vacant. Bar our three guards sitting on a sidewalk bench under a boutique roof's shelter. In spite of the laid-back setting and my pose, I felt uncomfortable as hell. After witnessing Kendrick's fantasies for us—the *between the sheets* part made me want to push him away. Far, far away. The *fighting side-by-side* part stopped me from doing exactly that. It was wrong, unfair, but I needed him. Couldn't imagine my life if he wasn't a part of it. If I lost him, too.

That eroding devastation crept back in and I blinked away the rising sun's light. Holding my breath, I stilled my thoughts and redirected them onto something useful. The torment was my driving force.

Confusion and anxiety rose and I let it pale my pain. In the back of my mind, I saw the sorrow on Caius's face, what appeared to be fear as he delivered his warning for me not to join light and dark. "What I don't understand, along with everything else, is why Caius doesn't want to restore all the damned along with his family. That had been the point all along, hadn't it?" A light bulb went off in my brain. "*All damned*. That's what he'd said. Maybe there's a way to save them all at once. That would eliminate the slow drain of restoring one by one. But what price could be so big he'd give that up?"

In the long, mottled shadow of the billowing tree next to me, Kendrick rubbed his thumbs over his temples. "Erzsebet's goal had been to save the damned. But..." No new fantasies snuck through, but a hint of desperation did. Worry that if he didn't unpuzzle Caius's warning, it would harm me in some way. "If he found out the price was his life to bring them all back, maybe he decided it was too much to pay."

"Then why warn me?" The fluffy, white clouds above shifted with a light breeze, creating doom-free images in the sky. Despite the view, I shivered. "He'd still need my life to save his family, wouldn't he? Why ramble on about this light and dark stuff?"

Kendrick went quiet, holding his breath for a moment. "I wish I knew."

"The light is my electric ability." Madam Rosalie had confirmed as much. "So what if the dark is..." I trailed off. My gaze left the clouds, flitting around the field and the thick trees that surrounded it. Shadows grew beyond those trunks and limbs. A shudder crawled up my spine. I sensed something but saw nothing. "Seeing the dead?"

Kendrick reclined next to me, keeping within the tree's shadow. "Or maybe there's another ability you still have to receive, like the light of the lightning, but dark in some way."

"I have an entirely different belief," a smooth voice announced as a shadow slid over me.

Kendrick and I both shot upright to find Marcus standing over us. The concrete angel fountain behind him made it look like he had wings. And his two guards waited yards back with ours outside the boutique. The look on his face as he scanned me over showed relief. My absence clearly hadn't gone unnoticed. From Kendrick, he knew our excursion hadn't gone well. But he didn't know it had been our last. And he didn't ask about it now. Like he sensed it was something I couldn't yet talk about.

Instead, he kept on with the topic of distraction. "If your power is the light Caius spoke of, then would it not stand to reason that the dark could be your other half? Your blooded twin."

Moving past the sudden surprise of Marcus sneaking up on us, my mind struggled with past and present. Being forced to move to the Armaya, along with Ty's disappearance had taken almost all my energy and actions since. Now there was no point in finding Ty. My heart ached anew, rebuilding the agony that pierced it from the inside like a knife stabbing over and over. My plight to uncover intel from Caius had distracted me and my pain. But it wouldn't budge now. And I didn't want it to. I didn't want to forget what I'd lost and what I had to fight on for. Holding on to the pain, I sharpened my mind, forcing my thoughts back to the issue.

I knew I had a twin, I'd seen Caius tear two babies from my mom's womb in a vision. Since discovering Caius was also my father, I'd learned Dorian wasn't really my twin. He wasn't related to me, Mom, or Caius in any way. But that didn't mean I still had a twin. "After Caius's sentencing he told me my twin died."

Marcus's brows popped. "Did he?" He leaned back against a tree and slid his hands into the pockets of his dark blue pants. One square-toed shoe was kicked over the other. "Words from the mouth of a traitor. You don't believe him, do you?"

I shook my head. "I don't want to."

Which meant I could still have a twin who was out in the world somewhere. And if they were this dark Caius was warning me about, I had to find them. I couldn't trust his warning. So far he'd given me no reason to trust anything he'd ever said to me. My twin could be in danger. They could even be the key to saving the damned.

I peered up, an idea drumming my heart with excitement. "If you're right, Marcus, then I have to find my twin."

"How?" Marcus questioned. "What can I do to help?"

Kendrick reared up with a smile, mottled shadow from the tree covering his face and neck. He knew exactly what I was about to do. "Get ready to contain some voltage. Amelia's gonna bring on a vision."

Marcus crouched down at the tree's base and clasped his hands. "Ready and waiting," he said with a smile.

Smiling back, I crossed my legs. Grass between my jeans and Vans tickled my ankles as I closed my eyes. After the bottles of Kendrick's blood I'd downed before seeing Caius, my electricity remained beneath my ribs, collecting like a spinning ball of glowing twine. The splash of the fountain and soft-blowing breeze remained, and I relaxed my mind.

Slowly the sounds faded and all that surrounded me was darkness. In the moving shadows that curled around me like living icky things, one stood out, curling around my waist. My hands caught and lifted it, and the black slime seeped into my palms.

Sudden light flared, blinding and all around me, stealing any depth to my surroundings. But I wasn't alone. Beside me and holding my hand was a guy, his skin soft and cold on mine. Shit-kickers covered his feet, black, leather and laced up the front, and dirty jeans covered his legs. My gaze traveled over his unbuttoned torn white shirt, seeing the slender plains of his pale chest and the black symbol painted on his skin. Recognition of the guy washed over me. But along with a need-to-know, there was disappointment. Standing with me was not my twin. It was the damned commander. And yet I felt no unease beside him, but rather anticipation and readiness.

Then my eyes flicked up to his face.

"Amelia!"

My lids flung open to see Kendrick and Marcus hovering over me. I was on my back, the white clouds moving behind their heads. The sound of wind-rustled leaves returned, as did the fountain's babbling. Grass prickled my neck and the backs of my arms. A metallic taste stained my throat and both guys looked worried as hell. "W-what happened?"

Holding each of my arms, they levered me upright. Kendrick held out a tissue as a trickle ran over my lip and down my chin. "Your nose started bleeding."

No longer across the street by the boutique, five guards stood close, partly shadowed by treetops. Their shifting stances were edgy.

Marcus lifted his chin to the guards. "She's fine. Retreat to your waiting posts." When they were out of earshot, Marcus let my arm go. "And then you lit up like a star and went limp. I caught you, but you wouldn't wake up." A look of curious suspense strained his young but sharp features. "What did you see?"

I took the tissue and held it to my nose as I recrossed my legs. "I have to go back. The damned commander—I almost saw his face."

"No!" both guys barked in unison. "You've never had bloody noses in the past," Kendrick pointed out. "Which means it was directly caused by bringing on that vision."

I couldn't argue the facts, but I had come so close and I wasn't about to give up. "Since when has a bloody nose killed anyone?" I leveled my eyes at both of them. Time-delayed hunger took up residence in my stomach. But it would have to wait. "I'm going to try again, and if either of you stops me from doing it now, I'll just do it by myself later."

The sigh from Marcus was a mix of irritation and resolution. "I guess it's better if we're here to intervene, to help if needed."

Kendrick was far from fine with this, but he knew I would follow through on my threat the minute he left me alone. Plus he wanted this over and done with so he could get some of his blood into me. "Fine."

Before either of them could change their mind, I closed my eyes and refocused my senses. Shutting down the sensation of my now gurgling stomach, I gritted my teeth. The black and shadows quickly returned, and I sought out the same one as before. But nothing stood out. None of them were drawn free of the swirling mass. It was like I'd used up the last vision, and now it had disappeared.

I blinked and the black faded, returning me to the field and both guys. My sight was hazy and more wetness trickled from my nose over my lips. The smell of what filled both guy's veins soared, but I shot my needs down. "The vision's gone. I can't bring it back."

CHAPTER 12

I completed a circle around the multi-tiered, carved-marble fountain that centered the castle gardens for the fourteenth time. The late afternoon sun—which meant early morning to vampires—reflected in the disturbed pattering water, blinding me every time I passed. A totally clear sky made the remainder of the rippling surface appear pastel blue. On waking after a crappy sleep, a request had been delivered to my suite. Uriel wanted me to meet her here. Considering the *why* behind the request made it impossible to stop burning up the grass-edged path around the fountain. Either she'd found out I wasn't taking Kendrick's vein, or she knew I'd been sneaking off the compound. The two bottles of blood I'd drunk before coming here churned up my stomach. I was totally screwed.

My current two guards stood a few yards away from me, one to my left and one to my right, both blocking manicured hedge arches from separate garden alcoves. And both sheltered by thick umbrellas. Like all royals bar me, they still felt uncomfortable when exposed to UV rays. Even if they weren't hurt beyond being slowly drained of energy.

I glanced around as I waited for Uriel to arrive. From this vantage point, the east end of the castle soared above a border of perfectly placed trees and trimmed hedges. The moss-growing stone wall was filled with Gothic windows, providing a view of the balcony and terrace doors to my suite's lounge. Which for what was in view, only took up a fraction of that section of castle. Its presence was formidable and dominating, a stark comparison to the gentle calm of the garden.

Heels clinking across a cobblestone path reached my ears and the female guard to my left bowed and stood aside. Uriel appeared through the arched entry, while small birds chirped and scampered about as if announcing her arrival. Her green dress with her fiery red hair made her seem like part of the gardens, adding to their color and life. Uriel dipped her head, looking eager below a green umbrella. She lowered onto the fountain while her shielded guards stood back. "Thank you for meeting me here, Amelia."

She eyed the space next to her as if demanding I fill it. "Oh, ah, not a problem, Lady Aswind." I rushed to sit, legs aching at the release from pacing.

Uriel chuckled. "Amelia, please, call me Uriel. Among The Seven and when not on public display, we generally lower the formalities."

"Sure. Okay." I placed my hands on my knees, realizing I was wearing jeans, a tank, and my hoodie. Now that I was one of them, was I expected to dress up twenty-four/seven? Marcus didn't, beyond looking sharp and tidy, and right now Uriel didn't seem to care. The look on her face was curious and still somewhat guarded. "So you wanted to ask me something?"

Uriel smiled, red lips parting to reveal pure-white teeth. "No.

The opposite, in fact. I have much to tell you." She nodded to our guards. "Garden outskirts, please."

The slightest nod from all four had them moving away through the exits and disappearing around hedges and shrubs. I wondered when I'd have that much power over them. And when they'd stop feeling like my jailers rather than my protectors.

Uriel turned her attention back to me. Sadness clouded her bright eyes. "After your vision during my family's funeral and subsequent question regarding the late Lady Bathory, I suspect I know what you saw. I was reluctant to reveal much at the time. Though it has now come to my attention that you have visited your father. The relay of your line of questioning to him, along with your reaction to the vision of my own father, has proven something to me. You are not operating with that murderer, and you are also in the dark."

Total relief released my almost cramping muscles. While I felt horrible all over again for what my vision—come too late—had cost her, paranoia at the rest of what she'd said kept my lips pinned shut. So Uriel didn't know about my blood habits or my disappearances. Though it seemed that where Caius was concerned, my actions had been under close watch.

"I believe that you at least know some of what Erzsebet was up to. So rather than rely on a liar's words, I hope to offer you some truth. Long ago, my father had volunteered to help Erzsebet in her plight to save her lost children." Uriel watched my reaction as if deciding whether her words were news or already known. Satisfied, she continued on. "She used him in her experiments, which is how he received the electric ability."

I let my hand dip into the fountain's cool water, firing small sparks from my fingers beneath the surface. I thought back to Mom's auction and recalled the red-haired vampire who'd gone against Caius in a bidding war. Uriel had bid on the jewelry box back then. She'd seemed intent on winning the item. The same one Erzsebet had owned when she'd conducted those experiments. Had Uriel known what Caius's plans were all along? Had she known I was in danger? "You knew about the vial inside the jewelry box and that Caius meant to inflict this power onto someone."

Instead of denying it, Uriel nodded. "I did. Though I suspected he'd use it on himself. Not knowing you were of his blood, or even pure, I never imagined he'd use the contents on you."

"Then you know what this power I have is meant to do?" I held up my wet hand while sparks danced up to my fingertips. "To restore a damned vampire to living again."

Surprise shifted Uriel's gentle features and her head tilted a fraction to the side. She studied my face, the calculative look sending anxiety through me. Shit! She'd known about saving Erzsebet's children, but had she not known they were damned? Did she not know what this power could do? Was she going to spill the news to the rest of The Seven?

"You do not know," she finally said.

Her response confused me. "Know what?"

Uriel gazed out at the gardens as gentle wind rustled their leaves. The considerate look on her face shifted to resolve, a decision made. "Erzsebet's plan was not merely to save her daughters. My father would not have sacrificed himself for only that. She believed this power"—Uriel reached out to take my hand, inhaling at the small currents that escaped into her flesh before I forced them back—"could break the damned curse, resulting in the permanent elimination of all damned."

I pulled my hand back and frowned. "I thought the damned could be created through full consumption."

"They can. Though my father believed that breaking their curse would not only revert the damned to living, but that it would also prevent that change from ever taking place again."

Worthwhile cause or not, there was something I needed to know. Something that could again change my life. "Will you tell the others about my power? What it was meant for?"

Uriel rose and used two fingers to whistle for our guards before looking down at me. "The RVC is not aware of why my father died, nor did they know of his power and its potential. For now, while the how of your ability is still unknown, this may remain between us. Though if it's answers you seek, Caius is the only other who would have documented this knowledge. Everything he once owned here is now yours."

"Why tell me all this? Why would you keep this secret?"

Uriel sighed as she reached up to catch at a gold locket around her neck. "Erzsebet and my father did attempt to break the curse." She opened it and held it out for me to see. Inside was a photo of the man I'd seen Erzsebet infecting. "The power she forced into him, the power that now resides inside of you...it killed him. Before you reveal anything to our colleagues, you must first be sure you are willing to sacrifice your own life, if that is what is required."

I FOUND myself outside Caius's cell after my meeting with Uriel. I stared down at my hands, watching as small sparks appeared before sinking back into my skin. This power had killed Lord Aswind. Would it kill me, too? I had to find out, and as Uriel said, there was only one man alive who could have documented the answers I needed.

But I wasn't going to re-search my suite or step foot in his office, which I'd avoided up until this point. I was going to attempt something new. To cut through the BS and get down to the truth. And Caius wasn't going to have a choice.

With our bond shut down on my end, I was alone. Kendrick had no idea I was here. And from his lack of presence, I assumed he was asleep. Still recharging after days of worrying about me. Only my shadows and the prison guards knew I was here, but they kept their mouths shut as I nodded for them to open Caius's cell.

The scenery hadn't changed, I saw as I stepped inside. Stone and nothing but the glow of a naked bulb. There was a drip, drip, drip as water fled the recently showered cell. Lying on his back, Caius glanced my way. Genuine surprise widened his eyes at the sight of me. He pushed upright, tattered shirt and pants wet and clinging to his blue-veined skin. "What a surprise, my dear. To what do I owe this pleasure?"

Being here on my own—even though it wasn't the first time—I felt exposed and vulnerable. Chained or not, I was alone in a room with my murderer. Knowing what I'd come here to do unnerved me, and goosebumps rippled from the back of my neck down to my feet. But I wasn't backing out. "Lord Aswind was Erzsebet's guinea pig. She used him for her cause, and he died in the process." I felt my hands tingling with stronger waves of static. "This power you inflicted on me, it's what killed him."

Understanding flashed across Caius's unshaven face. "You wish to know if you will suffer the same fate."

I said nothing, waiting for him to offer up—or refuse—an explanation.

"Whether you die is solely your choice, my dear." Caius struggled to push himself up off the ground before resting his weight against the wall. "When it comes to the matter of your power, that is."

"Did Lord Aswind have the same choice?"

"No. The power alone was too much for him to contain. He could never have survived it."

"Why? What makes me different?"

Caius supported his weight and took slow steps toward me. His chains rattled as he came as close as the restraints would allow. "That I cannot tell you."

Being only a foot away from him was way too close. My body wanted to run, but raw determination to seek the truth kept me planted. If Caius wouldn't offer up the answer willingly, I'd extract it from him. At least, that was the plan.

Flesh crawling in anticipation, I struck out and caught his wrist, letting out little currents to stop him from reacting. I stared into his widened eyes, needing to know the secrets he hid. I didn't know if a conscious vision was possible. Didn't know if touching a person could bring one on in the same way touching an object did. But I was going to try.

As my strength ebbed, my vision turned black. I couldn't hold it back and I couldn't stop the dark void from taking over. I saw flashes of events playing out before my eyes. Erzsebet bottling her own blood, brow creased with determination. A damned with its fangs embedded in her arm from behind bars. One she made no attempt to fight. Erzsebet crouched over a dead body, her mouth bloody and red eyes full of conflict. Erzsebet handing two identical, rubber-stopped vials to a watery-eyed, but fearless boy. One filled with red, the other with black. A quick, tight hug was shared before she locked him under the stairs. The last flash revealed a grand interior, empty of both movement and life. Red painted the walls and bodies lay strewn at every angle.

My eyes flung open with a gasp to find myself still standing. Caius was right before me, curiously watching. Breathing hard, I snatched my hand away and backed up, wondering why he hadn't stuck out or hurt me. The unwanted compassion I felt for the boy in the vision, given a purpose beyond his years, was like a personal betrayal.

"You saw what she did." There was no question, just unwavering insight.

I nodded and slipped my hand into the pocket of my hoodie. My hunger was rising and that little voice in my head wanted me to take the only person on offer in this room and bleed him dry. *Yuck.* "Erzsebet bottled her own blood, her vampire *and* damned blood," I said, mouth watering and fangs sliding free. "She gave them to you as a boy and locked you away before everyone was killed. *Why?*"

"Among other things, the contents of the vial I forced on you needed to contain both vampire and damned blood…from the same source. It also needed to be given to a descendant of the donor to work, before they breathed life. Infecting you was my only choice."

I spoke quickly so I could get the hell out of there. "But you won't tell me how to save the damned, or what choice I must make to live or die?"

Caius sighed deeply as he backed up and slid down the wall, wet shirt riding up. I could almost believe the look on his face was despair. "I can only advise you to stop on this path you are beginning down. No good will come of it. Especially not to you, my dear."

I FLEW through the door to my suite and slammed it on the guards. Urgency to search the entire place rushed through my veins while punishing hunger demanded attention. I shot from the foyer into the lounge room and fell to my knees before the bar fridge. Just short of tearing its doors clean off the hinges, I stared inside.

Empty.

"Dammit!"

The main door creaked open then and quick footsteps brought my head up. Kendrick stood in the opening to the foyer, jaw set and arms crossed over his chest. "Want to tell me why you're absolutely starving after two bottles, oh, I don't know…about an hour ago?"

Busted.

In my run back here from Caius's cell, Kendrick had been in my head without me even knowing it. Had he been awake the whole time? I stood on shaky legs, hands going to my hips. "You know why." He wasn't my keeper and I wasn't apologizing for where I'd been. I took a few steps forward, picking up the scent of his blood and…something else. I froze. "You've been down in the catacombs again."

"What?" Kendrick looked away with a shake of his head. His hands fidgeted with his navy polo, and then he stalked past me to perch on the edge of the couch. Irritation radiated off him. "No. It must be the shirt. Same one I had on yesterday. And don't change the subject."

"Right." Except I could swear he'd had a lighter blue polo on when I caught him exiting the catacomb entrance. I nudged at his mind, and all I got was a nudge back. Yesterday had been a turning point that had felt as extreme as jumping off a cliff. Maybe I was just wrong.

"So are you going to help me, or just give me hell?"

Kendrick's tough-guy exterior cracked. The fear he had for my safety overrode his pissed-off mood as he came over and plucked an upturned glass from the cupboard below the TV and flipped it the right way up. His intense silvery eyes met mine as he bit into his wrist and held it over the glass rim.

The scent of his blood escalated around the room, overriding that

157

dank and something-else smell wafting off his clothes. My gaze locked on the vibrant, glossy trickle as it slowly filled the glass. Rapt with hunger—and suddenly something stronger—I envisioned taking Kendrick by the elbow and bringing his bitten flesh to my lips. Licking. Sucking. Tasting.

"Amelia."

"Huh, what?" The fantasy fled as the glass was lifted up to my face. One of my hands was clutching Kendrick's elbow while the other claimed his bleeding wrist.

"Are you okay?"

Realizing I was biting my own lip, I released my fangs' hold, as well as my hands. I snatched the glass and backed up, almost tripping on the shaggy rug as my face burned. And yet I knew I'd somehow, subconsciously, locked down the fantasy as it had happened. I shook the memory away as fresh guilt rose up. "Yeah. Fine. Just really thirsty." Then I drained the glass.

Awkward seconds turned into the longest minute of my life. From the look on Kendrick's face, he'd read into my strange actions. Knew those silent seconds when I'd taken his arm and been transfixed on his wrist that there had been heat and desire…beyond my need for his blood. He didn't bring it up though. Instead, he took the empty glass from me—without meeting my eyes—and placed it on the white marble coffee table, giving me a little nudge. "We, ah…" He cleared his throat. "We need to know more about how Lord Aswind died. What caused his ultimate end." *And what could cause yours,* he thought, but said out loud, "What choice you have that he didn't."

Despite being grateful for him changing the subject away from my distorted emotions, I dreaded where this search was leading to. Caius's office. The place where Caius had compelled and fed from me before erasing the action. The place he'd led me to before knocking me out with a diamond paperweight to carry my body down to the catacombs. My heart raced at the thought of going back there. "I—"

"I'll go." With a squeeze of my arm, Kendrick retreated to the foyer. He turned back as he opened the main door. "You search the library tower."

The door swung shut behind him, and what felt like a boulder's pressure lifted off my chest. I'd just dodged two bullets. Owning up to my fantasy that left guilt swimming in my veins. And stepping into a place in the past that reminded me of hell. Now there was just the possibility of my future grisly death to try to prevent. Lucky me.

Task set, I climbed the white spiral staircase edging the lounge room and siding the walkway to my bedroom. Beyond the exposed stone ring below the wooden floor, and the railing around the central-placed staircase, was a hexagonal-shaped room. With floor-to-hip-height shelving, it was jam-packed full of books. A break in the shelving was filled with a red velvet chaise, stocked with two round pillows. Above the shelving, windows made of dark-tinted glass stretched up to the domed ceiling.

Regardless of the lavish and beautiful surroundings, I hated being up in this space. Of everything that had belonged to Caius before his imprisonment, the one thing I'd ordered the staff to leave untouched in the entire suite was this library tower. It wasn't hard to imagine Caius up here, stretched out on the chaise as he spent hours plotting and scheming. Is this where he'd decided to kill me?

I shook off the foreboding and started with the top left, pulling out one book after another. I'd been through every book here since this became my place to call home, but I'd never found anything more on what Caius had done to us or why. Still, knowing I had a choice that could be the death of me, and with Kendrick tackling Caius's office, I had to give it one last search.

As minutes bled into hours, I moved meticulously from one book to the next. Each was pulled out, pages flicked through, held by the spine and shaken, then replaced on the shelf.

When I got to shelf number five, I was well past the order of pulling out one book at a time and putting it back in its place. Instead, I resorted to ripping books from shelves, doing my check, and dumping them on the ground when they weren't what I was looking for. With the last handful of books, I let out a cry of frustration. I picked up and flung an elemental book. It hit the stair railing on one edge and spun until it smacked into the exposed edge of stone that underlay the wood-planked floor.

A hollow sound rang out and I followed the direction. A stone had shifted. Pressed back a quarter-inch at the colliding force.

I hurdled the mess of books at my feet to meet the spiral stairs and reached through the railing to the moved stone. It was a rough rectangle, like the others, and as big as my head. Wedging my fingers along the sides, I jiggled, and the stone began to slide forward. With measured force from both hands, it slid free to leave a black hole in its place. My hand shot into the dark void and felt the edges of something rectangular. I pulled it out to find a wooden box. It looked extremely old, the wood plain but carved with a single mark to prevent opening it without a key. I tested the mark, trying to pry the lid open, but got nowhere. Then I noticed that the shaped metal around the keyhole was brass.

A light bulb went off in my head. I knew how to open it.

I shoved the box up onto a stack of books and ran downstairs and into my bedroom. From atop the bedside table, I grabbed the jewelry box, forcing myself to ignore the stab my heart took on glimpsing the photo of Ty propped against the lamp. That same clink rose in my mind from the time I'd picked the gold box up at the auction. I knew the vial had been inside then, but after Caius had gifted me the item, the key had been left in its place.

I plucked the brass key with its looped-handle design out and threw the jewelry box onto my bed before racing back up the spiral stairs. The key fit like a glove as I shoved books back to perch on the top step. A click announced the lock's release. The lid swung open without protest, and I peered inside before pulling out an old notebook with a velvet-swathed cover.

Opening the cover, I reared and took up residence on the foot of the chaise and propped my knees up. *Erzsebet Bathory* was written with an inked quill, and a contents page outlined the notebook's details. There were titles for experiments and one caught my eye.

I carefully turned the frail pages until I found the one I wanted.

Last Attempt to Break Curse: During the test to break the damned curse, the expelled power returned unto Lord Aswind and instantaneously killed him. Attempts at resuscitation failed. Blood transfusion also returned no life signs. On opening the deceased, I found his internal organs to be burned, including his heart, and much damage inflicted on all areas throughout his body. I conclude that the power once expelled is too great to re-contain.

Having seen a dead Pure Blood on that cold steel table at the Anchorage Hospital Morgue, I shuddered at the thought of Lord Aswind being cut open and inspected like a meaningless slab of meat. Like all he had been was a means to an end. Not an important man with a family he was leaving behind.

The main door opened and then shut, and light feet patted across stone before the spiral stairs creaked. Kendrick poked his head up through the opening. "Office is clean," he said, seeing the book in my lap.

Through the distance from Caius's office up to my suite he'd seen the words I'd read from the notebook. And he'd come to his own conclusion on what I'd uncovered. He took the book from me and reread the passage. "There's only one choice I can come up with out of this."

Reading into his thoughts, I twisted on the chaise to glance out through the windows. It was still relatively quiet down there, the cobblestone streets almost empty, except for the few shop owners opening up their stores. With less refracted light from the sun over the horizon, the Victorian street lamps had lit up.

Caius had said he no longer wanted to save all damned. That the cost was too great. So with everything we now knew, there was only one thing that made sense. "I think you're right. Breaking the curse *is* the choice. Which means I can only restore one damned at a time."

Kendrick sighed and climbed the discarded books to sit beside me. He patted my hand, frowning as his lips parted. "If you were aware of the steps it would take to do it."

CHAPTER 13

"What do you mean—if I was aware?" I leaned forward to take the book back from Kendrick, wondering if I'd missed something.

Then the street lamps blacked out.

Warm yellow light gone, shadows grew as night rose. I froze, twisted on the chaise and panned left to right. "Could the twilight sensors malfunction—?"

Sudden heat burned my wrist, blazing from the pendant.

Kendrick squeezed right up beside me, scanning the darkening streets. "Something's coming."

What I saw next made my heart falter. More and more vamps appeared with the disappearing sun. But they weren't alone. Down on the street, dark figures slid around the sides of buildings, stalking them without a sound. Across from the angel fountain, others skulked along the tree line. My vampire sight refocused like binoculars. Sickly pale skin. Hoods covering faces. Predatory movement.

A deathly shiver cascaded down my spine and I leaped up. "The damned!"

Kendrick was right there with me. "What the hell. There's no alarm."

The furthest away damned entered houses on the town's outskirts. One approached Dorian's blue front door. My blood ran ice cold as it slipped inside.

Then—louder than any alarm—a chorus of screams cut through the air.

I launched downstairs and into my bedroom, flinging open two of my weapon crates. Desperate fear for my brother's life and everyone else's made me want to hurl. "We get to Dorian first."

Kendrick nodded through the opening as he reached the foyer and jammed a stool into the main door, effectively locking it. He doubted I'd pull through losing someone else I loved so much, and the thought terrified him. "No one will stop us now." Then he tripped the manual alarm.

As the piercing sound swept through me, I snatched up my whip and palmed a silver dagger, a gun, and a stake. I flung the dagger at Kendrick as he reached my terrace doors in a blur, and he caught the projectile by the hilt. Banging on the main door escalated as I shot to the balcony.

A crack of wood rang out as we leaped down to the ground.

The arched, iron-braced doors further down the castle flung open and guards streamed out. Uriel was right behind them. "Kill the damned. Defend the castle!"

With the guards armed to the teeth, I handed Kendrick the loaded gun and we darted into the garden. For every damned that appeared around the barricading hedges, Kendrick shot it down with a silver-exploding bullet. My stake finished the job.

More and more kept appearing, coming at us with nothing but

their nails and fangs. But the element of surprise was over. And they were on our turf.

As I staked my ninth damned, we'd reached the garden outskirts. Battle cries as well as ones of terror filled the air as vamps ran from danger. But the guards dominated the attack, three to every one damned. For now they had it under control.

A block behind them, the first residential houses started. Not for the first time, I wished I had that eerie "twin connection" with Dorian. Except we were no longer twins. We weren't even related. We never had been.

"We head straight for Dorian's."

A stray damned came at me and Kendrick dropped it with a quick stabbing twist of his silver dagger. Ash ballooned out like a smoke bomb. "Got your back."

"Thanks."

Without further words, I darted through the stone archway and down the main street. Kendrick was right behind me.

Sudden flames flared inside boutiques and cafés. Then a crack and a boom burst out multiple shop fronts. Kendrick and I ducked as glass shards speared our way and fresh screams filled the air.

"Multiple explosions!" Kendrick screamed as we scrambled upright.

But I didn't reply. Could barely breathe as I stared at the scene before me. Because I'd seen this all before: the fire, the panicked people...*the damned*. When I'd just started taking Kendrick's bottled blood and I'd managed to bring on a vision. But instead of passing out, my memory had faltered. My body hadn't yet fully recovered with the start of my new diet.

"This is my fault. This is the vision I lost."

Kendrick gripped my shoulders and squeezed. Fierce certainty edged his unwavering stare. "Don't do that. This is *not* your fault."

True or not, I could wallow in guilt later. We needed to get to Dorian, and there wasn't a second to waste. Dread that we'd be too late lit my muscles on fire and I grabbed Kendrick's hand. "Let's go."

We took off at a dead run, rounding street bends and battling—

A bright flash of light erupted in the distance behind the street of houses we were on. A sonic boom pulsated the atmosphere, catching our bodies and slamming us back into the road. Damned, vamps, and guards were thrown too.

My ears rang as I scrambled to my feet along with others who'd been floored. My dread turned into total panic. More smoke billowed up in the distance. "That came from Dorian's direction."

Kendrick jumped up and pushed me forward. "Go, go, go!"

With feet pelting the ground, in seconds we reached Dorian's kicked-in, blue front door and shot inside. The still-hot pendant at my wrist blazed with repetition. Warmth gathered inside the house and smoke clouded the air, making it hard to see. Without electricity, there was no light. But I didn't need it to figure out where Dorian was. The scent of fresh blood poisoned the air, leading me straight to the kitchen.

When I reached the entry, the first thing I saw was Vanessa in a heap to one corner. The small table beside her was snapped as if she'd been thrown into it, and half alight with billowing smoke. A silver stake lay just out of her reach. She was unconscious, but I could hear her steady breaths over the sound of gushing water.

My focus shot to the other side of the kitchen. A burst pipe over the sink sprouted water like a fountain. Singed cupboards were cracked and hanging off snapped hinges.

When my eyes lowered, I almost fell to my knees.

A set of legs stuck out from behind the kitchen bench. A hint of sports shorts was visible, wet with more than water. The feet were bare and pale, big like Dorian's. A crimson pool surrounded those legs—and a hooded figure crouched over the body. With their back to me, I couldn't see their face. But after a silent, frozen moment, they lowered Dorian's torso down to the stained, wet linoleum.

Tears clouded my vision and I clutched the stake in my hand tighter. My other hand rose, collecting a ball of electric energy into my palm. That monster had just fed off my brother. Killed him. "Get the fuck away from him."

With his dagger ready, Kendrick stalked forward. "She said, get the hell off him."

The crouching figure turned and pulled his hood back.

The electricity at my palm instantly receded at the unmistakable face staring up at me. "Marcus?"

My knees buckled, but I stayed upright, my hand clutching the stake so tight my bones felt like they were bending. My eyes flicked to Dorian's lifeless body and the pool of blood that coated the linoleum around him, then back to Marcus. Yellowing bruises marred his face, and the front of his hoodie was torn. More blood covered his gray pants from kneeling in the stuff. But dark torrents also ran down the front of his white collared shirt beneath the hoodie. My stare lifted to the patchy blood marking his neck. A long gash was steadily knitting back together. Had he been attacked, too? Had he just gotten here before us to find Dorian already dead?

"How? What…"

Kendrick's hand on his dagger held tight, but he didn't move—could only utter, "What happened?"

Marcus held up his hands and slowly stood. His eyes darted to Dorian with a look of fear, then back to me. "I'd just left *Bite* and compelled my guards away so I could take a walk alone. Then I heard the screams. I was on this street and saw Dorian's door standing open. I rushed inside and fought off the damned attacking him. He was so cut up, but he wasn't gone yet. I tried to save him." His raised hand went to his bloody neck. "I fed him my blood."

A shuffle tore my stare from Marcus. Vanessa let out a groan and touched a cut on her head. Then her eyes grew wide and she scrambled across the lino. "Dorian! Oh, God." She patted his body with shaking hands. With a shuddering breath her tear-filled sapphires found Marcus. "Did you kill it? Did you kill the effing damned who did this to him?"

Before he could answer, I recovered from the shock and stumbled forward, sliding through the blood to Dorian's other side. His sports shorts and muscle shirt were shredded. The damage was so vicious it had not just slashed skin but had severed through muscles to expose internal organs. With the severity, it was impossible to tell if he'd been bitten, too.

I ran a hand down his bloody face to his neck. My fingers paused as I felt something. Could it be? With all his injuries was it even possible? A weak and tiny blip registered beneath my fingertips. And there it was again. *"Dorian?"*

Behind me, Kendrick and Marcus crept closer.

Opposite me, Vanessa clutched Dorian's hand as if praying. "Please," she sobbed. "You have to be okay."

Dorian's eyes moved behind closed lids, then they cracked open. "Amelia? Vanessa?" He tried to sit up, but with a wet tearing sound he grunted and collapsed back down.

"Shh, don't move." I glanced down at his shredded body to see that through the blood, nothing fresh leaked out of him. "Thank God. You're going to be okay."

He ran his tongue over his lips and swallowed. "Whose blood am I tasting?"

Marcus moved to squat beside me and clasped Dorian's hand with a smile. "It's mine."

A chorus of shouts and screams traveled into the house from out on the street. No longer the sounds of distant battling, but close and desperate. The Armaya was still under invasion. And unlike earlier, it didn't sound like we were winning. Vampires with jobs, duties, homes, and families were dying out there.

I jumped up, a burning need to fight and protect lighting within me. "We have to help them." I stalled at the sight of my slowly recovering brother. "Will you—?"

"Not if you stay here instead of kicking some ass," Dorian cut in.

Kendrick threw Vanessa his gun and made for the front door. The last thing he wanted was for the damned to storm the house while Dorian was still recovering. "The damned are everywhere," he hollered back. "We need to get out before they come in."

Marcus swooped up the stray stake from the ground and stumbled before getting vertical. "Vanessa, stay with Dorian while he heals." He shook off a dizzy look and narrowed his eyes when he noticed me watching him. "I'm fine," he said before I could ask how much blood he'd fed Dorian. "Let's kick some damned butt."

With Kendrick's gun beside her, Vanessa shredded a tea towel to treat Dorian's wounds, who nodded as if to say, *go get 'em.*

Satisfied he'd be okay, I took off after Kendrick with Marcus behind me. Out in the street, vampires had vacated their homes and were now fighting to hold back the damned. Some held silver-coated weapons, but most were fending off attacks with objects they'd yanked from their houses. Guards were out here, too, fighting to save lives.

Kendrick whipped out his dagger and began defending the unarmed. At the same time, his free hand coaxed sudden gusts of wind that knocked the damned back from their prey.

Marcus went straight into the fray, stake wielding to kill injured but still-living damned.

I joined the battle, staking already-engaged damned. Then I lashed out my electrified whip at a distant damned that was a second away from taking a fresh victim. The civilian scurried to safety and the damned turned on me.

Whip still connected, he tugged me forward and smashed me down into the road. On top of me in a flash, I threw an electric punch. The damned hissed and hit back. Stars danced in my vision and its lips curled back from its fangs in preparation.

But I wasn't dying like this.

Hearing the sizzle of my whip around its torso, I drove my stake up—

The damned squealed and leaped off me as fire scaled its entire body. It ran but fell, engulfed by licking orange flames.

Its dying scream lifted the hairs across my neck as I sat up. "What the…"

Marcus stood statue-still in the middle of the cobblestone street. The stake was now tucked into his bloody pants, and his hands were held up. One by one, damned exploded into sudden pillars of fire. Their screams filled the starlit sky, as did the disgusting smell of their melting flesh.

Victorious cries began to ring out as the remaining damned fled. But I didn't stop fighting. Instead, I sprang up and staked any damned in my reach. The more we killed now, the less we'd have to take down later. And the less that could regroup to plan another invasion.

I kicked down the damned I was taking on and landed on his chest. "See you in hell," I spat, then drove the stake home. A spurt of black sprayed out to coat my face, then the body turned to ash beneath me.

Throat sawing with rapid breath, I jumped up, ready to continue my killing spree when a strong hand caught my wrist.

"I think that was the last one," Kendrick said, breathing hard and his face red.

Around us, people had started moving back to their houses while guards inspected the dead for survivors. Relieved the battle was over but with adrenaline still pumping, I placed a hand along Kendrick's cheek. Bruises and cuts covered his face and his own blood patterned his torn-up polo. I knew he was, but I asked anyway. "Are you okay?"

He smiled, pinching the hem of my tank as countless stings registered from my own injured body. "As long as you are."

"The city center is clear," Marcus called as he appeared around the bend. I took a step back from Kendrick as he jogged down the cobblestone street. When he reached us, he ran a hand down the side of his dirty face. "We'll need to organize a mass funeral for all—"

A shriek cut through the air, killing the last of Marcus's words. It had come from the castle's direction. Outside in the gardens.

We responded in a flash, speeding down the street and through the first stone-bordered entry. Taking off in different directions, we cleared the maze-like paths and alcoves. Pure despair struck my chest as I neared the fountain centering the gardens.

Kendrick was already there, and Marcus appeared through an arched entry as I rushed in.

Two female guards lay lifeless on the path, their throats torn out. Three swords lay scattered on the grass. Two clearly belonged to the guards, being the same all guards were armed with. The third sword was different, with gold and jewels coating the hilt.

Kendrick was in the fountain, red-tainted water up to his waist, and cradling...

A woman dressed in a saturated indigo gown. One with detailed stitching and made of silk. She was one of us, I thought as Kendrick's entire world shattered and split him in two.

With careful and gentle arms, he levered her up and smoothed the wet, golden-brown hair from her pale face. Her eyes were open, vampire blue and lifeless. Her mouth gaped, and a bloody gash in her jugular seeped crimson down her chest.

"Oh, God. No."

Serafina Baldassare. Kendrick's mother.

Kendrick lifted his head with tear-filled eyes. He choked on his words. "She's...she's dead."

CHAPTER 14

The next day I found myself trapped in the boardroom with the other crowned royals. Guards stood to attention against the walls. A mix of twenty-eight males and females in total, now that each of us had been assigned a protective detail of four at all times. The Baldassare throne sat glaringly empty, except for the gold-hilted sword strapped to the back.

A ball of anxiety batted around my chest. I didn't want to be here, stuck in this position and dealing with formalities. Kendrick needed me. Since yesterday, he'd put a block on his emotions. Still, some of the agony broke through. And even in its diluted state, it suffocated me to my very soul. I could only imagine the pure hell Kendrick was going through. In spite of having had a rocky relationship with his mother, he had always loved her. He'd never known his father, and as family went, she was all he'd had.

I sent out, *you've always been family to me. I'm here for you, always,* hoping it would make it through. I despairingly glanced to the oversized Gothic windows that peered out to the path before the garden hedges where even more guards patrolled outside.

"As our top-trained guards, you have all been offered this new position." Uriel's commanding voice made me flinch. I caught her hard stare softening as she glanced to the Baldassare throne and up to the guards. "Repeat your sworn oath to accept this privilege."

In chorus, every guard announced, *"By my royal blood, I pledge to protect my charges from any and all danger. To risk my life to save theirs. And to die by my sword if I fail."*

Lord Paole opened the cover of the binder in front of him without looking up and signed the inducted list of guards. "Oath accepted. You are all excused to take post outside the door. Baldassare guards, you are to situate yourselves outside the Baldassare suite." The heavy doors closed behind the last exiting guard. "Now, the funeral for Lady Baldassare. It will commence tomorrow at two a.m. in the main hall."

"Agreed," everyone replied, except for me.

Instead, the image of Kendrick carrying the hefty weight of a gold casket filled my mind. I wished I could help lighten the heavy burden. But tradition only allowed family members to cart the dead to their farewell. I could barely breathe at the thought. "Agreed."

Lord Strigon saluted his blood-filled glass and took a sip. "The remaining deceased will be honored at a pyre in the main field."

A split-second image of the royal heir who'd been burned alive for loving a lycan flashed across my mind. Ty's grandfather. With Kendrick's emotional devastation, my own at losing Ty had been on the back burner. Now it was a fire being blasted by oxygen, scorching my never-healing heart. I talked around the clenching of my throat. "You're burning the dead?"

"With the possibility of damned infection, it is the cleanest and most respectful way to dispose of the bodies," Lady Rasputin said, her face showing as much emotion as stone. "Without witness of their families, all deceased will be beheaded and placed in the pyre. All agreed?"

Marcus shared a look with me while everyone else voiced their agreement. From his sigh and pursed lips before he glanced down at his hands on the round marble table, it was clear he'd expected this. Growing up here, he knew the process. That didn't mean he was any happier about it than I was. But we were out-voted.

"Kendrick will need to be crowned during the late Lady Baldassare's funeral," Uriel said with clear regret. "Showing strength amongst us is important in this fearful time. Though I would like to suggest holding a ball to formally welcome not only Kendrick, but also our two other newest members, Amelia and Marcus. Two weeks should allow for grieving before the event. What say you all?"

"Agreed," the others voiced, while again Marcus and I remained quiet. I couldn't believe they were talking about a showy occasion when so many had lost so much.

"Now on to our last point for this meeting." Lord Paole frowned, then glanced down at his binder. "Our alchemist was among the many killed yesterday. Now we have no one to replace his wards around our perimeter."

Uriel got up and sashayed in her green gown over to the closest window. With her hands clasped tight, she stared out at the mountainous horizon the sun had dipped below. Even without the bright orb, the sky was still light. "The alarm sounded, but we need better warning. New wards set up miles from our perimeters so we have time to prepare."

"The damned didn't set the alarm off." I'd seen the damned from my library tower before rushing to get weapons. The alarm hadn't sounded until Kendrick pulled the lever himself. "They were already inside and stalking the streets when I saw them. Kendrick was with me and pulled the manual alarm in my suite."

"You must be mistaken," Lord Strigon said, eyes narrowing at me. "The wards trigger the alarm if a wolf or damned even steps one foot inside. They also weaken them as they pass onto our grounds."

"The damned were outnumbered," Marcus pointed out. "But they sure as hell weren't weak."

"Marcus is right," Uriel said, turning her gaze from the clear sky that had slowly begun to darken. "I fought myself, and the damned were as strong then as they were at Portsmouth. And our wards have been checked. Unlike at Portsmouth, they are still intact. They haven't been tampered with."

A memory tickled my subconscious. The time I'd gone to spy on the PVC with Ty and Troy. Pain struck my chest, remembering what Ty had looked like then. A flash of him dead across my lap followed. I swallowed to hold back tears and forced my way past the pain to focus. Back then, to get us all inside the PVC's walls, Troy had needed to drink my blood to prevent setting off the ward-triggered alarm. Ty hadn't—because he was already part vampire. I'd continued using that same proven weakness by giving Marika vials of my blood to get her onto castle grounds without detection. "What if the damned ingested vampire blood to avoid setting off the alarms?"

"How are you aware of that loophole?" Lady Rasputin demanded.

I stopped breathing, guilt all over my face. "I, um…"

"I told her," Marcus cut in, now knowing how I'd been sneaking Marika in for the past months. The look he gave me told me to keep my trap shut.

Lord Strigon waved a dismissive hand. "In any case, it doesn't matter. Our wards cannot be passed with simply any vampire's blood. It must be Pure, and not only Pure, but also one of The Seven who has consumed all of our blood through ritual. The only other blood that could suffice is from one of The Seven's spawn born after the ritual."

A shiver cascaded down my spine. The only options were that it was Caius's blood. It could even be my twin's, if they were alive… and even if they weren't, I doubt that would have stopped Caius from draining a newborn's veins. The other option was that it was mine, if Caius had kept and stored my blood when I was a child, or even under compulsion later on. Was this break in our security and danger to our people all because of me? Was this yet another thing I could add to my *you screwed up royally* list?

Marcus pushed his throne back and strode to the door, pulling only one side inward. "There is another way they could have gotten in."

A girl with long, red hair and sapphire-blue eyes stepped inside, wearing designer jeans and a red leather jacket.

Vanessa smiled at me, but she addressed everyone. "I believe a temporary alchemist mark could grant the damned entry."

"The damned can't be marked," I blurted out then cursed myself. I'd discovered the fact when Vanessa had tried to mark me. After what Caius had done to me, I was part damned on a cellular level. Any tattooed marks faded as soon as they were inflicted. But I didn't know if this was common RVC knowledge. I peered around the marble table.

Marcus gave me a stern look while the other royals glanced my way then back at Vanessa.

"No," Vanessa agreed. "But I think they could swallow something that had been."

"Regardless of your theories," Lady Rasputin said as she leaned back in her throne with authority. "This is a private meeting and we were not informed of any *visitors,* Marcus."

Marcus didn't backpedal or apologize. Instead, he smiled. "Before he passed away, Vanessa's grandfather, Mr. Aquinas, had been my family's private alchemist for almost a decade. Fully trained, Vanessa is trusted by myself and by Amelia, and has a symbol that will prevent any non-flesh marks from being effective. I believe she would be a valuable asset if made the Armaya's new alchemist."

The other royals began discussing whether taking her on was a good idea, and what security checks would be necessary before she was formally appointed. They each knew the name Aquinas, and most trusted their rumored work.

Rather than joining in, I turned to Vanessa. Even though her grandfather had assisted the Vladimirs, she had never hidden the fact that she supported the wolves first and foremost. "You don't actually want this, do you?"

She shrugged. "The damned need to be stopped. If I can do anything to help that, I will. Besides, with Dorian staying here, I hardly get to see him."

"Then it is settled." Uriel clapped her hands as the others quieted down. "You'll begin immediately, reinforcing the wards while we do a background check. Permanent residence while employed is non-negotiable."

BESIDE ME, Kendrick said nothing and his mind was closed off. But I didn't need our link to know what he was going through. Even if his reddened eyes and blank stare didn't portray enough, his actions had. Since finding Serafina dead two days ago, he'd remained by his mother's bed, holding her cold, lifeless hand and staring at her unresponsive face. It had taken much convincing to get him to allow me to help him dress for today's funeral.

I felt so utterly helpless. Could barely draw in full breaths in this stupid, tight gown as I watched him suffer. I wanted to steal his pain, to somehow take it from him and into myself. To do something other than rub his back or hold his hand in support. That comforting shit did jack-all, other than remind him I was still here. And after what he'd lost, that was so far from enough. Still, even as I held my own tears from him and pretended to be strong, I had to accept there was nothing more I could do to ease his pain.

Which I guess turned our tables.

Kendrick had been the one supporting me and backing me up since finding out Ty had died. The pain of losing Ty still radiated through every fiber of my being, but somehow I was functioning, somehow putting one foot in front of the other each day. And with Kendrick's grief, I had to be stronger. I had to pull him through this. It was my turn to carry him, to help him see that a future did still exist for him.

Now upright and dressed in an all-white suit, Kendrick pushed open the terrace doors.

"No, wait—"

And stepped out onto the balcony without a backward glance. I reached his side as he laid shaking hands on the thick, carved balustrade. Short of flinging my hands over his eyes, which I considered, I couldn't prevent the view he saw. The sight of the lush hedge-like maze of the gardens, the many secluded and well-planted alcoves with stone seating, and the vine-covered shelters. Glowing in the ghostly twilight, the tiered fountain centered it all. The one Kendrick had pulled his mother's body from. The one that was now dry and quiet without the patter of overflowing water. The one that was no longer stained with streaks of red.

Kendrick stopped breathing for a long while, one single tear sliding down his face as I covered his hand and squeezed. The breath he finally raked in was shuddering and full of sorrow. Wind ruffled his golden-brown hair like gentle fingers. "I still see her there," he croaked, clutching the balustrade hard enough to almost crack the polished stone. "I mean, I know she's back..." He glanced halfway over his shoulder, but squeezed his eyes shut and retreated before he could catch sight of her corpse on the bed. "There...but I see her down there. Face up. Eyes so still...unfocused. The chunk out of her neck. The blood. I—I see it all."

I wanted to say something, anything to make him feel better, to ease the agony wrecking him that I felt but a fraction of through the bond. But there were no words that could ease his suffering. Nothing could make this alright. So I just wrapped my arms around his waist and held tight, like I'd never, ever let go. "I know you do."

The creak of the main door to the Baldassare suite opening, cranked Kendrick's head around. The sound of clattering as something was wheeled in had him tearing free of my hold and racing inside.

Kendrick froze with me behind him and stared vacantly as two guards wheeled a gold coffin into the bedroom. They opened the lids in silence and strode to the canopy bed, moving to pull back the pure-white covers.

"No!" Kendrick lunged forward and caught one of the guard's arms and shoved him back. "No one touches her but me." He bared his fangs. "Get out!"

I said nothing as the guards both nodded and backed out of the room. The click of the door shutting released the breath Kendrick was holding. I stood cemented to the spot, my heart breaking as I watched my best friend sling his arms under his mother's body. He hoisted her up and winced as her head rocked back, swaying side to side. Moving awkwardly, he managed to reposition her head to support and cradle her against his chest. Each step toward the coffin felt like a stab to my heart, which must have meant Kendrick's was being pummeled with metaphorical brass knuckles fitted with spikes.

He lowered his dead mother's body into her eternal resting bed and fixed the arrangement of her gold burial gown. With a kiss to his palm, his hand covered the cleaned but shredded flesh at her neck. Vampires didn't heal after death. Then he pressed gentle lips to her forehead. When he stood back, a tear slid down his face. "Good bye, my mother."

I swished in my white and gold gown to stand behind him, each quiet step of my hidden Vans thumping like rude bombs to break the mournful silence. My arms came around his waist and I held tight. With my head resting on his back, I heard the elevated beat of his broken heart and his shallow, quick breaths as he tried not to break down. *Whatever you need. I'm here for you. Always.* Levering up on my toes, I pressed a kiss above his collar to his neck. Then I released him to head to the other side of the coffin.

Before I could take one step, Kendrick caught my arm and tugged me back against his chest. His lips crushed over mine and his hands came up to capture my face as I gasped. With his eyes squeezed shut before my wide ones, it was over within seconds. Kendrick's hands fell to his sides and he stepped back. "I'm sorry. I…just needed to feel something. Something other than…" He threw a fist over his chest and held it to his heart. *"This."*

Breath shaky and heart racing, I was shocked but I wasn't mad. My emotions were on a roller coaster, one I couldn't look into with everything else that was going on. On a lot of levels I'd needed something other than the constant despair of life, too. But I wasn't sure if I was ready for this. "You don't need to apologize." I backed up and around the coffin and grasped the center handle. "Are you ready?"

Kendrick nodded and forced a pained smile before lowering the coffin's bottom and top lids. "You may return," his voice cracked as he called through the opening to the foyer.

The guards re-entered and coasted around the granite table in the foyer and into the bedroom. One guard waited, hands clasped behind his back while the other retrieved the gold cloak draped over a high-backed armchair. He carried it held out over his forearms and faced Kendrick, the embroidered elemental designs that matched every other crowned royal's cloak visible across the back. A cloak that was only worn by an heir at the funeral of their ruling deceased.

My best friend nodded and the guard fastened the cloak over his shoulders. With one hand, Kendrick gripped the opposite handle and we lifted the heavy weight. With slow steps, we left what had been Serafina's bedroom and headed for the open main door.

Kendrick walked on in silence and I kept pace. When we reached the top of the grand stairs that led down to the main hall, Kendrick paused. The tribe of eight guards behind us remained mute. Quiet murmurs cut off as vampires rose to their feet from the pews below.

But Kendrick took no notice.

Instead, his thoughts went to his mother's cloak that hung like a heavy burden over his shoulders. Inside the soft folds, his free hand had brushed across something sharp-edged beneath the fine silk material. He reached inside the concealed pocket and pulled out a small card. Still supporting the weight of the coffin, he unfolded it and every single one of his muscles tightened and strained. He fully dropped the wall blocking me as he read his mother's handwritten words in his head.

DEAREST KENDRICK,

From the beginning, you were everything I hoped for. Strong. Smart. Brilliant. An heir to be proud of. And I am proud. You will make a grand ruler. This is what you were born for. I may not have been very clear in showing it, but I could not be happier witnessing everything you have become and everything I know you will now become.

I love you, my son.

A SURGE of determination filled Kendrick, and his slouched, depressed stance straightened. On the inside, his heart was raw, his mind a mess, and his body drained from lack of sleep. But he wasn't going to let it show anymore. He had been born for a purpose, and the last thing he wanted now was to let his mother down. She'd had faith in him...and she had loved him. Though she'd never said the words out loud, reading them on that letter had meant everything to him.

"Time for your funeral, Mother."

Total pride and relief at Kendrick's strength gave me hope. For him taking the first step to get over this loss, and for him finding his place in our ever-changing world. Still, I didn't know what to say, so I kept my mouth shut and glanced down into the main hall.

The other crowned royals were in their places on the stage, sporting their own ceremonial white, black, and gold formal attire.

The colors to honor the dead. In comparison to Caius's trial and my crowning, the hall was quite empty, except for the extra guards stationed around the perimeter. Through the open, heavily guarded main doors, I could see why. Smoke billowed high into the two a.m. sky, rising from behind the royal gardens, streets, and houses. Most of the town's people were out there on the field, watching their lost family members burn on the pyre. Those who had shown for the royal funeral were waiting.

You ready? I asked without speaking. It was a stupid question. And I held back the urge to clutch the amulet hidden below my bodice. No one was ever ready to give the final goodbye to a lost loved one. I knew that better than anyone.

Kendrick nodded and crooked his chin out to his four guards. "Raise the coffin."

The guards followed his order, taking possession of the gold box and raising it up high.

I met Kendrick's side and took his hands, peering deep into his eyes. "You have and always will be strong. You're my rock. And I'll be yours."

Kendrick almost smiled. "You are my family now. My everything." Then I let go and he stepped under the raised coffin, taking hold of the sides. With a curt nod, the guards released the weight and stood back. Kendrick clenched his jaw and his knees and shoulders creaked, but he showed no weakness. Then organ music rose from below, being played from beside the stage.

With one last glance, I rushed down the white marble steps before him. As I beelined toward the pews, I caught sight of Dorian and Vanessa sitting centered to the left. Dorian tipped his head, fully recovered and looking vibrant despite his somber expression. Vanessa held tight to his hand, appearing almost guilty at her relief of Dorian's safety when Kendrick's mother had been taken.

I pursed my lips as I passed and mounted the stage to take my throne. Above me, a chandelier lit up the platform, and more lit up the rest of the hall.

Kendrick began his descent then, taking slow but steady steps down the center of the grand staircase. The crowned royals and now standing-in-support extended family members, watched in silence as Kendrick carried the coffin all the way to the hall's front. A few rows back, Dorian and Vanessa sent regretful looks my way as he passed and mounted the steps to the stage with trembling legs. Then the guards helped Kendrick secure the coffin onto its stand, where he planted his feet and stood strong and ready. His mind was spinning a mile a minute, but I couldn't get a read on him.

Uriel reached the podium with glassy eyes. "Welcome all to this dark day. Your presence here will not only honor the recent loss of Lady Serafina Baldassare's life, but it will bear witness to the crowning of her royal heir. Her son and only family, Lord Kendrick Baldassare." She tilted her head and curtseyed at Kendrick. Then she resumed her place on her throne.

Marcus, having volunteered for the position during an RVC meeting this morning, cleared his throat and rose to face Kendrick. His suit was white with gold, and his stare was filled with under-standing compassion. He'd been there when Kendrick found his mother dead, and watching his friend now was clearly affecting him. "Lord Kendrick Baldassare, we summon you here to stand before the RVC, not only to honor the passing of your mother, but to be crowned in her place and recognized as one of The Seven. Have you come here of your own free will, ready to take your rightful place among us?"

Keeping his hands still at his sides, Kendrick commanded his voice to emerge without weakness. "Yes, Lord Marcus Vladimir. Of my own free will, and ready to take my rightful place imposed by my blood."

Marcus went to the table covered in crimson silk and retrieved Uriel's donated-for-the-occasion silver sword and the jewel-encrusted gold chalice. He then started toward the last throne where Lady Rasputin sat and began the process of cutting each royal's wrist so they could bleed into the cup. When Marcus reached me, the look on his face was seemingly blank. But something behind his eyes shone through. Marcus had been through this process to be crowned, too. He had also stood on this stage at the funeral for his whole family. Farewelled every last one of them with no one by his side to pull him through.

I held out my arm and Marcus sliced over the scar left from my own crowning. When the bleeding stopped, Marcus placed the chalice back on the table and sliced open the old scar on his own wrist. With his blood now added, he completed the ritual by cutting Kendrick before handing him the full chalice. "Kneel before your people and repeat the sacred oath."

Kendrick did as directed and repeated the words his mother had taught him as a child. "I vow to uphold the laws of the Royal Vampire Council, to be honest and true in all my actions, to seek justice and mercy for all that come under our laws. As long as I live, I vow this all."

The audience rose up and applauded, relief across many of their faces at welcoming their new ruler. Dorian and Vanessa didn't share their relief, keeping their somber expressions.

Marcus returned to his throne and Kendrick left his mother's side to place the empty chalice back on the table. Without needing instruction, he crossed back to his mother's coffin and opened the top lid to expose her face. After a brief pause, he strode to the podium with a stony face. The audience sat as his strong and level voice filled the soaring hall.

"Two days ago my life changed. As did many others. As will how our world continues to operate. But Lady Serafina Baldassare never did anything without reason. I stand before you all today as her reason. Her creation to fulfill her crowned role in her absence. All my life was devoted to learning our ways, our histories, and our customs. I will not fail when filling her shoes. I will rise to the challenge..." Kendrick's speech continued, detailing all the sacrifices his mother had made for our race, how our survival and prosperity was the focal point of her existence. Then he went quiet and reached into the concealed pocket of his cloak. Without pulling it free, he remembered every single word. *Strong. Smart. Brilliant.* She'd been proud of him and believed he would honor their name by being a grand ruler. And she had loved him.

In his silence, the thoughts that had been spinning around his mind coalesced into a plan. A plan he relayed to only me through our bond. *I want to set up a team to hunt and take down the damned, before they take any more of us.*

I'm all in, was my instant response. I was all for taking action. It was a hell of a lot better than sitting around and waiting to be attacked. There was just one thing standing in our way. *And if the RVC vote against us?*

Then screw the RVC.

Kendrick lifted his head and peered over the audience. His face transformed from reminiscent and strong to vengeful. "We have lost so many and the numbers are only increasing. This way of living, with fear and death always around the corner, is going to end. The damned must be stopped—no matter what it takes. If I have to stake them all myself, I will!"

CHAPTER 15

our of The Seven watched me quizzically as I closed the boardroom doors and came over to my throne. Not included in those four was Kendrick. Now re-dressed after laying his mother to rest in the Baldassare tomb, his fingers drummed the marble table. Being his idea, he was rearing to get this underway. So set on his decided mission that he wasn't about to let protocol or protection stand in his way. And I was glad. Watching him suffer had torn me apart. This driven purpose that had overridden his pain was a leap in the right direction. Besides, we couldn't continue doing nothing. Hiding out here wasn't doing anyone any good. And it sure as hell wasn't safe. After the invasion and Serafina's funeral, the others had to know that.

Marcus, who sat past Uriel to my right, nodded up at me. We'd let him in on our plans and he was all for it. Ready and willing to back up our argument and set off after the damned, too.

I remained standing in front of my throne, hands pressed into the cool marble as I leaned forward and met each of the royals' gazes.

"I'm sure you can all guess why we called this meeting. It's time we took action."

"We need to seek out the damned and stop them before it's too late." Kendrick's dancing digits stopped to smack down on the table, rattling the crystal glasses and decanter. "Before our race is overthrown and culled to extinction."

"I agree—"

"When you say we," Lady Rasputin cut Uriel's vote short, "whom are you referring to exactly?"

"The Seven and our guards," Marcus supplied, tipping his chin up at me in support. "And whoever else wishes to join the assault."

"Assault?" Lord Paole lifted his brows in distasteful surprise. "You mean for us, The Seven, the only leaders of our entire race to personally invade damned hideouts?"

At my nod, Lord Strigon tabled his crystal glass with a clank. "I'm all for taking action. But even I can't agree to this. Some of us are the last of our line. Without our leadership the race is helpless, without law, direction, or protection. We may as well lay down our throats and ask them to tear us apart."

"So as usual we do nothing?" Kendrick shot to his feet, throne legs scraping against stone. "We sit behind our tall walls, pretending we're untouchable while they keep coming for us, slashing our numbers with each strike? If that's going to be the result here, then screw you all." His voice rose with anger and desperation and the royals all stared at him like he'd gone mad. "And screw this council and all your ridiculous laws."

Still standing, I shoved my heavy throne back further. Come hell or high water, there was going to be action. "We won't stand by and pretend to rule while we just lay down and wait for death. With or without you we're taking action. Just try and stop us."

There was another scrape as we stepped out and strode to the exit. I caught Marcus in my peripheral vision. Right here and now, he was ready to follow us to the ends of the earth.

"You only need one vote." I turned to see Lord Paole, Lord Strigon, and Lady Rasputin staring at the three of us. But that voice hadn't been any of theirs. It belonged to Uriel, still perfectly seated with only her folded hands on the table in view around the back of that tall, carved wood. She spoke again. "Come and retake your seats. I have something to say."

Intrigued but nowhere near ready to back down, I nodded to Kendrick and Marcus and we retook our places at the huge, round table. "We're not changing our minds."

"And I don't expect you to." Uriel smiled, hidden sorrow gleaming in her unwavering stare. "Though I do agree that something needs to be done, I cannot agree to what you have suggested. As Lord Strigon pointed out, our leadership is above all. Without it, our race will not exist for long."

"*We* won't exist at all if we do nothing." Kendrick went to stand up but Uriel's next words kept him planted.

"So I propose that two of you follow up on a number of leads we've been tracking."

"Where?" Marcus said at the same time I said, "Two?"

Lady Rasputin kept her hard eyes on Uriel. "You wish to send them to Portsmouth to look into the leads the PVC has been investigating?"

"Better that than having half our council run off without a plan." Lord Strigon seemed to be on board.

But one thing hadn't been determined or set out in black and white. "You said two."

"More reports have come from Anchorage, but Lord Strigon and I will follow up on those." The Lord nodded, and Uriel got up and glided to the center window, staring out at the billowing smoke rising in the distance from the still-burning pyre. When she turned back around, she looked to me, her expression regretful. "With regards to the Portsmouth leads, you and Marcus will go. I am sure he will volunteer to supply your dietary needs. Kendrick, I am dearly sorry. You are to remain here with the others."

Kendrick rocked back in the throne that had belonged to his mother, outrage turning his pale face red. "I won't stay behind. You have no right to even…" He broke off, hands balling into fists as he relived what he'd so recently lost. The sight of her face-up and floating. Wading into the red-stained water. How ice-cold her gravity-free body had been. The sight of those lifeless silver-blue eyes. "She was my mother," he choked out. "I deserve the right to avenge her."

And there it was, the unsaid reason Uriel would agree to Marcus and me taking off, but not Kendrick. In his current state, the wounds of his mother's death were too raw, too new, and too blinding. Even now I saw red through Kendrick's vision as he glared at the other royals. He wanted vengeance, payback, to run into hell with no intention of ever coming back out alive. He was a liability and a risk to himself…and anyone who cared to keep him from harm's way.

"I agree to the terms." The words left my mouth on a whisper, and I could barely believe I'd said them. Barely believe I was backing them up.

Kendrick's venomous glare propelled onto me like I'd just become his worst enemy and the cause of his suffering. Like he hated me as deeply as he did the monster that stole his mother's life. Like he'd never forgive me.

I'm sorry, Kendrick. You're not in the right state of mind to avenge her death. And I won't let you die because your head's not on straight. I'm doing this to protect you. Please understand.

"Screw you."

With a belting hand, Kendrick shoved his throne over then stalked to the doors and threw them open.

Each stride was like a hammer to my heart. Of all the times I'd metaphorically run into a burning building, he'd been there to back me up. Yeah, he'd argued to protect me, but he'd still been by my side when I refused to listen. He hadn't taken irrevocable action to stop me from finding Ty. Instead, he'd had my back.

He turned back to look at us. Eyes like death lasers on me, he spat, "Screw you all." Then he slammed the doors behind him.

As the wood splintered and the windows rattled so hard that one cracked through the center, my heart was racing so fast it felt like it was about to explode. Squeezing my shaking hands into fists, I failed to keep the emotion from my voice. "When...when do we leave?"

Uriel patted my shoulder as I forced myself up on shaking legs. "A private jet can be fueled and ready to leave Anchorage International by eight a.m."

SHORTLY AFTER TEN P.M. the next evening, following our private jet flight from Anchorage to Boston, we finally arrived at the Portsmouth Council. Gravel crunched under the Bentley's wheels, the feeling mimicked in my stomach. I felt sick over leaving Kendrick behind. Absolutely gutted at what I'd done to him, even if the reason *had* been justified. The backpack strap I clutched made me feel like a user. The remaining blood bottles Kendrick had stocked my bar fridge with lay tucked in amongst my zip-up hoodie. Because like he'd speak to me or offer to fill more after my betrayal.

To top off my self-induced gut ache, my anxiety was through the roof.

I hadn't seen my mom since Caius's trial. She hadn't called, and I had been glad. Dealing with our broken relationship was way down on my list of priorities after everything else I'd been through. But now we were here. And with only turned vamps to man the councils, she would be, too.

The Bentley's back door swung out and a shock of light from a tall path lamp streamed in, no longer blocked behind the midnight-black window tint.

"You did the right thing," Marcus said, sympathy in his teal-flecked eyes as he reached his hand out to me. "Voting against Kendrick." In his black pants and a black collared shirt he looked smart, but the weapons strapped to his belt painted an entirely different view. The tightness of his mouth showed his unease at seeing my regret. "It had to be done."

I took Marcus's waiting hand and slid across the buttery-soft leather seat. My own weapons clattered as I straightened, and the backpack clinked as glass touched glass. "You don't have to keep telling me that."

Marcus smiled. "Start believing it, and I won't."

Across the parking lot and down the long curved path, the tall arched doors were wide open. Two guards marked the entry and more dotted the tree-shrouded and manicured lawn to either side. Our own guards' footsteps were almost soundless as we began walk-ing, and I kept my focus ahead. Another figure stood centered at the doors, her nervous expression becoming clear as we made our way over.

Mom's tightly clasped hands broke away from each other, looking confused as they swung wide to embrace me before changing course to return to her side. Her fingers pressed down her pencil skirt, and then rearranged the hem of her blouse. "Marcus." She smiled but looked more like she wanted to cry, which only intensified as she caught sight of my weapons. "Amelia. It's so good to see you."

Out of habit and maybe a little sympathy, I came forward and curved my arms around her. She responded instantly, her arms going around me and squeezing for a split second like she'd never get the chance again. The embrace felt off, nice and needed on many levels, but uncomfortable and alien at the same time. Her guilt was the third wheel, and my lingering—I don't even know what you'd call it—the fourth. I stepped back a little fast and shook my arms as if they had pins and needles. "Hey, Mom."

Marcus looked out of place stuck in this uncomfortable reunion, his brow furrowed and jaw tight. Still, he covered the growing awkwardness by shaking my mom's hand and motioning for us to go inside. "You have some leads for us?"

"Oh, right. Yes."

Going inside the hall, I had to blink a few times to see what was actually there. Last time the marble had been a trash heap of bodies and glossy blood puddles. Shredded curtains had framed the windows and every glass pane had been shattered. The clear slivers had been scattered among the once-living debris along with wood from the many cracked and broken chairs. I saw it all now, down to the sprays of scarlet and black that had painted the walls like a Gothic art display. Smelled the acrid scent of death in the air, too. I blinked hard and held my breath. With my heart drumming, I dared to open my lids. The horror had vanished, leaving the hall spotless before me. Same mammoth table surrounded by chairs. Same windows that reflected the candlelight from enormous wrought iron chandeliers and were framed by red velvet drapes.

Mom's council colleagues watched us as we walked in, gawking at the black, tight-fitting clothes I wore. Not to mention the utility belts at our hips decked out with stakes and blades. Definitely not the usual attire for crowned royals. But we weren't usual royals. We were the next generation, and things were beginning to get with the times now that we held almost half the power on the RVC.

Our guards followed after us and stood at even intervals around the rectangular room. Rather than sitting at either end of the long table, I went straight over and picked up a stack of loose papers. Sightings, reports, a list of names…vamps who'd been murdered in and around the state.

"Are these the leads?" Marcus asked, picking up a loose sheet from further down the table.

"Yes," Mom nodded. "We've had our guards staking them out, gathering intel since the attack here. They've been quieter of late, but they're still worth looking into."

I took the sheet from Marcus and scanned the addresses. My eyes popped. I knew almost every one of these locations. Along with Kendrick and Mr. Malau's wolves, I'd invaded them and taken out every damned that had hidden and killed there…way back before focusing our search on Anchorage. All bar two leads were dead ones.

For a second I thought of Kendrick. Had I tried to protect him when there wasn't even any danger here? Or had I kept him from losing it at being sent off on pointless leads? Either way, I couldn't reach him now. The link between us was barricaded shut—from his end.

And there were still two leads that might be worthwhile. But first…

I drew Marcus away from my mom and the other council members and kept my voice low. He already knew we'd been taking off with wolves to scope out damned hangouts. There was no point keeping the extent of my excursions from him. "They're dead leads. All bar two. Kendrick and I cleaned them out months ago."

Marcus nodded, eyes shifting to the watching council members then back to me. "Didn't know you'd ventured out of Alaska." No annoyance showed in Marcus's features. He smiled as if impressed. "Well, we can't tell them most of the leads are dead. But who knows. Maybe some damned have come back. We should check them out anyway. And at the very least, there are two new ones." Turning back to the waiting council members, he clapped his hands together. "No rest for the wicked. Tell your guards to get ready to set off."

While the others did as they were ordered, my mom glided over in her quiet and refined way. "You're going with them?" Although the outfit and sharp silver decorations were a dead giveaway, I nodded. "Is that what you want?"

Pressing my lips together I nodded.

Mom sighed slow and deep, looking like she wanted to tell me I couldn't go but knowing she had no say in the matter. Good or bad, I was my own person now. With a brush of her hand down my arm, she squared her shoulders. "Please be careful. I love you, Amelia."

"I know, Mom. Love you, too."

I THOUGHT of Kendrick for the millionth time as I sifted through the muck at our last damned lead. Five days had passed and there was still a lockdown on the bond. There was no confusing why, though. He was still pissed at me. I was pissed at myself, too.

Every location before this one had been just how we'd left it. Abandoned and with no sign of the damned or any new victims. The first fresh one had been a total bust, and this one, it seemed, was not better. Kendrick hadn't been ready to jump into battle with a clear head. But there was no threat to endanger him. Now our friendship hung on the edge of no return. And I had no one to blame but myself.

I kicked at the decrepit remains of a rotting couch with exposed beans and foam puffing out. What a waste of time. Beyond the dirty, cracked windows the sun was setting over this slummy part of Manchester.

Our guards and the extra ones we'd borrowed from the PVC milled around the many apartments in this three-leveled junkie dwelling. All looking for something that just wasn't there. Through our searching we'd crossed just a few humans. Marcus easily compelled them to take a long walk, forget seeing us, and to never touch drugs again.

"Clear like all the rest," I called out in spite of the heat coming off the pendant. It had been warm for the past half hour, but we'd uncovered nothing. It was clearly malfunctioning. "Guards, get the cars ready!"

I pivoted towards the exit—and my Vans froze I motion. The face nose-to-nose with mine stole my breath. *Ty.*

I blinked in disbelief and my eyes widened at the random damned staring back at me. Oh shit!

I reached for a stake but never got there. The damned tugged the tail of my belt and it clattered down to the bare concrete. My fist drove up and got caught in his chilling hand. The other seized my throat, fingers catching my hair and ripping strands from my scalp. He drove me into the wall, already-cracked plasterboard giving way and pinning my free arm.

The damned licked its lips and smiled.

But that wasn't going to last. Voltage grew inside of me and shot in spears to—

A long, silver dagger struck through the two inches separating the damned from me. Sizzling edge to the damned's throat, a pale hand yanked it sideways. The bone-deep cut sprayed black oil across my face. The damned's smile vanished. Its hold on me relented and it clutched its spurting neck as it tipped and fell.

In its place stood Marcus, stony faced and fangs fully extended. He wiped the dagger across his black pants and holstered it. Then he reached out to touch my face, doing his best to smear the black away. He spoke over the fish-flapping damned at his feet. "Are you hurt?"

Physically? No. But my ego was bruised. I'd been so distracted by my guilt, I'd let a damned get the jump on me. "I'm fine." The sound of the damned choking on its own blood affected my body like nails down a chalkboard. Not that it was dying. Only a stake or twisted silver blade through the heart or full decapitation would accomplish that.

Noticing my wince at the sound, Marcus whipped his dagger back out. "He doesn't deserve the peace, but for your benefit, I'll put him out of his misery."

Marcus dropped to his knees, dagger raised over his head as I registered a scent.

"Stop!"

Marcus froze, blade tip a breath away from sinking into the squirming damned's chest. He planted one knee on the damned's shoulder and peered up. "What for?"

I knelt, seeing the source of the scent. Dark ruddy blood splatter stained the damned's dirty T-shirt. The potency was almost undetectable because it was old. But I knew the source. "That's lycan blood."

I whipped my iPhone from my hoodie pocket and dialed Mr. Malau.

"Amelia." Surprise lifted his voice while something darker edged it. "I can't talk right now, I'm in the middle of—"

"I've found a damned in Manchester who's covered in old lycan blood."

Mr. Malau went silent, and then his voice broke through. "A silent alarm was triggered from Harper's dorm room a few hours ago. I'm stuck at Anchorage International waiting on the next flight. I—I can't get through to his phone."

Panic and shock had my heart racing. "Hold tight. I'm on my way."

Still holding the dagger, the frown across Marcus's face was intense. "What's happened?"

"I don't know yet." I grabbed his hand, plunged the dagger into the twitching damned's chest and twisted. "But I gotta go." I jumped up and hammered out into the hall and down the chipped concrete stairs.

Marcus caught my arm at the ground level. "Amelia. Talk to me. What's with the sudden panic?"

Outside, the guards were filing into the cars we'd come in while gentle rain spat down from the darkening sky. They were heading back to the PVC, but I wasn't going with them. Not anymore. "I need a car. I have to go to New Hampton."

"Why?" The question wasn't concerned or even curious, it was demanding. When I kept quiet, unsure I should say anything, Marcus said, "You know you can trust me, Amelia. With anything."

After all we'd been through and him covering our tracks, I did. But I didn't want to drag him into this. It wasn't something he'd approve of.

Marcus strode to the door hanging on one busted hinge and hollered through it. "Leave a car and four guards. The rest of you, get ready to return to the PVC."

"It's Ty's brother," I blurted, moved by his unquestionable

support. "He's gone missing from boarding school in New Hampton. I need to check it out."

Rather than showing disgust that I was still associating with lycans, Marcus smiled with his eyes. "Make that two cars and twice the guards," he called out. When I went to argue, he spoke over me. "Don't bother, Bathory. I'm not backing down. If you're going there, I'm coming with you. Subject. Closed."

WE ARRIVED at the New Hampton Boarding School for the Elite about an hour later. Standing in a second-level dormitory hall, Marcus spoke under his breath to our guards. "You will remain out here. Keep watch and compel any humans away."

At his raised brow at me, I peered out the window ending the hall. The manicured grounds and surrounding classroom and dorm buildings were still clear of movement. The second-level hall we were loitering in was clear, too. Being post nine p.m. it must have been after curfew for the few kids that hadn't gone home to family for summer break. I took a deep breath, mentally preparing myself for what we were about to find, then nodded.

With power and restraint to keep the noise level down, Marcus slowly cranked down on the handle to dorm room sixteen. Hand ready on his dagger's hilt, he stepped in and flicked the light switch.

With my own fingers curled around my stake, my breath sucked in. My free hand went to my throat. Hope and despair battled inside of me.

The place was a bombsite. Books and binders from shelves were scattered across the ground. Sleeves of paper, plastic pockets, and folder dividers were among the ruins. A shelving unit that must have fit against the wall between half-torn manga posters had been pulled down. Academic trophies of all shapes and sizes, along with medals added to the whirlwind mess. A bed tucked against one wall had the covers torn back and sported numerous tears and blood drops across the white linen. There was no doubt that there had been a struggle in this small room.

A fight-for-your-life one.

If humans had heard and inspected the commotion, they must have had their minds wiped. Or else the place would have been swarming with cops. Or been a graveyard of bodies. Maybe it had all gone down when summer classes were running, keeping all but the few passersby out of earshot.

Of everything I could see, one thing gave me hope. The amount of blood was small. The attack had ended with Ty's brother being knocked out. Because if the attacker had just wanted a meal, his body would have been left. Which meant Harper was alive. For now.

"Hey, look at this."

I turned back to Marcus, who stood by an upturned caster-wheeled chair. The desk behind him was neat to the point that it almost looked untouched. A laptop lay centered on the wooden top, a screen saver of shifting manga pictures coloring the black screen. "That's odd. How did that survive?"

Marcus shrugged and righted the chair. "Have a seat and let's find out."

Hurdling the damage, I slid into the padded chair while Marcus kept looking around. Letting my fingers do the walking, I found a bunch of files in 'recent items,' all of which appeared to be school projects for different classes. I opened folders and snooped through them. "There's nothing…" I paused in my sentence, noticing the Mac Mail icon in the line of applications at the bottom of the screen. Click. Open. Scroll. My jaw dropped at the sight of a folder in the sidebar named *Ty*. My hands shook over the mouse pad. Click. Starting over six months ago were a number of emails from Ty.

My heart shattered in my chest. My breath caught. The image of Ty laying face up, mouth frothy and eyes red, branded my vision. I didn't let it linger, though. Instead, I clutched the amulet so hard I swear it could have shattered, and scrolled back to the earliest and began reading.

The emails started with regular hellos that Harper slammed as being cruel jokes. Then one came, mentioning a song Mrs. Malau used to sing to them as children. Ty had said Harper didn't really remember his mother. But from his sudden email replies, he sure as hell remembered that song. One the emailer claimed their father had taken to humming since her death whenever it was quiet. Which must have been the one he'd always hummed when training me. Then the emails just stopped, none coming in but Harper sending more out, trying to reach his brother who was meant to be dead. Then one last one came through, but Ty's name wasn't on the bottom of it. An address was.

"You found something."

Marcus's voice coming from right behind me made me jump and I twirled on the chair. The emails didn't make sense to be from Ty. He was a prisoner and dying in my vision. He wouldn't have email access. But the damned commander could have. And he was after hybrids.

"Someone was in contact with Harper pretending to be Ty. The emails end suddenly." I swallowed past the terrible words I had to say. "Around the time Ty died."

Surprise widened Marcus's eyes. "How do you know he's dead?"

I shuddered as that horrible image seared across my quick-blinking eyelids. Tears were swarming, but I wouldn't let them fall. "Saw it in a vision."

Marcus wavered, watching me as if waiting for something else.

"There was one more email well after the others stopped. An address. In Anchorage."

Marcus narrowed his sight at the open email on the screen with a flash of urgency. "We need to tell the RVC. This could be our link to the damned hideout."

"No. We can't." I knew Marcus wasn't going to like what I said next, but I wasn't backing down. "If they have Ty's brother, the wolves deserve first hit. The RVC won't worry about protecting a single lycan, you know they won't."

The lift of Marcus's lip over extending fangs said he didn't care about protecting a random lycan, either. And with the way he'd been raised, I couldn't blame him. Still there was reservation as he spoke. "Amelia, I..."

"Give me a few days. I'll inform the wolves and let them do their thing, then after they're gone, we'll tell the RVC if there's any damned left to go after."

A long and deep breath in then out through his nose. "Okay, but only for you. This is not for *them*."

"Thank you." I pulled my iPhone from my hoodie and dialed.

Mr. Malau picked up after one ring. "Did you find him?"

"No..." I revealed everything we'd found with quick words along with the address. The next thing I said was the equivalent to a silver lining stained by dread. "Whoever's leading those soulless monsters wanted Ty to be his damned hybrid. If they found out he had a brother..."

"They took him to turn him."

I shuddered at the alpha's perception, but I wouldn't let him go through this alone. "I can be back—"

"No." The single word held the finality of a bullet to the temple. "I don't need your help. This is wolf business."

With that the line went dead. Marcus's hand on my shoulder was all support, but the look on his face said, *that's what you get for dealing with wolves*. And he was right. Alliance or not, it was still us and them.

CHAPTER 16

*I*t was still the same day when we returned, but mid-morning, time when almost all vamps were asleep. Instead of heading for my suite and that huge central bath for a good soak, I stopped short in front of the Baldassare suite. With four guards stationed outside, I knew he was here. Desperate and anxious to see him, I fiddled with my long plaited hair. The bond was still shut down from his end. I had detected his short-lived mental presence as we pulled up to the castle's steps, but it had vanished in a flash.

He still hadn't forgiven me. And maybe he never would. Which I totally deserved.

He'd always been the strong one, the one who helped me go on when everything seemed hopeless. And I'd freaking left him. I'd failed him.

With a surge of guilt trapping my heart, I took a deep breath as I pushed the handle down and went inside. "Kendrick, please hear me out. I'm sorry—"

I froze as I glimpsed his mother's bed and the terrace doors through the foyer opening that overlooked the gardens. Even though he'd shut me out, I'd caught glimpses of him on our way home, out there and staring down at the fountain. Lit up by sunlight, though now blood-free, I knew he still saw the carnage. His mother's lifeless eyes open, and her shredded neck leaking red that tainted the crystal clear water.

Just as I was haunted by Ty, he'd always remember how he'd found her there.

Sounds in the lounge room drew me over and I found Kendrick. Stuffing clothes into a Burton backpack, he was visibly shaking. The smell of his blood was thick on the air. The bottles lined up across the coffee table explained why. He'd filled them all. Recently. For me. But the shaking wasn't from the extensive bloodletting alone.

His shoulders hunched and I took a step closer. He knew I was here. Still he didn't turn around. Fear had my breath escaping in a whisper. "Where are you going?"

With his back to me, Kendrick shoved a jacket into the backpack. Without sparing me a glance, he stalked over to a tall chest of drawers. He plucked out rubber-handled, silver stakes and stalked back to dump them on the couch beside his bag. "That lead you found at the boarding school. We never staked it out with the wolves."

Now I knew what that short presence had been about. "You were spying on me?" Kendrick kept right on packing and I rushed forward and grabbed his bicep. Underneath my fingers, his arm trembled along with his whole body. The need to seek vengeance for his mother's murder seeped through the bond. "You can't go there. Not like this. Not alone. The wolves will probably be there already."

Kendrick yanked his arm free with a glare and shoved more stakes into the bag.

As I watched, something occurred to me. He knew I'd come back, and he'd steered clear. "Were you even going to tell me?"

Kendrick swung the backpack over his shoulder. "You'd just try to stop me."

"For good freaking reason. Even if you somehow managed to fool your guards into believing you're holed up here when you're not, the ball is in less than a week. If you're not there, *everyone* will notice."

"It's a masquerade. They decided that during the meeting." He spared me a glance and blew air through his nose. "Oh right, you weren't there."

Like a dagger to my heart. But I wasn't giving in. I clutched my hands together in desperation. "I know, and I'm sorry. I shouldn't have left. But that doesn't mean someone won't notice you missing from the masquerade." I didn't really give a shit about the RVC's let's-pretend-everything's-okay appearances. My total concern was for Kendrick's life. "Kendrick, what you're planning to do—if you beat the wolves there—is a suicide mission. You know that, don't you? And what's the point? It won't bring your mother back."

"I know that!" Kendrick turned on me and stalked forward, face a breath away from mine. "So what am I supposed to do? Sit here and wallow. Follow their rules and watch from the sidelines while everyone else dies. Fuck that. I'm taking action. And if I die, then fine. I've got nothing else to live for anyway."

I gasped and stepped back. My heart that still ached as a constant reminder of losing Ty, felt like it had just been torn into confetti. My voice escaped on a choked whisper. "I'm *nothing* to you?"

Kendrick's face cracked with emotion and he came forward, hands going to my hips. "You're all I have left, but…" He let go with a slight shove and looked back through the lounge room's terrace doors. From this angle he could see the fountain's top tier overflowing with sunlit water. With the shape and location of this suite, every window and terrace door offered a clear view. He couldn't escape it. "Never mind."

I cupped my hands over his cheeks and forced him to look at me. "No. Tell me, *please.*"

After a long silent moment, Kendrick spoke. "Ty's gone. He died months ago—before most of our missions to find him. You've finally accepted that he's gone, and still you won't move on. You won't let your heart be whole again. You won't allow yourself to love. To heal."

"So that's what this is about?"

"No." He took a few steps back and ran a hand down his face. "It's about vengeance. Payback for my loss *and* yours. Because you'll never allow yourself to be happy again, and I'll forever be by your side wishing for more. As long as there was something else in my life to live for, I pushed my feelings aside. Told myself I could be happy just to be in your life, to follow your lead. In the back of my mind, I still hoped you'd one day come around. That you'd accept that you love me."

I went to argue, to tell Kendrick that he was my best friend and I did love him, but he spoke over me through quickening breath.

"I don't mean friendship or soul-bound love. I mean heart-racing, passionate love. I want that—*with you*. I know you feel the start of those feeling for me too, but you're never going to live down your guilt over Ty to give in to them. And I can't wait around forever. Seeing my mother dead in that fountain brought all of this to light. Life is too short. Vengeance is all I have left. Unless you want to give me a reason to live for."

My vision blurred and tears rolled down my face. "I can't do that. I—I just can't." Part of me wanted to throw my arms around him and kiss him, to release the feelings that had built between us over the past months. The other part couldn't let go of Ty and my guilt. But I wouldn't let Kendrick run off and die because I wasn't ready. "Give me a day and let the wolves take this one. If you still want to leave, we'll blow off the RVC and join the wolves if they'll take us. Or we'll seek out the damned alone. Screw the consequences. You can have your vengeance, but please don't throw away your life. I can't…I can't lose you, too."

Kendrick remained quiet for a minute or so, his breath slowing down from the speed it had amped up to. Then without warning, he drew me into his arms, his hand running over my plait down my back. He sighed long and hard. "Then we'll do this together."

FORTY-FIVE MINUTES after sundown the next day, I sat curled up on the chaise in my library tower. Hours of *yeah right you're not getting any sleep* left me deliriously wired. My head and heart were on a battlefield, bruised and bloody and fighting to the death. Neither would compromise between a life of battle and vengeance or one of possible happiness and love.

My iPhone in my hoodie vibrated and I jumped, then I tore it free and stared at the screen. I'd run out of time, and with no decision made, the choice was staring me in the face. Vengeance. I answered Mr. Malau's call, letting my gaze drift to the scorched resting place of the many dead beyond the town on the once-perfectly green field. I let my every hope and fear fall on a soul that could be saved. "Did you find Harper?"

"No." Mr. Malau's reply was clipped and without hesitation. A strong alpha in control and driven by a cause. "The address was empty, quite recently from the mess left behind."

Dread swam in my veins like I'd been injected with formaldehyde. 'Mess' meant only one thing. Bodies. Victims. And blood. "Did you find…was there any…"

"Harper didn't die there." This time a crack showed through Mr. Malau's stone-cold exterior with a deep and even sigh. "I could scent him there, but not his blood. They haven't changed him and they're keeping him alive…for now."

The trees edging the field in the distance swayed, and I remembered how I'd seen Ty there. But that had been my imagination. Because he'd already been dead. Now there was lingering hope for his brother, and with Kendrick's drive, he could get his vengeance while I made up for my failures. "Then you'll be sourcing new leads." Which was the only way Kendrick and I would be setting off anywhere.

While away, Uriel and Lord Strigon had followed up on closer-to-home leads. Problem was? Those leads were all the places I'd already infiltrated with Kendrick while seeking out Ty.

"And we're up for it, Kendrick and I—"

"I don't question your sincerity or motives," the alpha interrupted. "But I can't involve you in this. Wolves protect their own and I *will* find my son." I began to argue and he raised his voice. "You're where you belong, Amelia. As am I. Our truce still stands, but I will not endanger what's left of my family and race by being caught fraternizing with the enemy."

The call ended and I stared blankly at the screen, twisting on the chaise to prop my knees up. Mr. Malau's refusal and non-existent leads. A twinge of relief-clouded anxiety swept through me. Now there was no reason for us to sneak off the grounds and go against the *no royals may leave the compound* rule. At least not until we could source damned locations. Kendrick wouldn't be putting himself in danger. Which left the only thing he felt he had left to live for was me.

My head-and-heart battle reignited and an unexpected shock of tingles danced inside my skull. Kendrick, and he was trying to read my thoughts. But he didn't have to. Now was the time to be honest. *Mr. Malau cleared that damned location. It was empty when they got there. He thinks Harper's still alive.*

Oh. That's good, I guess. Despite his torrid feelings yesterday, I sensed a sliver of respite through the bond. Even more than that, I could sense snowballing guilt, but not the source. His mind and location was otherwise a black hole.

We can still hunt them down. Force the RVC—

I was out of line. Kendrick's words stole the spotlight, stage, and the microphone, and my lips parted in silent wait. *Yesterday. How I spoke to you. What I said. I know you were trying to protect me— even if it was a bullshit way of doing it—because every time you went after him, I wanted to do the same. I wanted to lock you up and throw away the key.*

I grabbed a pillow from the chaise and clutched it to my chest with crossed arms. *But you never did.*

Because I know you, Amelia. What you needed then to keep you going. I need something to keep me going now, too. I need it for my mother. But I don't want to die. And I don't want to lose you. In whatever way I can have you. What I demanded was wrong. Unfair. A total dick move. And I'm sorry. I can't force you to love me. I just wish...never mind. The intensity streaming from his soul to mine cut me from deep within. *You're all I have left now. I'm sorry I scared you. Whatever happens, we'll do it together.*

With that, the link to my best friend and soul's mate shut off and I was left with nothing but the smell of books and tear-filled eyes.

With a deep and burdening inkling, I trekked down the spiral staircase and into the lounge room. Pushing through the side terrace door, I reached the balustrade and peered out. Regardless of

Kendrick's words, I knew he wasn't okay. The last thing he needed right now was to be alone. As I caught sight of him from the left corner of the balcony out in the garden, I knew how right I was. Sitting sideways on the fountain's edge, his face was angled down at the water. One hand hung in the gentle flowing drops, while his other clung to the carved marble edge.

Close-by guards were nowhere to be seen. He must have escaped from his balcony to be there alone. In the place he'd found her... floating. I didn't need to read his thoughts to know he was seeing her stunned white face as he stared. That he felt alone as his broken heart hemorrhaged.

But he wouldn't be alone for long.

Down the moss-covered stone walls, guards were stationed on the ground outside the castle. The two below my suite had just turned away from each other to move back in the opposite direction. I took the opportunity and jumped, Vans landing without a sound. Then I hightailed it down the path to one of the royal garden's entries.

As I rounded a curved line of tall, manicured hedges, the pendant at my wrist turned hot. Sudden horror hit me like a volt of electricity. My first thought was of Kendrick. My second was that I was unarmed. If another attack was about to break out, I was screwed. But there was no time to turn back.

My eyes became seeking lasers as I darted and weaved, heart thudding energizer-bunny fast. The alcove to the fountain was empty. Kendrick was gone.

I pelted on, feeling lost in the maze of hedges. Desperate at the thought of anything happening to him.

Around another corner, I skidded to a halt.

Standing in the distance before the next bend was a guy shadowed by tall hedges. In the near darkness and without moonlight he was hard to make out. His hair was as dark as the shadows surrounding him, his flesh visibly lighter beneath a black T-shirt and jeans. Facing my direction, he remained still as a statue. I couldn't make out his features or see his eyes. "K-Kendrick?"

Something in his frozen stance struck me as unnervingly familiar. And then I saw the hunting boots. My stare locked on its target and my Vans planted to the spot. It couldn't be. My heart felt like it was about to explode. *"Ty?"*

His eyes shone ruby red, then he turned and disappeared around the bend.

A flood of images—Ty's frothy mouth, still body, and those dead eyes—flashed through my mind, making my veins hum and my legs tingle. I knew it was impossible. Ty was dead. I'd seen it play out twice. *What if I'm wrong?* The pendant was still hot, and it only ever heated up when danger was around. If that was Ty and he was damned, it would respond to him like any other threat.

The expanding hope in my heart fed my need to know, making me dart after him. "Ty!"

Shadows were everywhere as I dodged around the hedges and planted gardens, slinky and deceptive. Some took human form, just to dematerialize as I got close. Then I saw him, left of where I'd been running. Just passing through an arched exit to the road. "Ty, wait!"

I swiveled and took chase, leaving the gardens and pelting down the cobblestone road. Houses whizzed by as I sped down quiet backstreets. When I met the grassy field, I heard the angel fountain's pattering and saw shop owners opening up down the main street. I kept to the trees' shadows, losing the darting figure through thick trunks. Then my Vans caught on a tree root and I went sprawling. I scrambled to gain footing, catching myself on another wide tree edging the grass. My eyes darted, scanning all around. There, past the pyre remains at the end of the fifty-yard lawn, I saw him. He stood at the tree line, his back turned, his body leaning into the frame of a small gazebo. One that was cloaked in shadow by over-hanging trees.

With careful, quiet steps, I gulped as I neared him. My hand slowly reached up to his shoulder. "Is it really you?"

The guy unhinged himself from the gazebo frame and spun, fast. His expression was surprised, his features shielded in shadow. "Geez. I didn't even hear you."

The pendant instantly turned cold and my heart sank, shattering my hope with an internal explosion. Even in darkness, that voice was unmistakable. "Kendrick."

He moved forward with a look of relief, leaving the darkest of the shadows. "Were you looking for me?"

I held back the tears, internally yelling at myself for being so stupid. So delusional that I'd allowed myself to believe Ty would just show up here. Piece-of-crap pendant. Or had that been my imag-ination too? I shouldn't have given in to the sliver of false and irra-tional hope. Because I knew what the reality was. Ty was dead. Gone. Never coming back. Pain struck my heart in a vicious wave. I pressed my palm to my chest. "Ah, shit."

Kendrick tilted my face up with his hand and his eyes narrowed. "Are you okay?" Worry creased his forehead. "You look like you've seen a ghost."

"I'm okay."

It was a total lie. Without Ty, nothing was okay. And now I was driving myself insane. Seeing Ty in shadows, in stranger's faces. Letting myself believe that he could still somehow be out there. The point of no return was close, and I had to make a decision. Get lost in the past and what I wish could be. Or decide to live again. Well, as close to living as I could manage without Ty. Kendrick was staring at me, his frown showing how much he wished he could get inside my head.

"I'm okay," I said again. Then I studied Kendrick's face, feeling my way into his open mind. Through all of this he had stood by me, risked his life to help me search for Ty, and bar a few slips, he'd never forced his feelings. His needs. After his desperate declaration yesterday, I knew the feelings he had for me were still there, strong and potent. And I loved him, too. Not in the way I loved Ty. That was a once-in-a-lifetime thing. Still, the emotion was there, the attraction. I'd die for him, just as he would for me. And if I lost him, too? My final reason for living on would be gone. Kendrick was my life now, my future.

I stepped closer, leaving a wisp of air between our bodies, and placed light hands on his waist.

Kendrick's breath drew in. "What are you doing?"

I let one hand trail up his stomach and chest, reaching his face and tilting his chin down. My voice was throaty, unsteady. "I'm ready."

Kendrick didn't move, his body turning rigid as glass. "For...what?"

Using my toes to gain height, I leaned up, getting closer and closer. I let my mouth brush against his. "To move on. *With you.*"

A jackhammer took up residence in Kendrick's chest. "Are you *sure*?"

I nodded, my body moving closer to eliminate the air between us. "Yes."

Kendrick's hands came up, cupping my face and his mouth closed over my bottom lip. I gasped at the sensation and taste of him as his tongue touched mine. It delved in deep, and my hands gripped the sides of his shirt, holding him close and reveling in the slow passionate strokes of his tongue. His body against mine was hard.

His breath in my mouth was sweet. The hunger radiating off him was almost tangible, coaxing my own desire free.

What am I doing?

The unwanted question sent guilt lancing through me, creating a maelstrom that fought against my rising passion. I gasped and froze, my hands no longer pulling Kendrick closer by his shirt. He pulled back instantly, breath as ragged as mine and face tipped with caution.

"I...I..." What the hell could I say that wouldn't result in hurting him?

Kendrick looked sidelong at the bench that bordered the internal wall of the gazebo. "Let's talk." We moved to take a seat and he nodded slightly as if making a decision. "You don't have to say anything. It's okay. I know you were trying. We—we can just forget this happened."

"Forget about it?"

That pain inside my chest soared, dulled only by the glimpse of Kendrick's own emotions that slammed shut. He wanted to be with me, more than anything. But he didn't want to pressure me into something I wasn't ready for. He didn't want to take advantage. If he only knew that he wasn't the one who'd be taking advantage. I was. I needed this. I needed to be close to someone. Accepting that Ty truly was dead, I needed a reason to go on. Just like he did with his mother now dead. If it was love that could keep me on this earth, then there was only one person's who could even come close to what I'd had with Ty. And since figuring out how to cure the damned had been a total bust, the only other option was to turn cold and ruthless, devote my life to seeking and killing all damned with him alongside. But I couldn't do it. I couldn't watch him become what I knew that would turn us into. Looking at Kendrick now, the hope in his eyes was clear, even if the lid was sealed on his emotions.

"I don't want to pretend we didn't just kiss." I ran my hand up his jaw, letting my fingers thread through his golden-brown hair. "Look, I...I love you, but I can't promise anything." My hand dropped. "This is...*shit*. What am I trying to say? Um, it's hard, you know." With my words failing, I let loose a few blocks in my mind, carefully revealing just the parts I wanted him to see. How I wished for a future with him, but how I didn't know even with time if I could ever get over losing Ty. How what I could offer now was watered down at best, compared to what I'd had. After feeling the prodding of Kendrick reading those thoughts and feelings, I dared to look up. "Is that...I mean, could that ever be enough for you?"

A beam of hope like streaming sunlight radiated off Kendrick, and he smiled. "I will always be..." He let the sentence hang in their air, bringing his lips to mine. Slightly parted. Hungry, but restrained. "Exactly what you need me to be. I'll never leave you."

CHAPTER 17

I hit the ground as a rubber floor mat came hurtling my way. It sailed overhead, smacking into the back wall and falling in a heap. "Missed me."

After hours of combat training, everyone else had vacated the gym ages ago. Sweat dampened my black Under Armour gear. My opponent did well to hide his fatigue, instead looking eager to keep going. Good thing, because the last hour had been dedicated to physical sparring, and I wasn't even close to being done.

Time to bring out the big guns.

I smiled and jumped up, flinging one hand forward. Blue lightning streamed from my palm at my opponent.

Kendrick launched just in time, gripping an exposed ceiling beam. His smile was cheeky and infectious. "Close, but no cigar." His eyes clouded as he dropped and a crate of weapons across the room began to rumble and shake. Pockets of wind sprang up from the box, sending individual daggers, machetes, chains, and swords my way.

I leaped left, right, into the air, and ducked to evade each deadly assault.

As one box emptied, its contents now littering the ground or stuck between stones in the wall behind me, the next crate began to rattle. A gust of wind coalesced into a small whirlwind that disappeared into the crate. Then it rose, bringing every weapon up and into its spinning vortex. Kendrick dropped to the ground and made a sweeping gesture with his arm. The whirlwind turned faster as it edged toward me. I sent voltage its way, firing individual weapons out with each strike.

But I wasn't fast enough.

A sudden shift in movement redirected the spinning vortex into a forward-thrusting deadly assault of air. I twirled sideways, barely evading the edge of sharp blades and machetes that hit the stone wall with a clank before clattering to the ground. Strong hands caught my arms and spun me on the spot. A bare foot kicked my legs out from under me.

"Oomph." The air escaped my lungs as I fell back onto hard wooden floors. The rubber mat from here—along with many others —lay strewn about the gym, on top of each other or half up against the walls.

Then Kendrick was on top of me, legs straddling my hips and hands pinning my shoulders down. I fought back, tearing his white T-shirt as I prepared to send a punishing volt down each of my arms.

Before I could release the power, Kendrick dropped his face, catching my lips with a quick kiss.

My voltage instantly receded at seeing how I'd looked to him a second before. Wild, excited eyes, glistening skin, flushed cheeks, and reddened lips clamped between my teeth with determination. It'd been impossible for him to resist.

He sat back up in a flash, looking sheepish but not moving to dismount me. "I, ah…" Color flared across his cheeks while a million things he could or should say swamped his mind. "Was that okay?"

He'd been dying to do that. Not only since two days ago in the gazebo and my decision to move on with life. But forever. After spending the time in between attending meetings, where no new leads had been found, we'd slogged out our frustrations here. Expended our energy until we collapsed side by side on the gym mats and crawled back up to our suites. All the while, our relationship had repaired and strengthened. Still, now that there was no one standing in his way, Kendrick thought taking this step would have been easier. But he knew I wasn't ready to just go full-on. The memory and my lost hope for Ty were still in the forefront of my mind. The last thing he wanted was to disrespect that.

I looked away from his handsome, worried face, trying to sort out my head. The memory of Ty had been driving me crazy since my delusional sighting. The pain of knowing he was truly gone hadn't let up. The only reprieve was when I was totally distracted, which being with Kendrick and focusing on something like training seemed to do. I knew I needed to move on, and I knew I loved Kendrick. I always had. He was my best friend, my soul's mate. But he was so much more. He was my rock. My soft place to fall. I needed him.

"It was…"

I lifted my gaze, still trying to put the words I needed to say together. As I reached the tear I'd ripped in his T-shirt, I paused. His chest was visible beneath the material—pale, smooth, and well-defined. I could hear his heart racing and detect the sweet smell of arousal tainted by musky caution coming off his skin. My body responded without my permission, emitting the same sweet and musky smell. The scent of his blood became stronger, too. My mouth watered, fangs peeking through my gums. Despite the bottled backup, he'd supplied his fresh blood both this morning and yesterday in a glass topped to the brim. But our energetic training with the use of powers had drained me. Renewed thirst stripped my throat of moisture.

Unable to read me through the bond, Kendrick interpreted my pause as uncertainty. He swung his leg over my body to sit with propped knees beside me. "It's fine. Really."

"No. It's not." I sat up and reached out, touching his jaw. The wall I normally kept in place, dropped, letting Kendrick in on my needs.

"Oh, right." Kendrick pulled away and rose, going to a crate next to the glass doors. He picked up one of the bottles from its top and unscrewed the lid. "I can fill one of these."

I came up behind him and put my hands on his shoulders. "That's not what I had in mind."

I'd kept my promise all this time, even at the cost of my deteriorating health. But Ty was gone. My aching heart had finally accepted the horrible truth. I'd suffered this whole time and would forever feel the devastation of losing him. But I had to go on, had to find a way to stop the damned before they killed us all. I had to be strong. The Oracle needed live Pure Blood.

I brushed my hand from his neck down sideways to his shoulder, pushing his T-shirt aside. Kendrick stopped breathing as I came closer, my chest meeting the tight lines of his back. My lips found the right spot at the base of his neck and my fangs fully extended. I paused, waiting for any uncertainty from my best friend—who was becoming so much more than that.

Kendrick reminded himself to breathe. "Soul and blood, I'm yours. Always."

There was no going back from this. And right now, I didn't want to.

My fangs sank in and the taste of him filled my mouth, hot, peppery, and alive. At the same time, something else happened. The pain of my bite sliced through him like a blade on fire. It was something I should have anticipated. But in my hunger and angst of doing this with him for the first time, I'd forgotten. Vampires weren't meant to feed from each other. The pain he now felt reinforced that fact.

I was hurting him.

I went to pull away, but Kendrick grabbed my hand at his waist. "Don't stop."

Breaking through the initial pain, another sensation took over. Pleasure. It warred with the sharp sting, the knowledge of me drinking his blood sending undulating waves from the bite, down, down… The link to his emotions shut off suddenly, but not before mine could react.

Heat warmed my body too, the desire so alien because I wasn't feeling it for Ty. My fangs receded into my gums and I pulled my arm free as I stepped back.

Kendrick turned, a flush coloring his cheeks and expression wary as if he expected me to bolt from the gym. "You okay?"

My pulse began to slow with my breathing while my mind raced. My lingering feelings for Ty made what we'd just done feel awkward and wrong. In stark contrast, our reaction to each other had felt incredibly right on so many levels. It was a step between us that had needed to be taken for so long now. One that we had now broken the ice to.

I took a step forward and curled my arms around Kendrick's waist. "As long as I have you…yes."

AT THE TOP of another gilt, marble staircase, I kept my lace-gloved hands clasped tight against the bodice of my flowing black, silver, and purple gown. Through the eye holes in my intricate black mask, I searched the mingling masked crowd below. So many had gathered for the masquerade ball that the baroque-styled ballroom was packed. Like my gaze was a magnet, I was drawn to one man and one man alone.

Kendrick.

The past few days had been like a dream. A beautiful, happy dream. Every possible waking minute had been spent together. In RVC meetings sharing glances across the marble slab. In one of the smaller training rooms, exerting ourselves with combat training to the point of breathlessness. And swapping between TVD, The Originals, and snowboarding marathons in our suites...

Warmth cascaded up my neck and across my cheeks. The short and lingering kisses had been nice. Not full-on or pushy, but really nice. My breath caught now, remembering what often came next. The slow sinking of my fangs into his neck. The heat that I held back and that he struggled to cage as I drew deep from his vein.

I felt happy for the first time in so long now. Excited for the future.

At the same time, a knot of eager anticipation swirled up my insides like a twister. The force was laced with nerves that grew by the second. Watching Kendrick down there, debating among a group of council members, he looked confident and in his element. With his mask over his forehead, his eyes shone more silver than blue. A common vampire sign of emotion, or was that anticipation? The tailored suit he wore fit perfectly, except for the collar covering only one of the closed punctures up his neck.

I had begun to descend into the crowd of lavishly dressed and masked vamps when Kendrick caught sight of me. A sudden smile brightened his already happy face and I pointed to my own neck.

Kendrick shrugged without hesitation. He knew I was pointing out the visible mark I'd left on him, but he didn't care who saw it. Vampires didn't usually feed from each other, unless maybe in romantic situations. And he wanted our world to know where we stood.

So did I.

Continuing down with my destination set, I weaved through the crowding vampires. Suspended from the ornate ceiling, thousands of crystal drops from the many chandeliers cast sparkling light over the extravagant space.

When I reached Kendrick's side he smiled and kissed my cheek before nodding to the others around us. "You all know Lady Bathory."

They murmured welcomes and inclined their heads as I greeted them back. Then as their discussion started back up, I laced my gloved fingers through Kendrick's and tugged him aside. My other hand caught around his neck and I tippy-toed in my purple-laced Vans. My lips crushed over his, hard, soft, and everything in between. People noticed, murmuring around us. But I didn't care. And neither did Kendrick as his arm snaked around my waist and he dipped me back to deepen the kiss.

When I regained my footing and broke away, I was dizzy. My lips throbbed and heat dyed my face.

Flushed too and breathing hard, Kendrick looked bewildered. "What was that for?"

I couldn't stop the smile that spread across my face. "Just letting everyone know where we stand."

A council member from Portsmouth engaged Kendrick then, and

after a squeeze of his hand, I took the opportunity to slip away. Now an automatic function unless I wanted Kendrick in my head, the link to my mind shut off like a vault locking. I passed the dance floor and waited at the bar for my turn to order a double vodka topped with blood. Sudden fresh anticipation and nerves made it feel like something was trying to burst from my ribcage. I ignored the feeling and less than a minute later a glass was handed over and drained.

With Dutch courage, I pulled my iPhone from the hidden pocket in my gown. Sending out a little nudge, Kendrick looked up and found me through the moving crowd. I blew a kiss across the ballroom and hit send on my iPhone. He flinched at the vibration of his own phone and slid his hand into the pocket of his black pants. Pulling it out just enough, he discreetly glanced at the screen. Through his eyes I saw the pre-typed text I'd sent.

'Alone time in my suite l8er 2nite?'

Red spread like wildfire across his cheeks and he shoved the phone back into his pocket before anyone caught sight. *"Are you sure?"* he mouthed.

I wasn't proposing sex, and Kendrick knew it. But I was hinting at a step further than what we'd already taken. The thought terrified and excited me. But I was ready. I wanted to do this. I wanted to remove the doubt and uncertainty between us and what we were fast becoming. I wanted to finally give myself permission to move on. *I am,* I sent through the bond.

With one last smile, I turned back to the bar. That last drink hadn't quieted down the crescendo of my nerves nearly enough. "Same again."

~

WHEN I'D HAD A SECOND, third, and ordered a fourth drink, my nerves were still going haywire. The glass came quickly and I raised the cool edge to my lips, about to empty the contents. But then I paused. Paranoia crept through my bones like a hair-raising chill that refused to let up.

Someone was watching me.

I spun and scanned around. The dance floor was a spinning display of waltzing couples, moving with silent grace and weight-lessness. Masked vamps stood on the opposing side, all watching the elegant display. Except for one. Between the constant and barri-cading movement, a single guy stood on the dance floor's edge. In an all-black suit, the pearl-white tie around his neck stood out. Iden-tical to the one I'd seen so long ago around his neck at Mom's auction. My breath flat-out stopped. A black mask covered his face bar his lips and chin. A devilish smile curved his mouth. One that hinted at cold calculation with a touch of pissed off. In the flickering candlelight, his dark and glossy eyes watched me.

I knew those lips, that chin, those eyes...

Oh dear God.

Without looking away, I slid my full drink back onto the bar. With slow, measured steps, I moved through the people surrounding the dance floor, my gown swaying around me. Every step was calcu-lated, cautious, eyes studying every inch of him I could catch between blocking bodies as I neared. Pale skin. Black-as-night hair. It was a delusion. An imagination. Just like all the others. It had to be. It couldn't really be him.

Ty was dead.

Still, my feet kept moving, bringing me closer and closer until I stopped right in front of him. My heart was pounding so fast, I thought it was going to explode. My lips parted, but nothing came out.

With that same cold smile, the guy bowed. Then he lifted his hand, gesturing for a dance. Above the mask, his forehead creased as though he'd raised his eyebrows in question.

Without thought, I took what was offered, gasping at the ice-cold touch of his unusually pale flesh. His familiar, but black eyes sparkled. Not gold like Ty's. Not red like a damned. Then everything became a blur. We were dancing, twirling around and around, my gown flaring out and my head spinning. The faces of everyone around us became a rush of color and masks. One hand was on my hip; I felt the callouses of the other as he gripped my hand tight. My stare stayed frozen on his, unable to look away. I reached up slowly, fingers gliding up his black suit to rest along his neck. The skin there was cold, too. A few small scars visible. The hair soft like I remembered. "It's not really you."

The guy smiled, and I held my breath. Had I just said that out loud?

Before I could stutter an explanation—because there was no way this was actually Ty—he leaned in. His stubble scratched my cheek and I closed my eyes. "I've missed you."

That voice was something I could never mistake. My eyes flashed open the exact second his touch faded. The space right before me was empty. Nothing but dancing couples and watchers from the sidelines. Trying to control my breathing, I looked around frantically. I was still in the middle of the dance floor, alone. My hands went to curl into fists, and I froze. There was something pressed into my palm. A note. In *his* handwriting.

'See you in your suite.'

Darting from the dance floor, I caught sight of Kendrick now in deep discussion. With the walls in my mind still rock solid, I hiked up my gown and took off up the grand staircase before my current guards could notice. I couldn't tell or alert him. He'd only think I was crazy.

Because this *was* crazy.

It couldn't be Ty. It was impossible. He was dead. I'd seen it more than I could live with. And I'd accepted it. I'd moved on…

Which meant I was actually losing my mind. Still, even knowing this, I couldn't stop myself. Clearing the steps, I flew down the other end of the extravagant corridor to my suite, speeding past the stony-faced portraits. Each passing second added to the rush inside my head.

My whole body was trembling when I reached my door, and I uncurled my clenched fingers from holding up the hem of my Cinderella gown. Rattled breath sucked in and out of my aching lungs.

Ready or not…

Chest ready to explode, I stepped inside and shut the door behind me. The foyer was pitch black, bar the slice of light coming under the door to light up the base of the centered table. Hand shaking, I reached to turn the lights on.

"Leave them off," a voice spoke from the shadows. That same unforgettable voice. But different. Alien in a way that made my blood run cold. A chilled hand curled around my wrist, demand in its tight squeeze.

I froze, forgetting to breathe. "This isn't real. Oh God, it can't be." My head began to swim and I sucked in air. *"You're dead."*

The grip on my wrist released, pressure finding my shoulders and turning me to face him. One of his hands rose, slowly removing my mask. "Am I?"

I cringed at the cold detachment in his tone. "No. You're dead," I repeated.

As if magically on speaker somewhere in the foyer, *Let It Die* by Three Days Grace began playing. I frowned, unable to pinpoint the source as I stared at his mask-covered face. In the almost pitch black, his glossy, obsidian eyes watched me with restrained want. My fingers twitched to rip away the cover, but I couldn't move.

He smiled, captivating and challenging, white fang tips peeking out. His voice was a whisper. "*Kiss me* and find out."

My eyes shot to his full lips, my own parting. They were exactly how I remembered them. In a trance, I leaned forward, closer and closer. Time slowed down, the music kept playing, and then…our lips met. Lightning-fast arms came around me, gripping my back and pulling me into his cold, concrete-hard body. His fangs scraped but didn't break flesh as his tongue invaded my mouth with consuming demand, full of animalistic desire. Only one boy had ever kissed me with such passion and hunger.

"*Ty,*" I gasped against his mouth. I threw my arms up over his shoulders, needing to hold him, to touch him, to keep him from leaving. But his lips vanished from mine and my arms collided. My lids flung open and I rushed to turn on the lights. The pendant above the foyer table lit up. I saw the hooks where my hoodie hung and the openings into the sitting room, lounge, and bedroom. But I couldn't see him. There was no one else here.

"Ty!" I called out and darted into my bedroom. But I never got there.

Suddenly my body was falling.

Broad hands shook my shoulders and rattled my head, while complete and utter panic bombarded me. "Amelia, wake up!" The voice that registered was desperate and rushed, but somehow comforting at the same time.

I shot upright, unexplained disappointment and confusion staining my heart. The feel of bedding and a super-soft mattress were beneath me. The stunning black, silver, and deep purple gown I'd put on for the ball still covered my body. A layer of cold sweat

WEB OF LIES

made the fabric cling in the under layers. "What happened? How did I get here?"

By my side, Kendrick clutched my clammy hands. "You fainted downstairs on the dance floor."

My mind felt like it had been whizzed in a blender. Then the haze lifted and I saw it. The dance floor and that eerily familiar guy. A flood of memory washed over me. Ty…it was Ty. I'd followed him up here, and… *Oh shit, what had I done?* Wait. My gaze shot through the opening to the foyer. I couldn't see the door. But light beamed through from the pendant over the table, swaying ever so slightly as if someone had rushed past. Fainted downstairs?

"But…" I hedged around the words I let out. "I remember coming up here…"

Kendrick shook his head, looking scared and on guard at the same time. "No. I carried you up here. Amelia, you were having a nightmare or something, you were screaming…" He looked down at our hands, wincing as if in pain.

I had to know. "Screaming what?"

"His name."

I gasped and looked away as those guarded silver-blues slid up to mine. With his mind open, I sorted through Kendrick's memory. The scene below in the ballroom came rushing in like an avalanche. I'd been down at the bar having a drink. Then another, and another, and another. I'd walked to the center of the dance floor and stood there like a zombie, lips slightly parted. Then I'd collapsed. There'd been no masked guy. No Ty.

I squeezed my eyes shut and slid my hands free from Kendrick's. In my closed thoughts, I relived the sight of him. Our dance had been like a dream, running up to my suite a blur. And that earth-shattering kiss…

It hadn't been real. None of it.

Some of the shock and guilt of what I thought had just happened subsided, replaced by agony at losing Ty all over again. Deep-searing fear settled between my ribs. I'd tried to move on. I'd even felt 'happy'. Or thought I had. But I couldn't write off this oh-so-real delusion. Losing Ty had broken something in me. And I didn't know if it could ever be fixed. All signs right now were pointing to crazy town. There was no other explanation. It wasn't a vision. The events had happened in real time. While I'd been awake, before passing out.

Was my subconscious trying to hold on to what I knew no longer existed? I remembered hearing the music that'd played right before I kissed Ty. *Let it die.* I tensed up as I glanced at the picture of Ty and me propped against the bedside lamp. What a wicked way for my mind to illustrate that Ty was never coming back. And passing out like that? On my live-from-Kendrick's-vein diet, it didn't add up. Unless my needs were suddenly changing again.

Long, silent moments dragged on, nothing getting clearer or making sense. "I don't know what happened," I whispered eventually. "Sorry I scared you."

Kendrick wrapped his arm around me, pulling me close to his chest. He sighed deep and hard, any other link to his mind protected. "Maybe we should slow things down a bit."

I jerked out of his gentle hold and frantically rechecked the walls in my mind. Had he seen what I'd imagined? The undeniable attraction I still held for a dead guy. The way my passion had ignited at the scraping crush of his lips on mine. "W-why?" I stammered, clutching the purple covers beneath the flare of my gown and on the verge of tears. The last thing I wanted was to hurt Kendrick. Or to lose him, too. "It was just a dream."

Kendrick rubbed my back and smiled with acceptance rather than happiness. "I saw you drinking. I saw how anxious you were about spending time with me...*up here*. I think that's why you passed out. After everything you've been through, it was a stressor you weren't ready for." I went to argue, not ready to end this. Not ready to let this go. But Kendrick spoke over me. "Don't feel bad. It's okay. We have plenty of time figure things out. And I'm not going anywhere. We can just take this one step at a time."

Kendrick knew I still wasn't over losing Ty. I'd told him as much after I'd first kissed him. He just didn't know how far from over Ty I still was, and how close to the edge I was getting. And I couldn't tell him.

I squeezed my arms around him, ear pressed to his chest and hearing the quick, tortured beat of his heart. "You know I love you, right?"

Kendrick's lips found my forehead. "I know. And I love you. As long as it takes, I'll still be here."

CHAPTER 18

Standing on the once-sprawling green field across from the gushing angel fountain, I tied my hair back into a pony-tail. I was early, so it wasn't a surprise that he wasn't here yet. But as I smelled the sooty remains from the large singed scar left by the pyre, I couldn't stand still. After my delusion and Kendrick's reaction to knowing only that I'd been calling out Ty's name at last night's ball, I needed a distraction more than I needed air.

I kept on pacing, feeling like I could run a mile, but having nowhere to go.

Being early morning, the sun was still well above the horizon and falling slowly. Shops and boutiques surrounding the fountain from the other side were still shut up, and the curving streets were free of wandering vampires. My guards remained beneath the shade of a café awning, UV protected, but armed and ready for anything.

No new leads had come through since I'd returned from the PVC. And after Uriel and Strigon had cleared the Alaskan ones, the

RVC was feeling in control. With Vanessa now warding the compound and checking them every day, the strong laws on royal heirs being guarded to the point of stalking had relaxed. We'd even voted before the ball to allow royals to leave the compound if accompanied by a trained guard.

Without warning, my delusion last night resurfaced again, replaying Ty's words, the feel of him, and that kiss. My knees buckled, but I kept on moving. The replay was pure torture, and I still hadn't told Kendrick. He was being so understanding and patient. The last thing I wanted to do was rub my everlasting and never-fading feelings for Ty in. But I couldn't forget. And I couldn't let go.

"Thought you were out here already," a deep velvet voice spoke as Lifehouse's album *Smoke and Mirrors* began playing on my iPod's loudspeaker. A long shadow grew next to mine, and I turned to see Marcus standing before the breeze-swaying oaks that lined the field. In white and black training gear and bare feet, he appeared eager to start, and only minorly uncomfortable from the warm sunlight. But curiosity edged his face as he watched me. "So why the change of venue?"

The question he didn't ask was, *where's Kendrick?* He'd seen me kiss Kendrick and though he'd left the ball before it happened, he'd heard about me fainting. When I'd asked him to meet me out here today for random training late last night, he hadn't asked questions. But he clearly had them.

I went to my iPod at a tree's base and paused the music. Then I caught and held the amulet hanging around my neck. "I've started something with Kendrick, but I can't forget about Ty. I'm just so muddled up." A flash of my lips connected to Ty's scored my mind. I shook my head. "I just…"

"Say no more." Marcus squared off against me, knees braced

and empty hands ready. We'd agreed to purely physical and weapon-free sparring. "One order of supersize distraction coming up. Ready Bathory?"

A wide smile spread across my face and I let my movements reply, doing a spinning kick aimed at his face.

Marcus caught my foot and smiled. "Gloves off, then."

He threw my leg down with such force that I did a full flip. Reflexes kicking in, I landed in a crouch on one foot, my other straight out to the side. Then I swung my leg and took out his ankles.

Marcus fell back, knees bending so his feet found the grass as his back did. With the momentum, he used the strength in his legs to propel up to his feet.

Anticipating the recovery, my fist drove forward.

Marcus's hand shot up, palm catching my hit. He kept hold and spun me, arm coming around my waist to catch me. I was stuck, back flat against the strong plains of his toned chest. With his chin resting on my shoulder, his mouth was right next to my ear. "One-nil."

"You wish."

I stuck my butt out, gripped his trapping arm, and yanked.

Marcus went flying over my back to land on his. With the momentum, his T-shirt had risen, uncovering his side below the ribs. A small white line glistened in the sunlight, an inch long and perfect in its straightness. Then it was gone as he sprang back up.

"Your scar," I said, backing away. I hiked up the bottom of my black Under Armour tank. A mirrored line marked my skin above the waistband of my leggings. I never looked at the scar. Never really let myself think about it. Because I knew where it had come from. Caius. When he'd sliced that scalpel over my body after he cut me free from my mother's belly. In my vision, the cut had seemed to vanish, becoming invisible with the blood that cloaked my tiny body. In reality? I wore the proof that my vision had been real, and that I had been that baby. "Caius did this to me. When I was born."

Marcus forfeited his fighting stance and frowned. "And you think...?" His lips parted and he walked past me into the shade of a tree, leaning into it with one arm. With his head shaking, his hand on his T-shirt covered the scar. "Caius didn't do this to me. My father did. The day he returned to bury my mother. It's common ritual— even one he couldn't refuse his heir. A blood offering from the old to the new."

Disappointed, I glanced down at my Vans and pushed down the hem of my tank. "Oh."

"That doesn't mean Caius didn't experiment on me. It just means he didn't do *this*. It doesn't make me who you want me to be."

Yeah, I thought. Because according to Caius, my twin was dead and gone.

"Now I think that's about enough reminiscing on deadbeat dads."

Before I could utter another word, Marcus bared his fangs and flung me around into the tree he'd been leaning into. "Round two?"

Happy to do anything to get Caius off my mind along with everything else, I smiled. "Read my mind." Then I uppercut his chin with an unintended bolt of electricity. There was a crack and I followed through with a roundhouse to his ribs. With Marcus no longer holding me against the tree, I spun out of the confined space.

But Marcus was ready.

His bare foot burst into flames as he booted it into my stomach. The connection felt like a sucker punch, my legs and arms straight in front of me as if I were a doll being torpedoed backward. My back struck a tree across the other side of the field, and the amulet around my neck flung up at the impact. The long chain slung around the trunk and snapped. Then gravity intervened and I dropped to the ground, exposed tree roots instantly bruising my butt.

Groggy, my head fell back against the rough bark, my back and shoulder blades aching as Marcus rushed over. The fire had singed my tank and created a few holes, but any minor damage was already healing.

"Shit, I'm sorry. Did I hurt you?" He knelt before me, concern wreaking havoc on the sharp lines of his face. "Your electricity hit and I got carried away."

"I'm fine." I held out my hand and he rushed to help me up. "I like that you spar with me like I'm a guy, powers and all." The next words I said tugged at my heart because they sounded so much like something Ty would say. "The damned won't take it easy on me just because I'm a girl." I went to catch the amulet when I remembered it snapping off.

"Oh, here." Marcus bent to pick up the stone from the tree's base, then dropped it like he'd just been bitten. "Shit!"

A burnt smell lifted before being carried away on the breeze. I grabbed Marcus's hand to see a brand across his palm. The stone had seared straight through layers of his skin. My gaze shot to his wrist. The silver-faced Rolex he usually wore wasn't there. "You're becoming allergic to silver?"

"Uh, yeah. It's slowly becoming a problem."

Immunity to silver was one thing Marcus and I had shared, which I'd put down to being a result of Caius's experiments. Even if Marcus didn't. As I retrieved the amulet, I wondered if I would start to develop the normal vampire allergy, too. I tucked the stone and broken chain into my pocket. For now, my immunity held.

"What is that stone anyway?" Marcus asked, teal-flecked eyes curious. "It looks ancient."

My heart in stone against yours. I reined in the overflowing emotion that came with remembering the car ride when Ty had given me his mother's necklace. "It's just a memory."

A FTER MARCUS LEFT twenty or so minutes later to feed his growing hunger, I couldn't help where my Vans led me: the back of the field and the gazebo. The one I'd chased what I thought was Ty to. And the one where I'd taken a new step with Kendrick. *Dammit!* On top of that brain-smacking memory, this place reminded me of the setting Ty had created at the lookout in our long-ago dreamscapes. It also replayed in vivid clarity my first consensual kiss with Kendrick.

I squeezed my weary eyes shut. I didn't want to think about any of that. My earlier distraction was now gone, and short of going with Marcus to *Bite*, I needed another. And I had the exact one to make all the other confusion melt away. My twin. It was time to find out what had happened for real. Was he dead? Alive? And if so, who and where was he?

I lowered myself onto the bench inside the gazebo and crossed my legs. Resting my elbows on my knees, my eyelids slid shut. The sound of tree leaves rustling in the breeze remained, drowning out any other city sounds. Behind my closed lids, I saw foggy images of Ty and then Kendrick. Keeping my delusional dream—or whatever it was—of Ty from him felt wrong. But I didn't want to hurt him. Didn't want to see his disappointment at hearing how much my heart was still divided when one of them wasn't even alive.

"*Argh!*"

I put my hands around my skull and pressed the heel of my palms into my eye sockets. *Shut up. Shut up. Shut up.* With every ounce of concentration, I pushed all the internal torment back and blocked it out, centering my focus. Static began to build, slithers sliding down my arms and legs. I reined them back in, refusing to let anything spoil this attempt to numb my mind with purpose.

The black void that resulted minutes later was like a sudden fresh breath, a weight lifted from my heart and soul. Feeling more in control, I allowed something to get in. Almost happy at the invitation, the shadows twirled around my body. The sound of them sliding over and around each other in a playful fashion was almost comforting for the first time. My hand lifted, and a single shadow slinked down my arm and created a swirl in my palm. Then, like a parasite, it tunneled its way into my flesh.

The dark cavern that suddenly surrounded me was familiar. And totally wrong. Fire pits with flame-carved edges lent flickering, murky light to the dank space. The smell of compacted earth filled my nose. This was the wrong place. The wrong time. The wrong truth. Far from what I'd wanted to see.

With a much smaller line of damned standing before me, red eyes focused, I knew I had no control to escape. And I knew whatever I was about to witness needed to be known.

Not in my own body, I paced in shitkickers, my hands shoved into the pockets of raggedy jeans. The voice that escaped my throat was male, youthful, and almost daring anyone to challenge him. The voice of the damned commander. "We are at a disadvantage after attacking the Armaya. Numbers are what we need." The body I was in stopped pacing and bellied up to a damned centering the line. "Send word to all that remain. Until we strike, we must rebuild. No full consumption. No killing royals. We turn every vampire we encounter. Every. Single. One."

I was suddenly inside the body of that centered damned, the commander's mug right up close. That face with its contours, those lips, that hair color, the cut…it was unmistakable. The only thing that didn't match was the feral stare that pegged the damned I now inhabited. It was all wrong, glowing red pupils with darker chips. I'd seen those eyes before too, but not in that color.

Oh my God. The damned commander was…

I gasped as my eyes flung open, seeing the sunlight gone and twilight rising. With rapid blinking, the surrounding field, trees, and frame of the gazebo returned. Eerie tingles crawled up my spine and I shot up and spun around. Feeling a localized chill, I looked down. Was that the hard press of fingers left around my wrist? With a blink, my sight refocused fully. The marks were gone. I turned in a circle, eyes darting. Beyond the wind-swooshing trees, my guards were assisting a café owner in bringing tables and chairs outside.

And…Dorian was at the street entrance to *Bite*. He peered side to side, up and down the street, Victorian lamps highlighting his serious face. Then he was gone as he slipped inside.

Vanessa wasn't with him.

With a frown, I sat back down on the bench. That was strange, but I felt like there was something important I was forgetting. I pressed my thumbs to my temples and massaged with slow circles. Wasn't I going to bring on a vision? Had I already done it? Sudden hunger hit me like a semi. Sure as hell seemed like I had. I pressed harder with my thumbs and a strike of pain penetrated my skull. I couldn't remember.

GROGGY AND FEELING like my eyelids were weighed down by sand, I blinked then shifted. Halfway arched up from the bed in the dark, the feel of smooth satin froze me. My heart pounded like a drum.

This wasn't my bed. And I hadn't fallen asleep in Kendrick's room and bed. I knew that much for sure. Spending time with him over the rest of the day had been slow and steady, just a few timid kisses and some hand holding in between taking his blood. I wouldn't have blurred the lines by crawling under his covers after the decision to slow things down. That type of setting was no longer a normal place to watch movies from or hang out lying side by side. It was the 'go zone,' the place that took everything we were slowly becoming to the next level.

I took a deep, testing breath, trying to keep calm. A distinctly stale smell filled my nose and lungs. This definitely didn't smell like Kendrick's suite that was now packed with his mountain of boarding gear and magazines.

Paranoia had my skin prickling as I sat up further and rubbed my eyes. Willing them to focus in the pitch black, I found a generous room fitted out with a small round dining table, lounge area, stand-alone bar...and a large black rectangle across one wall. A solid, roll-down blind blocked the window.

My paranoia shifted into panic, imagining exactly what type of creature needed absolute cut-off from sunlight. I grabbed the pendant at my wrist and it was cold. Not even a hint of warmth to indicate danger.

Sudden light had my head snapping sideways and my senses amping into overdrive. The sconce above the dining table had flashed on. My eyelids stretched wide, and my ears strained to pick up any direction of sound to indicate the threat. Except there was nothing. No movement. Nothing visible beyond the light-created shadows of the room.

"Hello, Amelia."

My heart wrenched from my chest and I spun on the bed, scrambling back until I fell and hit the ground. He was perched like a predator atop the bed's headboard, and still as a statue. *Ty.* His red eyes marked me with a frozen, calculated stare. His lips were slightly parted as if pleased. Between them, long pointed fangs glinted.

"Is it really you?" I barely breathed. A battle began between my heart and mind. My heart wanted me to leap off the ground and wrap my arms around him and never let go. Its opponent was vampire survival kicking in, that instinctual voice that said, *run or die.* But was this even real? Could I actually believe my own eyes? Or was this just another desperate and insane delusion? If the pendant's lack of heat was any indication, it pointed to the latter.

Regardless, I slowly stood, sight locked on Ty. There hadn't been a single movement. He hadn't even blinked. For how still he was he could have been a statue. "Ty?"

In the blink of an eye, the space above the bed was empty. Ty was gone. A gush of air that ruffled the window blind was the only indication he'd moved. I went to turn, but his hands were already on my hips, strong and hard as steel. "Welcome home, beautiful." The words from right behind me were gravelly and cold, a threat of capture.

Despite the fear pounding through my veins, my body responded, warming at his touch. My mouth spoke without permission. "It happened, didn't it?" All this time I'd known there was very little chance he was still alive at all…and that alive wouldn't actually mean living.

The grip on my hips relinquished. I turned, expecting him to be gone again. A figment of my imagination poofed into thin air. But he wasn't. He just stood there in that same statuesque fashion, eyes watching me. No *now-you-see-me, now-you-don't.*

I studied those features that were imprinted on my brain. It was all on show. Strong jaw line, full lips, thick hair, and his bare chest that I remembered every contour and line to. Most of the scars, I remembered their length and shape, too. I ached to reach out and see if they were real. But those eyes...

If this was real, if that was even possible after all I'd seen, I had to know. Was there any of the old Ty behind that predatory stare?

I slowly lifted a trembling hand, not taking my eyes off his as I laid it across his cold, pale chest. Breath escaped my lungs in despair. The scars were real. But there was no heartbeat. "You're damned."

A slow, devious smile crept across Ty's lips. "I'm stronger and more powerful than you could imagine."

I blinked, forcing back my tears. I'd seen a vision of Ty during the turning process, seen the pain and agony he'd suffered. I'd seen him refuse to take life to continue his existence as a damned. "What did they do to you? How did they make you...I mean, I saw it in a vision. You refused to kill. You decided to die."

Ty's brows arched with the slightest hint of surprise. "I did decide to die that day, but there was an intervention." He retrieved a shackle from the bar and pressed it into my hand, one that matched what he'd been restrained with in that warehouse. "Let me show you."

The moment the cool metal touched my skin, the surroundings warped. Concrete rose up, lit by fire from the body furnace. The basement level of the warehouse Ty had died in for the second time. On the ground next to the crying damned boy lay Ty. His eyes were open, red as fire, and froth bubbled as it dissipated from his mouth and chin.

From a few feet away, a pair of hard hands gripped my upper

arm and thrust me forward with booted strides. A knife's blade slashed across my throat and I gurgled, choking on my own blood. Except I couldn't taste anything. Because I was inside that royal girl's body, reliving the events after Ty had refused to feed.

The guy behind the girl I was trapped in shoved her twitching body down so the blood pouring from her neck flowed into Ty's gaping mouth. Then he knelt and connected her cut throat with Ty's lips. The wet sound of air leaking through the gap in her throat continued and her body began to tremble.

"Time to wake up, flea bag."

And then it happened.

Draped over Ty's body, I felt the tension return to every scarred inch of him. Saw his dilated pupils shrink as his face shifted to the side. His hands came up in a snap—not to push the girl away, but to pull her closer. There was a crack of his jaw as his mouth opened wide and his fangs sank in.

Locked in his death grip, I didn't feel the punch of his fangs or the draws he took from my neck. Even if this hadn't been a vision, I couldn't have felt it. The body suffering this fatal end wasn't mine. It was that girl's. What I did feel was enough though. Her twitching body starting to grow quiet as the wet suck of air from her throat suddenly died off. Then her racing heart stopped.

Dead.

Ty killed her.

The room returned like I'd just been dropped from the moon. I gasped as my conscious mind caught up to reality, my stare locked on Ty.

"So now you know." Ty smiled, and it was unfamiliar and heart-wrenching all at the same time. "But here's the twist. If not for your actions before Caius drove that sword through my heart, I wouldn't have survived beyond my last breath there."

My entire body felt numb, cold swamping from my head down to my toes. "My actions…?"

The memory of Ty spluttering on my blood after being stabbed through the heart by Caius's sword resurfaced. He'd been too close to death to even swallow a single drop. Or so I had thought. And Vanessa's alchemist mark had prevented the damned blood he'd ingested from mixing with the poison from all the bites he'd suffered. Without damned or vampire blood in his system to mix with the poison, the bites he had endured should have been fatal. Though there was another way blood could absorb into someone's system. I'd seen it myself when closing fang marks on the cruise doctor I'd fed from. A choice I'd made that had resulted in my blood-sourcing promise to Ty.

"When you told me to save you…I thought you didn't, I mean, you couldn't swallow. But you were so cut up. My blood ran from your mouth, down your chin, your neck. It absorbed in through your wounds."

"No."

Ty reached for my jaw, calloused thumb grazing my bottom lip. I stopped breathing and he leaned in, lips meeting my ear. Without warmth of breath I didn't feel him speak, but I couldn't miss his words. "That night, you fed me your blood so I could imprint you and escape the chains, then again to help me heal. Your blood that is both vampire and damned, that can cure poisoning of ingested damned blood, but not what already exists in its own make-up. Without that, I would now be rotting away in the ground. What you did in that cell cured the damned blood poisoning, but the mark didn't stop your blood from mixing with the damned venom. It gave me a loophole. *You* made me what I am."

~

I SHOT UPRIGHT, my senses heightened by the fear drumming through my veins. My hand swung out and knocked something to the ground with a crash. With the sound, a door swung open and lights beamed on. Not only the foyer's but also the decadent chandelier centering the room. In less than a second, guards appeared in the room, swords slicing free. My fear eased and I took a shuddering breath. I was in my four-poster bed and my suite.

Without Ty.

With the light, I saw with the guards the smashed lamp I'd knocked over, the photo of Ty that now lay flat on my bedside, and the twisted mess I'd made of my sheets. Goosebumps prickled over my skin as a cool draft blew in from the open door. My dark T-shirt and shorts were lathered with sweat and stuck to my body, accentuating my small breasts and... I grabbed the purple and silver striped sheet and pulled it up to my neck. *Freaking nipples.* "I—"

Before I could utter my total horror at what they'd seen and tell them to get the hell out, Kendrick flew into my room. His own entourage blazed in behind him with their swords drawn. The blocks in my mind reinforced as he pulled to a stop, registering the lamp and lack of an intruder. In spite of his relief at the non-threat, he caught on that I'd had a nightmare, and that my guards had just gotten an eyeful. Two of which were male.

Kendrick faced my guards, relief cut short by an inkling that cut him up on the inside. "Just a broken lamp. Return to your post." Then he motioned to his own. "I'll be out shortly."

When the door clicked shut, Kendrick lowered onto the edge of the bed and took my hand. Even with the memory of me looking down to see my breasts on wet-tee display, his expression was serious. "You..." He sighed hard and dropped his troubled gaze to our joined hands. "You dreamed of him?"

"I..." Kendrick had clearly picked up on something, whether it was just my reaction or a glimpse of what had happened. But sitting here now, one thing was clear. I wasn't starving. If what I'd seen had been a vision, I would be ravenous. So was it just another delusion, or was there more to it? A dreamscape? It had all seemed so real. So tangible. The smells. That room. Ty. He had seemed the most real. And what he'd said made sense. That if not for me he'd be rotting away instead of damned.

Despite the twinge of hope that flared, anger overcame it. There was no proof that any of it was reality. My mind could just be fucking with me again, giving me a silver lining for something that was dead and gone. And until I knew for sure, I'd keep my mouth shut. I had already hurt Kendrick enough. That was vividly clear as I looked up at his guarded face and saw the uncertainty in his down-cast silver-blues.

Kendrick squeezed my hand. "It's okay." As he caught sight of the photo, he winced before quickly shifting his focus back to me. "I know letting go is hard for you. I know becoming *us* will take time. Don't think for a second I want to rush any of this. We'll go at your pace. Unless you've..." He gulped. "Changed your mind..."

He let the sentence hang in the air, the turmoil that my actions and feelings were causing him tugging at my heart. My head was a mess, and whether what I'd seen was real or not, I didn't know what to do. I didn't want to break Kendrick's heart. And I didn't want to let him go, either. But if Ty was... "I haven't changed my mind," I heard myself say as if hearing a stranger speak. "I'm just adjust-ing...I guess."

Kendrick half smiled. "Want me to stay and keep the nightmares away?"

My lips parted. "Oh, no. Thanks. I'll be fine."

Dismissing the rejection, Kendrick released my hand and leaned in to kiss me. It was short and sweet, with no demand whatsoever. "Okay."

I watched him back up into the foyer toward the door, feeling like a piece of shit as he stepped out. He didn't know what I planned on doing, and I wasn't going to tell him, either. Not until I had the answers I needed.

CHAPTER 19

J paced in my suite before the sitting room window that looked down at part of the royal gardens. A shooting star streaked across the sky below a full moon, as if hinting that my earlier wish for answers was about to come true. And maybe it was.

It was late morning and only forty minutes until midday mandatory training. For now, Kendrick was off doing his own thing after showing up earlier to give me his vein. I'd gone ahead with it, and felt like the worst person in the world during and after. I wanted my delusions to be real. Would give anything to get Ty back. But not at Kendrick's expense.

And now I was running out of time.

I thought back to the brief call I'd made after Kendrick had taken off last night. From the card I kept in my jewelry box, I dialed the Boston number and it picked up after a few rings.

"Madam Rosalie. Fortune Teller Extraordinaire."

"I need answers, and don't even pretend you don't know what this is about." The extended pause evoked no dispute from the old woman, but I wasn't taking that as proof. And I wasn't accepting an explanation over the phone when she could lie. If she spun shit in person, I'd compel the truth from her. "I've organized a flight from Boston International. A driver will deliver you there, and another will bring you to me. Come willingly or under force. It's your choice."

There was a raspy clearing of a dry throat. "Then I guess I will see you late tonight, Amelia."

"That's tomorrow in my world," I replied and hung up.

With all the questions after my delusional, or not-so-delusional dream with Ty—on top of what happened at the ball—I needed answers. Was I just losing my mind, or was Ty alive?

A light tap sounded at the main door. *Finally.* "Come in."

The door swung inward and one guard came through the foyer to the sitting room. She stepped aside revealing a much smaller and frail woman. "Your guest, Lady Bathory."

"Thank you." The guard bowed and backed up to the door, closing it behind her. I caught the old woman's wandering eyes. "I'm glad you came."

Madam Rosalie scoffed. "Did I mistake the lack of choice in your summons?"

I took a seat on the cloth couch and she came forward, slip-ons pattering on the bare stone before hitting the rug. Wearing a velvet skirt and long-sleeved embroidered top, she lowered into a wing chair. "No. But you know why I needed you to come here."

Even though it wasn't a question, she nodded, her messy, gray bun bouncing on her head. "You cannot leave this place alone. A ruler among seven and of many, but you cannot follow your own lead."

Sly old woman. But she wasn't here just because I couldn't leave easily; she was here to fess up. "Cut the crap and tell me the truth. You lied about Ty. You said he was gone. You said—"

"Tut, tut, tut." She waved a bony finger in my direction. "I never said he was *gone*."

My heart leaped beneath my ribs and my vision blurred with manic possibility. "Then he is...he's not..."

On the coffee table between us was a hot pot of tea with cups and saucers that I'd had brought up by the kitchen staff. Madam Rosalie ignored the instant demand in my shaking voice, leaning forward to pour herself a cup.

The suspense made me feel like jumping out of my skin and my fangs bared in threat. "Tell me *now*."

Madam Rosalie narrowed her gaze at me defiantly. Then she picked up the cup to take a sip, her ringed fingers clinking against the china. "This Ty you speak of is not alive. He died in your arms."

My clasped hands squeezed tighter, nails biting into my flesh. Riddles. Freaking riddles. Every second of my life after this would be hinged on her response to my next words. "But he's not dead."

"He is dead, in many ways." Madam Rosalie took another slow sip, the time passing like long seconds before a guillotine was triggered. "Though he does still walk this earth."

My jaw went slack. My eyes no longer saw Madam Rosalie sitting beyond the coffee table and the room surrounding us. Instead, I began churning over everything that had happened over the last few days. I wasn't losing my mind. My broken heart wasn't conjuring up imagined moments that I wished were true. On the ballroom floor, it had really been Ty. So much like I remembered and yet so different. He'd held me and we'd danced. Then I'd followed him up to my suite and taken his dare.

My fingertips lifted to my lips, running from one side to the other. That kiss had been real.

Then I'd encountered him again when I'd woken in that unfamiliar room. He was so cold, in touch and in personality. He was different. Damned. Trailing my hand down, I gripped the amulet, now fixed after a quick trip to a jewelry store in town before the old woman's arrival. Everything he'd said had been true. Ty was damned because of me. The only way all of this could be possible was...?

The answer hit me like a stake to the chest. Dreamscape. Somehow Ty had altered my reality during the ball and forced me into unconsciousness. Forced me into his dream and mind while I'd still been awake. Then he'd come for me again in sleep. The fear of being unable to control my own consciousness or what I thought was real, terrified me. Would Ty come for me again? And if he did, what would he do to me? Even more terrifying was the thought of him never coming after me. Of disappearing again—for good.

My vision snapped back to here and now and I glared at the frail woman. "You *lied* to me. You told me he didn't exist."

"The boy you love does no longer exist," she said, repeating what she'd told me at her shop. "His body is animated, though his heart does not beat. His soul is fractured. He is fundamentally changed. He is no longer who he used to be."

"You knew that's not what I was asking when I came to see you," I snapped. Anger turned up my body temp and sweat bulleted over my brow and back. Because of her words, I'd given up on Ty. Given up my hope. Given in to my simmering feelings for Kendrick. And broken my promise. "I needed to know if I was searching for a ghost. If he was still out there, how I could save him. In your bullshit cryptic way you mislead me. *Why?*"

Madam Rosalie placed her teacup down on the white table and laid her hands over her crossed knees. "If you knew this boy was still out there, you would not stop until you found and saved him.

That I could not encourage. I have seen that making this boy's heart beat once more will trigger a chain-reaction of events. I cannot see far enough to know the final outcome. Though in the interim, the lead-up will cost much to those in the crossfire. Still, I can see now that this sequence of events is impossible to stop. The path is set on its course. Ty will not leave you be. He will come for you."

My hearing shut off after she said, *Making this boy's heart beat.* Those words couldn't be misconstrued, the result was clear. "So there is a way to save him? To restore a damned?"

Madam Rosalie nodded, "There is—" when the main door to my suite flung open.

Kendrick barged in like the sky was falling. The door slammed shut behind him and his worry for my safety changed course. He registered the fortuneteller with surprise and paused in the archway. "What's going on? Why is she here?"

Busted. In the suspense of uncovering the truth, the walls around my thoughts had started to crack, hairline fractures snaking through the mortar that held the bricks in place. With a mental snap, the wall was once again impenetrable. I rummaged through Kendrick's open mind, and found the source of his panicked and sudden entrance. He'd felt my anxiety, my trepidation, my hope, and my shock. I let out my held breath. He had no idea what had caused those feelings. He didn't know Ty was alive. Finding out this way might have been better. And my lips parted, ready to blurt out the truth. Only nothing came out. I couldn't make my voice box line up with my lips. Because apart from Ty being alive, I didn't know what to say. I didn't know what this changed, what I felt. I wasn't ready to have that conversation.

Madam Rosalie spoke over my fish-mouth silence. "Your girl-friend wants to know if there is still a way to save—"

"The damned!" I shot up from the couch and smacked my knee

on the coffee table. The half-filled China cup tipped and tea flooded across the white-painted wood and over the edge. There was a trickle followed by a *drip, drip, drip* as it pattered down onto the shaggy rug. "If there is any way I can restore the damned."

Kendrick sucked in a quick, almost undetectable breath and his eyes widened before narrowing with a frown at me. Failing to break through my mental block, his gaze slid to Madam Rosalie. He leaned into the jamb, crossing his arms over his chest and kicking one DC over the other. "Even if there was a way, you're human. You couldn't possibly know—"

"Actually, I do, Kendrick." After a tense moment that had a muscle ticking in Kendrick's jaw, Madam Rosalie shifted a smile my way, flashing a missing front tooth. "That light inside of you, the one you now control. That's all you ever needed to save..." She paused, perception gleaming in her beady black eyes. "...*them*."

The light. You must accept the light. It's the only way to save him. Madam Rosalie's warning from back at the fair instantly took me back to the council hall on that fateful day. Ty lay dead, his life-less body sprawled out on the blood-slicked floor. His face was slack and his body was covered in red and black stains and so many wounds. I was screaming at him, pumping his chest and watching more and more blood stream free. Then the instinct came to me, the need to send my volatile lightning straight into his heart. To use my hands like a flesh-and-bone defibrillator. I screamed when it didn't work, when I realized that taking my rage out on Caius had drained my power.

I blinked rapidly and cold drops fell from my eyes. Slowly my hand rose as blue sparks collected down my arm to my fingertips. I'd failed to save Ty then, but I had another chance now. And I wouldn't give up. "This power is the key. I've thought it was all along. But I don't know how to use it."

"Your power can do many things," Madam Rosalie said in her usual cryptic way. "Restoring a damned to life is but one of them."

For a second, I saw all the damned I'd taken down with my lightning. Some in battle. Some in my restoration attempts. None had survived in the end. My stomach dropped, seeing all of those murderous creatures reduced to nothing but ash. I'd taken out so many. And I'd been able to save them all along? Guilt rose like a tidal wave up my neck, but I forced it back down. There was plenty of time to suffer that failure. Right now I needed to think to the future, to bringing Ty back. *"How?"* The sound from my throat was barely a croak. "How can my power restore their life?"

"I do not know the details." The old woman lifted her chin and nodded at Kendrick whose causal pose had straightened, along with the set of his mouth. "But your boyfriend does—and he's known it all along."

My fists clenched and I paced to the back of the couch, one hand clawing into the patterned backrest. "Guards!"

Kendrick shifted out of the way as eight guards— panicked as if the room were suddenly on fire—plowed into my suite.

I pointed at Madam Rosalie, feeling like my irises were blazing with fire. "Escort my guest back to the town car and have her safely delivered back to her Boston shop. Wipe her memory of our location." The shit was about to hit the fan and I didn't need an audience.

Madam Rosalie said nothing and rose to hobble after two guards with another two following behind.

"Leave us," Kendrick directed to the last four, who complied in orderly silence. Through the bond, regret and fear sat like poison in his stomach. But he didn't dare move or speak. Just stood there like an accused dragged to the slaughter.

When the door shut behind the last guard, I couldn't even look at him. I was a breath away from tearing him to shreds with my bare hands for lying to me. He was supposed to be the one I could always count on. The one who always had my back. The one I could *trust*. "What the fuck, Kendrick?" With my eyes down, his flare of regret suffocated me. I glanced up to see the same emotion marring his face as he stood just inside the room, his back against the jamb. "This whole time. This whole freaking time. You knew I could restore them and you just kept letting me go around killing?"

Kendrick lunged around the couch, hands going to my waist. With how our relationship had grown recently, the touch was too intimate for the deception. I stepped out of his reach and he sighed, his expression morphing with despair. "I wanted to tell you. I was going to. But then I thought about the consequences. You were already willing to risk your life to find and save Ty. If you knew you could save them all one by one, you'd never stop. You'd keep going until you died in the process. It was selfish, not telling you. I know that. But I couldn't lose you. And I couldn't bear to see you throw your life away because of what your prick of a father had done to you. He gave you this power. He put this responsibility on your shoulders. You shouldn't have to carry the weight."

"So I should just let them all remain damned? They're our race's main threat and there was a way to stop them. A way to save the ones who'd been infected, not turned by their own choice." Again I saw Ty the moment after his body stopped convulsing when he'd refused to feed. He'd made his choice, but someone had intervened. Stolen his right to die a hero and made him into a monster. And I had given up on him.

"Saving them would never stop," Kendrick said, interrupting my mental kick to the head. "Any vamp can decide to turn. Whether what we've uncovered about breaking the curse is true or not, you can't stop that. Not without killing yourself."

I shivered, remembering my vision of Lord Aswind being infected before what may well have been the attempt that killed him. Kendrick was my best friend...now my boyfriend as Madam Rosalie had said. But that didn't mean he got to decide my life for me. And beyond my anger at his betrayal, I wasn't sure what I wanted to do in this moment. About the damned. My power. Or even Kendrick. In all the uncertainty though, I knew there was one thing I needed to accomplish. Ty *would* be saved. "Tell me how to restore them." The demand in my voice was clear but Kendrick hesitated, face straining with resistance. "Tell me or I'll go out on my own and try everything until it works or I die."

Kendrick's shoulders slumped and his head dropped forward. "Okay." He held out his hand to me, looking at it rather than at me. *Please trust me,* the whisper came through the bond. "Come with me?"

His love, despair, and hope seeped into me, and even though I was still pissed, I didn't refuse the gesture. With my hand in his, sparks fired with emotion that I didn't bother to hold back. He led me out of my suite, down the grand corridor to the back hallway that led to a number of guest rooms. Eight guards shadowed us as we walked, their swords clanking with their marching strides. Down one of the two opposing back stairwells, we met a familiar corridor. The one that Caius's old office came off.

Ice formed in my bones, but I went along, stopping only when Kendrick did in front of a guarded door part way down the corridor. Marcus's office. Where I'd encountered Kendrick slipping out and picked up that unusual scent on him. My hands pulled free with one last strike of static.

Kendrick grunted but said nothing, then he knocked twice and a smooth male voice called out, *"Come in."*

He pushed the door wide and the many lit candles around the

office flickered at the air disruption. Their flames highlighted the windowpane behind the desk where Marcus glanced up from. Looking from me to Kendrick, his eyebrows popped and he closed the binder in front of him. "You both look serious as hell. What's going on?"

Kendrick gulped. "She knows."

Which meant Marcus was in on this, too. Hurt and betrayed, I couldn't even speak.

Marcus stood and came around the desk. As he clicked his fingers, every candle flame extinguished. A dull glow from the lanterns in the hall lit the unmistakable apology across his angled features. "Then I guess it's time. We have something you must see."

CHAPTER 20

*W*ith a tight squeeze of my hand, Marcus went to the open door. "Wait out here," he ordered the twelve guards now crowding the corridor. "You are not permitted to enter this area under any circumstance." After closing the door, he glided past the Chesterfield to a wall unit on the left. On a higher shelf he slid a book out one inch. With barely a sound, the shallow unit slid sideways on invisible tracks to tuck behind the sofa. Wall lanterns sparked with fire beyond the dark void, revealing a stone-walled chamber and spiral staircase. Marcus pursed his lips with uncertainty. Then he entered the void and began descending the black metal stairs.

Feeling like a dog for deceiving me, Kendrick's hands found my shoulders. He couldn't hide his fear that his lies would cost him what we'd started, and even more so? That the truth would endanger me. "I know you're pissed with me. You have every right to be. But please don't hate me."

My head was a total mess, and I was angry beyond words. Two

of my closest friends had kept secrets from me. Ones that could have changed my past actions and affected the many damned lives I'd snuffed out. Still, after everything we'd been through, I knew that sometimes things happened and loyalty didn't always make honesty clean-cut. Keeping Ty's existence from Kendrick was huge, and I was going to tell him. Just not right now.

Kendrick's hand guardedly slid down my arm and I let his fingers lace through mine. "I do trust you," I said.

As we clambered down after Marcus, déjà vu in reverse sent a shiver down my spine. This spiral staircase was identical to the one I'd climbed after surviving Caius's attempt to kill me. When we stepped out of the recess in the wall, a tunnel spanned out from either side. Stronger apprehension tightened my chest.

My hand rose to my neck, scratching and then gripping. It felt like I had just swallowed a fist full of glass shards. This place had too many memories, horrific memories that I didn't need any encouragement to relive. "W-why are we down here?" I choked out.

A dank smell still permeated the air, but it wasn't as gag-inducing as I remembered. The inch of rank water that had covered the stone ground was mostly gone, leaving the stone damp in places —which explained Kendrick's wet footprints when I'd run into him in the main cells. Exactly the same or not, it didn't matter. This place reminded me of hell. Of Caius's fangs deep in my throat. Of the agony as my body chilled and my heart gave in. Of my last breath before my lights blinked out.

Kendrick released my hand and hugged an arm around me. "Nothing down here can hurt you anymore. I promise you that."

He linked his arm through mine and hauled me along after Marcus. We covered a labyrinth of twists and turns. Between locked cell doors, dusty, grimy wall lanterns I hadn't noticed on my last visit burst into flames the second Marcus passed.

When we reached what appeared to be a dead end, two lanterns crackled to life with fire. The orange glow illuminated the space, revealing a wooden, iron-braced door. I gulped. It was identical to the one Caius had imprisoned me behind.

Who or what in the hell was I about to walk in on?

Kendrick unhooked his arm from mine and removed a large iron key from his cargo pants and held it out. A memory clicked into place. The time I'd caught him exiting the catacomb entrance in the main cells. He hadn't been looking for clues. He'd been coming down here to see whatever was locked behind this barrier.

Marcus took the key and slotted it into a plate on the door. "It's time to discover another piece of the puzzle in what you are." The locking mechanism clicked and he faced me rather than pushing the door in. "For the record, we only kept this from you to guard your health. Baldassare had wanted to tell you in the beginning when we arranged the secret transportation, but I talked him into staying quiet, at least until we knew more. And when your health deteriorated…" He said no more but lifted his apologetic gaze to me in question. "Are you ready?" At my nod, he slid the unlocked iron bar back and nudged the door. It creaked open, revealing a room lit by a single bulb. "She's in here."

Kendrick's hand found mine and we followed Marcus inside. This cell was larger than the one Caius had killed me in, but less putrid, and it didn't reek of death and decay. There was a toilet in the right corner of the cell, along with a sink. And in the left corner was a bed. Unlike the chain-suspended cot that had been in Ty's cell in Portsmouth, this one was actually framed and had a covered mattress that didn't appear stained or soiled. Instead, it had clean linen and even a soft-looking pillow.

Centering the bed was a girl, sitting with her knees together. Her head was dropped, short, blue-black hair hanging over her forehead as she stared down at the pages of a book. She wasn't chained or restricted in any way, and the sight of black veins across her pale flesh made me freeze.

Unconcerned, Kendrick stepped forward and knelt before the girl. "Raven, I would like you to meet Amelia."

The girl's head lifted slowly. Her pallor was chalky, and more spiderweb veins snaked across her small, oval face. The color of her irises was unusual, mainly silver-blue, but hers held tiny chips of maroon. *She's a vampire?* I studied her features more closely. There was something strangely familiar about her. "Have we met before?"

Raven's lips parted with a broad smile that revealed the tips of her tiny fangs. Then she launched, the bed creaking as she flew across the cell to capture me with her arms. She squeezed my body as the hardcover she'd been reading—The Secret Garden—clunked to the stone. I struggled against her for a moment before realizing she wasn't attacking me. She was actually hugging me. "Thank you," she cried. Her grip on me loosened and she peered up at me, eyes shining and cheeks wet. "Thank you for saving me."

"Saving you?" I wriggled free and backed up, hitting the wall. "What are you talking about?" I looked from her to the others.

Kendrick had his hands shoved into the pockets of his black cargo pants, unable to keep eye contact with me. Marcus blocked the doorway, his gaze focused on Raven while nodding. "Show her."

Raven undid the top three buttons of her white blouse and pulled the light material aside. An area of exposed flesh was revealed, almost centering her chest and just above the cover of her left breast. There was a patch of scarred flesh that reminded me of the starburst I'd been left with after falling through the cabin basement.

"You were one of the damned who attacked the Armaya?"

"No," Kendrick answered. "This happened back in Portsmouth."

My eyes were still set on Raven's exposed and marred flesh.

Something about the mark tickled at my subconscious, telling me that I already knew the answer to the question I was about to ask. "Who did that to you?"

Raven let the fabric go and it slid back to cover the scar. "You did."

"What?"

Memories pumped through my head as if sent by the volumes of blood my heart was now forcing at speed through my veins. In an uncontrollable quake of what felt like time and reality splitting, I was back in the Portsmouth council hall, stake thrusting tip first into the chest of a damned girl. The stake snapped through a rib and struck her heart. The girl's face contorted and she flew across the room at the force. But I didn't see her body instantaneously combust. Instead, I spun away from her, knowing I had stuck her heart, knowing I had killed her. She was one more I'd killed, and one less left to take down.

"I staked you," I whispered, voice so soft it was almost inaudible. The girl standing before me was an altered mirror image of the damned girl I had killed during that battle. But there was a distinct difference, more than the lack of her red-rimmed eyes, something that stood in the way of the fact that I had taken this girl's life. I could hear it. Apart from the steady heartbeat coming from Kendrick and Marcus, I could hear hers. Her heart was beating. She was not just animated like only a damned could be, with the cold and non-beating heart of a monster. She was alive. "But I killed you."

The girl shrugged. "Yes—and no."

She sat back on the bed, and Kendrick took up the space beside her. Being a restored damned, he showed no concern being close to her. Instead, he seemed rather acquainted. "When you staked Raven, something else happened."

And that's when it clicked. I recalled the scent I'd picked up on

267

him and sniffed. It was hers. All those times he'd been inexplicably missing now made sense. All those months he'd been sneaking down here, visiting her behind my back. A glare transformed my face, but I pushed my resurfacing anger aside. I needed to remember what had happened that fateful day, but my brain refused to cooperate.

"Amelia." Marcus clasped his hands and moved to stand before me. "Don't you see? What you did during that battle saved her, caused her dead heart to beat again."

I winced at the memory of failing Ty that day. Of knowing what he now was. And yet I had saved this girl who had tried to kill me, who had likely killed over a dozen living vampires in that hall. Ty had set aside racial grudges and put his life on the line to save his sworn enemies. Ty had deserved to live. To be whole. What had she done to deserve a second chance?

"You killed people, vampires," I said suddenly, steel-hardened eyes narrowing at the girl named Raven. "Do you remember every life you took while your heart was as black as coal?"

The girl's eyes diverted with a shudder as she stared down at her hands in her lap. She frowned at them, then buried them into the pockets of her beige, drawstring pants while she scuffed her bare feet through a groove between the stones. "I remember *everything*."

Raven never decided to become damned, Kendrick spoke through our bond. *It was forced on her.*

Deep inside my heart, I wanted to hate this girl more than I had ever wanted to hate anyone. Even more than I could hate Caius. But I couldn't. Looking at her now as she gingerly retrieved her novel and held it tight—like it was her most valuable possession—her earlier vibrancy had deflated, now bordering on guilty caution. She wasn't even a shadow of the monster that had attacked to kill. She was just a girl, maybe fifteen, but with maroon-speckled, tear-filled eyes that spoke volumes to the condemnation of all the heinous acts she had committed as a damned. This wasn't her fault. She had been a victim too.

Still, all of this aside, how had staking her restored her mortality and conscience, when every other damned I'd taken down was obliterated?

Kendrick stood and walked behind me, hands finding my shoulders with a squeezed. *You know the answer.* His unspoken words seemed to whistle through my ears. *You just have to allow yourself to remember.*

Terrified but receiving strength from Kendrick, I allowed my mind to relax, allowed the floodgates that I'd been trying to hold in place with my bare hands crumble with a flow of cruel memory. There was so much, things I'd already been unable to hold back, but so, so much more than that.

I heard the sounds of battle, the cries of people dying around me, of weapons slicing through resistant flesh. Bodies had piled up so fast, the spilled concoction of black and red blood infecting the pristine marble floor.

As I forced my way past the clutter, I found the memory I needed to make sense of this. The one that revealed the stark difference between every damned I had taken out with my stake, to this girl who now sat before me, alive and breathing. Raven had launched at me, fangs bared and aimed at my neck. Ty had intervened, leaped into the crossfire and taken her bite. The first bite of many he'd sustained by the end of the battle. With my whip, I'd tugged her off him, and then barreled her off Ty. Craze-blinded, she'd flipped me onto my back in the cold wetness of spilled blood. Her fangs aimed for my jugular. Then my hand gripping the stake between us shot up, sending her flying back into a heap of bodies.

"When I drove the stake into your heart..." I held up my hands that rippled with blue sparks. "A bolt of lightning erupted straight into the stake."

"Your power inflicted with silver jump-started her heart," Marcus said.

Kendrick's breath was cool in my ear. "It restored Raven to life."

In spite of the ground-shattering news, an obstacle stood in the way of this being true, throwing a spanner in the works. Before Raven had torn a chunk from Ty's thigh and I'd taken her down, Ty had clamped onto her, werewolf teeth and all. The proof was there in the healed serration of teeth and canines along her arm.

"You still should have died."

Kendrick came around me fast as Raven's eyes widened and her arms wrapped around her body. He blocked my view of her, his open mouth and frown one of total disbelief. "Amelia, that's not fair. Raven had no control when she was damned. She never meant—"

"I didn't mean she deserved to die," I cut him off. His sudden protection of her irked me, but not as much as his assumption that I'd wished her dead. He was supposed to know me better than I knew myself. How could he even think that? "Ty bit her," I said, forcing my clenched teeth apart. "Even if my power restored her, the bite should have killed her."

Kendrick's shoulders slumped and he felt instantly bad for his assumption.

Marcus went to hold Raven's arm out and inspected the scars. "Interesting." He dropped her hand and leaned against the wall, seeming to consider the possibility as he propped his foot up against the stone. "Although she would have still been damned when bitten. A death sentence to vampires, but only debilitating to damned. Being restored while infected could have cured the bite's poison."

"I guess that makes sense," I said, backing up to the door. A split-second decision had entered my mind and even without lack of urgency, I felt the need to get this out in the open.

Kendrick followed after me, about to apologize for his wrong assumption of my character, when he caught on. My thoughts locked down too late and he grabbed my bicep and spun me back around. "No. You can't do it. Who knows what they'd do to Raven."

Knowing something silent had passed between us, Marcus's interest piqued. "What who would do to Raven?"

I heard a creak and saw Raven had shifted to the edge of the bed in suspense. This would affect all of them, but it needed to be done. For all the lives I'd taken when I didn't know any better. And for Ty. "The RVC needs to know about Raven. They need to know that there's a way to save the damned and that my power is the key."

"Amelia, that's not a good idea." Marcus stepped under the single bulb that lit the cell, blond hair gleaming and hands up in anxious reasoning. "We've already seen the effect a vision can have on you. Even with your diet changes, you are weakened every time. Restoring life will surely take a much greater toll."

Kendrick came up close, hand cupping the back of my neck and eyes intense with fear. "After the PVC you were out for days. The tranq was only supposed to knock you out for six hours. *Six hours.* And if you start restoring the damned at the RVC's will, you don't know what will happen." The rest of his spiel was silent, for my ears only. *Caius warned you'd do this. Try to save them all. Sacrifice yourself until it killed you.*

"So you think he was right to take me out early?" I batted his hand away and snarled. "To save me the suffering!"

"I didn't say that," he shot back. "Everything I've ever done was to keep you safe."

"By taking away my right to choose my own path." I paced back and forth beside the door, seeing those monstrous faces turn from shock to smoldering ash. "I've killed so many, put down all those damned when I could have given their lives back. Now I have a chance at redemption and you all want to take that away from me. Why is my life so damned important—"

"I don't." Raven's quiet voice cut off my rant. Now standing, she pushed her black hair behind her ears then kept her hands bent over her shoulders. "I don't want to take anything away from you, Amelia. And I don't want to remain in hiding, either. I want to be a normal vampire again. I want to have my life back."

Kendrick touched her arm and I felt his fear. And something else inside me that I didn't want to cop to. "There's no guarantee the RVC will accept you," he said. "What if they just lock you back up?"

Raven shrugged and dropped her arms. "Then I won't be any worse off than I am now. But at least I'll have tried."

Silence stretched on as they stared at each other, and I couldn't stand another second of it. "So are we doing this?"

Raven smiled over Kendrick's shoulder at me. "Lead the way."

CHAPTER 21

J sat on my throne at the round marble slab that made up the boardroom table. It was about thirty minutes later after rounding up the RVC for my unscheduled but urgent meeting. Being a bit after midday, it was dark beyond the uncovered Gothic windows. Except for the full moon that cast silvery light on the path and bordering hedges to the gardens. As I waited for the others to sit, I was both anxious and ready. The wait was over. Now the ability I'd been altered for would be brought to light. Now the rest of the RVC would know I could restore the damned.

In the Baldassare throne, Kendrick fumed, cursing internally for me to change my mind. Worried more than he'd ever been for what would come of me if I didn't. But I couldn't. The RVC needed to know why Caius had tried to abduct me, and they needed to see the proof that I could save the damned and our race.

"Thank you all for coming," I spoke up when all eyes focused on me. "I have some crucial information that could change the future of our race."

"Interesting," Lord Strigon murmured. "Has a vision offered new enlightenment?"

"Not in this instance," Marcus replied as he placed his filled glass down on the tabletop. His eyes were almost pleading for me to back down, but the resignation across his face showed how likely he thought that was.

"I have discovered that Caius meant to use me, or my power, at least,"—I held out my hand and sparks trailed down my arm to my fingertips—"to restore damned vampires to life."

"It's a long-held belief that there is a way to cure the damned." Uriel sent a warning look my way. After losing her father because of the same power, she seemed to guess exactly what I was about to reveal. "There is no proof however that there is any merit to the rumor."

If Kendrick's continued voiceless argument still wasn't stopping me, hers wouldn't either, regardless of what she'd said in the garden two weeks ago. "But what if there were a way. If we can save some or even all of the damned, wouldn't that be the ultimate solution?"

"Even if this were possible, why would the traitor want to restore them?" Lord Paole questioned. "Death is much quicker."

With a sigh, Uriel gestured to one of the oil portraits on the stone wall behind where we sat. The painting made me recoil as I twisted my head to catch a glimpse. The one of a beautiful woman in a medieval gown, with blond hair, unblemished white skin, and a cold stare that could crack ice. "To return to life the late Lady Bathory and her daughters. He believes they all still roam this earth."

Lady Rasputin looked less than impressed. "And how, pray tell, did your *father* intend to achieve this?"

I cringed at her reference to Caius as my blood. "A silver stake to the heart with a jolt of electricity."

"Theories are all well and good," Lord Strigon said as he

glanced to the others. "Though in this crisis, we need to continue to take action. If another way is found in the process, then so be it. Until definite knowledge and proof of this damned-saving possibility is unveiled, we must make a stand in this war to preserve our race."

Marcus remained as quiet on the outside as Kendrick did, neither giving anything away to the others. If I decided to bow out of this confession, they were backing me up. Coming clean in the past had wreaked havoc on my life, and maybe it would again this time. Still, I couldn't keep what I knew secret when I could use the force inside me to save vampires who'd been forced into a damned existence. Like Ty. I now knew how to save him, and I knew he was still alive.

"It's not a theory. I have proof." I glanced over my shoulder. "Bring her in."

The doors swung inward and the black-haired girl walked over to stand beside my throne. With her drawstring pants and Kendrick's thin boarding hoodie on, she was mostly covered and her face was shadowed. Her wide eyes scanned all who watched and fell on Kendrick. Regardless of her obvious fear, she nodded as if reinstating her decision to back me.

I smiled up at her, glad for an ally. "This is Raven. She was at the Portsmouth Battle...as a damned. I staked her and hit her with lightning, and it brought her back to life."

I nodded up at her as the other royals stared. Raven removed the borrowed hoodie and the council members' jaws fell at the black veins across her arms and face. When she pulled her top aside to reveal the healed mark above her heart where my stake had struck through, Lady Rasputin shot up.

"Guards!"

Countless guards swarmed the boardroom, a few taking hold of

Raven. The rest wavered in silence for a command, weapons at the ready.

"Let her go." Kendrick was across the room in a second, breathing down the restraining guards' necks. "Now."

"You knew this threat existed?" Uriel accused, looking past me to him.

"We both did," Marcus answered. His throne scraped over stone as he pushed it back to rise. "We revealed her existence to Amelia less than an hour ago. It was her decision to reveal the restored damned to you all."

While the guards kept Raven pinned, who showed only fear and no hint of retaliation, the other council members' alarm ebbed.

"What will you do to her?" I asked, Kendrick's worry as he held his ground feeding my own. Although I'd wanted to reveal my ability, I hadn't wanted any harm to come to her.

Uriel got up and marched over to the girl. Her sapphire eyes studied her with intense curiosity. "Are you a threat? A danger?"

"N-no. I would never hurt a soul."

"But you have," Lord Paole accused. "You have killed vampires?" The notion seemed to sadden the royal rather than anger him. Another emotion tightened his features as he stared at her, but it was impossible to tell which one.

Raven didn't deny the accusation, and averted her eyes in shame.

"She was turned against her will," Kendrick spoke in her defense.

Marcus spoke up, too. "In the months Kendrick and I kept her hidden, she has behaved perfectly. She is not a threat."

"Then prove it," Lady Rasputin demanded. "Or we'll vote to put her down."

I shot up, ready to defend the girl, but Kendrick acted first. Fangs punching from his gums, he tore into his wrist. The savage gouge welled with blood that trickled all the way down to his elbow. "Release her," he snarled at the guards. "She's a threat to no one."

A tense moment passed and Raven didn't budge. There was no red glow to her irises and, as her lips parted, everyone could see only the tips of her protruding fangs. They weren't fully extended and desperate for the source on offer.

Uriel nodded to the restraining guards. "You heard Lord Baldassare. Release the girl."

In a heartbeat she was free—and still she showed no loss of control at the puddle of glossy red. Which was amazing. Even from across the room, I couldn't stop my mouth watering at the smell.

Lord Paole spoke before anyone else could. "I vote we mark and keep this girl under strict guard at all times for now."

With a curt nod, Uriel returned to her throne. "And as your deception brought her here…" She eyed Kendrick and Marcus. "One of you must assume responsibility for her."

Kendrick remained by Raven's side, wrist closing up and an untouched puddle by his DCs that tempted me with each residual *drip, drip*. He didn't argue the security measures. "I will," he said to my total surprise.

There were murmurs around the boardroom and then a string of "agreed" votes were voiced.

Uriel eyed two guards. "Escort the girl to the alchemist for marking, then deliver her to one of the guest suites. Do not leave her unattended, or it'll be your heads."

Guards led Raven from the boardroom. Her head twisted over her shoulder with uncertain worry at Kendrick. His body was tense as he returned to his throne, fingers pressing against the tabletop. But he nodded with encouragement.

I didn't miss her trust in him or the security she gained from his voiceless actions. In our world that she'd now re-entered, he was her source of comfort and safety. Their relationship had grown over the past six months in secret.

After all Kendrick and I had been through together, and with what we'd started to become, the deep-down sting I felt was real and unmovable.

Still, I couldn't dwell on it, at least not now. A bigger discussion needed to take place first.

The RVC was bickering over their decisions regarding Raven and whether further action was needed to reprimand Kendrick and Marcus. Lord Paole seemed to have sided with Uriel, but the others were now the second half of a debating team.

I raised my voice to speak over them. "Past decisions aside, there is a much more important issue we must vote on."

"And what might that be?" Lady Rasputin questioned, filling a glass and taking an exasperated sip.

Marcus folded his arms over his pea coat and cleared his throat. "Whether we stop hunting down the damned and killing them."

I smiled my thanks past Uriel to him, then I panned over the other royals. "We have a choice now. We can fight to catch and imprison them. With my power, we can give them their lives back and lessen the threat to our people."

"Amelia, I don't believe you have thought this through." Uriel rose and looked down at me, her expression riddled with concern and apprehension. "Having you use your power in that way is far too risky. Even if we had new leads and the means to imprison them, the damned are too dangerous to hold captive. And when they're vying for blood and you come to save the day, do you think they'll just stand still and thank you?"

"They'll tear her to shreds," Lord Strigon announced.

"Plus we don't know the full effect of using your power in this way." Kendrick's gaze slid up to me, then away at my shooting-daggers stare. "You already need Pure Blood. You barely functioned before it."

"Kendrick is right." Uriel reclaimed her throne and filled a glass before sliding it my way. "Amelia, you cannot think there will be no personal—and maybe irrevocable—damage done with each restored damned."

A murmur of agreement sounded and the same feeling swept through the bond from Kendrick. His stand on me risking my life in this way hadn't budged. The cost of this power and its use was still unknown. In his mind he recalled how I'd lay unconscious after the PVC attack. After restoring Raven. How the blood transfusion after restoring just one had still left me lights out for days. He feared restoring on a regular basis could one day knock me out permanently. Like my vision had threatened to do.

Still I couldn't think of that. Couldn't do nothing when I had this power for a reason. After taking so many of their lives already, there was a penance to pay. And if I couldn't get them to agree to this, when they eventually found Ty, there'd be no hope of bringing him back to life. The drive that swelled my heart at the renewed chance of saving Ty also made it drop. I was a total piece of shit. Kendrick still didn't know Ty was alive. And even worse, I still didn't know what that meant for us. I rechecked the blocks in my head. Telling him now wasn't an option, and I needed time to think. Then there was Caius's execution, which I just remembered was set for tomorrow. Great. Another irrevocable change that I wasn't even nearly ready to deal with.

I forced my thoughts out of my head and found everyone waiting on my response to Uriel's concerns. "I...I don't know what will happen or what it will do to me. But my life is not above everyone else's. Everyone deserves a second chance. My mind is made up."

"Then we put this to a vote," Marcus announced to the others around the gray-veined slab. "All in favor of imprisoning the damned to be restored?"

"Nay," Lord Strigon voted, followed by Lady Rasputin and Lord Paole.

"Aye," Uriel said to my surprise. She shrugged at my questioning glance. "I said it was your choice, remember."

In spite of his desperation to vote against me, Kendrick knew what being in my position was like—when I'd voted to keep him safe here while seeking damned in Portsmouth with Marcus. He wasn't going to use the past vindictively, especially after the lies he'd already been caught in today. As always, he had my back, even if he didn't want to. "Aye."

Twisting to face Marcus, hopeful questioning strained my eyes. "I'm sorry, Amelia. I can't agree to this."

Hurt and in shock, different scenarios filled my mind. I needed to inform Mr. Malau about so much more than my power. With a reason to rebuild the rescue efforts, he'd come to my aid. Then it would be back to seeking out damned hideouts while Marika took my place. I'd be able to make up for all the lives I'd taken rather than saving. And I could finally do what Ty had believed I could do in his dying moments. *Save him.* Though there was a big obstacle standing in the way of half of my mission. Mr. Malau would never agree to rescue all the damned we encountered. He'd only back me up to save Ty.

On top of that, I hadn't told Kendrick Ty was even alive. It wasn't fair to keep this from him. After hiding Raven's existence from me, I knew how deep that deception cut from the person you trusted most. By Caius's execution tomorrow, I told myself. I'd have to come clean and sort out my head by then.

"What would it take to make you all reconsider?"

My head snapped up at Kendrick's voice. Though he couldn't

access my thoughts, he'd been reading my silent reaction to their vote. He knew how guilty I felt for killing so many damned, when all along I could have been saving them—even if he didn't have a clue what else was stirring my conscience. He suffered his own guilt for lying to me all this time, and for the many lives he'd taken, too. But he didn't regret the kills. When it came to a choice, protecting me over them would always win out.

"There will be no reconsidering while the option is to restore the damned one at a time," Lady Rasputin said.

"I agree," said Lord Paole. "They are hard enough to kill, let alone catch."

Lord Strigon tapped the marble tabletop, looking deep in thought. "Though perhaps we could revisit the vote if a full cure were found."

Uriel had been in the middle of taking a sip from her crystal glass, and paused. "You don't mean...?"

Glances were exchanged around the table; the only ones in the dark were Kendrick and me.

"There is an old rumor." Marcus cleared his throat. "It states that one day the powers of light and dark will join and break the damned curse."

My swell of excitement at the possibility vanished. I didn't know what the dark Caius had warned me about was. But Kendrick and I had uncovered clues about my power and its use. To break the curse, payment of my life was the price.

To save them all...I'd have to die.

CHAPTER 22

*W*hen I ran from my suite the next day, black and silver-laced gown swishing, I knew I was almost out of time. Every hour since the boardroom I'd spent mostly alone, stewing over how to tell Kendrick Ty was alive…and trying to figure out what that meant. I still had no clue, and I couldn't keep it from him any longer. But as I rounded the bend with four cloaked guards shadowing me, I saw not a single one outside the Baldassare suite.

I picked up the pace, hefting up the hem of my gown as my Vans pattered down the grand staircase to the main hall—

I plowed into Kendrick who appeared suddenly, his arm catching around my waist before I could bowl us over.

"Hey, you okay?" Keeping one arm hooked around me, he brushed the loose hair back from my face. Then he saw my whip curled around my waist, which at the last minute I'd put there for an unobtrusive sense of protection.

"Oh, I…" After taking his blood this morning along with another apology for his lies, my mouth still watered at his closeness. But he wasn't talking about any of that.

I noticed then the many people filing through the tall arched doors into the main hall. I was out of time to spill what I should have already come clean about. Revealing Ty's existence would have to wait. The pews were filling fast, everyone gathering to witness Caius paying the price for his crimes against our race.

I suddenly felt sick. I'd been so wrapped up in my own lies I hadn't spared more than a thought about today. But I couldn't stop the avalanche now.

Between the pews and the wall of Gothic windows, a small plat-form had been erected. Centering it, a large, square rock stood out like it was lit up by neon lights. The metal pail below had a spike of bile erupting up my throat. Before the end of this formal gathering, Caius's head would drop into the pail like trash thrown in a wastepaper basket.

In spite of my hate for him, I felt overwhelmed by loss.

Kendrick's hand caught around my nape and he dropped his forehead against mine. *You don't have to watch it.*

My constant, my rock. *I know.* I sighed, feeling like shit because I was still lying to him. I re-cemented my decision to come clean. Straight after the public display, I'd take him up to my suite and tell him. "Guess we better get on stage."

Kendrick took my hand and moments later we were positioned side by side on our thrones. He didn't let go, but I caught him looking at Raven, who smiled from the front row.

Before I could dwell on that, I caught sight of my mom in the crowd, eyes bloodshot and puffy. She'd come to watch the execu-tion, to see the man she'd once loved beheaded before her eyes. After knowing what he'd done to me, her harbored feelings for him cut me deep.

Dorian sat beside her in a collared shirt, while Vanessa—who looked almost prepped for a fight—wore the same body-hugging black she'd had on at Ty's funeral. He tapped my mom's hand in support, but the strain on his face showed how uncomfortable he was in doing it. She had been the only mother he'd known, and Caius had taken that and so much more away from him.

More guards entered the hall then to form a barricade around the perimeter. Being a formal execution, every guard wore a black robe that stretched all the way to the ground and had a hood to conceal their faces. It was custom, and as one of them would carry out the execution, it kept their identity from being known.

The pendant trapped between my wrist and the throne's wooden armrest flared with heat. Then it resettled to a dull and constant warmth. I didn't take too much notice. It had been acting up all morning for absolutely no reason. Or more likely, because the dreaded event was creeping in that would bring my attempted murderer within range.

From his own throne on my other side, Marcus pursed his lips at me and sighed as the crowd's chatter died down. "I guess it's time." He rose and strode to the podium and the remaining whispers died. "I welcome you all this day to witness the price Lord Caius Bathory will pay as a guilt-found traitor." He pointed to the guards beside the stage. "Bring forth the guilty."

One guard spoke into the handheld radio at his shoulder, then after a few moments a door to one side of the stage opened. Caius appeared, shackles chinking across the stone as two guards dragged him in. Morbid resignation creased his tired face as they forced him along the outside row of pews. The crowd murmured and some even booed as he was forced up the side steps and onto the platform. He caught sight of my mom then, and his expression transformed. The word *sorry* was mouthed from his dry lips and moisture sparkled from his eyes.

When they reached the large rock, the guards forced Caius to his knees behind the stone so he faced the crowd. Everyone twisted sideways to watch. His wrists and ankles were unshackled with gloved hands and one guard remained close by, their head tipped forward beneath their robe. The other returned to the uniformed line before the windows.

"For your treason in plotting against our race, you, Lord Caius Bathory, have been found guilty," Marcus announced. "The punishment to be carried out this day is death. Have you any last words?"

Caius spared Marcus a glare before he looked to me with desperation. "Heed my warning. If you do not, death is the only result." Then he threw his voice over the crowd while eyeing each of his old colleagues. "Someone else is leading the damned and your own blood will run in rivers through our city if you do not stop them."

With Kendrick's hand still holding mine, fingers laced through my own, the pendant flared again. I frowned down, ready to tear the malfunctioning stone off, but decided to wait.

As I glanced back up, Marcus nodded for the guard to retrieve the silver sword from the table siding the platform. The guard, with their face in shadow, nodded, then strode to retrieve the weapon with slow calculated grace. Transfixed, I stared as the guard repositioned behind Caius, weapon raised over their shoulder and ready to swing. Unplaceable suspicion had my heart racing as the guard shoved a booted foot into Caius's back, forcing his upper body to bend over the rock.

With his head hanging over the edge and ready to fall into the pail, my frown shifted. Caius glanced up to look me squarely in the eyes, regret marring his wrinkled face. "I am sorry, my dear Amelia, for all that I have done to wrong you."

The pendant flared hotter again, over and over. This wasn't a malfunction. And it wasn't responding to Caius who was seconds from execution and far from a threat. I let the feeling shoot through the bond and Kendrick's head cranked my way.

At the same time, Marcus had returned to his throne and as he sat, the guard tensed, body twisting back. The sword sliced the air and—

Missed.

The silver length pinged as it hit the stone instead of Caius's waiting neck. My unwanted relief-laced confusion was short lived. The guard threw off his hood to reveal red eyes, protruding fangs, and a monstrous face that broke my heart. "Now!" Ty ordered.

Bar The Seven's detail, every other guard circling the hall threw off their robes. Dozens of damned revealed themselves, no longer posing as castle guards. A succession of red peepers flared beyond the tall windows. The crowd shot up in panic and the main doors flung open before a waiting, blood-hungry army.

Ty pointed the sword tip at me, callous flashing in his eyes at the sight of Kendrick's hand around mine. He motioned with his free arm, and the damned flooded into the hall. "Kill them all, except for *her*."

"What the hell?" Kendrick jumped up at the sight of Ty. He saw my frozen shock at Ty's intrusion with the damned as he bared his fangs.

Blood-curdling screams and cries split the air. The raw terror was something that would forever stain my memory. The damned were everywhere, unarmed but for their nails and fangs. Having come to watch an execution, the vampires were unarmed too, except for The Seven and their guards.

The Seven unhinged weapons from the backs of their thrones

while Marcus called for everyone else to take hold of the decorated swords cross-mounted to the walls.

Breaking my stunned stare from Ty who hadn't so much as blinked, I tore the top layers of my gown's skirt off. Legs covered by a shorter underlayer, I uncoiled my whip from around my waist.

With the shock of their appearance and the speed the damned possessed, a few bodies already littered the stone ground. Some of the living fought back, while others made for the exits.

I wasn't about to let that number soar.

With my whip uncurled, I was ready to lash out when I suddenly realized I couldn't see Caius. In the distraction of seeing Ty in the flesh, the prick must have made his escape.

Kendrick shucked off his suit jacket and palmed a dagger I hadn't known he'd been packing. He threw it to Raven who, to her credit, held her ground to fight. Now weaponless, his eyes clouded, hands conjuring wind pockets that curled just above the ground to sweep damned off their feet.

In my search of Caius, I didn't see the damned girl clear the stage until she knocked me down. Kendrick booted her off me and I leaped up, seeing Dorian and Vanessa down the hall, protecting my mom with stakes. Urgency to make sure she stayed safe fueled my drive and I got back with the program.

Kendrick took on more encroaching damned as the girl sprang up.

I smashed my whip's butt into her nose, and she teetered. Then I looped the silver length around her neck and squeezed. Her wail cut off as the spikes embedded, black oozing as her eyes popped and her skin sizzled. For a second I hesitated as she clawed at the whip, hands burning at the silver contact.

Death wasn't the only option.

"You don't have a stake," Kendrick snapped, still conjuring mini twisters to keep the damned away. "Kill her, or I will."

I wanted to save her, to save them all, but I knew I couldn't. Even if I got a stake, there was only one heart my restrained voltage was being saved for. Ty.

"Sorry," I whispered to the girl, resolve to protect my mum weighing on my heart. I turned my head aside and tugged the whip tight over itself. With the crack of her neck and the tear that followed, I released one end. Her head hit the stage before her body did.

With no time to spare on remorse, I found Dorian and Vanessa. They barricaded my terrified mom behind them as two damned stalked their way.

I lashed my whip out to floor a damned whose red eyes marked me, and went to leap into the fray when four more appeared.

Knowing where I was trying to get to, Kendrick joined my assault, throwing damned off the stage with strong gusts.

They flew at the walls, into other damned, and catapulted into pews. But for every damned he sent flying, another jumped up to take its place. Trapped, we kept up the fight to get to them as I watched in horror.

Vanessa jumped and spun in the air. One spiked heel kicked out at a damned's throat. Surprised a human had gotten such a fast move in, the damned recovered quickly and slammed her to the ground.

Then it launched.

But Dorian blocked the way. The damned saw the stake heading for his heart and went to evade, but Dorian's free hand flicked out with command. Black blood spurted from its eyes and Dorian's stake hit the mark, bringing the damned down with a puff of ash.

The second attacker took the opportunity and went for my mom.

I screamed out, whip torso-trapping my own damned as Dorian

leaped up only to be knocked back down. The damned curled his hand around my mom's throat and her eyes grew too wide as he squeezed.

A roar vibrated the chandeliers and Caius appeared across the hall. Hands unshackled, he clawed at his tattered shirt and the marking on his back that blocked his earth ability. The stone beneath the damned's feet erupted like a sudden earthquake. Then Caius was through the battlers, barreling the damned off my mom. The damned sprang up and Caius's hands shook as bad as the ground beneath them. As bad as every wall around the hall that rattled the windows.

Caius's connection to earth.

But as the stone split, he didn't get the chance to bury his opponent.

The damned suddenly dropped to its knees, no sound coming from its gaping mouth as its hands lifted slowly then froze. Tiny cracks appeared all over its exposed flesh, growing like a frozen ice statue and cracking through.

Dorian stalked forward, trembling hand raised to keep control of the ice sculpture he'd made of the damned. With a booted foot, he kicked the frozen monster and it shattered into a million pieces.

The battle forged on after that, seconds bleeding into minutes of cut-down cries and air-slicing swords that rendered damned to ash with a twist of each hilt.

Below the stage, the other crowned royals fought with the still-living.

Kendrick leaped down into the masses to join Raven and the unarmed vamps she was protecting. I kept lashing my whip out from the stage, needing the distance to make my weapon effective and safe to the innocent.

Marcus was among the battlers, taking the damned down with ferocious speed and agility. His fire-lit sword only joined in on the action when his opponent looked close to the point of begging for death.

No longer on the execution stand, Ty had disappeared.

My sight darted and fell on Dorian, Vanessa, and my mom. With his ability now drained, Dorian was relying on his and Vanessa's stakes and agility. Still at the back of the hall, they were trying to stab a path to the tall open doors. Trying to get my mom to safety.

Caius was right there with them, fighting the damned back.

Helping them would give Caius a chance to escape, but their safety won out over the danger of him being on the loose. "Kendrick!" Through the bond I sent my need, knowing I had to contain my lightning for the moment I found Ty.

Kendrick's head snapped up over the battlers. Hands raised, his eyes clouded. A surge of power swamped the hall and every window burst inward. Kendrick flicked his wrists, wind throwing glass shards like knives at the damned that blocked the exit.

Dorian and Vanessa grabbed my mom and made a run for it. As they cleared the threshold, Dorian turned back and flung his stake with speed.

It sailed, rubber end over tip and my hand caught it as they disappeared. Caius was gone, too.

Then through the melee, a figure in hunting boots and worn jeans made my heart stop.

Ty stood statue-still at the mouth of the shoved and upturned pews. Attacking damned kept guards off him as he watched me with deadly intent. His bone-white fangs were bared and his tongue licked one with greedy promise. He strode forward then, fighters parting like a sea divided. His eyes tracked me with every booted step, a predator locked on its prey.

The moment I'd been so desperate for all this time was here. With a quick slice from the tip of my whip the stake was freed of its protective rubber. Restrained electricity surged from my chest down to my hand that clung to Dorian's stake for dear life.

This was it, and I was ready.

I had to be.

Fighting among the others on the ground, Kendrick felt my mental shift. The scene to come struck him with panic and he went to mount the stage.

Too late.

Damned blocked his way.

Ty shot right in front of me, so fast I couldn't track the move until we were face to face. An acrid, stale smell hit me as he spoke. "Missed you over the last two days."

Despite the threat and my intent, my body responded to him. My weapon-holding hands ached to touch his scarred arms and neck. My lips parted with breath, desperate to taste him. Still, my mind was on track and I smashed my head into his nose. In his stumble the stake aimed and drove forward. The electric tip pierced his chest and—

Ty's cold, calloused hand caught my wrist and squeezed, cracking bone. As the stake clanked to the stage, he elbowed me in the eye. Pain exploded and he clutched my throat hard, twisting my head to the side. His jaws split wide, fangs pointed and long as his mouth neared my jugular. "Time to join the superior race."

I flung my whip around his waist, catching-hand failing with my broken wrist. Kendrick screamed from far away and damned in the distance began to explode into fire pillars as Marcus fought to get closer.

Game. Set. Match.

The space was too great. The threat too close. I was about to lose everything.

Someone shot between us, breaking Ty's stronghold around my

throat. But not before his fangs could claim flesh. Not mine though. Caius's.

Ty tore his fangs free as Caius bit down on his forearm. He roared, gold sparking in his red irises as he cold-clocked the four-hundred-year-old vampire and threw him across the stage. He came at me and my whip sailed around his torso. Instant sizzling bubbled from his flesh as the spikes embedded through his T-shirt.

But that didn't stop his strangling hold from reclaiming my neck.

He caught and squeezed my broken wrist while electricity pulsed down the whip. He hissed and his fanged mouth gaped—

With a choking sound, he threw me back. Black started leaking from his eyes and nose as I hit the stage. And that's when I saw it. Now on the execution platform, Dorian's silver-sparking eyes were trained on Ty.

Staggering back, Ty's furious stare burrowed into my very soul. "Until next time, beautiful," he choked out. Then he shot across the hall to the open doors, hand clinging to the jamb as his legs quaked.

With a high-pitched whistle, the remaining damned ceased their killing spree. They sped toward him as he morphed into a giant wolf. Then they all disappeared in a black and gray blur down the castle's steps and into the trees over the road.

I collapsed, breath sawing from my lungs. The threat was gone.

And so was Ty.

CHAPTER 23

$\mathcal{I}$ stood at the balcony coming off my bedroom, cool wind batting my damp hair. With my wrist bandaged while the bone healed, I gripped onto the balustrade, throbs ascending my arm to my shoulder. I stared out at the field to that tree I'd seen Ty beneath all those weeks ago. He wasn't there now, but I expected him to show up at any moment. To come back and make good on his promise. He would be back. He'd threatened as much. And I wanted that, feared it just as much.

In a crumpled mess behind me lay my ruined gown, soiled by red and black smears and ash. My body was free of those remnants now. Washed down the drain in the quickest shower of my life. But the healing cuts remained, as did the many yellowing bruises across my flesh. All the wounds I'd sustained while battling without even noticing at the same time.

All the crowned royals had been sequestered to their suites for the time being, until the guards made certain there were no damned left roaming. I was alone in body and spirit. Because there was a block more impenetrable than the Great Wall that separated me from Kendrick. The suspicion I had on why planted what felt like a fist in my throat that refused to budge. But until I could see him face to face, I wouldn't know.

Abandoning one problem for the next, I stared down at my iPhone in my hands. A fresh wave of dread hit me like a cold slap. There was a task I desperately had to complete before the impending council meeting I was required to attend. The call I was about to make would change more than my life. Mr. Malau had to know his eldest son was alive. *Ty* was alive. The need for us to rejoin forces now existed. He'd take me on. And together we'd find him. We'd save him. At what cost, I didn't know. But it was all I could think of. And all that made that dread swim in my veins.

Now re-dressed in fighting gear—which, screw formalities, would remain my usual attire from this day forward—a sparkling array of deadly weapons covered my body. Whip, dagger, and stake. Guards milled around in pre-dawn darkness on the grounds outside the castle. More moved through the maze-like gardens while others could be seen in the distance, marching through the streets and weaving through the surrounding forestry. Many had been found unconscious, their robes stolen by the impersonators. Others had been found injured badly or dead, bleeding out and unable to warn of the incoming threat. Others had been bitten, infected with poison from damned fangs. But it seemed none had been infected with their blood to put them into the transition process. Still, the RVC had taken any bitten and moved them down to the cells. Until the effects of the poison wore off, they'd remain down there, as prisoners. The rest were on task—secure location. And they would keep marching until a plan was put in motion.

I sighed and bit the bullet, dialing Mr. Malau's number and raising the phone to my ear.

"I've not changed my mind," the alpha barked the second the line picked up. "Wolf business is wolf—"

"Ty's alive." The next words I spoke, the recounting of events and Ty's actions, had deafening silence radiating through the speaker. "Did you hear me? I said, Ty's alive. And if Harper is too, that's exactly where he'll be. With his brother."

"Are—are you sure?"

A father in denial, and I couldn't blame him. Regardless of his tough-alpha act, he'd been through hell over the last six months. Lost both his sons. And now there was a chance to get them back.

"He tried to bite me. Infect me. He came for *me*. So, yeah. I'm sure. Which means you have only one choice. Use me as bait. As the only means that can turn Ty back to the way he used to be. And if there's a chance for Harper, if he's still alive like Ty is now, I'll save him, too."

"You…" More silence passed, only the rattled breath of a father that was shocked beyond words breaking through. "You would do that for me? For them? For both of them?"

"In a heartbeat." There was no doubt, no hesitation, and no uncertainty. And this time, I wouldn't fail. "Just say when and where, and I'm there."

"Once-a-week infiltrations aren't enough. We need to hit this hard and fast." That drive and passion had returned to Mr. Malau's voice. That certainty that we could tackle the task ahead of us and come out on top. The sound of an alpha in his element. "I'll make the arrangements. I'll source the locations. We'll hit everything back-to-back. In four days I'll pick you up in the forest outside the walls. Marika will be in touch to relieve you."

I found that spot again, across the town siding the scorched field where beheaded bodies would soon be carted. In those minutes after my nightmare when Kendrick had stormed from my room, had Ty really been there? Had some of those other sightings been real? If he was coming after me, had he been keeping tabs on me all this time? I couldn't know for sure. But I at least suspected he had.

Now the time had finally come. We would find Ty and Harper. And we would save them. Screw the consequences. Screw the effect restoring their lives would have on me. I wasn't going to fail this time.

I sighed deeply, wrist throbbing as I clutched the amulet hanging from my neck. "I'll see you then, Alpha."

I hung up and went inside to my bedside table, pulling out the wooden drawer as I dropped onto the bed's edge. From inside, I plucked Ty's stake out and it gleamed under the lamplight. This weapon had been intended for Ty, given to me by his father when all hope had been lost. Now we had a chance. And there was one heart that this stake was intended for. One heart that it would make beat. Scratch that. Make it two hearts. Ty's and Harper's. This stake was reserved for them and them alone.

MY SIGHT SHIFTED to Kendrick again and stayed there for painful, drawn-out seconds. Still, he wouldn't look at me. Wouldn't even acknowledge I existed. The nudges I sent out through our bond were repelled back like being snapped by an electric fence. The only clue that he'd felt the attempts was the tight ticking of a muscle along his clenched jaw.

This had been going on since the boardroom meeting started. Me, sitting across the slab of marble, looking, waiting, hoping. It was like I was dead to him, a source of anguish he couldn't with-stand. With his blocks up, I couldn't read his thoughts. Had he found out I'd known Ty was alive? Was that why he was so detached from me? I didn't know. And it looked like I wasn't going to find out anytime soon.

The royals did most of the talking throughout the meeting. Kendrick barely uttered a word. They each aired their thoughts and opinions on what had happened and what needed to happen now. Beyond the tall Gothic windows, the sun was now rising over the mountainous horizon. A golden hue crept over the town toward the manicured gardens. The boardroom's thick blackout drapes were drawn, but by whom I wasn't sure.

I lifted my dropped gaze to Kendrick again as the wrought iron chandelier beamed on.

Still nothing.

So far I'd caught on that before the attacks more and more reports had come in of vamps going missing. Not killed or slaughtered like they had been, but MIA. At the mention, déjà vu had registered in the back of my mind. Like I'd heard that information before. But when I tried to think into it deeper, my head started to pulse like it had been sucker punched with a sledgehammer.

Now tasks had been set. A hall to be cleansed under royal and guard supervision in case any bodies reanimated. Beheadings to be carried out on all the dead, and a pyre to honor the families' losses. Guards' recoveries to be monitored down in the cells, and transitionees to be watched for. Lastly, every perimeter ward needed to be checked. To prevent another ambush, we needed to know how the damned had snuck through.

With the entire community on high alert, the enemies' message had been received. We weren't safe, and they'd come and take whatever they wanted—whenever they wanted. Unless we did something to stop them.

Now everyone was assigned their tasks. Mine was to accompany Vanessa to check the wards. Another possible task was to decide

Caius's fate. Despite my expectation, it seemed the traitor hadn't run. He'd stayed behind and let the guards capture him. Let them drag him back down to that cell and shackle him. After being bitten in place of me and biting Ty himself, he was now in transition. Being his daughter, the RVC had voted to give me the choice on whether he now lived through the process or died. After that? They were happy to let him rot away the rest of his existence.

I spared no thought for him now, or for the choice I had to make.

Instead, my gaze settled on Kendrick again. He was all I could think about, because as long as we weren't good, my life was in ruin. And for every second that I got no response, it felt like the air was getting thinner and thinner, my throat closing up, and my lungs squeezing in my chest.

Without me realizing, the meeting adjourned and the other royals stood up suddenly and made for the exit. Kendrick rose too, catching sight of Raven through the now open doors. She smiled, maroon chips in her irises sparkling as she waved.

I darted in front of him before he could step out. "Kendrick, please. *Please.* I need to speak to you. We need to talk about this."

His eyes slid from Raven and down to me, but there was no other movement. Not in his expression. Not in his body under his loose cargos and Burton T-shirt. Not in his open hands. There was no anger. No Sadness. No *anything*. There was just...emptiness. "I can't do this right now, Amelia. I need to go check on the guards down in the cells."

"I know, but—"

"Not now." The sudden sharpness of his voice had me stepping back and out of his way. And he spared not even a glance as he kept on walking out the door.

Concern riddled Raven's round features as he reached her, and she rushed to follow at his side as he stalked toward the main hall.

I stared after him as he passed the stage and disappeared around the bend. All that was left of his escape from me? His and Raven's shoe prints in the red and black blood and soot dirtying the stone ground. My eyelids slid shut over growing tears—then flung open as my iPhone buzzed from my hoodie's pocket. Body tight and with a single tear sliding down my cheek, I forced my shaking hands to retrieve and work the phone.

A one-liner from Kendrick. Not a message through our bond.

'Meet me at the gazebo at nine a.m.'

"You brought this on yourself."

I tore my gaze from the stage Kendrick had disappeared beyond and found Vanessa loitering in the corridor with four guards.

Hands on hips and covered in fitted black leather, one spiked heel tapped. "So how long have you known?"

Asking for clarification was redundant. I knew exactly what—or should I say who—she was talking about. Ty. Our one sore point since we'd first met. Hating how I felt like a pinned bug under her stare, I walked away. Minding the blood that had leaked from good and evil around the bombsite of smashed and strewn pews, I headed for the castle's iron-braced doors. "There've been sightings." Four guards flanked us as she followed, heels clipping stone with strong strides. They each held drawn swords in one hand and opened thick-skinned umbrellas as we stepped onto the landing outside. "I thought I was going bat-shit."

Which was a shitload better than believing that all those times, Ty had actually been there. Stalking me. Taunting me. Tearing me apart, physically and mentally. Because the reality was too cruel. To accept that Ty was—like Madam Rosalie had said—changed. The Ty I had and still did love with every fiber of my being was dead. And now that his replacement was out there, the fear that I'd never get the old Ty back terrified me.

"I never thought…"

A familiar face appeared up the stairs from the cobblestone road as rising daylight coated us. A knitted sweater and jeans over boots sheltered his body. A scarf covered his neck and dark sunglasses shielded his eyes, leaving only hints of his face exposed. From the set of his expression, he felt the sting that reminded all Pure Bloods of what they risked losing if they killed. Immunity from the sun. But something darker formed the frown lines across his brow. "Lamayli's safely on her way back to Portsmouth. And…I'm guessing the hot topic right now is Ty."

"She knew he was alive," Vanessa accused, going to take my brother's hand.

I blew air through my nose and stomped past her, jumped the stairs and marched down the road. Weaving through the shrubs then trees to the first perimeter, six sets of feet crunched over grass behind me. The barrier was made up of the same stone the castle had been built with, solid sections that spanned out between squared-out pillars of glossy, black marble.

I sighed and a broad hand over my shoulder had me turning to face my unwanted company. Dorian's jaw was set, his lips pressed into a tight line. "Is it true?"

"Fan out," I instructed the four guards with a sharp nod. When they were far enough away, I stared down at my Vans, the shoes I'd worn when I'd chased Ty through the gardens. A day and a week ago when I'd started something with Kendrick. When I'd convinced myself my eyes were lying. But this whole time I'd been lying to myself. And everyone else. "I didn't want to believe it. But yes." I sighed again, and the memory of Ty's dangerous and cold hands on me made me shiver. "It was all confirmed yesterday."

Dorian slung an arm around me and held me close. His exhale fanned over my loose hair. "So what's your plan now?"

I wasn't going into detail with the guards milling around. But I didn't need to. "Arrangements have been made."

"Then we're in." The accusation and some of the anger left Vanessa's face. Where motives were concerned, she apparently trusted mine. "But first…we need to secure the Armaya."

Thankful for the task, distraction, and their acceptance, I shrugged out of Dorian's hold and faced the wall.

Inside the perimeter, gold symbols were etched into the marble pillars. One glamoured the wall to make it appear as a ten-foot, electrified chain-link fence, with a rolling nature reserve beyond. Another mark gave anyone who got close a shot of electric pain. A deterrent for any humans that somehow made it past the first razor wire fence to this one, stopping them from climbing up and over. A blood symbol stopped anyone from entering who'd ingested one of The Seven's Pure Blood. Thanks to Vanessa. Another collection of swirls and lines prevented temporary or ingested marks from granting entry without setting off the alarms. One of the remaining marks weakened any non-vamps who passed. And the last triggered the alarm if any damage was done to the barrier from the outside. Every base had been covered.

"This one's intact," Vanessa said, running her hand over the engraved symbols.

"Only another thousand or so to go," Dorian said, now more comfortable with his girlfriend and ex-sister re-allied. Not to mention the borrowed shade of the surrounding trees.

For the alarms not to have reacted to the damned climbing the wall, one had to have been damaged. Which would mean someone inside the castle had let them in. A damned trying to disarm the wards would trip the alarm first.

"Great," I said, my thoughts still too stuck on death, Ty, and Kendrick to give much more of a response.

I walked on and they followed, talking quietly to themselves as we cleared one set of wards after the next. The process could have been much faster, but I wasn't in the mood to shoot around in a blink. I needed something to keep me moving, one foot after the other, to keep my brain and heart from imploding. Trying to figure out what to do about Kendrick, what to tell him about my plans with Mr. Malau... *Shit.* I kept on walking. I was screwed, heart, mind, and soul. Totally—

"Amelia, wait!" Dorian called after me.

I jolted out of my tortured headspace and whirled. *Dammit.* I hoped they'd been checking the marks, because I sure as shit hadn't. "Did you find a damaged ward?"

"No." Vanessa drew her hand away from the pillar's gold markings, her mind clearly spinning behind her sapphire eyes. "They're intact."

"So we'll keep going then."

Dorian frowned at me while the guards spaced out around us and the trees danced in a gentle wind. "We've already been full-circle, Amelia. Every ward has been checked. Not a single one was damaged. No one inside let them in."

"What?" Through my hijacked thoughts, I hadn't noticed the last hour or two pass. "That doesn't make sense. How can they all be set? The damned broke in *somehow.*"

Dorian put a hand out to lean against a tree and cupped the other over his jaw and chin. "Dug their way in?"

Vanessa shook her head, red hair swaying. "No. The same force field that acts like a dome spanning up from every mark also penetrates the ground."

"Like a sphere surrounding everything above and below the property," I said.

"Exactly." Vanessa tapped her lip, deep in thought. "Which means they got in some other way."

"What other way is there?" I slumped back against a cool marble post, propping one leg up. A slice of sunlight broke through the surrounding trees and warmed my skin.

"A mark," Vanessa blurted. She came closer and whispered into my ear. "After I put up the blood block, I sourced a combating mark. Just in case you needed it." She touched a pillar mark that prevented ingested blood of The Seven from working. "The mark I have is the only way to get in."

Vanessa wasn't giving too much away, but I knew exactly what she was talking about. Marika. For if and when I ever needed the cover again.

"The damned can't be marked," Dorian pointed out. A fact we'd all learned back when Vanessa had tried to mark me before we'd set off to rescue Ty from execution.

"Not as far as I know," she said. "But what other explanation is there?"

My leg fell off the marble pillar. "There is none. A mark is the only way. Which means the damned commander has an alchemist, and a way we don't know about to mark his army."

KENDRICK SAT in the gazebo with his back to me, facing the thick trees that grew beyond the field. His head was down, staring at his hands, and my link to him was so vaulted shut, a bomb blast couldn't have broken down the walls. But I didn't need the link to know what was bothering him. It had everything to do with me and that fact that Ty was alive. His protective detail saw my approach but made no move to announce my arrival, and there was no point in asking them to *take a walk*. After the latest invasion and all the deaths, a few yards was the most they'd allow. Same as the four guards who surrounded me, their steps across the marbled mash of vibrant grass and burnt earth as silent as my own.

With the beheading of bodies taking place during the remaining light hours, the pile of dead hadn't yet begun to be built. Thank God. With my reason for being here, I already felt sick enough without witnessing the headless being carted here for the pyre.

When I was close enough that my Vans touched the gazebo's shadow, I paused. I still had no idea what to say. Regret stained the slate of my soul like all the blood that had been spilled today.

"Did you know?"

I flinched at Kendrick's sudden question, my heart jumping into my throat. With a few deep breaths, I came around to the gazebo entrance, trying to ignore the tree-sheltered audience of our lingering guards. Kendrick's head remained down, face frozen in an almost-scowl at his hands. "I didn't know there was going to be an attack. I didn't know he was leading—"

"You know that's not what I mean."

Still no movement, no eye contact. Something inside me was slowly breaking. Even with his blocks up, the pain of loss pouring off him was monumental. He was hurt, confused, and everything else because of me. Because I'd let truth become deception. Taken what should have been words between us and left it to cruel fate. He thought he'd lost me now that Ty was alive. Had he? I didn't know. But I did know what he was asking me. Before the attack led by Ty, I had known he was still alive. "Yes."

That one simple, soft-spoken word made him jerk like I'd slapped him. Still he didn't look at me. "You lied to me?" Disbelief colored his quiet, harsh words. "You were just stringing me on. Using me."

"No." I bounded into the shelter and dropped to my knees, clutching his hands. A few small sparks escaped my fingers before I could rein in the static. Kendrick didn't even seem to notice. "I was going to tell you. The dream I had during the masquerade ball, especially with how it all happened. I never even thought it could be real. I thought my mind was messing with me. But then the second one? I wasn't sure anymore. That's why I brought Madam Rosalie here." Looking up, I found his eyes tunneling down into mine and I quickly looked away. "That's when I found out they weren't just dreams."

"Dreamscapes."

I dared to look up, that severe expression now a vacant stare that reeked of realized acceptance.

Kendrick pushed my hands aside and stood. "It was good while it lasted."

I all but lunged for his hands and pulled him back down. "Kendrick, stop. Wait. I never said we were over. I just..." Words died in my throat, because I wouldn't lead him on. I couldn't profess my love and make promises that might lead to breaking his heart even more than I already had. And I wouldn't lie. Not again. I dropped the floodgate wall I'd perfected holding up. Memories and feelings poured out, a dam breaking its banks over the city of my mind. Everything was on display, the good, the bad, and the regretful. Nothing was hidden. "See for yourself."

Staring into my eyes, Kendrick hissed, seeing into the core of my very soul, reliving every moment and emotion that accompanied it. It all played out in our minds at the same time like a movie, our surroundings and the guards becoming nothing more than noiseless shadows. Every moment I'd spent seeking Ty out, my hopes and fears with every useless lead. My developing feelings for Kendrick with his forever-loyal support, even in spite of the times he'd done things behind my back. My internal struggles with my promise to

Ty, and the aftermath when I truly thought he was gone forever. As the beginning of our redefined relationship played out, Kendrick's lips curved. They fell moments later at seeing my dreamscapes with Ty. The kiss he'd dared me to take. The how of Ty's continued existence. Lastly, he saw my desperate need to find a way tell him everything I'd kept hidden, without breaking his heart or obliterating everything we had been and had now become.

The replay shut off when he reached the moment from just before when I'd crossed the field to come talk to him. The sun had inched higher above the horizon, long tree and gazebo shadows shrinking by the second. Our guards, still keeping close watch from the shadows of trees, opened umbrellas above their heads to block the rising sun.

Golden light bathed Kendrick's pale face in warm tones, making it look like he had a tan. The tingle of being exposed danced over his face and neck, but he didn't reposition himself. He just sat there, his own thoughts unreadable and body so still I shivered at the memory of seeing Ty in that same frozenness. If not for the small rise and fall of his chest, I could have believed he was a beautiful, broken statue.

And I'd done the breaking.

When the lack of response continued, I slowly stood up. Tears made the scenery and Kendrick's face look like I was viewing them underwater. I blinked and turned away, cold drops rolling down my face. "I'm sorry. I'm so—"

Before my first steps away could meet grass, a broad hand caught my wrist. I spun into Kendrick, our faces so close his cool breath ruffled my eyelashes. "You're falling for me."

It wasn't a question, but I nodded with a sniffle. I couldn't deny the true feelings I now harbored for my best friend. Feelings that had grown into so much more than friendship.

"But you still love him. You don't know what your heart wants."

"Kendrick, I—"

"Love isn't black and white." His free hand cupped my neck and his thumb slid over my jaw to my bottom lip. "It's a spectrum. It's not right or wrong. It just is. I can't fault your feelings, and I can't make you choose. But consider this. Madam Rosalie said it herself —*'The boy you love no longer exists.'* Ty is alive in a way, but he's not the same. He's damned. His soul is fractured. He doesn't love you anymore. *He can't.*"

But I can save him now. The thought was all hope and despair wrapped up in a tight ball that batted around in my chest.

"And I'll help you."

My head cranked up, eyes searching Kendrick's. *"Why?"*

"For a chance." His hand dropped and he stared out at the scorched center of the field. Now rich and vibrant with increasing sunlight, fresh green blades patched the scarred earth. After sundown and hours of burning, the earth would be as black as damned blood all over again. "We'll find Ty and you'll restore him, make his heart beat and realign his soul. If he returns to himself, if his love for you lives again, I'll stand aside—if that's what you want. If it doesn't—and if you still want me—I'm yours."

My hands came up to rest over his chest. Beneath his toned pecs and rising and falling ribs, his heart was suffering a battle of its own. "Why are you doing this?"

A ghost of a smile curved his mouth. His gaze returned to mine, warmth radiating from his silver-blue eyes. "Because I love you, Amelia. I want you to be happy. In whatever way that comes."

CHAPTER 24

*A*fter the two a.m. funeral pyre, I made my way to the cells. My whip, dagger, and stake clattered at my belt, echoed by my four shadows' swords as I descended the stairs. Smoke from the burned bodies wafted off my Under Armour gear, so pungent I was sure washing wouldn't cleanse the tight material. And I didn't mind that. The deceased needed to be remembered well beyond the point where their bodies had combusted into ash.

With the RVC's vote, I had a decision to make. But like hell if I'd figured out that one yet. I didn't know if I could bring myself to restore Caius, my attempted murderer, my father—any more than I could just stand back and let the transition kill him. Good thing I had some questions I needed answered first to buy me some time.

Facing Caius's cell door, no order was needed for a guard to unlock the solid barrier. When it swung wide, the same throat-constricting smell of bleach ballooned out into the round waiting area. I covered my mouth, breathing through my fingers as I went inside alone and shut the door. With the prisoner restrained by marked silver shackles that bolted to the wall, the guards had accepted exclusion. But I knew they were listening and waiting right outside the unbolted door.

Sitting on the uneven stone ground in his same disheveled clothes—now bleached clean of black and red blood—Caius glanced up. He was in transition, slowly becoming damned until the point that taking a vampire's life would complete the process. Or kill him if he didn't. The evidence was clear in the graying of his flesh, visible on his face and neck and through the slashes in his dirty shirt and pants. It was also obvious in the color of his pupils—no longer dull silver but rimmed with red. And the long stretching breaks between each of his heartbeats, and the lack of breath that passed through his pasty lips. His frozen scowl accompanied the sizzling red welts at his wrists from his restraints. But as his bleary eyes met mine, the pain in his expression lifted, as if in appreciation. "Ah, my daughter. I wondered how long it would take."

I hated that he called me that, but I had more important things to discuss. "Take for what?"

"You are here to demand answers." Caius winced, then almost smiled, shifting to clasp tight hands over one propped knee. "You need to know why I did what I did…before my brain fries from the transition—or my living body dies. Why I saved your mother. Why I took that boy's bite for you."

"And why you didn't go with the damned?" I hoped for the truth, but I didn't expect it. Caius had always been a flawless weaver of lies and deception. "Why let the guards catch you so easily?"

"For the latter, I wanted to be caught. With what I now know, I have no place with those creatures. As for Lamayli? Keeping her safe was an act of love. Because even after all we've done to each other, I do and will always love her. And as for you, my dear daughter—"

Caius's face pinched as he listed sideways and curled in on himself, heaving. Bile sprayed out across the dark stone, tainted by blood. He twisted onto his back, head smacking stone and knees knocking. Violent convulsions overcame his body, rattling his shackles but keeping the distance between us from shrinking.

Instinct made me want to rush forward, to help, somehow. But I kept my Vans planted. This was Caius, and though the tremors seemed real, I wasn't about to fall for a trick. Wasn't about to let him take me as his victim to turn his already still heart to permanent black stone. Plus watching this jittery display threatened to take me back in time to a memory I didn't want to relive again.

Less than a minute more and with a final full-body quake, the tremors receded. Caius sagged against the stone, gasping as his slack head tilted. "A s-low process," he stammered, struggling to slide his body sideways and back to meet the wall. "Though the break between fits is rather fast."

He grunted, still twitching as he used his frail arms to lever himself up against the wall, knees propped and arms draped over them. He coughed and blood sprayed across his arm. With a shaky wipe across his mouth he became still once more.

"It was my instinct," Caius rasped. He coughed blood again but seemed beyond the effort of smearing it away with his dirty hands. "To protect you."

Shaken out of the shock of watching Caius convulsing, I stepped forward and clenched my fists. "You're full of shit." I suddenly had the urge to hit Caius, for all he'd done to me and everything he'd taken from me. "You're the one who drained the life from my fucking veins, asshole."

"Which I am glad you survived," Caius snapped, looking anything but. He sighed hard then coughed, lungs refusing to draw air. His shaking hands ran down his face, smearing dirt streaks across his cheeks. "I saved your life because aside from who you are to me…I knew what was intended for you. That you would be turned. Not killed. For a purpose you would then be powerless to refuse."

When he paused, it was as if he were waiting for me to question his claims. But I'd heard this rant before. This cryptic, bullshit rant. If he'd wanted to lay it all out in black and white, he would have. "Are you done?"

"No." A short moment of hesitation passed. "I have a favor to ask."

There was the ulterior motive I was waiting for. The one I knew had been the drive to his seemingly heroic actions. Once a traitorous murderer, always a traitorous murderer. "And that is?"

Caius's red-ringed eyes drilled into me, determined and almost hopeful. "Find our family and restore them. You owe me that—"

Caius's face twisted and he slammed sideways, skull cracking on the stone. Convulsions took over, even more violent than before. And they didn't let up. Minutes passed as I remained rooted to the spot. Five. Ten. Still, it didn't stop.

Watching from mere feet away, I couldn't keep the past from flooding back. Though I knew where I was and who was suffering, I suddenly saw Ty. Convulsing in that warehouse, his teeth chattered. His skull hit the ground over and over. His arms were ripped with muscle but powerless to help. Then his mouth frothed and he became still. Dead, or so I had thought.

With a hard blink, the memory faded. The convulsions still had control of Caius's body, his brittle bones knocking the ground and wall beside him, and his skin grating over the rough surface. He grunted and groaned, the guttural sounds torn from his throat. As it went on and on, I wondered if it would ever stop—or if Caius would still be alive when it did. With each new tear in his clothes, more and more grazes covered his body. Blood began streaming from the cuts, being expelled in a rush rather than leaking out. Then froth spurted from his mouth. Like it had from Ty's. Caius, my murderer, and the man who'd taken that lethal bite for me yesterday, my father, was dying.

Sudden urgency, the understanding that I'd lose the option possibly in seconds had my mind made up. I may never forgive Caius for everything he'd done. And he had to pay for the lives he'd ruined. Still, deserving or not, I wouldn't be responsible for his death. Someone else could make that call.

I tugged a silver stake from my hoodie and lunged at Caius. Flattening him on his back, I lifted the silver over my head. Then I drove the stake straight into his heart with a release of blue voltage. Light exploded around us, and then Caius's body slumped. His eyes stared up at me, red-rings fading to vampire-blue. Blood no longer poured from the cuts covering him.

With a twisting yank, I pulled the stake free, jumped up, and stumbled to the door. God, I was suddenly dizzy. And starving. My legs felt like putty. The air in my lungs was dense, weak of oxygen. But I didn't dwell. Didn't listen for his first breath. Didn't wait for his heart to reanimate. "I owe you nothing," I said as I slipped out.

SITTING cross-legged on the edge of the garden fountain, I squeezed my eyes shut so tight I began to see stars. With a quick trip back to my suite, I'd downed four bottles of Kendrick's blood. With everything going on between us, it had been his idea to revert from taking his vein. To take that crossed line off the table. To remove complication and temptation until I could figure out what I wanted, or should I say who. Even with his hidden emotions, I knew it had hurt him to offer the change. Still, he didn't want to pressure me.

Appreciation aside, the alternative couldn't compare. I felt dehydrated, like my arteries were pushing around sludge. But at least the jitters after restoring Caius had died off. And my voltage was still on recharge.

Good thing, with what I was planning to do.

I hadn't asked Caius anything about the damned commander's location...or Ty. One, because he wouldn't have spilled anything. And two, if I wanted concrete intel and not full-of-shit words, I had a better chance of digging up clues myself. Mr. Malau was already on lead-seeking duty, but waiting just wasn't in my nature.

Which is why I'd snuck out here alone.

Every day Ty was out there—especially after I'd given up on finding him—was one day too many. I'd made promises to him and I'd broken them. I'd sworn to his father that I'd save him, and I'd failed. I'd begun a relationship with Kendrick and taken his vein. I was a cheater and a liar. And there was only one way to make up for it. I'd find Ty and I'd restore him, make his heart beat again like I'd done to the damned girl, Raven. Like I'd now done for Caius. And after that? I didn't have a freaking clue.

The not-quite full moon was lower in the sky, its glow illuminating the surrounding trees and manicured hedges. With the noise of the fountain—and all the mess inside my head—getting to that black void was grueling. Keeping Kendrick out after sneaking from my suite was taking a toll, too.

I pressed my palms over my sockets and added pressure. The stars turned into starbursts, a beautiful display of white-light fireworks. But it was working. The noise of gently flowing water, soft breeze-rustling leaves, and distant street sounds faded. That remote black emptiness rose, blocking out everything. Tightness strapped over my chest, the feel claustrophobic as the blackness caved in.

No shadows. No slime.

My breath sucked in and became barricaded in my lungs, unable to exhale to draw fresh air in to feed my body oxygen.

I was drowning.

I scrambled for air before a hole punctured through and my surroundings cleaved into focus. In a grand room of stone, dark carpet, and mirrors, I saw a four-poster bed with a crib lined up by its side. Red silk draped from the canopy and decorated the mattress, covering a panting and heavily sweating woman. Her dark blond hair was splayed over mounds of silk pillows as well as plastered to her forehead. She grabbed the red covers with long nails and wailed, her fangs peeking out from her gaping mouth.

This didn't seem right. There was no damned. No commander. No Ty.

A shadow moved from an adjoining room to her side, their back to me as he clasped her hand. The way he moved and the mature build of him locked my attention. His hair was salt and pepper, his ash-colored suit with red trim, pristine. "You must breathe through the pain," the man said in a voice that was thick with concern.

With a jolt, I couldn't confuse who'd said those words, even with his back turned and that hint of abnormal emotion. Caius.

The woman nodded with wide eyes, her hand in his clutching so tight her knuckles looked ready to split skin. Her face pinched and she began hyperventilating. "Oh no, no-no-no. It's coming." She shoved the red covering down, a white nightgown covering her swollen belly. "Right—" She pressed back into the pillows, face scrunching as a scream tore from her throat.

Caius kept hold of her hand while her free one splayed, grabbing onto the bedding like it was a cliff's edge and she was about to fall.

"It is time to push." His free hand grabbed a towel from the stack on the end of the bed, tousling it before draping it over her propped knees. In the position he sat, he blocked the view between her legs. The woman held her breath and pushed, her face turning tomato red. More sweat sprouted across her brow and even soaked through her nightgown from her chest. The pushing continued, taking the color from her complexion and leaving her sickly white. She released her breath again, and this time slumped against the pillows, eyes spacing out at the red canopy above. "Stay with me," Caius grated, body tensing. "Push. *Push again*."

The woman's head lolled side to side. Was she about to pass out?

Caius leaned forward, shoulders connecting with her shins as he snatched her hands, and pulled. "Push!"

Levered up, the woman cried out before clamping her lips shut. Blood spurted from where her fangs punctured and a grunt replaced her agony until there was no sound left. When Caius released her hands she dropped back against the pillows, face lost in the padding. Another towel was grabbed and wrapped around the newborn that had a thin halo of dark hair.

Caius moved to the side, vigorously rubbing the baby's chest and body. *"Breathe dammit."* His hand ran over its cheek, his index finger going to the baby's throat. His shoulders slumped. Relief or despair? He slid a duffel bag out from under the bed and placed the wrapped baby inside, leaving it unzipped before carrying it from the room. There was the sound of a door I couldn't see opening, then quietly closing.

Minutes passed as I stayed in the vision, my stare locked on the woman lying on the bed. Her face was slack, no muscle control to hold an expression in place.

She was dead.

The unseen door reopened and shoes treaded over soft carpet.

Caius appeared through the opening, the baby still wrapped in the bloody towel in his arms. Had he revived it? A sudden cry filled the quiet room and my heart lifted with relief. The crying continued as Caius placed the bundle down and unwrapped the naked baby. He held him up before his eyes. But something was wrong.

This wasn't the same baby.

With such pale hair, the strands were almost invisible against its scalp. Not so dark they were almost black. A pink line marked the stomach on its tiny body, too. I stared in confusion as Caius placed the now quiet baby into the dead woman's arms with care. He collected blood from the sheets onto his palms and smeared it over the baby's clean skin. A scalpel appeared from the inside pocket of his suit jacket. "Time to play your role—my son." He bent, lips brushing the baby's forehead. Then he sliced the pink scar that swelled with instant red. The infant's cry cut the silence as Caius straightened. "Guards! Call for help!"

"Oomph." Sudden rising pressure knocked the air from my lungs and propelled me back to reality. Darkness blinded me, taking away my sight while my other senses compensated. Something soft-yet-prickly tickled the backs of my arms and neck. A constant patter broke the surface of water somewhere nearby. Cool air feathered over my exposed face and arms, carrying with it the scent of fresh bark and cut grass. A familiar metallic taste stained my tongue. My eyelids cracked and I went to sit upright, but my spinning head brought me back down.

With a few long deep breaths, the spinning died off. I levered up on shaky elbows and wetness trickled over my lip into my mouth. I wiped it away, realizing I was on the grass at the base of the fountain before seeing the red smear across my arm. Bloody nose. And...*ow.* A grinding gut that demanded attention. But after what I'd witnessed it would have to wait.

Unlike some of my other visions, I knew with total clarity what I had seen. Caius had left no doubt with his words, *Time to play your role, my son.*

I'd seen Lady Vladimir holding that baby before. In a photo.

I knew who my twin was. I had been one of three that Caius had used in his more recent experiments. A scar from that was now an almost invisible white line across my stomach. The mirror of that mark had been re-cut into the fair-haired baby by Caius. The man who'd raised him when his own supposed father couldn't bear the sight of him.

Marcus wasn't the last surviving Vladimir. If the birthed baby had survived, Dorian likely was. Marcus, with his Caius-fed lies, was the son of a traitor.

My true twin.

CHAPTER 25

I took off through the garden, not bothering to scour the castle for Marcus. With the regular RVC meeting canceled in the wake of the pyre, and with the time of day, something told me exactly where I needed to go to find my twin.

Taking to the streets, I pelted to a place he was a regular at. Fear at how he'd take the news pounded my heart as I pulled to a stop outside *Bite*. Pumping club music radiated through the walls out to the street. The red neon sign flashed above and I pushed through the doors, revealing the club's raging belly. The lights over the dance floor were strobing, while the outer booth seating was dark and moody. Vamps milled around the bar being served, and I glanced away from the others who filled the many booths. Each had company: a human they were snacking on in plain sight.

None of them were Marcus.

Still, the view made my mouth water and fangs throb. The gurgle of my gut almost cut through the loud pumping music.

I didn't turn away, though. A strange sensation, an inkling that I was right where I needed to be, had me weaving around the velvet-swathed lounges to the centralized bar.

The bartender caught sight of me and ignored a guy he was serving to rush over. He dipped his head. "Lady Bathory, what can I get for you?"

Before finding Marcus, I needed to strap a leash on my hunger. Preferably before the dizzies came back. "Tall glass of whatever's freshest."

A nod and a smile, and a few seconds later I had a glass of human blood in hand. Chugging and benching the glass, I retreated to the shadows by the back wall. Sharpening my senses, I glanced around again, certain he was here, somewhere. A quiet sound froze my swiveling gaze. It had come from the opening to my right, the hall that led down to *The Pit*. Someone was down there.

No bouncer blocked the way, and I checked that no one was looking over before hurdling the velvet rope into the corridor. The quiet noise was louder here, the sound of wet lips on flesh. There was a scent, too. Fresh blood. I kept moving forward, curiosity set on overdrive with that strange sensation daring me to keep going. Gentle light grew as I crept down the curved stairwell, the kerosene wall lanterns throwing devious shadows as I met the landing.

I sucked in my breath.

The same partitions were set in intervals around the curved wood-braced chamber, with seats positioned between each divider. The humans who were meant to be sitting dazed in those seats weren't there. Their bodies, male and female, lay strewn about the ground, throats messy and the smell of blood thick in the air. Three guards' bodies lay among the carnage. My voice escaped in a quiet rush. *"What the hell?"*

The guy holding up a fourth guard he was hunched over with his fangs buried deep in, dropped the body and spun. A snarl of threat scored Marcus's face, which fell with instant guilt at the sight of me. He blinked slowly and breathed in deep, making not a single other movement. "What are you doing here?"

Words fought their way up my throat but died before they could escape. Face a bloody mess with red streaks from his mouth down to his neck and staining his white shirt, was my brother. My twin. Seeing those bodies and knowing what he'd done made me want to puke. *"W-why?"*

"I didn't. I mean..." Marcus came forward and clutched my elbows, fear rather than fierce threat driving his expression. "It's not what you think." He looked to the bodies. *"Listen."*

I tuned my hearing past the pounding of my own heart to pick up something else. Faint heartbeats. The humans weren't dead. And neither were the guards. But they weren't without needing help. They'd been consumed to within an inch of their lives. "You've almost drained every one of them."

Marcus released my elbows and dropped his head, staring down at his shiny shoes. "My hunger, it's...been growing. Every. Single. Day. It's like no matter how much I take, it's never enough."

I understood that feeling well, had suffered with my own hunger needs from the start, and again with every change to my powers. Hunger for blood was a result of being a vampire, but his and my abnormal need for more than normal sustenance was a result of something bigger than us. It had been forced onto us because of Caius's experiments. Because of our powers—

"You think I'm a monster," Marcus said suddenly.

"What? No." I reached out and squeezed his shoulder. When I'd almost killed, I hadn't been condemned for it. I'd been offered help and support. And this wasn't who he was, any more than any of that had been the real me. We were pawns in a deadly game of chess. "This isn't your fault."

Marcus's head snapped up, surprise dancing in his teal-flecked eyes. "How could it not be?"

There was no going back from this, and there was no way I'd ever want to. The truth needed to come to light. Good, bad, and ugly. "You believe your mother died while giving birth to you. But she didn't. It was all a lie. That woman was never your mother. And that scar proves—"

"Amelia, no." Marcus stepped back, square-toed shoes hitting a body and preventing further retreat. Frowning up from the mess he'd made, he shook his head. "We've gone over this before. The cut is a birth ritual—"

"That Caius re-cut the day you were supposedly born. I saw it all." I tapped beside my eye. "Lady Vladimir birthed a dark-haired baby. One Caius switched for his blond-haired son. A son who already had a scar that he reopened that day. Don't you see, Marcus? He passed you off as hers. Lamayli and Caius are your parents. His experiment created this hunger in you just like it did in me. Marcus...you're my twin."

Marcus stood frozen for a long time, expression masked as I waited. After minutes that felt like hours and had my heart doing suicide jumps in my chest, he thawed. One hand extended to clasp mine. He lifted our joined hands between us to eye level. Streaks of renewed power escaped from the ball I kept locked up inside my chest, drawn to his touch despite my restraint. But unlike every other time we touched, the power didn't disappear into his skin. Instead, it drew something out of him. Red volts that slid up his arm to our joined hands.

Before I could ask he explained. "Happened during the first Armaya invasion. Light split up from the ground."

I remembered that sonic boom and the glorious light that had exploded with it. "You didn't tell me."

"I didn't want to burden you. You already had so much going on. And I didn't know what it meant." Marcus smiled, and the drying blood across his chin cracked as a result. "Now I understand this undeniable need I've felt to protect you. To take action when Caius intended to kill you. It's ingrained in me to keep you safe." He drew me in, hand pressing my head to his chest. "My sister. My other half. My twin."

STEPPING out of my twin's embrace, I frowned at the unmoving bodies lying twisted on the ground. Each heartbeat was still detectable, quiet but detectable. "Now what do we do? With them? With what we know?"

With a deep frown, Marcus knelt down to one of the humans. "First, I'm going to fix what I've wrought." He bit into his wrist and pressed the punctures to her mouth before glancing up at me. "Have you told the RVC? Dorian?"

I hadn't thought that far ahead. "You don't want me to?"

The girl's heartbeat went from weak to steady and Marcus sighed. "I need time to process this. For my entire life I've known who I was. Who I was born to be. Now I'm the son of the traitor." Satisfied at the first recovery, he moved to the next human and fed them his blood. "Plus right now we have two votes. If the others discover we're both Caius's, we'll only have one, and only one seat for one ruler. And what about Dorian? If he is this Vladimir, the long-lost son and the only living descendant, would he want to take all this responsibility we now share onto himself?"

That I didn't know, but it wasn't my place to decide. "Then we talk to Dorian. He has a right to know."

"I agree," Marcus said as the second human's weak heart

strengthened. "Let me finish fixing what I've done here and then we'll find him."

A short while later all the humans had been treated and their minds scrubbed. As had the guards who Marcus compelled to wait outside the club. I led the way back up the stairwell and corridor and over the cordoning rope. Since I'd ventured downstairs, the club had gotten even busier. The dance floor was a flood with pale, non-sweating bodies, and most of the booths and lounges were filled. To my relief, most of the extra patrons were enjoying their fill from a glass, rather than from living donors. Still, with the few mouth-to-neck-or-wrist actions on going, I was glad to make it to the door and *so* ready to leave. The sight reminded me a little too much of whose flesh I'd been surviving off until recently.

"Hold up." I spun to see Marcus pointing to a booth in the back corner of the club on the other side of the central bar. "Isn't that Dorian?"

Far from needing to squint, my eyes widened at the view. "What the—?" I took off in his direction, dodging a guy who stood up suddenly and a group that was taking their sweet time to get to the bar. When I reached the booth, I put my hands on my hips. Marcus stepped up right beside me. He'd been right. It was Dorian, and he wasn't alone. His hands were all over a woman who definitely wasn't Vanessa, and his lips were sealed over her neck. *"Ah hem."*

Dorian slowly removed his mouth from her neck, waving a dismissive hand. "Got all I need on tap here, thanks."

His head lowered, ready to retake the woman's punctured neck. "I'm not a *freaking* waiter!"

That got his attention, head snapping around to see me. "Amelia!" He reached into his jacket and pulled out some notes before pressing them into the woman's hand as he leaned in to close the punctures with his tongue. "Thanks, gorgeous. We're done here."

The woman slid off the seat, leaving Dorian to himself. "What are you doing here?"

"Me?" I still couldn't believe what I'd just seen. This was classic old Dorian. Player Dorian. Dorian who could charm the pants off anyone and get them between the sheets. Since Marika had broken his heart, he'd changed. And he was far from unattached. "Does Vanessa know you're here?"

Dorian shrugged. "Food's food, whether it's in a pretty package or not. And my relationship with Vanessa is none of your business."

I stared in dumbfounded silence. This was not my brother. Well...that was right, wasn't it. But that wasn't what I meant. This wasn't the guy I'd seen mature over the last year. The Dorian before me was someone I didn't quite recognize. Was he acting out because he didn't feel like he belonged? Was he just reverting to old, comfortable ways?

"We have some news for you," Marcus said, breaking through the pulsing music and our stalemate stare. He slid onto the opposite side of the booth, leaving enough room for me to slide in after him. "It's about your bloodline. Your heritage."

Conflict forgotten, Dorian's interest peaked. "Really? You know who I am?"

No. Not at all, I thought. Though on the outside I nodded. "I think so. I saw it. Caius switched Lady Vladimir's dark haired baby with a blond one. Marcus was the baby passed off as a Vladimir, just like you were passed off as my brother. Which I think means..."

Marcus steepled his hands in a creepy way on the tabletop that gave me chills. The action was so like Caius and the times I'd sat across from him at his desk. "You must be the one true child born to the Vladimirs."

Dorian remained mute for a long while, a vacant stare on his face. A glimmer of sadness peeked through. "They're all dead. And I never even knew them." More silence. Then a flash of almost-anger transformed his face. "And what? Now I'm this person who's supposed to have a predetermined role?"

"It doesn't have to be that way," Marcus said, voice reasoning as he leaned back into the padded booth. "We haven't told anyone yet."

"Then don't tell them."

The Dorian I knew never hid from anything. Never shied away from life and all its challenges. "It's not that bad, Dorian. And I'll be there to help you. Being on the RVC gives you a voice, gives your family's line a vote."

"It also makes me a prisoner. If you tell them I could be a Vladimir, the only one now in existence, what do you think they'll do? Every royal is a prisoner here, except for me. Pure Blood by blood test or not, they don't know what line I belong to. They don't really believe I'm one of them. But if you tell them this…"

"He'll be a prisoner, too," Marcus said. "Unable to leave the compound without permission or sneaky measures like the rest of us."

"And what if it's not even true?" Dorian added. "Do you want them to exhume the dead lord or lady to prove that I'm theirs?"

I got up out of the booth and started pacing. I didn't know what to say, what to think. What to do. Letting Dorian bury this felt so very wrong.

"Look, it's up to you." Marcus slid out of the booth and ran a hand down my arm to still me. The buzz of energy was palpable between us, but nothing was visible on the surface. "If you want to tell them, I'll stand by you. If you decide to keep this on the DL for now, then so be it." He nodded to Dorian. "I'll leave it up to you both."

A new, louder beat than before started up and a smoke machine pumped fog around the dance floor. Marcus strode away through the growing crowd and haze, leaving us alone in the club's back corner. I met Dorian's eyes, the boy I'd believe was my brother until seven months ago. "Are you sure about this?"

"I've seen what it's done to you. How hard this whole lifestyle change has been." He slid across the seat and stood up, hands catching mine with a squeeze. "That's why I've stayed here. But I know nothing about how to rule." I began to argue, saying that I hadn't either, but Dorian talked over me. "And I don't want to learn. As long as Marcus is fine in playing the role, the one he was conditioned for his entire life, I'm happy to remain the outsider."

With a deep, unsettled sigh, I knew Dorian had made up his mind. And I wasn't sure if there was any good in trying to change it.

Dorian dropped my hands to sling his arm around my shoulders. "Besides, I'm no good in helping you save Ty if I'm locked up in here like the rest of you."

Despite Vanessa saying they were on board while checking the wards, we hadn't spoken about it further. "Really? After what happened, what he ordered here, you still want to help?"

Dorian shrugged. "Unless you plan to give up—"

"Never."

Dorian's arm around my shoulders squeezed. "Good, then. I have a plan. Just give me twenty-four hours."

CHAPTER 26

I found myself back inside the castle after walking Dorian home and wandering the streets and gardens. After sneaking back over the balcony to my suite and refueling hours ago, I'd ended up here outside Kendrick's door. Eight a.m. and sun out. Castle sleeping, but my mind wired.

So much had been unearthed today. The truth of the past. The identity of my twin. The connection and instinctual trust I had in Marcus now made perfect sense. We were blood, brought into existence together but separated for all this time. Now we had a chance to get to know each other as siblings.

In spite of the happy reunion, lingering confusion fogged up my mind. The side of Dorian I'd witnessed just didn't sit right. More than his reverting actions, something had seemed off. But I wasn't sure what. And now I was here, mere yards of stone and space separating me from the one person who'd been absent from it all, but who I was dying to tell.

With guards stationed at even intervals on either side of the door and my current ones joining suit, I pushed my way inside, closed the door behind me, and took a deep breath. My palms sprouted moisture and my lungs felt tight. The news I had was epic, but the state of our relationship was strained at best.

Shaking off my uncertainty, I padded around the foyer's white granite table and through the archway to the living room.

Empty.

Two voices drifted over from the right, and my head snapped sideways to glimpse into Kendrick's bedroom. The walls were plastered with Three Days Grace and Red posters, and a few snowboards were propped against the stone. The canopy bed he'd sat by holding his mother's hand before her funeral was no longer there. Instead, his bed from his old room with its tall wooden headboard sat in its place. The blue and orange striped bedding was crumpled. Kendrick sat there, legs stretched out and upper body propped back onto his elbows. Beside him was Raven, stomach down and legs bent up with her feet dangling. Her chin rested in her hands as she watched the wall-mounted screen playing snowboarding races.

"When there's more snow, you'll take me out there, right?" Raven glanced sideways at Kendrick and I saw her face, black hair shiny and eyes shimmering with so much more than excitement.

Kendrick smiled at her so genuinely it made me pause. There was no grief in that smile, no worry or concern. With everything he'd gone through, from risking his life to helping me save Ty, to being thrown into battle, to losing his mother and being forced into a life of custom and expectation, to having his open heart shredded by me, he was...*happy*. I hadn't seen him look at me with such true happiness even when I'd kissed him and told him I was ready to be with him. Even then I'd gotten a standoffish, *I don't know whether to believe this* look.

With them both facing the television, his head was near her legs and he leaned over to nudge her dangling feet. "I promised you I would months ago. I never break promises."

Ouch. As if that didn't sting. I'd only found out about this girl days ago, and he'd made promises to her months ago? That interaction between them in the catacombs had been real. And comfortable. Trusting. All those times I hadn't known where he was, and when he'd been blocking me, all added up to the closeness they now shared. He'd been hanging out, having fun…with her.

I backed up—and bumped into the white leather couch, making a collision sound and almost tipping foot over head onto the cushions before righting my balance.

"Amelia?" Head twisted over his shoulder, Kendrick frowned at me before swiveling around. "Hey, I didn't hear you come in."

Raven scrambled to sit up, her face turning beat red. "Oh—hi, Amelia."

I dropped onto the arm of the couch, pretending that's what I'd been trying to do. "Sorry, I didn't mean to interrupt or anything."

"Interrupt?" There was no embarrassment or guilt on Kendrick's face. "You weren't, we were just…" He trailed off, scanning over my exposed arms and legs. I looked down, noticing the darkening blue veins spanning like concrete cracks over my skin. "Ah, Raven, would you mind…"

"Oh, right." She scooted off the bed and shook her head, making her short black hair sway. "Yeah, of course. I should probably turn in for the day anyway. Knowing the sun's up is making me itch." She half waved at me as she headed toward the door. "C'ya, Amelia."

A moment later she was gone and Kendrick was standing before me. "Taking my blood from a bottle isn't doing enough."

"It's not just that," I said absently, unable to get the sight of Kendrick and Raven from my mind. "I decided to restore Caius.

And," I said, talking over Kendrick's instant frown, "I had a vision. I know who my brother is."

Carefree expression now dead and gone, Kendrick clenched his jaw. The *I would have come with you* was thought rather than said. "Let me see what happened. With Caius...and your *brother?*"

Dropping the necessary blocks, I waited for Kendrick to sift through it all—bar what I'd found Marcus doing in *The Pit.* All the while my mind remained preoccupied with other things. Like how quickly my presence had changed him.

When he'd seen it all, Kendrick took my hand and I followed him to sit on the couch. Focusing past his fear of me endangering myself with Caius, he let the bigger bombshell take front and center. "Wow. And Dorian doesn't want to come out? Marcus is happy to continue playing his role?"

"Yep," I said. But in the back of my mind I was wondering: by hanging onto what we could be, was I stopping him from truly being happy?

"Hey." His hand came up to cup my face. "What's wrong? You're not happy Marcus is your brother?"

I curled my fingers around his arm and pulled it down, staring at the veins snaking up his wrist. The scent of his blood disrupted my thoughts and my fangs poked through my gums. "No. I'm glad it's Marcus. It explains so much. It's just..." While I fought through my hunger to string words together, Kendrick waited, not moving or saying anything. I peered up to see worry creasing his face. "I don't want you to risk your life when you could be happy, without me."

"Without you?" Kendrick grabbed my hands and held on tight, my reasoning leaking through the bond. "What do you—" Over my shoulder he saw the mess of his blue and orange striped bed and the snowboarding that was now paused on the massive screen. "Raven. You think? No, Amelia. It's not like that. She's a nice girl, well not

really a girl, ninety years damned give or take. She was laying low with the one who infected her before they came across some newly turned damned and got recruited. They were two of only a few she knew about that had existed under the guise of rogues. But that's not the point. I've only known her for six months. You've been my best friend ever since I can remember. And I love you." I went to argue and his strong hand cupped the back of my neck. "*I love you.* I was wrong to give up so easily. To act like I didn't care if you went back to Ty. I do. I want you. But I want you to want me, too."

Quick as a flash he released my neck and bit into his wrist. Blood welled and slid down his arm to his elbow. Eyes transfixed, I couldn't look away. That rich red, the sudden increase of scent like a balloon had popped, was irresistible.

"You want me too, *don't you?*"

The need in his voice matched the need of my body, a void that wouldn't be sated without action. *"Yes."* In a trance, I took him by the hand and elbow and ran my tongue up his forearm. What I was doing broke through the haze. Oh God, I couldn't stop. And worse? I didn't want to. When I reached the source, I bit down.

Kendrick cradled me against his chest, stroking my hair as I took his blood. His lips brushed my forehead. "I'm not giving up on us. On this. Not until you tell me it's over."

I FINALLY FELL into a fitful sleep hours after leaving Kendrick's suite to return to my own. Everything that plagued my mind—from the Ty sightings, his horrible actions and character transplant, to my undeniable feelings for Kendrick and taking his vein—finally dimmed as a dream took over.

Everything was quiet here, my mind numbing until the walls of the Portsmouth hall rose up around me. Shattered windows looked like open mouths with jagged teeth. Bodies and blood painted a scene of quiet, peaceful carnage after a battle that had run its course. I was back in that moment after the damned attack. Alone, save for the still body that lay beneath me as I knelt in the wet.

Lost in the silence, I ran my hand down Ty's handsome and motionless face. Not knowing if I'd ever see him like this again terrified me. Made this reenacted dream beyond his death sacred and heartbreaking all at the same time. When my fingers stilled across his cheek, my surroundings flickered, slow like a faulty bulb at first, then faster. The flashes strobed until there was nothing but light. The surroundings were gone. Only Ty's body straddled beneath me remained.

Color and definition crept in: three dark walls, a curtain-covered doorway, and a daybed beneath me. Ty's skin was no longer shredded and covered in black and red wet patches. Blood no longer painted his chin and neck. The hole in his chest had vanished. Despite the lack of sound from a beating heart, his pale face held clear muscle control. He looked peaceful. Sleeping rather than dead.

Oh, God. This wasn't a dream.

I jumped up only to have Ty's strong hands catch my forearms and force me back down. His eyelids flung open and his crimson pupils drilled straight into me, hungry for blood and so much more. In a flash, he arched up on the bed, ice-cold lips pressing against mine.

For a second, I got lost in the moment. Lost in the fact that this was Ty and he was kissing me. I kissed him back, my entire body alight. Then I froze. I knew what was coming next. Because this was the dreamscape I'd suffered before.

I tore my forearms free and Ty's cold, calloused hands shot to my waist and flipped me onto my back. Now straddling me in nothing but jeans with his rippled chest bare, Ty smiled. Long fangs peeked through his pale lips. "Hello, beautiful."

With morbid realization I recognized my surroundings. Trapped in this small room, the bulb above splashed Ty and me in red light. The daybed beneath me was soft. This was one of the feeding rooms at *Pulse* in Anchorage. Not where Ty was actually hiding out.

I refused to gulp as I remembered in vivid detail the death and destruction Ty had ordered over a day ago at the Armaya. I never thought being trapped in a dreamscape with Ty would elicit fear in me. But after everything I'd seen, I was scared.

Combating that rational fear was a surge of relief at seeing him. Of attraction I couldn't control or cage. Because even as my mind screamed for me to run, to somehow find a way out of this conjured prison, my body tingled to close the space between us. To get up close and test whether there was anything left of the guy I still loved so deeply.

My brain commanded my lips with savage force and my voice escaped in a choked whisper. "You killed people. You ordered those damned to kill everyone. How could you?"

Those piercing red eyes didn't leave my face, regarding me with desire and curiosity. Like he couldn't understand what I was accusing him of. Like he hadn't even been there. He frowned and shook his head, then his lips parted with a split second of hurt. "I killed no one. Not a single vampire. I was there for you. Only you." He glanced away, squeezing his lids shut. "But orders are orders. I had to obey."

"You were compelled?" I looked at Ty's hands. They didn't hold me down, but instead lay gently against my stomach. I didn't try to pull out from under him as I glanced back up. Was the Ty I remembered hidden behind that dangerous stare? Was he dying to break free? "Tell me where you are. Where I can find you. Please, Ty. I can save you now. I can bring you back to life."

The amused smile that spread across his full lips struck me like a blade through my heart. "Do I seem dead to you?"

I went to edge upward and froze as Ty's rough hands splayed out, curving around my waist. "You know that's not what I meant. You're damned, but I can fix that."

"What if I don't want to be *fixed?* I will live forever, strong and frozen in time."

I couldn't stop the words or sharp tone that spewed from my lips. "As the exact thing you lived to cure the world of. As someone else's puppet. That's not you, Ty. You're a warrior. A hero."

"Such a hero that I couldn't save myself, let alone the girl I love." The intensity in his expression, the passion and anger, broke my heart. Then it was gone. "No. I won't return to being that weak mongrel. I'm stronger, more powerful. Unstoppable…" His hold on my waist softened, thumbs moving in a circle to hike my top up. I gasped as Ty spoke. "A being that can give you everything you need and desire. Who can love you for all eternity. Who can protect you and keep you safe…*always*."

My lips parted with breath, words lost. Ty released my waist and slid his hand up my body and around my nape with possession. The growl up his throat was both a warning and a promise. One that frightened and excited me. And one that had me freezing like a deer in headlights. His body came down on mine, trapping me against the soft bed. Then our mouths met, his tongue taking advantage of my parted lips and slipping inside. The taste of him filled my mouth and my body responded against my will, coming alive at his rough touch.

Oh God, I had waited so long for this. Fought to find him and know he was alive. To have him back in my arms and to feel his hard body against mine and his addictive kiss on my lips. Any rational thought about what I was doing, where I was, or what I needed to be doing fled my mind. It was like I couldn't think past the right now. Past what I could see, touch, and taste. It consumed my every thought, my every need. Here in this moment, Ty was my everything. Nothing existed beyond that. The need inside me wasn't rational, the hope, the love. It was unstoppable.

I was lost to him.

Still locked to his lips, my arms flung around his back, nails scraping down the many scars there and feeling his every muscle bunch and release beneath my palms. My body undulated against his, the hard icy plains still a perfect fit against mine.

Ty's eyes pulsed with red intensity and I felt his next words as if he were mirroring my own mind. "Tell me you want me, you need me."

Locked by his stare, I couldn't refuse, even as his fangs grazed my bottom lip and he slid kisses from my mouth to my neck. There was nothing beyond those few words and the tangle of our embrace. Nothing that resonated deep within me more than that burning need. It was the core of me, everything that had kept me living on with hope. "I want you." My head turned, lips finding his bicep, needing to keep the passion escalating. "More than...*anything*."

His hands slid under my top to my back, unclipping my bra as he licked my neck. "Tell me you want me to taste you, to feel the life of your blood coursing through my veins."

Alarm bells went off, halting my digging-in nails and separating my lips from his bicep. I spluttered through ragged breath, "You-you want to turn me?"

Even with the sudden rigidness of my body, one of Ty's hands continued their exploration to slip under the side of my bra, heading inward. "No. I want to show you what true ecstasy can feel like.

339

What it could be like for us now." His hand slid over my breast, fingers toying with me. "Don't you want that? Don't you want *me?*"

My head battled with my heart while his other hand trailed from my back down my waist and hip to my thigh. One side of me knew Ty was damned, not the same as before. The other refused to accept that fact, feeling only the touch of his lips and the slow caress of his calloused hands. A monster could never be so gentle, so passionate. Turning damned was a slow process, even after taking life. The insanity crept in over months and years. How much of the old Ty, the one my heart ached for, still remained?

"I give you my word." Ty's fangs grazed my jugular, tongue sliding over my perspiring skin. "Just a taste of what our future could hold. Let me show you."

Panic and desire swept through me, the feelings at odds with each other, fire and ice battling it out. Then a simple truth registered in my mind. My eyes blinked up at that red bulb, then darted to the curtain-covered exit that even if I ran to wouldn't get me out of this. *This is just a dream.* Anything that happened here wasn't real. Wasn't dangerous. It wasn't everlasting. And this time, my heart was going to win. Breathing hard, my answer was a throaty whisper. *"Yes..."*

I braced for his fangs to plunge into my jugular, but the sting of punctured flesh never came. Instead, Ty kissed my neck, slow and sweet. My heart galloped in response and my hands explored the hard plains of his back, encouraging and inviting. Ty's kisses continued, becoming rougher as they moved up my jugular and along my jaw to my lips. Then our tongues met and a sudden sting had me jolt in surprise. Ty retreated a few inches, face hovering above mine, black hair hanging over his forehead. The taste of my own blood registered on my tongue, and he smiled, dipping his head to take my bottom lip between his. He sucked for a second, and then his eyelids sprang open, the red blazing like a flare…in anger?

Rough hands reclaimed my waist and hard lips my neck, nipping as he trailed down to my cleavage. My breath caught at the sudden animalistic change that teetered on aggressiveness, words of protest trapped on my tongue. Ty tugged at the neckline of my tank and bit down, fangs punching into my skin. A split-second lance of pain struck through me as he drew hard. Then white-hot ecstasy flooded my veins with a shot of dopamine from his bite. My back arched in response and I dug my nails into his rock-hard arms that held me down, unable to catch my breath. His bite released with a growl that had me sagging into the soft bedding and panting as his mouth trailed down my body, fangs tearing through my tank. His cold and wet tongue snaked out as he reached my navel. It licked to my side, then over my hip, hands shoving the leg of my PJ shorts higher as he curved into my inner thigh. An ice-cold chill exploded with his bite, radiating through my bones and tingling all the way to my fingers and toes.

The sudden release of his fangs had a whimper escaping my throat. Like a predator, he crawled back up my body, pressing the hard bulge beneath his jeans into me. His vibrant red eyes drilled into mine. "You want me. You want all of me."

There was nothing I wanted more. "Yes, all of you."

A wicked smile curved his full mouth and he collected my hand, extending my index finger up before slicing the nail across his neck. The incision swelled and wept with blood. Black. Glossy. Blood. "Taste me. Join me," his smooth voice coaxed.

And I wanted to. I needed to. Anticipation had my tongue gliding over my bottom lip, my body arching up closer to that tempting torrent of glossy— The scent of Ty's black blood hit me. Not addictively rich and irresistible, but wrong. The rotten smell of decay. I pulled back, my nose scrunching up. "Your blood. It's changed."

"Turning changes a lot of things, Amelia. But it's still me." Ty's palm came up to rest over the healing punctures on my chest. "I know you feel it in the racing of your heart. You want me. You need me. Bite me and join me *forever*."

Like a plate-glass window shattering, everything that had just happened registered past the haze over my mind. Everything I'd just done hit me. As did what Ty was trying to coax me into doing. No. Not coax. Compel. Only a damned's blood mixed with damned venom could turn a vampire. Except this was a dreamscape. Or at least I thought it was. I scrambled back, head knocking into the curved wooden end of the daybed and leaving Ty's hand to fall away. "I won't let you turn me."

Ty laughed, an emotionless and horrible sound. His fingers clawed into the bedding on either side of my legs. "And here I thought you were going to make this easy. Guess I should have known better. But Amelia, you can't resist me, at least not forever. And I won't stop. This will end one way or another. Sooner or later. I promise you that."

I SHOT up straight as an arrow, minimal ambient light around closed drapes creating ominous shadows around me. Reaching out, I clicked my lamp on, highlighting my bedroom in the Bathory suite. The sheets were hanging half off the bed like they had tried to escape my fitful sleep. My heart drummed like it wanted to burst from my chest.

It had been a dreamscape. Not real. But Ty had been trying to turn me. Why?

Panic made my whole body feel like it was crawling with insects. Not breathing, I dared to peek under my tank and saw clear supple and unmarked skin. I whipped what remained of the sheet away from my legs. "Oh, thank God." My inner thigh was clear, too. Free of punctures, of the proof of what I'd allowed to go on.

Through the receding panic, the feeling of being watched settled over me. I wasn't alone.

I tugged the sheet back up as I found the source. My heart sank like a stone as I caught a shadow standing in the entry from the foyer. "Kendrick!" The walls were crumbled in my mind and I slammed them back into place.

Way too late.

The mixed emotion radiating off him in palpable waves matched the pummeled disbelief across his face, the tight clench of his fists. He'd seen my initial interaction with Ty when he'd kissed me—and I'd kissed him back. He'd seen me betray him.

"I...I..."

Kendrick turned to storm away and I leaped up, stumbling on the twisted sheets before rushing over. Catching his wrist, I spun him around. "I'm sorry. I got caught up. I was confused."

Refusing to look me in the eye, Kendrick glared as he saw my bed, like that's where Ty had been lip-locked to me with his body on top of mine. His jaw clenched. "And that makes it *okay*."

The steel in his voice made me step back as if his words had been shoving hands. And I almost wished the verbal strike had been a physical one. My heart had broken over losing Ty. I knew how devastating that pain was. And now I'd inflicted an equivalent onto my best friend. My boyfriend. Given him the hope he'd been wishing for all his life and stolen it away. Nothing I could say or do would make what I'd done *okay*. Because before the compulsion to accept his bite, I had given in to him.

My throat tightened as tears distorted my sight. "I…I tried to resist."

Kendrick tugged his arm free of my grasp. "Well, as long as you *tried*."

He went to leave then spun back. Terrible curiosity burned within him, the need to know every detail of what had happened. "Tell me."

I gasped at the request, the anger in his voice. "Kendrick, no—"

His hand shot up to clutch my nape and his thumb forced my face up. A flash of images penetrated my mind. Kendrick ruling by my side, us fighting together for our people, sharing a suite, a bed, the rest of our long lives. All his hopes and dreams for us that I'd ruined. The snarl through his lips was pure agony. His eyes bored into mine, pupils enlarging instantly to eliminate his silver-firing irises. "Drop the block. Let me see it. Now."

Compelled, an unstoppable rerun of events flashed through my mind, streaming like a broad telecast straight into Kendrick's subconscious. Ty's lips on mine. Me kissing him back. The passionate nips that trailed across my cheek to my neck…down my cleavage… His teeth sinking into my breast…trailing down… down…licking up my thigh and—

Kendrick almost pushed me away as he snatched his hand back and stalked into the foyer.

"Kendrick, wait!"

With a leap, I caught his wrist and Kendrick spun, hands clutching my shoulders and driving me back against the wall. One hand moved to slide roughly down my shoulder, fingers hooking my tank aside. He glared down at where I'd let Ty bite me, seeing the proof that wasn't there. His stomach turned over what felt like hot lava. "You let him bite you. You let…"

"It was a dream. It wasn't real."

Overriding his anger at the intimate replay was his fear for my safety. "And what about the next time, when it's not a dreamscape?" His tight fingers released my tank as he paced a few steps to the foyer table, making my heart sink with each forceful step. He turned back just as suddenly to face me. "What the hell were you thinking?"

I wanted to throw myself forward and cling to him. I wanted to point out that I'd allowed Ty to bite me because of compulsion. But I didn't. What I wanted didn't matter, and it was clear Kendrick didn't want me to touch him in any way, especially not after who my hands and fingers had been gripping to. And if I was being totally honest? I couldn't swear I wouldn't have let it all go down even if I wasn't coerced.

"I wasn't thinking. At all. It was stupid and selfish and *I'm sorry*." I clasped my hands together, desperate for him to feel the regret I propelled through the bond.

Kendrick closed off his thoughts without hesitation, along with anything I let through.

"I don't know what I can say to make things right. Forgive me. *Please*."

Kendrick's eyes squeezed shut, pain resonating across his handsome, broken face. Those damning images slipped through again and again: the way I had touched Ty and the things I'd let Ty do to me, plaguing his thoughts. As his lids lifted, he shook his head. "I must have been delusional to think you could ever get over him. That you could ever *love* me."

The first part was true. Even when I'd accepted that Ty was truly dead, my love for him hadn't faded. I'd acted on impulse at my first consensual kiss with Kendrick, then instantly regretted it. Straight after I'd been honest, laying my feelings out to him with total transparency. Kendrick's acceptance of taking what little I could give had swayed me. But I shouldn't have let it. He'd been hurting after the death of his mother and been clinging to anything he could hold onto with his bare hands. Even the second-hand and sub-par love I could offer.

My voice cracked as I spoke. "I do love you. You know I do."

"But you're not *in love* with me. You never have been and you never will be."

I sank onto a padded stool against the curved stone wall, dropping my head into my hands. I wasn't about to start lying. Not about this. Despite hoping my feelings would one day blossom into *that kind of love*, I knew they hadn't even begun to scratch the surface on that front. Which made one thing vividly clear. I had taken advantage of my best friend. I'd filled the loss of Ty with the hope of something I knew in my heart could never compete.

"More than anything," Kendrick whispered as he made for the exit.

I glanced up slowly and wiped the moisture from my cheeks. "What?"

"He asked you." Defeat saddened Kendrick's voice. "You said more than anything. You want him more than anything. You need him more than anything. Real or not, you let him bite you. You were ready to give up everything, your mom, Dorian, Marcus...me." He took a backward step toward the door. "I—I just can't..."

"I'm sorry," I said with a sob, standing but not moving any closer to him. A gulf separated us now that had nothing to do with physical space. "I didn't mean it." Which was the truth. I loved Ty, more than anything. But that didn't mean I would give up everything and everyone in my life for him. That I would give my living life up to be damned so that I could be with him.

Kendrick shrugged and gripped the door handle. "It doesn't matter. You meant it at the time and your feelings were real." Even with his back to me, the movement of him clutching his shirt over his heart was unmissable. He glanced over his shoulder, eyes focused on the ground rather than at me. "I can't even... I need to be alone."

As he slid silently out, closing the door behind him, I knew the rest of the words he couldn't say.

I can't even look at you.

The link between us vanished, severed by my selfish actions. An impenetrable block replaced the invisible ties, a screaming sign from Kendrick that spelled out what he wanted without question. Absolutely nothing to do with me. I couldn't blame him. I'd created all this mess on my own. It was now mine to live with.

CHAPTER 27

A knock ratta-tap-tapped at my door the next morning and my heart took off like a start gun had been fired. I tore my stare from the cobblestone street beyond my bedroom balcony and rushed toward the sound. Being late summer and close to sunset, bright refracted rays lit up the surrounding mountains and kept my suite from being dark and gloomy like my thoughts. Now hope of who stood outside my door soared, while anxiety for our discussion to come filled me with dread.

Since Kendrick had stalked off earlier, I hadn't seen or heard from him. Even as I made my way to the door now, the feelers I sent out through the bond hit a roadblock. Another series of knocks sounded against the solid wooden barrier, and my chest constricted as my hand shot out to swing the door wide.

My heart sank.

A female guard stood holding a crate with filled blood bottles. "Lord Baldassare delivered these almost an hour ago, my Lady.

Thought you might want them refrigerated now that they've cooled."

"Oh, right." I took the crate, the wood and glass clinking against my waist-height dagger and stake. "Thanks."

Totally dejected, I footed the door shut and slid down the carved wood onto my butt. Staring down at the bottles, I felt hollow. Kendrick was still looking out for me, still willing to keep my diet and supply needs secret. But he clearly couldn't stand the sight of me. So much so that he'd left the bottles at my door rather than bringing them in and chancing a face-to-face.

I rubbed my temples, the background throb in my skull intensifying. Hours of thinking had kept me playing out the conversation I knew I needed to have with Kendrick in every single scenario. Because we couldn't go on like this. Connected by blood and soul and so fundamentally separated. I was a mess, and even if I couldn't read Kendrick, I knew where we stood was killing him, too. Still, none of the mental play-outs had ended well, and all I'd gotten out of the round-and-round mock-up conversations was a headache.

I couldn't let it go, though. This last nine or so sleepless hours had been hell. And unlike most of the times past, I wouldn't wait for him to seek me out. This time I would make it right.

I pushed the crate aside, took a deep breath, and fled my suite. My guards snapped to attention, tailing behind without a word. Down the corridor, the lack of protection outside Kendrick's suite told me what I needed to know. He wasn't there. I followed the bend around, but when I reached the grand stairs down to the main hall, I swung right. If Kendrick was as brain-effed as I was, I knew where he'd be—killing his mental problems with physical exhaustion.

The narrower corridor with doors to guest rooms led to opposing back stairwells, and I took the one down to the training facilities. The gym took up one length of the long corridor and the training rooms were opposite, thick glass doors keeping sparring sounds to a minimum. I glanced inside each room as I passed, seeing most of them empty and only a few vamps training in hand-to-hand combat. Marcus was in a room halfway down the hall, throwing daggers at a stuffed dummy with exact precision. He tipped his chin as I passed, but kept on throwing.

I walked on, then stopped dead at the last room, my guards halting a few yards back. The guy and girl in sweaty clothes inside looked like they'd been sparring for hours. Though they weren't anymore. With short black hair, I recognized Raven lip-locked to a tall, toned guy. Her arms around him felt their way under his T-shirt and up his back. The guy pulled her closer, golden-brown hair gleaming under the fluorescent lights as he gripped her butt. My hand shot up to cover my mouth, eyes transfixed as the two turned an inch. I knew who the guy was, even without the clear view of the side of his face.

Kendrick.

His long fangs and Raven's more petite ones glinted through their joined lips. Their rushed breath sped up—then Kendrick's eyes flung open and his pupils locked on me. He turned rigid while Raven hiked up his wet T-shirt. A second of pain—or maybe even regret—passed over his sweaty face. But it didn't last. Renewed anger blazed in his irises and he hissed, pulling Raven closer and kissing her harder.

Instant tears sprouted and I tripped over my Vans as I darted for the exit—

Dorian appeared around the bend and caught me. "Hey, I found you." The animation drained from his face. "What's wrong?"

I swiped my fallen tears away. "It's—nothing." Dorian had his own issues now that he knew he was the only Vladimir. He didn't need to be sucked into mine. "Can we just go?"

As I pushed on his chest, his whole body tensed. He snarled over my shoulder, fangs punching free in threat. "That prick. How dare he—"

Dorian went to storm past me and I clamped onto his taut arms and shoved him back. "No, please. This is my fault. I just wanna get outta here." I held Dorian back, the look across my face pleading.

Finally he let his breath out through flared nostrils. Instead of asking why it was my fault, he tilted his head to crack his neck. "Fine. But if you decide you want mince meat made out of him, you come see me first." He pointed from the adjoining corridor to the training room he could no longer see inside of. "I don't give a shit what you did. *That* isn't okay."

"Wanna talk about it?"

Beside me, Dorian kept up with my quick gait as I cleared the labyrinth of corridors with the tall order of being directionally challenged. His tone was clipped, his expression as each wall lantern lit up his face, pissed yet sympathetic. The stride of his boots slapped the stone as he stuck by my side.

The scene of Kendrick making out with Raven replayed in my subconscious for the millionth time on cruel never-ending repeat. The lack of space between their bodies. Her hands sliding up his back. His on her ass as he pulled her harder against him.

I stumbled and Dorian reached out to balance me, but I yanked free and picked up the pace. I didn't know how far what they'd been doing would go. After what I'd let happen with Ty, rationality told me I had no right to find out. My heart disagreed. It felt raw and pummeled, on the verge of imploding. Betrayal sat like cancer in my gut, a living thing that grew by the second. I felt cheated on. The exact way I'd made Kendrick feel after kissing Ty and letting him sink his fangs in to drink my blood. For what I'd done, I deserved his actions and more.

But, God. If payback wasn't a bitch.

"I guess not then."

I stopped suddenly, pent-up energy screaming to drive my legs on until I wore them down to bloody stumps. I faced Dorian, but there were no words. At least none I could manage to string together. But then I remembered the way Dorian had shown up outside that training room unexpectedly. "You were looking for me."

"I guess timing is everything. And seeing as you're in desperate need for a distraction..." Dorian rolled up the long sleeve of his V-neck and turned his forearm up. A symbol marked his flesh, clearly new by the pinkish skin around the gold lines. "This was my idea, and Vanessa came through. With *this* we can force Caius to spill the commander's name and Ty's location."

Letting the distraction take over, I held his arm and took a closer look. The mark was much like the one to boost compulsion, with the outline of an eye with intricate pupil and iris. Except there were two eyes, the second larger with the first one inside. "How does it work?"

I released his arm and Dorian rolled his sleeve back down. "The larger eye represents the person marked so they can compel any vampire. Even an old-ass royal like that dick, Caius. Vanessa reckons it can even break through a vampire's compulsion to get to the truth. Like we failed to do with mom—I mean Lamayli—when Caius had her marked."

In spite of the potential of what this meant, I squeezed Dorian's shoulder. "Mom still sees you as her son," I said. "She raised you and she loves you. She doesn't know about Marcus."

Dorian shrugged the subject and my hand off. "Instead of getting into a big D and M on the whole orphan thing, how 'bout we chuck it in the too-hard basket with your love triangle?"

I wanted to help him feel better, but fair was fair. Dorian didn't want to talk his grief out any more than I did. "Deal."

Dorian smiled then patted his arm. "Let's put this bad boy to use."

I led the way on in silence, gathering my bearings to take us from where we were to where we needed to get to. The few minute's walk to the cell's entry had everything I'd been distracted from rushing back.

I clenched and unclenched my fists over and over, the sting increasing as my nails sliced then disembedded from my palms. If Kendrick wanted to move on, to have nothing to do with me, I wouldn't stop him. Not because I saw this rosy ending after I somehow miraculously saved Ty. Not because I wanted the easy way out. I did love Kendrick. As more than a friend. It wasn't the same as my love for Ty, but that didn't make it any less. Just different. Unique. Still, I had no right to suck Kendrick back in. To damage his life any more than I already had. He deserved to be happy. Not second best. And not brought into my mess of a life and put in danger.

"Amelia, you okay?"

I almost stumbled again and realized we were at the bottom of the stairs surrounded by a curved wall of cell doors. Dorian was watching me with concern, so like his normal self, and so different from the glimpse of him I'd stumbled across at *Bite* yesterday. The return to normal was a silent relief with everything else that was on my mind.

"I'll be fine." I shoved every other feeling, thought, and image down and locked them away, tossing out the key. Right now I had a job to do and a promise to keep...I hoped. "Let's just do this. I need...to do this."

Dorian instructed a prison guard to unlock Caius's cell and the two of us entered and shut him and my four guards out. Inside was the same, cold stone on all sides and a strong aroma of bleach—which I was almost getting accustomed to, I realized with a start. There was a dripping sound from a fresh spray down. The one difference was Caius standing in the corner. No longer sickly, his pale skin was iridescent and his face appeared younger and less wrinkled. Even his eyes had changed, now bright silver-gray and filled with more life than I'd ever seen.

Caius smiled and stepped forward, not needing the wall for support. "My dear daughter. To what do I owe this visit?"

Dorian made fists out of his hands and took a booted step forward, sole slapping the wet stone. "You're going to tell us where we can find the damned."

Caius paid him no attention, keeping his focus on me. "That you know I cannot divulge, my dear."

I strode around Dorian, coming face to face with my father, the traitor, and my murderer. After everything that had happened, seeing a different, yet still-twisted side of Caius and restoring him, I no longer feared being around him. "This time you have no choice. You will speak." I clutched his jaw and sidestepped as Dorian came forward. My other hand clamped around the back of his head, holding it in place as he reached up to free himself. "Go for it."

Dorian's eyes locked on Caius's as I held on tight, his irises sparking with silver and his pupils dilating. "Tell us the main location of the damned. Where they're commanded from."

Caius stopped struggling, the defiance that creased his face melting into abject indifference. I released his jaw as it went to part.

"Anchorage...old street. Maples overhang sidewalk...red brick...abandoned..."

"The address." Dorian edged closer, stare burrowing hate-filled lasers into his ex-uncle. "What's the address, asshole?"

Caius's open mouth twisted and he gagged and spluttered. Dorian shook him and demanded a compelled answer while I stared on. The gagging continued and Dorian drove Caius back against the wall. Air *oomphed* from the old vampire's lungs as my brother's frustration peaked. "Cut the crap, you piece of shit, and talk. Where are the damned and who's commanding them?"

"It is—" The gagging graduated to choking and Caius's hands went to his throat, clawing as if trying to pull someone's strangling grip away. When his face began to turn blue-gray, eyes rolling like marbles, I lunged forward and yanked Dorian off him.

The cell door swung open as Caius folded over onto his knees and retched. Marcus strode in and swung the door shut behind him. "Thought you might..." He caught sight of Caius and frowned. Anger flashed in his eyes. "If you'd told me you were going to torture the bastard, I would have come along."

"We're trying to find the damned hub," I said as Caius tipped sideways and let out a last cough, eyes blinking as if he were seeing stars.

Dorian peeled his sleeve up to reveal the mark Vanessa had given him. "With this."

At Marcus's raised brow, I explained the workings of the mark. Then I glanced back at Caius who was now propped back against the wall and sucking air like he'd just surfaced from underwater. "It should have worked."

Caius grunted, breathing hard. Fangs flashing, his stare went from Marcus and settled on Dorian. The glare that narrowed his eyes was fierce. "Do not go with—" His breath caught and he coughed, beating a fist against his chest. Glazed eyes turned on me. "Do not trust—" More horrible choking, followed by a cough that sounded like a lung was about to burst from his throat. *"Him."*

Marcus took a few steps toward Caius, hands clasped before him as he squatted. "Cat got your tongue, *father*."

Caius's now bloodshot eyes flickered to me then back to Marcus. "You—"

"Amelia figured it out," Marcus said in his nothing-fazes-me voice. "She told me yesterday." He knelt before Caius, seeming to study his face with curiosity. Seeing the man whose blood ran through his veins for the very first time. "Though I'm not into sappy reunions where you're concerned. So why don't you tell us why Dorian's mark can't make you spill your guts, traitor?"

I expected a mocking laugh or a snide comment. Maybe more choking. Instead, Caius looked at me, his chin tilting up. "I cannot speak the name of the commander or the damned location…even if I wanted to. Damned compulsion prevents it."

MARCUS CLOSED the two of us inside his office, leaving our guards outside. A lingering hue over the horizon offered minimal light through the tall window behind his desk with its open drapes. He cleared his throat and sat on the Chesterfield, clasping his hands. With a furrowed brow, he said, "I saw Kendrick with Raven."

Great. Feeling like I'd just been staked, I shrugged out of my zip-up hoodie and took the spot next to him on the sofa, minding my dagger and stake on the leather. Dorian had taken off to find Vanessa so they could work on a new symbol that could break through damned compulsion. So it was just the two of us.

"It's the reason I came looking for you." Marcus touched my

hand and a spark lit up at the connection. "Want me to go teach the moron a lesson?"

Knowing who Marcus now was to me, I wanted to get to know him, but the issues of my life refused to give me peace. The scene of Raven wrapped in Kendrick's strong arms flooded back. I blinked it away, depression weighing me down. I didn't have any leads to locate Ty and I'd screwed my relationship with Kendrick. After a solid minute of silent head-fuck, I blurted, "I kissed Ty...in a dream-scape. More than once. And I...I let him..."

More silence as my throat constricted, and Marcus waited patiently, no judgment or disdain across his chiseled face. As every candlewick around the room suddenly sparked with flame, their crackle filling the mirrored room with sound and gentle light, I remembered his guilt and desperation when I'd found him in *The Pit*. He'd been scared to admit what he'd done, but he'd been totally honest. My twin had trusted me with his deepest, darkest secret.

"I let him bite me," I whispered, eyes darting to gauge his disgust.

There was none.

Marcus picked up a dagger from the table with engraved mark-ings up the hilt and began scraping under his nails. Without looking up from the silver blade that reflected candlelight up onto his face, he said, "You want to save him. To restore him like that damned girl."

A flash of her hands up Kendrick's back broke through, and I winced before shutting it down. "That's why Dorian and I ques-tioned Caius. He must know where Ty is. And I can't save him if I can't find him."

The dagger clanked as Marcus replaced it on the glass table before lounging back on the Chesterfield. One arm slung across the armrest to prop up his head. The other stretched out along the backrest. "Since we're being totally honest..." His smile revealed the tips of his white fangs, which made me wonder if his increased hunger kept them exposed rather than retracting. His next words stopped me from asking. "Since we touched after you found me in...*The Pit*, I, ah, have felt this build up of power." He fisted his collared shirt over his heart. "In here. I just have this overwhelming feeling that..."

Marcus scooted closer, his bent knee meeting the side of my leg. He took my hands and blue and red sparks emerged, mingling together like they were playing. "That I need to connect—"

The view of my twin's cautious face was suddenly gone, replaced by red hair and Vanessa's pixie-like face. With my forearm upturned on a small table between us, she drilled into the flesh with her homemade tattoo gun. Her sapphire eyes were focused and determined.

There was something wrong though.

Next to the arm getting inked was a dagger. One I swear I'd seen just before. And that wasn't all. The arm Vanessa was drilling into wasn't chalky-pale and slender. The skin tone was darker but without rich pigment, leaving it gray in pallor. A damned, but unlike most. Muscle corded from their scarred upper arm all the way down to their masculine hand.

Vanessa flicked the drumming gun off and swiped a black-stained cloth across the inner forearm. What was left behind stunned me. An intricate and thick mark that was as black as old oil with only a shimmer of gold. The arm flexed, fingers splaying to curl into a loose fist.

"This'll get you past the wards." Vanessa stood up and the eyes I saw from sent their gaze at a mirror mounted behind an old wooden door.

Ty's gray face stared back at me, red eyes glowing. "Good job."

A voice even colder and more ruthless than Ty's spoke from the shadows. The commander's. "Now mark the rest of them."

My eyes blinked open and I saw Marcus's face before me. No longer holding my hands, he cupped my face. "My touch gave you a vision. Didn't it?" When I nodded, he let his hands fall away while watching me with excitement and concern. "What did you see?"

The image of the tattoo gun held by Vanessa returned, followed by Ty's red eyes staring back at me. Remembering that faceless, cold, commanding voice made me shudder. "The damned are being marked," I coughed, swinging my legs up and under my butt. My arms wrapped around my body to stop the internal shiver that wanted to take over on the outside. "That's how they got in without setting off our wards." Which Vanessa set, my mind echoed.

Marcus's brows popped before his gaze narrowed. He slid to the edge of the sofa, candlelight from around the room reflecting in his considering, teal-flecked eyes. "Who's marking them?"

"I…"

The confession caught in my throat, Vanessa's name tasting like poison on my tongue. I couldn't out her. Not yet. There had to be some explanation. There just had to. I knew her. I trusted her. She was dating Dorian, had moved to our vampire community despite her allegiance to…the lycans. To Ty. *Oh Shit.* Had that loyalty carried on even after Ty changed races, after he'd lost his soul and become damned? Or was she being coerced? Either way, there was something I knew without any doubt. Vanessa—on a conscious level or not—knew where to find Ty. One way or another, she was going to take me to him.

Mind made up on my next move even with how horrible it made me feel, I shook my head. "I didn't see who did the marking."

I stood up abruptly—mind racing for an excuse to leave without having to out Vanessa or lie to my twin—and swayed. Dizziness overcame me and I collapsed back onto the tight leather, holstered weapons digging into me. Sudden ravenous hunger clawed at my stomach, and the taste of blood registered on my tongue. Mine, dripping from my nose over my lip and into my mouth. I lifted the sleeve of my hoodie on the cushion beside me and swiped it away.

"You need blood." Marcus bit into his wrist and held his arm out to me. The punch of blood in this draft-free room tore a hiss from my throat. "Here. Take mine." At my straight-out refusal he frowned like I'd just insulted him. "I'm your brother, Amelia. Your blood. There's no reason to refuse, and with how things are with Kendrick…" He let the rest of the sentence hang in the air unsaid.

My need to argue waned as my vision went from carousel to still. I instantly became aware of the sound of blood coursing through Marcus's and my veins. Ty's problem with me taking from someone else had been that he'd felt like I'd cheated on him. Betrayed him. Which I'd now more than done to him with Kendrick and vice versa. But there was not a single iota of intimacy between Marcus and me. Even before knowing he was my twin, none had existed. Marcus's argument was right.

I took his arm and peered up. "Are you sure?" His eyes narrowed in a *do you really need to ask* way as my fangs lengthened. The punctures began to shrink, stealing that punch of blood from the air and striking urgency through me. I lifted his wrist and created a seal with my lips. A few long pulls delivered a double stream down my throat of what was becoming my favorite drug. Vampire blood. The taste was so rich and potent, and distinctly unique from Ty's and even Kendrick's.

Hunger and pain receding, I released the connection to his skin. I ran my tongue over my teeth as I let go of his arm, Marcus's potent blood striking the taste of my own from my mouth with its individuality. "Thanks."

Marcus shrugged. "Don't mention it."

He leaned back to kick his feet up onto the glass table, and the heel of his square-toed shoes knocked into something. As the length of hard metal spun on the table and slowed, I couldn't help but stare as it shone with candlelight. The dagger. The one Marcus had been fiddling with before, was the same one I'd seen in my vision.

My breath caught for a nanosecond. "Where did you get that dagger?"

Marcus's lips parted and he tapped a slightly extended fang with his tongue. "Vanessa gave it to me after I got her the alchemist job. Made it especially for me, she said." He raised a single brow. "Why do you ask?"

I swooped the dagger up. "Oh, it's just—"

An image scored my subconscious, bringing me to my knees on the plush white rug. The silver dagger in my hand buried up to the hilt in Marcus's chest, glossy scarlet leaking out as he collapsed to his knees.

I blinked like I'd just been maced, the unlimited candlelight returning in a hazy glow. I held back my gasp and kept a firm hold on the dagger as Marcus gripped my arm to help me up onto the coffee table's edge.

"What happened? Are you okay?"

The guilt I'd felt over lying to my twin about Vanessa's part in marking the damned burst like a popped balloon. "Guess I'm still vision drained." There was no hesitation in my voice, no wavering. Because I could see the writing on the wall. I'd go after Vanessa and find Ty, and Marcus would be along for the ride. Like he'd insisted on when Harper had gone missing. To keep me safe. And in return, his life would be challenged. Someone was going to stab him with *this* dagger. And I wasn't going to let that happen. To him. To anyone. Not anymore. I'd seen the effect my mission to save Ty had

had on Kendrick, and I couldn't do it to him any more than I could do it to my own twin.

It was time for me to back myself up. Alone. No more risk of casualties.

I stood, and my own dagger clanked against my holstered stake. With sleight of hand, I tucked Marcus's dagger behind my back, hilt down into my waistband. Then I retrieved and shrugged on my hoodie to conceal the blade. I wanted to see if I could bring back who had plunged the blade into my brother's heart. And even if I couldn't, at the very least I had possession of the deadly weapon. No one would be able to use it against him. And so help me if it was Vanessa. "Do you mind if I take off? I've got some mental stuff to sort through."

With a speculative look, Marcus shrugged, swinging his feet off the table to plant them on the rug. "A rest is probably a good idea, too. But if you need me—you know I'll always back you up."

That's what I was afraid of, which proved I was making the right choice. "I'll let you know." I trekked to the door, and with a quick wave I slipped out.

CHAPTER 28

"I'm tired and I don't want any interruptions." I narrowed my eyes at the four guards outside my suite. One hand was above my head, curled around the door's wooden edges. The other sat like a warning above the dagger at my hip. "If anyone comes looking for me, send them away. No exceptions."

Shutting them out, I chucked on clean black jeans, tugged on my hoodie and knelt down at my weapon crates. In less than a minute, I strapped a holster to my thigh to accommodate Marcus's dagger—which I'd failed to pick up anything else from throughout the day—and filled my utility belt with as many silver stakes as I could fit. Bar one slot I kept free for now. The hook at my back already accommodated my whip.

I knew how to find Ty and I wasn't turning back, for anything or anyone. I wasn't coming back without him. And if I failed? I wasn't coming back at all, but at least I wouldn't have taken anyone I loved down with me.

I sat on the edge of my purple-covered bed, plaiting my hair and eyeing the three bottles of Kendrick's blood I'd left on my bedside. With a deep sigh, I emptied the vibrant red contents. Kendrick, whatever he was now doing with Raven, was still blocking me. Good. Even with my own blocks in place, it was added cover. A fail-safe to keep him out of all the mess that was mine and mine alone to fix. And that he clearly wanted nothing to do with.

Since my visions with Marcus this morning, I'd attended my usual training and RVC meeting between hiding back out here and trying to bring on more visions. No luck on the third eye stuff. And the rest had been hell. Kendrick hadn't spoken a word to me. He hadn't even looked at me. And for his sake, I hadn't even tried to connect. He was better off without me. If history proved anything, he'd be happier, too.

I opened the drawer then and held my breath as I pulled out a length of shiny silver. Ty's stake. With a kiss to the cool metal and a silent prayer, it filled the last hole in my utility belt.

Ready or not.

With one last look at the suite that had formerly belonged to Caius and was now my home, I crossed to the balcony and climbed over the balustrade. It was seven-thirty a.m. and well past sunrise, but had been light for over two hours with early September twilight. The vampire community had shut down, and there'd be little to no one out and about. If this went the way I'd planned, no one would come looking for me until well into tomorrow.

A backward drop over the balustrade had me landing on the path outside the moss-covered wall, darting into the gardens, and hooking a right to the nearest exit. A brisk walk down the quiet backstreets had me standing in the shadow of a wind-ruffled tree across the road from Dorian's. My initial plan had been to question Vanessa, to call her out. But I had to get this right.

Ty's life depended on it.

With the sun climbing higher in the sky, the streets were empty, the blackout curtains on all the houses drawn shut. The only reprieve from the ultraviolet light was the fluffy white clouds that propelled dark patches onto the street and house roofs. Dorian had to be inside, which meant Vanessa should be, too.

I crept across the cobblestone street and down the left side of the house to the first window. Around the edge of the curtains, I squinted to glimpse the living room. TV with moving color on a small table. Boxes with 'Vanessa's stuff' in black marker on them. And as I twisted my head sideways...the edge of the worn sofa where Vanessa sat in my closest view. Her legs were draped over Dorian's and her downcast head blocked out most of my brother's face as she fingered through the thick book in her lap.

Dorian was nuzzling into her neck, one arm around her shoulders and fingers toying with her long hair.

Instant dread weighed against my heart. If Vanessa was playing him and pretending to be on our side, it would wreck him. He'd already lost his mother and gained a dead family with unwanted obligation. He felt he'd lost me too as his sister, even though nothing could be further from the truth...well, until I went after Ty and chanced not coming back alive. But I couldn't pretend I hadn't seen what I had. There was no mistaking my vision, just the why was unknown. But not for long...

I lowered from my tippy toes, ready to go knock on that blue door when the pendant heated up. On instinct, my head snapped sideways to the street, scanning for lurking danger. But it was too bright; the damned would never make a move during slow, painful incineration time. Which meant the threat was something else. Something close.

With my heart suddenly drumming, I reared up and peered back inside. Something was about to happen. The now constant heat of the pendant promised it. And if Dorian was in danger, if Vanessa was about to pull a villain move, I was armed and ready to fight.

Hand going to the hilt of my dagger, what I saw next stopped me from breaking in through the window.

Dorian and Vanessa were consumed by a passionate lip-lock. Her hands shoved his T-shirt up and his fingers were laced through her red locks. But then those digits turned from loose into a rigid fist. He yanked her head back, giving me a clear view of his blank yet horrible expression, mouth parted and fangs exposed.

Rooted to the spot, my eyes widened as Dorian jerked Vanessa's arm out with his free hand. His bared fangs came down, gouging torrents along her skin and shredding her alchemist marks.

Including one for anti-compulsion.

With the popping of Vanessa's eyes and the cry that peeled from her throat, Dorian released her hair, hand clamping across her mouth to cut off her scream as he captured her gaze.

I zeroed in on his jaw movement as he spoke, my hearing blocking out everything—the distant birds chirping, creaks as houses warmed in the sun, wind rustling trees across the street. Everything but the sound of his words.

"Ty wants you at the location. Take my M5. It's waiting by the gates. Go now."

In numb shock, I watched as Vanessa tugged on her red leather jacket, covering the destroyed marks on her forearm. With total vacancy in her eyes, she zombied off the sofa and from the room. A click and a creak followed by a knock announced her exit through that blue door. As the clip, clip of her heels down the street grew quieter, I spared a glance inside.

Dorian hadn't moved, but with remote in hand he turned the TV on and sports colored the screen. Like everything was normal. Like he hadn't just injured and compelled his girlfriend to a location no one but the damned commander and his minions were meant to know about. He lounged back on the sofa, kicking up his boots— No. Not just boots. Shitkickers. Black, leather, and from the looks, steel-toed. Just like the ones I'd seen the damned commander wearing in my visions.

I shrank back, mind reeling as I blindly headed down the street to the field's edge. Dorian, the boy who'd been my brother for our first sixteen years of life. It couldn't be him.

Except it was, wasn't it. What I'd just seen proved it.

Dorian was the insider. The one who'd led the damned through our wards with his Pure Blood. The damned commander.

A swift weave through the surrounding trees brought me to the perimeter. I bent at the waist and heaved up what was left of Kendrick's bottled blood. With a swipe of my arm across my mouth, I leaped over the stone boundary. Even though my sneak-outs to infiltrate damned locations had died off, I'd left my Ducati hidden in the empty horse shelter a few miles from the outer perimeter. I picked up the pace, moving at full vampire speed through the thicket.

The clues I'd dismissed surfaced from my subconscious then, events filling my head with noise. Before moving here and Ty's death, someone had been keeping tabs on me—at home and at school. When we'd found the cabin burned to the ground, Dorian had stayed home, knowing where we were going and why. My mom was marked while Dorian was home, supposed to be looking out for her—by an unknown alchemist. At the same time he was apparently hooking up with Vanessa. The holiday bookings separated me from Kendrick. It had created an opportunity to turn Ty and kidnap me while pointing to Caius as the instigator. It had endangered Kendrick's life and seemingly Dorian's, too.

Now he was refusing to let the RVC in on his bloodline and rightful position because it would restrict his freedom. His ability to come and go unnoticed. I recalled the time I'd opened my dazed eyes while sitting in the gazebo and seen a handprint across my arm. Dorian had been down the street from the angel fountain, eyes shifty as he entered *Bite*. Then there was his split personality with that blood donor in the club, and Caius's warning after Dorian had tried to compel answers out of him—on a location he'd just sent Vanessa to.

Had Dorian been acting against us this whole time? Was he the enemy in disguise?

I reached my Ducati and fired up the engine, running a reminiscent hand along the insignia. *Soul mates.* My head and heart were at odds with the life I was leaving behind, and—with who I was leaving behind, too. I kissed my fingertips and pressed them to the silver-scribbled metal. *Goodbye, Kendrick.* With a single escaping tear, I rechecked and reinforced the total and impenetrable block around my thoughts, emotions, and physical form. I was on my own now, body and soul.

Letting everything I'd just unearthed pale my grief, my inner drive to get to Ty swelled. Still, my heart ached in reply, unable to accept the damning proof against the boy who'd been my brother for sixteen years.

With a curse, I rolled the bike out and wheeled it down a dirt path to the only road that led to and from the Armaya. Waiting in the bushes with a headache coming on strong, a few minutes passed before the rumble of Dorian's M5 reached me. The shiny, black Cabriolet appeared then, rolling swiftly down the road.

Zipping up my hoodie and mounting my Ducati, I followed at a distance through the forest, the speed and bumpy terrain doing a number on my thoughts, my bike's shocks, and flailing my hood and plaited hair behind me. All those moments replayed, all the clues, all the proof. But even with all the damning evidence, there was one thing that didn't add up. How had he gotten all the way to Russia to slaughter Lord Vladimir, his own father, and gotten back for training the next day? Commercial flights wouldn't have been quick enough. Marcus had proved that when he'd arrived with help to find them all dead. But if you were somehow commanding an army, would it really be that hard to commandeer and cover up the borrowing of a private jet? To move you and a horde of undead across an ocean? I guess not.

It was a few hours later when we reached Anchorage and Vanessa pulled up along a quiet, old weathered street that looked like it never saw traffic or passersby. Killing my Ducati's engine way up the road before she got out, I stashed the bike behind a dumped sedan with slashed tires and a cracked windshield. Keeping to the shadows of the many draping maples that bordered the old street, I skulked closer.

Vanessa turned away from the street to disappear through a metal gate along a red brick wall. The pendant warmed as I reached and peeked through the wrought iron bars. A three-story redbrick hotel soared from beyond, the sign above the entry reading *The Avondale* with a few letters missing. With half the dirty windows boarded up and a few cracked and a *Keep Out* sign chained to the gate, the place looked abandoned.

And totally familiar.

The exact details Caius had tried to spill when Dorian had pretended to use that mark against him. He'd tried to reveal Ty's location—and he'd tried to warn me.

My heart ached anew at the thought of Dorian. He'd known

Caius wouldn't—couldn't—talk even with the mark. So why the pretense? Just more acting to keep up the charade?

I opened the creaking gate and stepped inside with a wince. This was my one and only—and final—chance to save Ty. There was the option to call for backup. Which would just endanger more lives and potentially blow my cover. Or there was the option to act. No one knew I was here, armed and ready. Not even Ty, who had to be inside. I had the element of surprise, and I wasn't going to waste it.

Up the chipped, maroon-painted concrete steps, I released my dagger and slipped through the door into the old hotel's rundown foyer. Surrounded by dark shadows, I caught movement above the open area with a central, forking staircase leading up to the left and right—Vanessa, with her fingers trailing along the carved wooden balustrade to the third level. Other distant sounds of movement reached my ears, not coming from the adjoining rooms, but down the hallway past the stairs. Voices. Boots treading over ground. Crackling from a fire.

I tiptoed around the central wooden table, scanning for soundless threats as I mounted the wooden stairs with quiet speed. As I cleared the second floor, I kept that mop of red hair in my sight until I lost her around a bend.

Now on the third floor, the creak of a door opening and closing led me around the same curving balustrade. I checked behind me again as I holstered my dagger and palmed Ty's stake. Then I grabbed and turned the clear glass doorknob, and cracked the door open.

Darkness prevailed as one beating heart registered. I didn't dare say a word as my sense of smell picked up something too. Not just Vanessa. And not alive.

This was a trap.

I struck out with Ty's stake as the blunt force of a loaded fist belted into my cheek. My head snapped sideways with the crack of my neck and my legs turned to liquid. Concrete arms caught me and cold breath fanned over my face as Ty growled, "Welcome home, beautiful."

Then it was lights out.

CHAPTER 29

*P*ain rocketed through my neck that was bent at an awkward angle. And that wasn't all. I locked down the impulse to tilt my head upright and kept my slow rhythmic breathing in check in spite of the fear that had my heart racing. A loud whirring sound pounded my eardrums while numbing prickles scraped my inner forearm.

Keeping knockout still in my sitting position, my fuzzy eyes slitted open. A satin-swathed bed jutted out from the far wall. The wooden headboard made my heart stop. The same one Ty had been perched on in his tell-all dreamscape. A loveseat butted up against a powder-blue wall. A roll-down blind kept the day or night locked out, though which I wasn't sure.

My other senses caught up as my vision became crystal clear. Apart from my own, there was one heartbeat and one set of lungs that inflated and exhaled. A warm, fine-boned hand lay across my wrist.

Shifting my eyeballs as far right as I could manage, I found the source. Vanessa's forearm was bandaged and her red hair was tied back. The glow of the wall sconce above the table beside us highlighted one side of her face and her downcast sapphire irises. A glass pot was there too, filled with black liquid that she dipped the tattoo gun's needle into while perched on the edge of her own chair.

"I know you're awake," she said without looking up from the mark she returned to drilling into my arm.

No longer wearing my hoodie, my hands strained to dart to my waist and my weapons. But they never got there. Tied down with engraved iron, the chains pinned my arms to a metal chair. My Vans scuffed what felt like thin carpet, but got no further as my sight snapped down. Not only were my arms and legs tied, but another three loops of iron kept my ribs strapped too.

My breath hitched. That wasn't even the worse of it.

My utility belt was gone, along with Marcus's dagger. All my stakes? Gone. Including Ty's. *Shit.* I was trapped and out of silver—in damned territory. On the damned commander and Ty's turf.

Something else was off, too. That feeling of having something missing when you wore it twenty-four/seven. There—my naked wrist. The pendant was gone. My warning of danger—gone.

Unarmed and without warning or not, I tugged at the chains, making Vanessa frown as she tried to finish the marks on my arm. "Why are you doing this?"

I struggled harder when she didn't reply, but short of tipping the chair over, I wasn't going anywhere fast.

"Vanessa!"

Her stare lifted a fraction, unfocused and blank. Then it dropped again to continue the last line of the mark she was on. "Almost finished."

Compulsion. Strong, mind-bending compulsion.

With nowhere to go, I dared to inspect the sequence of symbols along my inner forearm. In the same black I'd seen Vanessa inflict onto Ty in my vision, these marks weren't fading like the ones she'd tried to give me back in Portsmouth. I didn't recognize any of them, but sudden suspicion had me dropping a brick in my mental wall to see if I could reach out and connect with Kendrick. I wasn't going to let anything through. I wasn't going to bring him into this. I just—

Nothing.

I dropped another brick. Then another. Then the whole wall. Still nothing. Not even the sense of Kendrick keeping me out. Just vacantness. One of the symbols had severed my blood bond.

Knowing I was in deep shit, I rescanned the room. One door. One exit. Unless I broke out through the window. But that still involved getting free of these chains. Perhaps I could get through...

"Vanessa, look at me. I can get us out of here. I just need you to look up."

Vanessa shut off the tattoo gun then, the whirring snapping off with a click. She held the machinery in her lap and her focus lifted. "All done."

I threw every ounce of compulsion at her, my stare penetrating hers. "I need you to unlock these chains. Right. Now."

The blank look on her face didn't budge. Either the damned compulsion she was under was too strong, or one of my tattoos was a compulsion blocker. Either way, I had a hope's chance in hell of getting through to her verbally.

Vanessa went about her business, unplugging the gun's cord from behind the table as my mind raced. When she tabled the machinery to slide a black case out from behind her chair, the needle tip gleamed in the sconce's light. Silver. The needles were silver. More filled the velvet molded inside of the case, I saw as she propped it open on the table. They ranged in size and length, filling a separate clear plastic container.

As the container was moved to the table's edge and the lid opened to accommodate the gun's needle, I thought on my feet. Or rather, on my butt. What I needed was out of reach, but like that was going to stop me.

Summoning strength, I rocked out then in, the chair's backrest knocking into the small table. Rocking from the sudden contact, the top smacked the wall and repelled back our way. Just the way I'd planned it. Tilted off balance, the case and container went sliding off the wooden edge along with the pot of black ink. The gun thudded as it hit, while the needles pinged and the black ink sprayed across the thin carpet and began soaking in.

Vanessa responded to the disruption in slow-mo, staring at the scattered mess at our feet. She lowered with zombie grace and got to work packing up.

She was so souped up on brain-fry she hadn't noticed the way the container had tipped. How its contents had rained down so close to my restrained right hand. How my clenched fist had unfurled to catch just one thick, sharp piece.

My fingers squeezed tight.

Now I had a fighting chance.

The heavy stride of boots registered outside the room I was trapped in. I tensed against my restraints, listening to the pitch of tread that neared in rising steps. Climbing the staircase. The sound gained small distance, only to shift and pick up pace to come this way. Landing cleared and balustrade passed. My fist squeezed around the silver needle as a chink preceded the shifting of the lock.

The door opened and Ty strolled in. Scanning me over with anticipation, he tucked a black-handled semi-automatic into the back of his waistband. He spared a glance down at Vanessa who rose with her packed-up equipment. His brow arched at the soaked-in splash of black ink. "I heard a thud," he said, hunting boots striding over to stand before his old friend. He tilted her chin up, irises and pupils unchanged as he captured her gaze. "Was there a problem?"

Packed case hanging by the handle, Vanessa made no physical movement. Her voice was monotone as she spoke, and I held my breath, fearing she'd somehow caught on to what I'd done and was about to rat me out. "She knocked into the table. I packed up. The markings are complete."

Ty raised a brow over his shoulder at me. "Trying to escape?" His fangs gleamed as he smiled. "You'll be free soon enough. Leave now, Vanessa."

Without a glance or a word, she carted her equipment out and shut the door behind her.

Now alone with Ty, my heart stammered and I suddenly felt hot. My blood raced with adrenaline. Run, fight, speak.

Still chained, I had only one option. And I was floundering.

If there was any chance at breaking through to him, appealing to the guy he used to be and could be again, I had to try. "It's not too late, Ty. You can still be my hero. You can protect me, you just have to let me—"

Ty shot forward to kneel before me. His strong hands landed on my thighs and slid down my jeans. My breath caught at his touch, his closeness, the way he kept his eyes on mine. A key was retrieved from his pocket, and then he was behind me in a flash. Metal slotted and turned and the chains around me clanked as they fell loose. I didn't dare move as he stood in front of me again, preparing only on the inside to strike.

"I'm not who you think I am, Amelia." Ty pulled a Zippo from his leather jacket, clicking the lid open and shut as he walked to the loveseat and slumped onto it. "That guy you're in love with isn't here anymore. It's just me."

I dared to shake the chains off, feeling lighter as they clanked to the carpet. A few steps brought me closer to him, but not too close. "That's not true."

A cigarette followed the lighter, and with the butt between his lips, Ty flicked the lighter open and lit up.

"You're smoking," I couldn't stop from blurting as burning tobacco stained the air.

"It's not like it's going to kill me," Ty said with a shrug. "But that's why you're here. Isn't it? To release me from this abominable existence, to stop the death and destruction I am unleashing on vampires." He took a drag and shrugged out of his leather jacket, standing to close the space between us. "Well I have news for you." Smoke puffed out with his words, and my throat clenched as I refused to cough. "I like what I've become. So what if lives get lost along the way, when each one I take strengthens me. Don't you see, Amelia? We can be together now. We can rule both worlds, side by side."

I stood my ground, refusing to give in. Refusing to let my one empty hand reach out and touch him. "You can't be serious. You can't really want to live like this."

"But I do." The light from a tall lamp beside him emphasized his driven expression. A fanged smile parted his lips and tendrils of smoke drifted out. "So there are only two options you have to consider. Though after what you've done," he said, top lip curling with a snarl. "I really shouldn't give you the choice."

Struck by the sudden and dangerous look I didn't understand, I let my curiosity get the better of me. "What I've done?"

"I've seen how you were with him. *Kendrick*." That look suddenly made sense. Jealousy. Boiling, revenge-seeking jealousy. "At the shack in Palmer. At the Armaya. Then my suspicions were cemented. When I drank you...I tasted *him*."

"H-how?" was all I managed to croak.

At the emotionless look in his eyes and lack of reply as he took another drag of his cigarette, I replayed all the sightings. Of all the times I'd felt like I was being watched, or thought I'd imagined seeing Ty at the Armaya, two stood out in vivid detail. The time I'd seen him from my balcony at the field. Then in the basement in Palmer that led to old tunnels. There he'd changed into a stranger and left me bleeding out. I hadn't been losing it...well not completely. Those times *had* been him.

And I knew now how he'd done it. "You imprinted another damned."

"Among others. Told you I'd never abandon you." His cold smile broke my heart. "Now, your two choices, which I'll give you total control of...without persuasion. Join me and rule by my side, or..." Shrug without words.

A hard lump climbed up my throat and I gulped it down. Back in our last dreamscape my feelings had been so raw, so true. I'd let Ty bite me, drink from me, even knowing what he was. I'd suspected then, and now his words, *without persuasion,* confirmed it. Ty had compelled me. Tested my resistance, my weakness to him turning me. And that's what joining him now meant...me dying, my heart ceasing to beat.

"And the second option?"

Ty bent to tap the ash from his cigarette into a glass bowl on a side table. "Would not be my choice, but, if you give me no option, then so be it." He reached out to touch my arm and my fist cranked tighter around the silver needle. "Amelia, I won't let you live without me. If you refuse to join me..." He returned the cigarette to his lips and took a long draw, staring at me as if to say, *fill in the blanks.*

The message was clear. I was dead one way or another.

White smoke curled from Ty's mouth and his voice was seductively smooth. "You belong to *me*."

And there was the cold, hard truth. The fact I hadn't wanted to believe but could no longer delude myself with. The Ty I was still so inexorably in love with was gone. What was left was this empty shell that was my enemy. Someone who wanted to possess me, not love me. I sighed, scanning over every part of him, committing all those little details to my memory bank. I knew the choice I had to make, and I would fight until my last dying breath. If I couldn't save Ty, I'd have to kill him…or die trying.

"Then I choose death. But don't expect me to go down without a fight."

A feral smile transformed Ty's features as he butted out his cig. "Wouldn't dream of it."

Ty leaped first, which I expected and managed to dodge. But he was fast, so fast, and came at me again. His calloused, iron grip caught my shoulder and I threw an uppercut to his nose. A faint crack sounded and Ty laughed. "Thought I'd taught you better than this. But you're no match for me." He licked over his fangs and snarled. "Victory's gonna taste good."

In a split second, I studied my options. I knew Ty, had fought with him back in our training days. I knew his moves. Unfortunately, he knew most of mine, too. His heart didn't beat and he wouldn't tire like I would. If I was going to get the upper hand, I would have to act fast. I needed to subdue him if I was going to have any chance of saving him. And I had to do it without wasting my voltage. Which, thank God, I could still feel swarming inside of me.

Ty lunged again and I dropped to the ground, punching my knee into his crotch. Ty grunted and staggered, for only a second. But it was enough for me to pull up and swipe the gun from him. With a dangerous smile, he rose so the muzzle was pressed to his ash-colored T-shirt.

Right over his heart.

With a full magazine of bullets—if they were silver—I could kill him. End it now.

But I hesitated.

The plan had been to slow him down, to create an opportunity to pierce his heart with electric silver…but would the thin silver in my palm be enough to do it?

Ty grasped the gun and turned the business end back onto me. "I knew you couldn't do it." He cocked the gun. "Last chance to change your mind. So what'll it be?"

I struck out hard, knocking the weapon from his hands and it went skidding under the bed. He countered with an irritated growl and an elbow to my jaw. "Keep that up and I'm going to end up hurting you."

I ignored the explosion of pain and planted a strong kick into his stomach. "Ditto."

That won me a slight groan, but it wasn't enough. Ty grasped my shoulders lightning fast and threw me at the wall.

I hit and fell, air belting from my lungs and bones aching. Still, I managed to land crouched on the ground just beside the window and its thick sun-blocking roll-down.

I had to act fast. But I didn't want to kill him. I just needed the upper hand.

As Ty leaped for me again, I sprang to my feet, retracting the blind a few inches up.

Thin light streamed inside the half boarded-up window. Even with the dark glass and caked-on dirt, Ty cowered away as it hit him. He hissed and growled, arms shooting to his chest out of the light as he writhed in agony. Then he tripped, catching the blind's drawstring. The cover shot up higher and he collapsed on the ground, bathed in setting sunlight.

Drowning in terror, I rushed to Ty, placing a hand on him to spin him around.

The hissing stopped and Ty rose off the stained carpet. With his head dropped he laughed with amusement. "Do you really think I'm that stupid?"

I backed up slowly, my jaw gaping. Ty was unmarked, unburned. Completely unharmed. "How is that possible?"

Ty's head slowly lifted, a fanged smile spreading across his lips. "Double glazed, one hundred percent UV-resistant tinted glass."

He stepped forward and I held my clenched fist to my heart, fingers squeezing around the silver length. Invisible power streamed from my chest to the one place I needed it. If I failed, this was it. For both of us.

Ty struck out and clutched my neck, tilting my head to expose my jugular. "I wish it didn't have to come to this…" He leaned in, mouth parting, deadly fangs so long…

I flicked the silver out and plunged it into his chest with voltage. Ty flinched at the last second and I missed his heart, the needle sizzling as it sank just below the mark. With the silver embedded, he flew back at the shock of electricity. I sprinted for the door, the one that had never been relocked.

I was out of options.

I couldn't beat Ty without killing him. And with that release of power and the loss of my only weapon, I couldn't save him now.

I escaped as Ty roared my name, hurtling my body down the flights of stairs to the foyer. I needed to get armed fast. But I needed a plan. Being unprepared before almost got me killed. And I wouldn't make the same mistake twice. Wouldn't get so consumed on the location of Ty without considering my next step. Before night broke, I would be back. And so help me God. I would be ready.

About to propel myself through the front door, a voice jarred me to a stop. It wasn't Ty's. And it wasn't a stranger's. The callous intent that sent a shudder through me identified the speaker without confusion. I'd heard that same chilling tone more than once before —in visions commanding the damned and from the late Lord Vladimir's murderer. The puzzle pieces had already fallen into place. It had to be. Only one person's compulsion had sent Vanessa here and led me to Ty.

Oh dear God.

Horror and the need to see him with my own eyes had my Vans taking me past the stairs' landing and down a dark hall to a cellar door. In spite of my measured steps, the stairs creaked as I clambered down. Beyond the cellar I'd seen in my vision, the concrete hallway was narrow, with rope hanging from hooks, and stacks of old newspapers taking up foot space. Ones that headlined missing persons and brutal unsolved murders. At the last second, I shrank behind a door and peeked through the quarter-inch gap to find an earth-reeking tunnel.

"Prepare and gather our numbers. We have a message to deliver, and we need it to be unforgettable."

A group of five damned stood in a uniformed line, before a wooden table with what appeared to be an unfolded map. From this distance and angle, I couldn't make out the finer details. But I had a sinister suspicion that I knew the location.

I couldn't see the face I was looking for, either, but then that voice came again, sending an arctic shiver up my spine and into my skull. *"It's about time everyone learned my true identity. And what a way to make an entrance."*

With a nod from the five, a chorus of booted feet came marching my way. Going gecko-flat behind the door, I held my breath as the damned climbed up the stairs and closed the cellar door behind them. I crept around, back grazing the earthy walls to get a clear—

"Amelia, I know you're there."

My heart couldn't decide if it wanted to race or stop altogether, and my brain felt like it was on fire. Sweating instant bullets, I entered the cavern where flame light danced from a single fire pit.

Sitting in a solid, black marble throne, was the person I'd sought to identify for all this time. His name left my mouth on a choked breath. *"Marcus."*

CHAPTER 30

he first words that wanted to come out of my mouth were, *why are you here? Who's making you do this?* Because this was Marcus, my brother by blood, my twin. He couldn't really be... Except he was, wasn't he? Hearing that voice and knowing it came from his own mouth, the same voice I'd heard in visions that had been so familiar and yet so alien. It had never been Dorian's. It was the voice of the damned commander. The voice of the Vladimirs' slaughterer.

In dumb shock, I just stood there, making no move to arm myself or prepare to fight. Of all the images and questions that ran manic through my head, only one thing could escape. *"Why?"*

Marcus looked up at me thoughtfully, no concern or regret at me finding him out, but rather glowing satisfaction. "It's what I was born to do. As were you. We are two halves of a whole." He stood, his hand sliding off the throne's armrest and picking up the dagger that had been hidden below. The same one I'd taken to keep whoever had hurt him from plunging it in deep. He sheathed it at his waist, and with another step his face caught the only light that shone from the fire pit. "The frontier of vampire evolution."

"You knew all along. That I was your sister and you were Caius's son." I dared to meet his stare and gasped at the color of his irises. Blood red with darker specks. He wasn't damned, his beating heart and the times I'd tasted his blood was proof enough. "Your eyes."

"A result of what our father made me." A nonchalant shrug. "And I'm not wearing my contacts. Wouldn't go down too well to walk about the Armaya without them, now would it."

At the admission, all the memories I had of the damned resurfaced. The commander ordering his minions to seek and slaughter royals. Leading the slaughter of the Vladimirs and killing the lord— who he'd known wasn't his true father. Orchestrating a killing spree on the Armaya. Eradicating all of Uriel's family. Sending Ty to turn me...or was that bite actually intended for Caius all along?

My brain pulsed, feeling like it wanted to explode. It couldn't all have been him, my twin. It just couldn't.

The Portsmouth Council flooded back, the smashed-up hall painted in bodies and ash and black and red blood. Caius had claimed the PVC carnage hadn't been his aim. Had he been telling the truth?

"Was it all you, Marcus? All those vampires, the attacks..." The rest of my words hung unsaid in the damp, clay-smelling air, refusing to pass my lips, refusing to ask the unthinkable. I saw Marcus's face when I'd found him taking all those humans and guards in *The Pit*, the turmoil that had reverberated off him like a stain on his soul. A ruse to cover what he'd been all along. "Was it all an act?"

A pair of strong hands gripped my waist and spun me on the spot. Ty, and he looked seriously pissed off as I lashed out to get free. A small hole was left in his T-shirt where the needle had penetrated his chest. But the silver was gone. All that remained was a dribble of sludgy black blood down the ash-colored material. His deadly stare drilled into me as he released his hold.

"Oh, good. My second in command." Marcus chuckled, returning to his throne. "Looks like my sister did a number on you, Wolf."

"Our talk didn't go as planned," Ty said, fangs and canines long and deadly. He was close enough to breathe down my neck—if he still needed to. "She pinched a marking needle and tried to stake me with it. Won't happen again. I promise you that." He knocked past me to stand beside Marcus. "Now can we revert to force?"

"Not yet." Marcus's alien gaze traveled up to me, some of that old and familiar sincerity transforming his features. "These things take time, and all of this is new to you."

A missing puzzle piece rose with the whirlwind inside my head. The other half that had brought me to this hotel from hell. "Where's Dorian? What have you done to him?"

"Done to him? Nothing. He's in one piece at the Armaya where I left him." Marcus smiled. "Such an easy mind to bend. But helpful, nonetheless."

Dorian was completely innocent like Vanessa. A means to an end. I remembered the vision that had led me to my ex-brother and his girlfriend in the first place. "You delivered that vision on purpose, to lure me here." Marcus offered no answer, just a smile of satisfaction. With wheels spinning, I remembered my forgotten vision of the Armaya attack, then all the times I'd tried to uncover the commander's identity and been forced from the vision too soon, or lost the images I'd seen. "That was you, too. You stole my visions. So I wouldn't warn the RVC. So I wouldn't know it was you. Didn't you?"

Raised eyebrow, but not a single word.

I saw then for the millionth time, Caius's blade slicing through Ty's heart. His body had disappeared from that hall. Been taken for a purpose. To turn a hybrid damned. Caius had been trying to protect me. He had told the truth. "That story you told me of the vampire and lycan lovers, you knew who and what Ty was then. It was your plan all along to turn him."

"Since learning of your relationship, I'd been gunning for him. Your hybrid turning damned was purely a matter of time."

"So the cruise…the *snow lodge*."

"I needed your entourage out of the way. Though we both know that little plan fell through. Then you came out as the Oracle and the opportunity was too much to ignore when your wolf got himself caught. I needed the bargaining chip. In the state he was kept imprisoned in, I knew you'd give him your blood. His death was ordered before the attack, though our father saved me the trouble. As for everything else? It was all my doing, though not without reason."

Marcus stood, shitkickers striding slowly over the compacted dirt to meet me. The vulnerability in his red eyes stopped me from running or backing away. He touched my shoulder and let his hand slide down to my elbow. "I want to unite the races. All three: vampire, lycan, damned. I can control the damned. Stop the feuding. The bloodshed. Except the RVC will never allow it. Not with those stuffy royals calling the shots. But if we can have ruling power…"

After being shocked mute, Marcus's candid words forced my voice. "No reason will ever *justify* what you've already done." His actions had been deplorable. But I couldn't lay the blame solely on him. My Twin. I thought *I* had been the one who was cursed all this time, but he'd gotten the short end of the stick. All his heinous actions were fueled by what Marcus was. What Caius had engineered him to be. I put a foot of space between us, but still I didn't run. "I can give you both a chance...it's not too late to do the right thing. To make amends."

Ty resorted to that statue-still stance as Marcus backed up. "I'm not damned, Amelia. I'm just like you. Both races mixed together, but where you're a little more vamp, I'm a little more damned... well, a lot more. You can't restore me like you did that damned girl or our father." That smile, horrible, cruel and seductively smooth, crawled across Marcus's lips. "I am what I am. But if you join me, together we could be so much more."

The horrible truth I'd tried to ignore was staring me in the face with his red eyes. I felt it in his cold calculation and warped reasoning, down to that place deep in my soul that had recognized his essence from the start. Marcus had no conscience. No depth to understand how wrong everything he'd done was. With what he'd been given in life, I couldn't blame him. But I couldn't ignore it, either. Able to restore him or not, I wouldn't play along. I wouldn't stand by while he slaughtered the innocent. "I'm sorry, Marcus. I can't be your moral compass."

Blue lightning sparked across my flesh, gathering at speed to collect at my hands. Marcus's stare grew dangerous while Ty's body began to tremble, readying to shift forms. This time I was quicker, the internal and invisible prep giving me the element of surprise. A dying volt forked from either hand, one blasting into Ty and halting his transformation as he stumbled back. The second dwindling spark snapped Marcus's holster and sent his dagger airborne.

Hand striking out, I caught the hilt mid-air. I backed up while Marcus remained stationary, blade ready to cut flesh. In my peripheral view Ty snarled, teeth gritting as his body resumed its trembling and slow cracks rang out. My latest vision was about to come true. I just hadn't expected the instigator to be me.

Marcus's smile sent frozen shards through my heart as Ty

padded closer in wolf form, jaw snapping. Outnumbered, and powerless to save anyone, let alone myself, I had only one option.

Run.

Every residual spark I could muster flew at Ty, who let out a yelp as he went flying back into the gently curved wall. I lunged forward, dagger driving the assault. Marcus saw the attack coming.

And opened his arms in invitation.

He was going to let me kill him.

And damn me, I couldn't bring myself to do it. To be like our father.

I shifted at the last second, plunging the silver into his chest less than an inch from his heart. No cry erupted as Marcus collapsed. And I didn't stick around to see the fire in his eyes or the disbelief in his gaping mouth. I pivoted around and bolted from the cavern.

Marcus's bellow echoed up the dirt tunnel, voice full of command that promised death to anyone who disobeyed. "Stop her!"

Exploding from the stairs below, I broke into the foyer, eyes fixed on the wide front door. Just a few more bounds and I'd be outside, safe in setting sunlight. My hands reached out, fingers straining as they caught around the handle, pushed down and—

"Oomph."

The arm that appeared out of nowhere was an iron bar that flung around my neck, squeezing almost to the point of breaking bone.

I clawed at the damned's gray flesh as he pulled my back to his chest. The long ribbons left in my nails' wake swelled with black as his hold tightened. My voltage was DOA, and his other arm clamped around my waist and held tight. Fang tips scraped down my neck and I cried out as they plunged in deep. Water sprang to my eyes with the injection of venom that shot like speed-driven battery acid through my veins.

Marcus and Ty—the only existing damned wolf—appeared in a haze with a snarl and a bark.

Before the damned took a draw on my vein, Marcus was across the green patterned tiles. In a blur, he ripped the damned from me. One arm was torn off the damned with a sick and wet crack and hurled across the room. It hit the central table and smashed the ceramic vase to pieces.

Marcus's own mouth was on the damned's neck then as more damned appeared in the open entries to other rooms. They all stood in perfect stillness, glowing eyes watching as their comrade's jugular was ripped from its neck. A quick twist with Marcus's arms and the damned was beheaded with a squirt of glossy black. The head landed in place of the smashed vase, a gruesome replacement. Then the body was dropped, a severed hose of black blood spraying in pulses across the tiles.

Without that flood of dopamine, I felt like I was melting from the inside out. Like in minutes my flesh would ignite with fire. Sweat sprouted from my pores, drops forming to slide down my back. My vision blurred.

I wasn't about to let being stunned by shock and bone-striking pain stop me. With my hand flying over the serrated gouge in my neck, I backed up toward the door—then stopped.

Ty was now behind me, hackles raised and canines gleaming below his bunched muzzle as he guarded the exit. All the other escapes were blocked by watching damned.

They made no move as Marcus turned in a slow circle to meet each of their red stares. Like Ty earlier, blood coated his white T-shirt in rivulets that had stained down to the top of ripped jeans. But so much more had spilled. His chest below the torn cotton was smudged with his crimson blood, but the skin had pulled together, leaving a scar that looked like an old operation incision fully healed.

"That punishment will be inflicted on any of you, should you harm so much as a hair on her head." His arm flung out, finger pointing right at me. "Now declare your sworn allegiance—to your queen."

Each of the damned knelt on one knee, their glowing eyes locked on me as each fisted a hand over their silent hearts. As one they declared, "Hail forever, Queen of the Damned."

Unhindered warmth rose up as bones cracked behind me. A nod from Marcus was directed over my shoulder to Ty who stood tall in all his naked glory.

"Until the venom burns off, beautiful, sleep tight." Ty swung sideways, bent arm flicking up and elbow driving into my temple.

Brightness flared across my vision, then it was lights out.

CHAPTER 31

J awoke to darkness, feeling satin against my skin and padding beneath my head. Tucked in tight to a bed, I listened for sounds and heard nothing. That didn't mean I was alone. Ty could be as silent as a ghost, and like before when he'd knocked me out, as fast as lightning.

My hand slid along the satin, stupid heart drumming too loud as I groped for the bedside lamp. Finding the button, the light beamed on and I ratcheted upright.

Sight darting, I saw the vacant chairs where Vanessa had marked me, the loveseat Ty had sat on, the ashtray he'd used, the couch separating the bed from the door. My head craned around and my rising fear ebbed. Ty wasn't propped like a human spider on the tall headboard. He wasn't here at all.

The dizziness and fire that had swamped my veins from that damned's bite were gone. Working off that kind of poison took time. How long had I been out of it? Hours, a day, more?

I slung my legs over the bed's edge and padded in my Vans to the door. I gripped the knob and—locked. Not a surprise. But that wasn't going to contain me. At least not for long.

Grasping a throw blanket draped over the loveseat, I reached the window. Hand wrapped in cotton, I lifted the blind to reveal a deepening night sky and rising stars. With a quick jab, I punched out—

The window vibrated and a red symbol that had been invisible pulsed across the glass. Explosive power sent me flying back into the bar across the room. Wood splintered and glass cracked, cutting into my arms and clothes. I held back my hiss and swore as I scrambled up, watching the door in wait of Ty or Marcus to bust in at the noise.

No one came.

A few minutes passed as my stinging cuts began to zip shut, and still there was no show.

Maybe I was alone here. Being after dark, they could all be out hunting for victims. The thought of Ty or Marcus among a prowling, blood-hungry group made me cringe. But opportunity was opportunity.

Striding around the couch, I picked a chair up by it legs. With both hands I swung it sideways, belting it into the locked door.

Right before impact another symbol lit up. An invisible wave vibrated off the uninjured door and compacted the metal frame that propelled back at me. I ducked in time and it catapulted into the couch, tipping it backward.

Rage built within me at the confinement of being caged like a wild animal. Door, window…walls? There had to be a weakness. And I was going to find it.

All that filled this imprisoning room suddenly became a tool. A means to escape. And I didn't hold back. Every piece and every surface were fair game.

I went at the wall and retried the window and door, attacking with furniture to test every spot for that one weakness. Each hit ignited a reverberating shudder around the room and a glowing symbol. So I resorted to the mold-stained ceiling and thin-carpeted floor. No difference. No fissures to crack through. Just surfaces more impenetrable than foot-thick steel. But I couldn't stop. Couldn't accept that this was it.

I kept up my attack, moving faster, throwing harder, and air sawing in and out of my lungs.

Not fifteen minutes later, I sat on my butt, knees propped and arms levered against the carpet, angling my torso upright. Exhaustion wreaked havoc on my bones, making them throb after the thrashing I'd subjected them to. Slow-healing cuts covered my exposed flesh that was now teeming with darkening blue veins. My tank and second-skin black jeans were restyled with rents and holes. Around me, a dumpsite of broken furniture littered the once-orderly room: splintered wood, shredded couch material and foam, gnarled metal chairs and lamps, and a clawed blind that looked like a bear had mistaken it for a hunter.

In tired frustration, I picked up a splintered piece of wood that had been a leg on the small table between two padded chairs. With less than full power, I flung it at the wall. Right before the connection, a force field rippled out with the same glowing red symbol. Ricocheting wood missiled right back at me. I dropped flat on my back as the returned debris sailed over my head and collided with a pile of former furniture. Every attempt to break out of this room had had the same result. Every external surface had been reinforced with a series of swirls that repelled any attempt to break through.

I was trapped. Body and mind.

∾

FOR A LONG WHILE I sat on the ground, surrounded by my attempt to break free. With my body healing, the thoughts I'd repressed over everything I'd learned resurfaced. Marcus, my twin, was the damned commander and a murderer. He'd insured Ty's transition into a conscienceless monster. He'd used Vanessa to get his army onto Armaya grounds, and Dorian as a scapegoat to lead me here.

My thoughts played the events before Ty had knocked me out in reverse. My hand slid up to my neck, covering the almost healed serrated gouge from the damned now serving as a head ornament on the foyer table downstairs. For some reason, I was on the protected list. Untouchable…for the time being. But why?

Thinking back, I remembered the first words I'd heard before following the source to find Marcus: *"Prepare and gather our numbers. We have a message to deliver, and we need it to be unfor-gettable. It's about time everyone learned my true identity. And what a way to make an entrance."*

My eyes widened in understanding as I recalled the map and my suspicion of its location. The Armaya. Where no one knew who Marcus really was. And where he was ready to rip that little blinder off, quick like a Band-Aid. He had a message for them. The reveal of his true identity. After every other move he'd made, it wouldn't be a friendly meet and greet. It would be a shut-up-and-take-notice encounter while the collateral damage bled out on the ground.

And Kendrick was there.

Urgency tightened every one of my sore muscles and made my bones creak. I needed to warn him. Warn them all. Before it was too late.

Twisting my forearm, I picked up a splinter of wood and went to plunge it into my inked skin, intending to puncture and tear down, splitting the series of marks in two. Damaging them beyond usability like Dorian had done to Vanessa.

As the jagged tip drove down, a stabbing pain struck my skull and weapon-directing arm. I cried out, the intensity feeling like my forearm had snapped and my skull had cracked like an egg. Keeling over, the wood splinter fell as I curled up and clung to my head. Salty tears squeezed out of my pinned-shut eyes.

The pain began to recede then, and I took a shuddering breath. Lying sideways, I stared at the marks. I reached up, intending to claw them off with my bare nails. But as I got closer, a warning of what I'd just experienced began to rebuild with torturing force.

I dropped my intent and shoved my body upright. Maybe one of Vanessa's marks repelled damage, like the rest of this destroyed room. Either that, or I'd been compelled without knowing to leave them intact. Either way I was screwed. But for Kendrick's sake and all the other lives at stake, I couldn't give up.

I needed to see exactly what was going to happen. Because that's why no one had interrupted my demolition. They were all on a mission. Dread made it feel like I'd just been run through. It couldn't be too late. I had to find a way to stop it.

Dropping my knees, I crossed my legs and squeezed my eyes shut. Stars of light danced behind my eyelids, fighting the empty void I was aiming for. But they didn't hold out, my will overrode the distraction and soon enough all that remained was empty black. The shadows slid in then, curling around my body like eels underwater. But this time I wasn't going to wish the right one would curl around my arm and absorb into my hand. There was only one vision I needed to see right now, and I was going to take it.

Standing in frozen stillness, my silver-glowing eyes were the only things that moved apart from the shadows. I watched as they clustered and glided around me, waiting for the one I needed. They all looked the same, but as I watched on, a sensation caught my breath every other second. Right when one of the shadows slid over my heart.

My hand shot up, strangling the slippery eel it caught as my other hand came up. Bringing my palms together, the essence struggled for only a moment before absorbing into my skin.

I was suddenly in the boardroom, strong male arms folded on the round marble slab in front of me. I knew those arms like they were my own. Kendrick's. Sitting on his throne, he looked over the table at Marcus. Oh God, I wish I could see his face. A hint of emotion dyed his voice as he spoke. "Where's Amelia?"

There was something else I sensed, too. A tightening of his muscles like he was pent up with angst that he couldn't release. Just from speaking my name?

"She's feeling under the weather," Marcus said without hesitation. "Said to go on without her."

So Kendrick still didn't know I was missing. No one did. Had he tried to connect with me through the bond? Did he think I was blocking him now? If the energy I was reading off him was any indication, the answer was a big fat NO.

"As you called the meeting," Uriel spoke up from beside Marcus, "if carrying on without Lady Bathory is fine with you, I have no issue with it."

The other royals made collective noises of agreement that made Marcus smile. "Then let's get on with it." He clapped his hands and rubbed his palms together as if pleased. "With the ongoing attacks, you all know you are not safe. The Armaya is not safe. Will you surrender to keep your lives and that of all our people?"

Aghast, the other royals strained in their thrones while Kendrick's eyes narrowed. They all spoke at the same time.

"Where is this coming from?"

"We will never surrender."

"How can you even suggest such a thing?"

"We will find a way to beat them."

Kendrick spoke last, one hand dropping under the table to the blade strapped to his waist. Not actually linked to him, I didn't know what triggered him to move. An unconscious reflex, or the innate sense of impending danger? "You make it sound like there's an option. Like we have a choice to make."

Marcus stood slowly, hands going to the table's edge as he leaned forward. He looked from his left at Uriel and around to each royal's face. "Which you all just made."

His fist came down and cracked through the marble. The doors kicked in and damned flooded through as fire scaled up from the floor all around the room. The sudden live columns consumed the surrounding royal portraits, and blocked every door and windowpane.

A war cry bellowed from Marcus's mouth. "Kill them all!"

MY CONSCIOUSNESS RETURNED with a rush of anxiety, and my heart belted with the need to take action. As my lids flung wide, I went to jump up and gasped. The mess I'd made of the room was gone. Minimal new furniture now filled the space. All the surfaces were bare though, no excess decoration that could be broken if I turned the place upside down again.

The smell of burnt tobacco registered then and I saw him, sitting in an armchair across the room. A single lamp was all that offered light in the redecorated space, revealing the face of who watched me with restrained intent. Ty took a long draw on a cigarette and blew out, eyes narrowing. Through the clean-up, he knew exactly what I'd been doing. But did he know why?

With the room's transformation, it was clear I'd been out for a while, so connected to the vision that I'd had no idea what had been going on around my physical body. No idea that Ty had even been here. I went to sit up—and paused. Behind my back my arms were bound by rope. Was it unbreakable? Shifting without use of my hands or arms, I kept him in my sight.

In that frozen, could-be-a-statue thing he did, his eyes—rich with red hunger—were the only thing that gave away the fact that he was animated. As did the curling smoke from his parted lips. "Been a day since that damned tried to take a chunk out of you. Looks like you've recovered though. Well, mostly."

Hunger grumbled from my stomach then, as if trying to make conversation. The physical exhaustion of tearing this room to pieces and bringing on that vision had completely drained me. Not to mention overcoming the damned poison, and it being well over twenty-four hours since I took off from the Armaya. I dared a quick look at my chest and shoulders. Yep. Dark blue veins tracked over my exposed skin like cracks in pavement.

I was starved.

But I couldn't let my guard down, and I couldn't forget what I'd seen. I needed to get through to Kendrick, get warning out before it was too late. "Where's Marcus?"

Ty stood up and rolled his shoulders back with a series of crunches. "Took off over an hour ago. So it's just you and me. We've got the place to ourselves…well mostly."

Shit! The bloody reveal. My fear as to why this place had seemed empty had just been confirmed. Time was ticking and I had no idea how to get warning out. If I somehow managed to get the upper hand again, I could incapacitate Ty and take his phone. If he even had one on him. Or steal the key to escape this room. With the damned en route with Marcus, I'd have a better chance of escaping.

But then what? Even on my Ducati, I'd never get to the Armaya before them. But if I stole a phone…

"Guess you saw our next move." My jaw dropped as Ty waved a carefree hand. "Don't worry, it will be over soon enough. But now…" From his position, his gaze lit up as if sending laser beams into my own eyes. "Come. Sit in the chair opposite me."

Mind screaming, my body ignored my internal fight. With more struggle than usual, using balance and strength with my wrists bound, my legs forced me to my feet. Each step I battled, but it was no use. I was too hungry and weak to refuse his compulsion.

A second later I'd taken the seat opposite Ty as he lowered back down into his. A table separated us, small enough that his cold, gray hands could reach out and touch me if he wanted. "You must be starving by now. It must be all you can even think of."

The hunger I already felt grew into a wave of gut-churning pain, overriding my need to find a way to contact Kendrick or anyone at the Armaya. But not the need to free my wrists. With what little finger movement I could manage without letting on by shifting my arms, my nails began picking at the tough ropes.

Ty kept a close and pleased watch on me as someone knocked at the door. He butted his cigarette out on the bare wood of the table. "Come in."

Vanessa walked right on in—not needing to unlock the door to gain access. Her nothing expression and blank stare registered jack-all in particular as she came to stand between us.

"Vanessa," her name left my lips on a whisper, dread combining with the hunger in my gut. God. I could hear her racing heart. Could detect the scent of her coursing blood. I pinned my lips shut to jail my impulse to hiss.

There was no response from her though, no recognition as she lowered two crystal glasses with what smelled like scotch from the tray she carried onto the tabletop. She turned to leave.

"Wait," Ty demanded, freezing her in motion. His fangs like white bone daggers poked through his lips and clinked against the glass as he threw back the alcohol quickly. "Join us. But first, lock the door." He held out a key from his pocket and a few moments later the order was complete.

Vanessa turned back, nothing of her usual bubbly personality showing through. For all the compulsion she was under, she looked like she'd been doped up on some hardcore drugs.

Ty snatched the key back and pocketed it. Then he picked up her delicate wrist and held it out in my direction. His brows arched in dare, but the one word wasn't compelled. "Eat."

Coerced or not, my own fangs dropped from the roof of my mouth and pins stabbed at my churning gut. I leveled a glare at Ty while I clung to my weakening self-control. Vanessa was my friend, and somehow I was going to get her—maybe even both of us—out of this. I shifted in defiance, giving my nails a better angle to keep working at my restraints. "No. And leave her alone."

Ty smiled, flicking one of his long fangs with his tongue as he dropped her wrist. It thumped on the table before flopping off. "I prefer vampire blood, myself. Yours most of all." He held his open hand out over the table. "Give me your arm, Amelia."

In spite of the little thrill that swept through me at the memory of his passionate bite, I pushed my back into the chair. Never-ceasing love aside, this wasn't the Ty I loved. Plus I needed all the space I could get from Vanessa. "I will never willingly give myself to you again."

Another devilish smile. "Thought you might say that." He yanked Vanessa down onto his lap, flipping her hair over her shoulder and capturing her neck in an iron grip.

"Stop!" I cried too late.

Ty's bite into Vanessa's jugular made her flinch, and he dragged blood from her vein. I stared in horror, seeing the monster Ty had become. When his fangs slid free, red coated his mouth and tongue. "Not nearly as delicious as yours, but it'll do."

Vanessa didn't scream and made no move to struggle from his grasp, but silent tears streamed down her face. Almost as fast as the twin rivers that flowed from the punctures to stain the collar of her white, fitted shirt. Whatever she'd been compelled to do, she still knew what was happening to her.

I gritted my teeth, wanting to tear him apart. Hating that this is what he'd become: a monster wrapped in familiar packaging. Hating that my tied, clenched hands and thinning restraints were all that was keeping me from mauling her, too. I ground my teeth. "Let. Her. Go."

"And why would I do that...unless you'd like to take her place?"

Static gathered beneath my ribs, desperate to flood my hands and burn the rope. But I held it back. Once I was free, I'd need all the power I could get to knock him the hell out. "You disgust me!"

Ty yanked Vanessa closer and bit into her again with savage force. This time Vanessa's mouth gaped, but no sound came out. No cry. No scream. And Ty wasn't letting go. Hands clutching so tight and mouth an iron bear trap, he was going to kill her.

"Stop!" I shouted, my own hunger abandoned but unable to jump up from the chair with his mind control keeping me planted. "Take mine. Please. Just don't kill her. You'll never forgive yourself."

Ty dropped Vanessa to the ground and leaped at me, knocking the armchair onto its back. My skull smacked into the thin carpet, feeling the hardwood floors beneath that made my vision spin. He snarled on top of me, tongue licking up the column of my neck as he breathed me in. He reared back, hovering above me with his lips curled back from his fangs. Time slowed as he pinned one of my shoulders down—because I was no longer compelled to the chair— and lifted his own wrist to his mouth. My racing heart galloped as he tore into his own vein and held it out, black torrents trailing down to his elbow.

"Drink me and I'll let her go."

My lips pinned shut as icy drops pattered down onto my chest above my tank. The request wasn't compelled, but I knew what the end game was. To still my heart and turn it black. To make me a monster just like him. I couldn't do it, not willingly. He could take my vein, my life. But I'd never take his black blood.

Ty's nostrils flared and he growled, canines making a sudden appearance too as his eyes flashed with anger. Then he launched off me and onto Vanessa. It happened so fast I didn't have time to react as he ripped into her throat. With an agonizing roar, Vanessa's body dropped to the ground and Ty rose, turning his bloody face to me.

"Call my bluff? You lose."

I couldn't utter a word as I stared up at him in horror. The Ty I knew, the one I'd fallen in love with…was completely gone. What remained was a cold-blooded killer. That thing standing before me was an abomination. Seething down at me with total aggravation, it was an insult to everything Ty had been. And it needed to be put down.

Regret at what I knew I had to do weighed me down like stones under water. I shouldn't have provoked him. I should have surrendered to save Vanessa. Now there was no turning back.

Fury reignited my voltage, snapping the rope as I threw my hands up. The blue light streamed into Ty's chest as he snarled, plowing him off his feet and into the wall.

Right before hitting, the symbol flared and the force field came to life.

The pulse of power sent Ty's body back at me and I ducked, catching his arms and slamming him down onto the table. It cracked under the force and I leaped on top of him.

Grabbing a fallen glass, I smashed it into his eye socket without shattering the crystal—I wasn't trying to blind him permanently. It dazed him for a split second. Enough time to raid his pockets. The key. His Zippo.

I jumped up and went to race to the door—but something stopped me. More than the sight of Vanessa's body lying twisted on the ground. More than her vibrant blood pooling from her neck over the carpet.

Sniffling.

I whirled around and kept backing up to the door. Now on his knees, Ty wasn't advancing on me. He wasn't even looking at me. Instead, with one puffy and one good eye, he stared down at the rich color draining out of Vanessa. His gray hands reached out, one resting on her hand, the other gliding down her face. "I'm—*sorry*." His fingers stalled on the un-chewed length of her neck. Checking for a pulse? "I'm fucking sorry!"

Unable to look away, my hand behind my back stabbed blindly for the keyhole.

Ty's gaze shot up to me, crimson tears tracking down his face. His hands came together as if begging. "It's inside of me. I can't fight it. This monster…it's consuming everything that used to be me."

Horror and morbid regret plagued his bloody face. The expression was so true it broke my heart all over again. What I was seeing was real. Was Ty. The old Ty. The Ty who owned my heart. *"Ty."*

He crawled forward on his knees through Vanessa's pooling

blood, leaving smudges in the carpet as he neared. "Kill me, Amelia. Do it now. *Please. I beg you.*"

The scene was déjà vu of the time I'd been in that position, begging Ty to kill me...before the monster I was becoming took over. He couldn't end my life then, even before knowing me. But could I grant his wish now? My grip on the Zippo tightened. It was my only weapon. My only means to kill him. A flash of him burning alive branded my mind, so real I could smell the stench of his skin at it melted off his bones. So real that I could hear the tortured sounds from his throat as his life incinerated before my eyes.

I couldn't do it. Not this way. Not now.

My heart wouldn't let me.

"Ty, no."

The key found its home, but instead of turning the brass, I scanned the room. New bed and couch...and nothing else. There was no silver, why would there be. And I'd already used my voltage. Was there any left? Whether there was or not, this could be my only chance to save him. If I could just find where my weapons had been stashed. "Tell me where—"

"Get out!" Ty roared suddenly, vibrating the window and walls. Some of that cold calculation returned to his face and red eyes. His joined, begging hands stained with Vanessa's blood separated, fingers clawing into the carpet and hitting the wood below. As if he were trying to ground himself. Or readying to launch. His muscle-corded arms bulged with restraint. "Before I fucking kill you."

CHAPTER 32

I turned the key and shot through the door as Ty launched at me with a roar. The door slammed shut as Ty's reaching arms belted into it. Fear, as well as desperation to survive long enough to warn Kendrick, had adrenaline flooding through me. I shoved back as the barrier bounced open at his belting fight, and stabbed the key into the hole on the outside.

The door cracked open with force and Ty's arm snaked out. "Amelia!"

Bent at the elbow, he clawed to reach me, to catch me. I rammed my shoulder into the wood as he sliced into my arm. A shout penetrated the barrier and I bit back my own as Ty's arm was crushed. The door popped open again and his lax arm was pulled inside. Then it shut with another mighty push and the key turned, a click announcing the lock engaging.

Something slammed into the door from inside, and Ty's muffled roar cut short. If he got out, I was as good as dead.

I snatched the key from the lock as something rumbled not just the door but also the entire wall: a body being thrown at full speed and colliding before being catapulted back by the force field. The key slipped from between my fingers and bounced under the gap into the room.

Shit!

I dropped to the floorboards, glimpsing Ty's body rushing forward again. The key was inside, and if my fingers poke through, Ty would see it.

Heart pounding as he collided, I was out of options. I pivoted and launched over the balustrade, landing with bent knees in the foyer right behind the table. The bodiless damned stared back at me, a reminder to anyone who dared disobey my twin. My stomach lurched. Vile smells of decay hung in the air. But nothing else came at me, no damned and no Ty.

I pushed the acid vomit back down and raced around the table to the front door. There was no time to be sick. Not with the pounding that was still vibrating the entire top floor. It was only a matter of time before Ty found the key and broke through.

My shaking hands gripped the handle and pushed. *Locked.*

I backed up and ram-ran, my own body slam mirroring another of Ty's and throwing me back. I hit the table and it cracked and tipped, falling down beneath me. The head bounced onto my lap and I scrambled to throw it off, gagging at the touch of its deteriorating flesh. The same symbol had lit up across the door, and after sprinting to check, I found that every exit point was marked, too. Not a phone in sight or a weapon, either. I was unarmed and trapped. A rat in a maze. Up shit creek without a freaking paddle.

Accepting that there was no way to save myself, I stared down at the marks on my arm. My previous attempt to destroy them like Dorian had done to Vanessa's had failed. But I couldn't give up.

There had to be a way to contact Kendrick. To warn him before it was too late.

My fist clenched tighter with urgency—and felt the small, cold rectangle I'd been holding all along. Ty's Zippo.

Thoughts on speed, I saw a solution and raced down through the cellar door. With two lengths of thick rope and an armful of old newspapers, I reemerged, screwing up the paper before throwing it onto the splintered table. Then I tied one end of each rope to an anchor point.

The first went around the front door handle, which I hoped the ward would keep from breaking.

The other fastened to the solid post at the stairs' landing where I stood closest.

I tied the opposite ends around my wrists, only keeping enough slack for me to reclaim the Zippo from between my teeth. With a flick of my thumb, the lighter's lid clicked open, then I swiped back over the roller. The flame ignited and I let the Zippo fall.

An eternal second passed as more thuds rang out upstairs.

And then the flame caught. The newspaper went up quickly, heating smaller fragments of wood that grew the flame into a fire. The larger pieces took longer, agonizing minutes filled with crackling flames, rising smoke, and vibrations upstairs.

Tied over the slow-growing heat, I began to sweat, but I held my wrist out. As the heat turned into pain, something in me began to fight. Not to rid myself of these marks for good. But to save them from the fire. Against my will, my body spasmed, trying to tear the ropes from their anchors. But it was no use. I'd tied those double knots for a reason.

The crackling embers hit me as a bigger shard of wood ignited. The fire swelled and I bit my lip to keep from crying out as the flames coated my forearm like a dragon's licking tongue. Agony pinned my eyes shut, and my body sprouted sweat from every pore like it was trying to douse the flames. I shrieked inside my mouth, refusing to let it free, wondering if the damned felt the extent of this all over their bodies as they combusted after being staked.

The sounds of Ty upstairs belting into the wall and being thrown back died off as a buzzing in my ears took over.

The rope keeping my marked arm in the flames snapped, burned through by the fire.

At the sudden release my body fell back, butt hitting the tiles. Instinct had me cradling my arm to my chest as tears I hadn't realized I'd been crying dripped onto my bubbled flesh.

I looked down and my vision became hazy, my eyes rolling back in my head. I bit down on my bottom lip, breaking the skin and re-jogging my consciousness. As deprived of blood as I was, the damage was horrendous and showing no sign of healing. From my elbow to my wrist, the skin was bubbled and glossy. Parts had clung together as my skin melted while other sections separated, leaving holes that peeked through to underlying bone.

Vomit rose up my throat again and I turned my head, spraying bile from my mouth. My whole arm throbbed, so hot it felt like it was still melting away in the fire. But there wasn't time to find a tap for cold water. There wasn't time for regret.

I flipped my arm over. The marks that had scarred my forearm were no more. It had worked.

I cranked my head back to look up through the cavernous foyer. There was no sign of Ty. No sound of him, either. Heart thudding with urgency, I reached out through the bond, praying Kendrick wasn't still locking me out. *Kendrick, please. You have to hear me.*

In a mirror between royal portraits, I got a glimpse of him shoving one of my guards as he burst out from my suite. "Where the hell is she?"

He looked like hell hit by a truck. Twice. Covered in hunger veins, dark crescents lined his bloodshot eyes. Stubble shadowed his face and internal guilt rode him like a poisoned wave. After what I'd caught him doing with Raven, he blamed himself for me taking off.

But he hadn't heard me.

Was he still blocking me? I could see him, which proved something was joined between us. Something was getting through. And he knew I was missing. Being as weak as I was, my voice must be coming through on mute.

I concentrated everything I had left on making the words louder. *You're all dead if you don't let me in!*

Amelia? Instant panic claimed his deep voice and he stopped in mid-attack of driving one guard against the corridor. *Where are you? What happened?*

I'm so sorry. I never meant... Stop the groveling and get it out. His life comes before your relationship. Mess this up and he's dead. *You're all in danger. Marcus is controlling the damned. He's the commander. And he's on his way to execute you all. You'll be outnumbered.*

Amelia, wait. Marcus what? I saw through his eyes as he retreated back into my suite, closing the door on my now arguing guards. *You're coming through like you're on a bad phone line or something. Danger. Marcus. Outnumbered. I don't understand.*

I drilled my index fingers into my temples and squeezed my eyes shut. *Marcus is coming with the damned. He'll kill you all.*

An unexpected memory rose up. The wolves, Mr. Malau... I recounted the days. If my math was right after all the unconscious breaks, he'd be on his way to the forest outside the Armaya's walls with backup to break me out.

Warn the others and call Mr. Malau for backup. Kendrick, are you getting this—

A cold and hard, moving mass collided with me and knocked me over. Ty's weight pinned me down, his punishing hold on my shoulders slamming me into the tiles and his lower half nullifying my instant body convulsions to get free. "Warning your boyfriend won't save him. Even if you did get through, they're all dead."

I kept fighting beneath him, fists driving into his ribs that felt like I was hitting a cement block. My legs thrashed too, but the summon I sent out for sparks to light up my body, tapped nothing but exhaustion.

I cried out when his hold on my shoulders released and one arm came down like a beam across my neck. "T—" I spluttered and coughed on the rising smoke, unable to get any full words out. My fists gave up on the punching and shot out, patting the ground for something, anything. With my damaged skin feeling like it was peeling off as it moved over the tiles, warmth grew as I neared the mini bonfire. "Sto—" My windpipe choked closed as my fingertips found a jagged table fragment. They groped and strained, the wooden equivalent of a stake just out of my reach.

"You left me no choice."

A slight move from Ty gave me the quarter-inch I needed and a lungful of smoky air. My hand took hold, arm directing the makeshift weapon to that sweet spot between his ribs that would pierce his heart. It wouldn't kill him, but it would—

Ty's cold, hard lips came down on mine and my eyes flared wide in shock. His fangs hurt, pressed against my mouth. Wetness seeped from his lips onto my tongue with his rough, lapping kiss, the taste like rotting berries.

Ty's blood.

Heart drumming and sucking a lungful or smoke through my nose, I drove the sharp end of wood through his ribs.

Ty's ferocious kiss broke off, a hiss rasping from his black-smudged lips.

Tucking my knees up, I separated our bodies and kicked out with my feet. Ty flipped onto his back, the splinter protruding as I sprang up and went to run.

Ty was on me in a flash, chest against my back and arms capturing my waist. His fangs came down, sinking into that supple part at the base of my neck.

"Ty, no!" Feet kicking out as he held tight and burnt arm throbbing with scalding heat, I fought to strike out at him. But it was no use. Ty pulled on my vein, arms around me constricting as fire lit in my veins. I was burning...from the inside out. Venom. It was spreading through my body at an alarming rate, infecting me, mingling with the blood Ty had forced me to drink. Preventing that shot of ecstasy from numbing my mind and body "Ty...*stop*."

Weakness overtook my fight and my body went lax against the screaming in my mind. My heartbeat slowed and I felt the ground rising up. No, not the ground rising. Me falling.

Still draining me, Ty lowered to the tiles, his arms no longer squeezing, but holding me gently. The crackle of the fire still burning to the side, its flames, the shattered table and that damned's head all began to fade. The hole in my vision grew, being eaten away with black hopelessness.

As sight and feeling faded, the fire in my body turning cold, Ty's voice registered in my ear.

"You're mine now. Forever."

CHAPTER 33

*W*rithing pain undulating up and down my body tore me from unconsciousness and muted the feel of fire across my burnt arm. Too much light surrounded me, swamping my vision with piercing needles as my lids fluttered. Confusion-laced panic swept through me as I scrambled to remember what had happened before I blacked out.

What I was laid out on felt like sandpaper, grating against my skin as I clawed at the...sheets? My sight came back in patches, lids shutting against my attempt to see to avoid the striking light. I was on a bed, the one in the room Ty kept me in. Clamping my teeth over my bottom lip to endure the torture riding through my body, I arched up. The room looked the same as it had the last time I'd escape from it. New furniture and window blind, which was open with a starry sky beyond the tree line opposite the street. My hands went to my stomach, catching and squeezing at the feel of lava bubbling inside. I blinked again, the feel of needles receding as I noticed the only light source in the entire room. One lamp on the bedside table with a black shade covering the naked bulb. I squinted as I looked straight at the lamp, eyes forcing themselves shut.

In the wonderful darkness of my closed lids, the physical pain remained and soared without the added distraction. My bones ached from the death-grip hold on them, feeling like at any moment they could melt, turning me into a mess of flesh without a frame. Uncontrollable shivers took over and I fell back onto the pillows. My arms came around my waist and I rolled to my side, curling in on myself.

A voice broke through then, the source distanced and beyond this room as the sound of pouring water was met with a sizzling hiss. "She got through to him... No. I didn't... I know..." More sizzling, and then a creak as something cracked through. "Already done... Minutes ago... She won't be a problem anymore."

As Ty's report ended with what sounded like demolition, the events before blacking out rushed back. Escaping this room, the fire, my wrecked arm and its alchemist marks. Refreshed panic made it feel like a bomb had just gone off in my chest. Kendrick. I'd connected with him, but had my warning gotten through? I squeezed my eyes shut so tight I saw bursts of light, a never-ending fireworks display. Then I reached out through the bond and—nothing. I tried again and again, shutting down my need to react to the agony striking through me. But no matter how hard I tried, or how long I strained for, nothing came through. I couldn't connect with Kendrick. I couldn't even feel him.

My heart dropped and I let my lids slide open. The torturous waves riding my body had dulled for the moment, but that little win didn't even cut the surface of important. On the carpet, the red stain and smears were now a darkening rust color. Vanessa's blood. Because Ty had killed her. One dead, and now Kendrick.

Oh, God. Was he dead, too?

My hand slid past the amulet to my heart—and froze. I gasped. And realized I hadn't drawn a single breath since waking up. The reason was clear as I patted a palm against my chest. My heart wasn't beating, it just…wasn't.

In numb shock, I sat perfectly still, waiting for that bodily reaction that forced you to take a breath when you'd been holding it for too long. That tightening around your lungs that threatened to force you to breathe even if you were drowning underwater. I felt like I was drowning now. Not because of that feeling. But because it didn't exist. Out of habit alone, I sucked in air and—coughed like I'd inhaled water.

That same bomb explosion went off in my chest again, and I looked down. As if I could see through my own skin and bone. The color of my flesh had changed. Across my arms and chest above my tank, its snow-white was now a deathly shade of gray. The blue veins that had stood out like tree roots there, were darkening to black. That bomb had been my heart. Beating like it was fighting the black blood that was now feeding my body.

And losing.

I was in transition. Turning damned.

A renewed strike of horrid sensation overcame my shock, and I didn't fight the darkness that came over me like a sinister shadow. My eyes slid shut and all the tension that chained me released.

I don't know how long the infinite peace lasted. Had no control to end or keep it going. But then something changed.

A cool hand pushed the sweaty hair back from my face. The touch wasn't freezing like a damned's hands. It was barely a degree cooler than my own. Peeking through slitted eyes, I saw Ty's face. Damned hand then. Which meant my skin was almost as cold as his. Arctic compared to vampire cold. I was becoming just like him.

"What do you want?" I pulled upright on the bed and shifted

away from his touch. Not because I was afraid of him or what he might do. I was already half dead, more if you went by my heart which threw out a single unsteady beat. It seemed like that part of me had died already, the ability to fear, at least for myself.

Ty's head tilted sideways, blood-red eyes ticking over every part of me as if in fascination. But he said nothing.

I tucked my legs under my butt and, feeling an unusual sensation, I glanced down at my body. My tank and black jeans were stuck to my chest and legs with moisture. With a hint of salt coming off me, I knew the dampness was sweat. And it was all mine. My body fighting the process it was going through without relief. There was only one way to stop this, and I wasn't even sure if I did have silver that I'd have the energy to create a spark, or if I could even use the power to cure myself. The voice out of my mouth was mine, but it lacked emotion and dripped in snideness. "Enjoying your work?"

"Hardly."

My stability gave out suddenly as a strike of pure hell shot from my heart out through every inch of me. I tipped sideways, every muscle seizing around bones that felt like they were going to shatter. A tortured scream tore from my throat and pressure came over me. It covered my body with force, holding me down as I rode the pain like a roller coaster. One after the other, the waves continued, debilitating my body and scrambling my mind. It felt like I'd swallowed Vanessa's tattoo gun and it was going off at triple speed, painting my insides black. Seconds turned into minutes and minutes into what felt like hours.

When the hold on my muscles finally released, the pressure now cradling me loosened. Red colored my vision, staying even as my sight went from blurred to razor sharp.

Close enough that I could have felt his breath if he'd had any, Ty stared into my eyes. His hand was against my jaw, thumb running back and forth over my cheek. "You're okay. As long as it takes, I'm here for you. We'll get through this…together."

The almost-warmth in his voice had my head jerking back on the pillows. My heart let out a whopping beat as if to remind me of what I was becoming, of what he already was. "You don't really care about me. You just want to own—"

My jaw cranked shut, teeth knocking together at the force and sending splitting pain through my nerves up to my skull. The same convulsions took over as if I were plugged into an electric socket. My teeth chattered together before an arm squeezed around me, Ty's hand cupping my head to his chest. "It's okay. I've got you. It's okay. I've got you."

Whispered from his lips that touched my forehead and remained there, the chant repeated over and over. Time passed in slow motion, and through the agony, I became aware of every part of him that touched me. His other arm was curled tight around my waist, holding me so close to him the lack of space could have been intimate in any other situation. And if he wasn't my enemy. Lying sideways above the covers with me, each leg was slung around my hips and crossed behind my legs. His face was shoved down into the crook of my neck. Not with extended fangs waiting for a taste, but to limit the shaking there like every other part of him contended with in their space. Together he rode the wave with me, waiting until it died down again.

As I released air that had collected in my lungs, not from breathing, but rather from the fight to contain my screams, I stared back at the face that lowered to my eye level on the pillow. I remembered the vicious way he'd mauled Vanessa, then his heartbreaking plea for death. A tortured soul trapped in the body of a killer. I wondered —was some of the old Ty peeking through now, regretting what this new version of him had done to me? "Is that you?" I whispered with a croak.

Grief and indifference battled across his face. "I don't know anymore. I just...don't."

A door opening and slamming shut downstairs jolted me. Ty remained still, that light of life in his eyes fleeing.

"Repair and arm up!" Marcus screamed. "We're going to take out those fucking royals and their flea-ridden mongrels." Stomping boots climbed the stairs from the foyer, each step as loud as a mallet.

A blank look transformed Ty's features that chilled my already-frozen heart. He released my body and slid off the bed with a predator's grace. Keeping his gaze on me, he crossed to the door and unlocked it.

Fear of the unknown, rather than Marcus's approach, had me scrambling upright on the bed. He was back from the Armaya and pissed. Had the takedown failed? Had Kendrick survived? Or had his army simply failed to extinguish every life they'd planned to snuff out? Reaching out now, my link to Kendrick met vacancy. No sensations. No thought. No feelings.

The door flung inward then, and Marcus stormed through. Fury animated his expression. But something was off. A sheen dampened his forehead and grayed-out cheeks. It spread down his chest to soak through in splotches across his white shirt that was stained red and slashed through. Gasping for air, his eyes darted and blinked as if blurred. He looked undeniably ill.

Breath rasped from his lungs and he stumbled, gripping the doorjamb for stability. His red eyes flung daggers at Ty. "You incompetent, good-for-nothing dog. You can't even babysit a single damn vampire."

"She's not just any vampire." Ty stalked forward, getting up in Marcus's grill. "She's equipped and deadly. I trained her myself."

"Then you should know her well enough not to have fallen for her moves."

As I slid off the bed, Marcus moved without warning, grabbing Ty's biceps and flinging him across the room. He hit the wall and repelled off as I grabbed the metal lamp in readiness to fight.

But Marcus didn't advance on me.

Instead, he shot around the couch and hauled Ty up by his shirt. One hand struck out around his jugular and forced his muscle-bunching body back into the powder-blue wall. Ty bared his fangs and canines as his head smashed into the drywall. But he didn't fight back, instead taking the rough treatment as Marcus kept him pinned.

The door was open, free for me to run right through. But I didn't speed across the stained carpet. Didn't release my grip on the lamp, either. The hotel was teeming with damned, and in my current condition—waiting for the next wave of pain to hit—I had little to no chance of escaping. And even more than that, I couldn't leave Ty behind.

Marcus's jaw cracked open wide and I couldn't look away. Couldn't move, either. His fangs struck deep, and still Ty didn't fight it, jaw clenching as he took the pain and punishment. Ty's scarred arms at his sides strained, muscles bunching as black veins slid from his fingers up.

And then it was all over. Marcus tore his fangs free, gasping as oil-black blood trailed over his bottom lip and down his chin. A vibrant glow replaced the deathly sheen across his face and his stare pulsed red. Ty slid down the wall to the floor, dazed but conscious.

Marcus was in front of me in an instant. Like he'd disappeared and reformed at will. "Family," he drawled. "Can't live with them… but you can kill them."

I hissed, glimpsing Ty rise across the room. "Your wolf already beat you to it."

Cold blood-soaked smile. "I see that. It's about time. But you shouldn't have gone against me."

A need to know forced my next words. "Is he dead? Are they all dead?"

"They gave me no choice, especially after your warning." Marcus caught the side of my neck, his thumb forcing my face up to meet his stare. "Or didn't you see that much?"

I bared my fangs and felt an internal wave building up. I gritted my teeth. "I saw plenty."

Marcus shoved me back onto the bed and looked over his shoulder at Ty. "Regroup the army and be ready to leave at sundown."

Fresh throbbing suddenly vibrated my bones and I bit back a groan, refusing to lose sight of my twin as he marched to the door.

"Oh, and when you're done, put my dear sister out of her misery."

Marcus left then, and Ty took his place in the open doorway. He stepped outside, wiping the two black channels from his neck. "Back soon." Then he closed the way out and locked it.

AFTER ANOTHER LONG roller coaster of internal agony, one of many I'd suffered through, I willed my body upright on the bed. Every lean muscle bulged and shook with fatigued strain, but I pushed through it. Propping my knees up, I chained my arms around them to balance. I was weak and suffering, dying slowly and surely, but I couldn't give up. Marcus was more damned than I had been and he still had his abilities. His fire. His electricity. And I wasn't fully dead yet. The single beat every five or so minutes proved that. Plus I hadn't chowed down on anyone: a necessary step in completing the process from vampire to damned.

Now with a short reprieve that could end any second, I had to act fast.

Eyes shutting out the sting of lamplight, I forced out every possible distraction. I clung onto the diminishing pain that would soon enough rebuild with a vengeance and brought on the black void. Then I waited. No shadows came. No remnants of the past, present, or future that I could grasp onto and see an event through. Just empty blackness. I kept my concentration, kept looking, waiting…

Another wave began to build inside my marrow, striking out hard and fast. I fought to block it out. To hold it back. But I wasn't in control. My body wasn't what it used to be, it had changed. It wasn't mine to control anymore. Agony forced my mouth to gape with a scream I wouldn't let escape, and then what was still alive in my body gave out. I collapsed sideways on the bed, consciousness knocked out as if I were a fighter in a ring.

When I came to, the crippling pain was gone. The light sensitivity no more. Even without taking life, had the conversion somehow completed? Was I damned?

"Amelia."

The female voice emerged as the space surrounding me cleaved into focus. The empty boardroom with its round marble slab and seven surrounding thrones. The drapes were drawn with star-speckled night beyond the glass lighting up the garden's bordering hedges, where long figures skulked within the shadows. The person standing beside me appeared like a spectral force solidifying. "Marika?"

"Shh." She raised a finger to her lips. "Watch. I can't keep this up for long."

As vampires entered the room, royals filling their thrones, which included Kendrick...and Marcus, I knew what I was seeing. A recount of events in a dreamscape. Marika's. And I knew what was seconds away from happening.

Already standing, Marcus looked from his left at Uriel and around to each royal. Satisfaction highlighted his smirk, a clue to the horror he was about to unleash. "Which you all just made."

All hell was about to break loose and there was nothing I could do to stop it. No way to change what had already taken place.

Without a heartbeat, I stared in horror, not ready to witness the slaughter. Not ready to see Kendrick's life being taken before my very eyes. Confusion wormed its way in as Marcus's fist came down on the table with a crack.

Why was Marika showing me this? How had she seen—?

Damned swarmed in through the doors and fire scaled up from the floor all around the room. The live columns blocked every door and window as a war cry bellowed from Marcus's mouth. "Kill them all!"

The royals shot to their feet, suddenly brandishing swords like they'd anticipated the attack. The fire-coated windows shattered and wolves streamed in one after the other, deadly long canines latching on to the damned that struck out at the royals.

The wolf leading the assault was the biggest I'd ever seen. Even bigger than Ty.

Mr. Malau.

He flew onto the marble slab and I saw Kendrick swing out at Marcus with his dagger. There was no shock in his determined expression. Only anger and the need to fight and kill. He'd understood my warning and he'd gotten the wolves on our side. Allied them to fight for vampires.

Kendrick's blade scored flesh and red sprayed from Marcus's shoulder, but he struck out regardless. Mid-air his fangs gleamed, their mark bullseying Kendrick's jugular.

Mr. Malau dove between the two, his wolf skull cranking sideways and enormous jaws snapping shut around Marcus's side.

Which explained why he'd looked like death afterward. Infected by a lycan's bite. But that wouldn't be the end of him. Because he'd returned here—to be cured by Ty's hybrid blood. Like Raven had been at Portsmouth when Ty had bitten her back. Ingesting his blood there—not being brought back to life by me—had saved her from dying as a wolf-bitten restored.

While the two struggled, more and more screams filled the closed-in space. Smoke billowed up as the portraits were burned to charcoal, ridding clean air from the room. The doors had been broken in, letting some smoke out, but the flames acted like a fiery curtain, too thick for the guards to get through.

Still in the alpha's jaws and being thrashed like a ragdoll, Marcus hissed and brought his dagger's hilt down onto the alpha's skull. Mr. Malau released his hold and Marcus threw him at the wall with a crack of solid stone. His glowing eyes trained on Kendrick through the dwindling visibility. My twin batted the dagger from his hand and caught his throat. "You lose."

Striking pain tore my view of the room in half, an earthquake separating the scene like two pieces of a puzzle. I cried out, eyes shutting against my will and blocking out the sounds of fighting and life being taken.

Through slitted eyes and clutching my arms around me, I recognized my surroundings. The dreamscape was gone, torn away by the transition. I was back in the damned hotel, imprisoned in the same room.

Marcus had come back alive, but had the others survived? Had Kendrick? Had Mr. Malau?

Alone and trapped, I didn't know. And if I didn't make it much longer through the transition, maybe I never would.

TY'S EARLIER "BACK SOON" turned into hours, the time between slowing with the number of excruciating bouts and replacing them with gut-striking spears. The hunger that roiled through me was like nothing I'd ever experienced before. My fangs ached, fully extended and throbbing. They refused to retract. Even as I tried again now, the struggle to gain some control over them just sent that never-ending throbbing from each pointed tooth up through my jaw and into my skull. And my head was already pounding as if it had taken over the constant beat my heart could no longer make.

I doubled over again, arms wrapped tight around my stomach while the feel of ten daggers stabbed at me from the inside out. My head pounded so loud it blocked out any other sounds: the odd car passing on the street, strong wind batting against the window, and movement of almost soundless feet downstairs. From where I'd fallen asleep on the floor, I saw my tear-blurred surroundings through cracked eyelids. Legs of furniture and the bed's base with a sheet hanging on the ground. Small debris dotted the carpet, still left from my rampage. The smell of Vanessa's blood was thick on the air. At least I couldn't see the stain. In the position I lay curled over in, it was behind me, smudges from Ty's knees and all.

I didn't hear the door unlock, swing open and shut, or the slow steps that approached me from behind.

But I did pick up a scent. Blood. Not spilled, but thrumming through a living lycan's veins at that normal irregular beat.

The pounding got louder as I twisted upright, knees going to my chest and hands free and ready to act. My eyes widened. Ty stood right behind me, a dangerous look in his eyes and a hint of something raw and deep-cutting: heavily veiled desperation.

On registering the source of the lycan scent, I understood why. Held with a constricting hand around his bicep was Harper. Ty had had him all along. Had kept him alive, too. Uninfected. Harper's eyes were wide, his face full of fear. But that fear wasn't directed at me like the time we'd met at Ty's father's house. Now it was propelled at his brother, his body arching away so obviously that if Ty let go, the terrified kid would topple over.

Even though Harper didn't appear injured in any way, his jeans and T-shirt a little dirty but intact, the scent of his blood rose like a direct assault to my nostrils. That stabbing in my gut rebuilt with force and I dug my nails into the carpet to keep upright. My teeth came down on my lower lip to keep me from crying out. As I rode the torture train, Ty watched, his earlier empathy gone. I wondered what he was planning to do to his little brother. Turn him too? The only other hybrid in known existence. When the agony began to lift, I managed to splutter a half-coherent sentence. "W-why—what's he —here—for?"

Ty thrust the boy forward. "Time to join the program."

Harper landed in front of me on his knees, catching himself before he toppled sideways. Dark crescents lined the underside of his bloodshot eyes and his body trembled. He'd been a prisoner here since his abduction two weeks ago. From the bones jutting out through his T-shirt, I wondered if they'd fed him at all. Or had the only thing on offer been vampire blood and the promise of a new, soulless life? As he swayed and righted himself, it was clear the trembling wasn't just a result of fear, but also the strain his body was going through to keep conscious. He registered my face and hope flashed in his eyes. His lips moved with a silent plea, *help me.*

I reached out to him, doing my best to keep my throbbing fangs hidden and to ignore the grinding in my gut. The sound of his beating heart made it through the pounding in my head and my mouth watered. With my hand on his, I forced my scanning gaze from various vein-tapping points—his neck, inside elbow, wrist—and up to Ty. "Ty, don't do this to him. *Please.* He's your little brother. Don't make him like you."

Empty, dead eyes stared down at me. "That's not why he's here. It's time for *you* to join our program."

Harper cringed at his brother's voice, that sliver of hope dissolving into total fear.

Unlike Ty, he hadn't been conditioned all his life to be a fearless and brutal killer. He'd been sheltered from that future. Protected.

Despite how hard I tried, I couldn't keep my gaze from returning to the boy's neck. That delicious thick vein that pulsed along the side. Red clouded my vision, turning the entire room and my intended victim rose-colored. Because that was Harper's purpose in this visit, wasn't it? Living hybrid with veins of blood that I needed to drain to become just like Ty. Damned. "Oh, God...no."

That red must have turned my eyes crimson—or had that needy hiss escaped my own mouth—because Harper yanked his hand away and scrambled sideways past the couch until he hit the wall.

With his eyes darting between us, a primal need to take chase and kill exploded inside of me. I shot to the far wall, wishing the invisible wards weren't preventing me from smashing my fist through the drywall and anchoring onto a structural beam. A new wave of pain had me crumbling to the carpet and my bones aching with the need to give in. To take what my body needed. "I won't—do it. I won't take—his life."

"He dies whether you do or not." Ty shot to his brother and hauled him up. Harper cried out but was quickly subdued when his brother's eyes compelled control. "You're going to die. It's inevitable. And you're okay with that." Harper's shoulders slouched and he nodded. Ty let go with a quick release of a switchblade from his pocket and sliced across the boy's inner forearm. "Offer yourself to her, your life. You want Amelia to take it."

Harper padded in bare feet over to me, the fear now gone from his expression. As he got closer, the smell of his blood soared, poisoning the air of anything else. It was in my nose, my mouth. I could even taste it down my throat. With the red haze my vision was locked in, the blood sliding down his arm in rivulets looked so dark. So irresistible.

"Feed on him," Ty demanded. "Take him *now*."

A groan escaped my mouth as the boy knelt, holding out his arm. Everything in my body wanted what he had on offer. Needed it. Survival 101 for a transitionee was kicking in, awakening my inner monster and giving it power over my body and mind. Taking my shredded conscience and blowing it to pieces. Removing my fear and empathy as swiftly as if they'd never existed at all.

Shuffling forward on my knees, I took hold of Harper's heated flesh with both hands. The blood leaked onto my own skin, warm and alive—

A dam wall broke in me, snapping my last tie to humanity.

I couldn't hold back.

I struck out hard, smashing the boy's wrist to my gaping mouth and plunging my fangs in so deep they hit bone. I didn't care if I hurt him. Didn't care that my curled fingers were cranking so tight that I'd soon break bone. All that mattered—all that registered—was that delicious taste as it flowed with vibrant life down my throat. My taste buds came alive and I felt that stream quickly filling my gut. Felt the rush of Harper's rapid-beating heart in the pulses that were sucked from his vein into me. Energy grew inside me like a beacon. And then that rapid beat began to fade. Still offering every drop I was taking without fight, Harper would be my first victim.

And he sure as hell wouldn't be my last.

CHAPTER 34

*a*n explosion of wood and glass halted the long draw I was sucking from Harper's wrist. But only for a nanosecond. The entire hotel could be burning down, and I'd still have kept my death bite until the boy was tapped out.

Ty didn't share my single-mindedness. A snarl of irritation raked from between suddenly extended canines and fangs. He shot to the door and unlocked it as shouts and the clang of weapons and thump of bodies colliding drifted up from downstairs. "Looks like we have company. Finish up here and join us." Then he was gone with a rush, swinging the door shut behind him.

Without relocking it.

Mildly interested in the chorus of beating hearts I could now hear outside this room, I sucked harder on Harper's vein. His body had grown cooler, and without realizing it, I was now supporting his growing weight. The pain that had plagued me had vanished. The conversion was nearing completion. Without every last drop, the torture would return and I would die. My heart let out a giant beat as I readied to finish him off.

If you were a normal vampire.

The simple little thought slipped through the blood-hungry craze as the ruckus escalated downstairs. Kendrick's voice, and it had been loud and clear and driven by desperation. *But you're not, Amelia. You're the exception to the rule.*

A sense of Kendrick registered through the bond. He was *alive* and here, fully backed up with vampires…and wolves. As I slowed my hungry draws on the boy's wrist, the relief I felt to know he lived battled with my need to kill. My connection to him flickered like a candle flame in a building breeze, not able to see through his eyes, but able to sense his closeness and flashes of his conviction. He was here to fight and kill and to rescue me.

You're not a killer, Amelia. Fight the urge. Before it's too late.

With my head no longer pounding and my gut no longer grinding, I ignored the throbbing in my fangs and released my suctioning lips. No other messages came through, but a sequence of images did. Kendrick was on his phone in my suite's foyer as he paced. Drive creased his face as he made verbal threats—"Use that bloody crystal ball that's linked to Amelia's pendant and tell me where the hell I can find her!" More pacing around the central table, then he got a call back. His eyes stared blankly as he held the speaker up to his ear. They focused a moment later with a deep, burdening sigh. "Thank you."

So that's how he'd found me. By using my missing pendant's link to Madam Rosalie's crystal ball. With a shock of reality my brain joined the party again, now able to think past the lust for poor Harper's blood. Kendrick had never given up. And he'd gone through hell to locate me. And what he'd said was right. I was the exception to the rule. My blood was immortal, and maybe that made my body immortal, too. That and my electric power made it possible for me to restore the damned, the thing I was becoming. And I wasn't damned yet. I wasn't a killer. A murderer.

And I didn't have to be.

Feeling the strength I'd taken from Harper reviving me, I called up every ounce of my lingering self-control and held on to it for dear life. That light still existed in me, that sense of right and wrong. And as long as I was connected to Kendrick, there was enough of his soul to feed my fractured conscience.

I dropped Harper's wrist, needing a fast and clean break to get away, and went to jump up. The boy grabbed hold of me and my momentum hauled him up. But in his state, he couldn't hold on and fell back. I lunged out and caught him, that need in me rising at his closeness. "You're not finished." Harper held out his wrist, cut and gouged section exposed and still glossy with crimson. "I want you to."

Damning temptation had me biting my lip to keep my fangs from taking over. I wasn't killing this boy, not anymore. Keeping my supporting arm around him from tightening with possession, I caught his eyes with my pulsing ones. "Wake up. You don't really want to die. Ty compelled you. But help's here. We're going to get out of this alive."

Harper's feet planted on the ground, steadying his wonky balance. Though I was dying not to, I released my hold to go join the escalating sounds now rising up three levels. Harper blocked my way, gripping the couch's armrest to stop from collapsing. "You need this, *please.*"

"Harper, no." Apparently my compulsion was more than lacking, even though I was turning damned. "You're under Ty's comp—"

"I'm not." His mouth parted and his fangs and canines both slid free. "Not anymore. But if you're going to save Ty like my father said you could, you'll need to be strong. Stronger than him."

All this time, Mr. Malau had barely spoken about his younger son. But clearly he'd known every move we'd been making, and what the plan was to rescue Ty. This time, when Harper bit into his now healing arm and held it up, I bit back a hiss.

His knees wobbled and I slung my arm around him and hoisted him over to the bed. "I've already taken too much from you." God, was that my voice? Guttural and strained. "And—it'll help. You just need to stay here and recover." Far away from me.

Harper's eyelids drooped as I lay him down and covered him with the sheets. "Bring my brother back. I know you can."

"I will. I promise."

His eyes closed and I crossed to the door. With a quick move, I smashed one of the armchairs into the ground and tore off a leg. It wasn't silver, but with what was on offer, it would have to do for now.

I slipped outside, and as the shouting and battle volume increased, I quickly registered my surroundings. A hint of smoke tainted the air, having permeated the paint-peeling walls from the bonfire I'd lit. But I couldn't see the burn stain through the open horseshoe shape that made up the balustrade.

Because the foyer was packed.

Vamps and wolves slogged it out against the damned, cutting them down with swords and canines. But they were dropping, too. And a few stragglers were pushing up the central stairs to the second level. But for now, the top level remained clear.

With urgency making my quiet heart ache to beat, I pulled the door shut, hoping Harper would be safe inside. A burning need to find Kendrick had my blood racing as his own desperation to get to me registered through the bond.

He wasn't far away, and there was something wrong.

I spun back to the balustrade, ready to leap over the rail in search-and-kill mode, when a voice stopped me. "Amelia!"

I saw a stake sailing through the air and abandoned my makeshift one to catch the thing. At the same time I registered the person who'd thrown it. Kendrick.

A terrible weight lifted off him at having finally found me. The flash of pride he felt at knowing I'd restrained from killing Harper was short and sweet. Because as he spilled up to the top floor, I saw that he was far from alone. In the middle of fighting for his life, Kendrick's opponent wasn't just any damned.

It was Ty, pushing him around the opposite side of the balustrade and away from me. He spared me a glance, red eyes pulsing with encouragement like he wanted me to enjoy the show. Like he didn't see me as a threat. "Get your last yearning looks in now, *soul mate*. She's mine."

Ty thought I'd completed the conversion.

He thought I was damned.

With that knowledge, I gravitated toward them as the crimson faded from my sight. The mash of huge fur-covered bodies and gray-skinned damned below took an instant second seat.

Diagonal lacerations across the front and back of Kendrick's pale blue shirt were stained with blood. Equal wounds marked Ty with leaking black. But he was in better shape from the easy blocks and strikes he kept handing out.

Kendrick lashed out with a silver dagger, swiping it back and forth. But he wasn't attempting to knock Ty down and drive the weapon in. No. He was buying me time. Giving me the chance to do what I needed to do.

To restore Ty.

After all that had happened, his devotion and selflessness struck my soul. Angry, hurt, moved on with Raven or whatever, he would always have my back. Always want what was best for me. What would make me happy, even if that one thing made him miserable.

When you're ready, his unspoken allegiance swept through me along with his acceptance of any outcome from our actions.

My focus trained on what I needed to do. We had one chance at this, just one shot to save Ty's life. If we failed, someone would die for good. Kendrick and me, or Ty.

I crept forward with lethal planning.

Probably able to smell his brother's blood rising from me, Ty showed no concern as I approached. And with the noise below, he wouldn't hear that intermittent beat of my dying heart until I was up close and personal.

With both hands clutching the stake, a gentle sizzle manifested with the tingling of one palm. Warmth grew around my neck, too, down to where the amulet hung below my tank. The silver below the rubber grip on the stake and the amulet were burning me. Not as ruthlessly as it would a normal damned, but who knew how long that would last.

I tugged the amulet from below the cover of my tank and adjusted my hold to one hand, praying Ty hadn't picked up on the scent of my burning flesh yet. And that he wouldn't after what I was about to do.

Running a quick nail down the rubber grip, it sliced in two and peeled free, leaving only bare silver below. I had to get a clean shot and sink this stake in with all the voltage I was storing up. The rubber had to go. It would have blocked the currents.

I crept in close, but in their fighting they were never more than a foot apart. And jumping in to get a better angle would only give away whose side I was really on. I held my ground, hand stinging as the burning increased, my insides jumping at the pain.

A sudden bout of returning transition agony overwhelmed me. I clutched the railing, dropping the stake and catching it just before it clattered to the scuffed floorboards. The silver burned with renewed strength in my hand and around my neck, while the earlier turning sensations grew. I bit my lip to keep from crying out and pinned my eyes shut. If Ty knew I was still experiencing a fraction of my earlier pain, he'd know I wasn't damned. He'd know I hadn't killed his brother.

When the aching and throbbing lessened, I saw through slitted eyes.

Kendrick's dagger went sailing hilt over tip, leaving him unarmed. Ty raked down his torso, cutting deep with wide lashes. Wind conjured by Kendrick's hands separated them for a second. Then Ty sniffed the air and roared.

Like something had suddenly ticked him off.

Swinging a roundhouse at Kendrick's face, he knocked him to the ground. Suddenly on top of him, Ty pinned him down and leaned in with exposed fangs. Kendrick's lids drooped and his air ability died off. He was a breath away from passing out. A second from that deadly bite. "I'm going to enjoy this."

I leaped at Ty, aiming the stake between ribs in his back.

Ty's elbow struck back without warning like he'd anticipated my attack. The bone connected with my striking arm and sent the stake clattering away. I countered with a chokehold around his neck that was met with a laugh before I realized choking him would do no good.

He didn't breathe.

With a growl, his scarred arm swung over my head, grabbing on and flipping me off his back and onto mine. Then just as fast, he hauled me up and drove me into the wall.

The belting force rattled my head and made every bone in my body ache.

With one arm across my chest, Ty saw the welts from the amulet chain down to my cleavage. He grabbed my hand and lifted it high, seeing the healing flesh as he nailed his thumb into my palm. Dipping his head with a snarl, his tongue forked out, licking from my collarbone and up my neck. I struggled as he breathed in deep. He registered the missing red from my irises as my heart gave out a thud.

"You didn't drain the hybrid."

"I didn't kill your brother."

Ty showed no reaction to the jab. Instead, his enraged stare narrowed and a cold smile revealed his fangs. "Now we have a better substitute." He glanced over his shoulder at Kendrick who had recovered enough to prop himself back against the balustrade. He hadn't been bitten, but his many wounds were weeping, staining the blue from his shirt vibrant scarlet. Grating his teeth, he tried to push up, needing to take action to protect me. But his strength failed. His body had shifted into healing mode, sapping every bit of energy to bind his wounds.

As I sent out *stay put* to him, I shoved against Ty. I needed to help Kendrick and I needed to stay alive—for both our sakes.

But Ty caught my jaw and his intense stare claimed mine. Nothing in his eyes changed as he made his command through clenched teeth. "Time to complete the conversion—before my patience runs out. *Kill* your boyfriend."

Over the noise of battling that seemed locked below us, like this floor had been ordered out of bounds, my head heated up. With neurons firing inside, a fight warred on as Ty's compulsion overrode what was left of my conscience. I couldn't stop it, was powerless to keep the next sequence of events from throwing my body into action.

"Amelia, fight it." Kendrick struggled to his feet and gripped the rail with one hand. The damage to his body was taking a toll, the many healing lacerations still weakening him. "You're strong. You can fight back."

I wavered for a moment, that war in my head gaining casualties as my own thoughts and wants were chopped down. My hunger rebuilt with force, the sated taste of Harper's blood suddenly seeming like years ago. The burning around my neck died off without explanation.

Stepping out as Ty's hold on me fell, I faced Kendrick. *"I'm sorry."*

Blazing in front of him, I knocked him down, finding that jugular sweet spot and sinking my fangs in deep.

Kendrick didn't try to push me off. The wind power I felt collecting inside him wasn't released. Instead, he hugged me like he'd never get to again. *I'm not your boyfriend.* The simple sentence punched into my head, a brand across my brain that stopped my strong pulls on his vein. *I never really was. Your heart has always belonged to Ty. And it's not too late. He compelled you. Kill him. Kill your boyfriend.*

His honest words were a loophole. A strike of truth that mingled with what I'd been ordered to do. The need to complete what Ty had compelled of me was unstoppable. There was no getting out of it. But Kendrick was right. He wasn't my boyfriend. Even if he had kinda been for a short while, my actions with Ty had severed that possibility even before I'd seen him with Raven.

Something was slid into my belt loop below the hem of my black tank. Then Kendrick's body went lax in my arms. I was visibly shaking to keep that flow of his life pouring down my throat. To keep my long, pointed fangs buried in deep. But I wasn't alone in this. And I wouldn't be the one to end his life. Kendrick's arms thudded to the ground then and even though it killed me, I let his body slide down gently. Over the noise of battling below, I couldn't hear his heartbeat, which meant Ty couldn't either. With slow grace, I rose and pivoted, restrained hunger cloaking my sight red.

Ty smiled wide and held out his hand. "Ready to join me now?"

I nodded and stepped forward, lacing my fingers through his. The cut-short taste of Kendrick made my veins thrum, renewing the power beneath my skin. Power I needed to fulfill the compulsion still spinning in my head.

I was going to kill my boyfriend.

Ty took me into his arms with a kind of evil pride across his face. He kissed my hair and his strong arms became gentle as he released me enough to tilt my face up.

Was that a flicker of emotion in his soulless eyes?

My heart made no beat and I spared no thought about Kendrick lying still to the side. But feelings did break through the steel now barricading that part in me that differentiated right from wrong. Hope. The emotion no true damned could feel. A bloody tear slid down my face and I didn't bother to hide it. "I love you, Ty."

Ty went statue-still as he stared down at me, a flicker of recognition in his fiery eyes. A slight nod was the only signal he gave. A trick, or the old Ty shining through somehow? There was no way to know, and no second chances. I was going to kill Ty. Kill the damned part of him that currently lived.

With all the hope in the world about to burst my non-beating heart, I brought my curled fingers around the silver through my belt loop. My skin didn't burn and my hand shot up. At the same time, Kendrick shifted, sending all the built-up air he'd stored into Ty to pin him to the wall. Ty didn't struggle, didn't resist, and the stake sank in deep. The biggest volt I'd ever conjured surged from my palm, spearing blue light into his black heart.

Ty's arms came around me, a trap as his body lit up like a firework. Inky veins grew like cracks over his skin, and then he slid down the wall, the stake sliding free of his chest.

I stared down at him, no burn or renewed sizzle attacking my hand that remained cranked tight around the silver length. There was no movement, no breath, and no heartbeat.

CHAPTER 35

A wolf's bark echoed up the hollowed foyer as the sound of feuding damned, vampires, and wolves encroached upstairs, getting nearer by the second.

"We have to get out of the open," Kendrick said as the clouds faded from his eyes. Despite the blood I'd taken from him and his many still-healing wounds, he moved in a flash and swooped up his dagger. Then he looped his arms around Ty's and hauled him back, kicking in the door I'd come from earlier. "Come on."

Downgrading how grateful I was for everything Kendrick had done and was doing, single-minded fear made me want to scream. Right behind him, I staggered through the open door and slammed it shut.

My knees hit the carpet first, no longer able to hold my weight, but shaking like I'd just run a marathon. Liquid trickled from my nose and I dropped the stake as I spluttered a spray of red across my raised hands. The blood I'd taken from Kendrick's vein fought my full-body drain, while my hunger rebuilt with creeping strength. But

I wasn't worried for myself, even if Kendrick was now eyeing me as if waiting to catch me if I keeled over. I reached out, trembling fingers touching the right spot on Ty's neck.

Kendrick crossed the room as a bare-footed stumble brought Harper over from the bed. "Is my brother alive?"

Kendrick's think-on-your-toes-and-risk-your-life plan had worked. It had kept me from completing the transition and had given me time to get through to Ty. To save Ty...I hoped.

A punch of blood struck the air and as I whirled, I caught Kendrick holstering his dagger. He returned from the table between two chairs—one standing and one that I'd smashed—and thrust a full glass at me. "You need this."

With fangs throbbing and rose-color tainting my sight, the hunger I'd ignored roared from my gut. I snatched the glass, drained it fast, and then forced the red-stained shell back at him. Spinning back to Ty, I replaced my first two fingers along his neck. "Come on, dammit." There had to be a pulse. There just had to. But he was lying there so still, so cold. Nearing battle sounds and bloodcurdling cries made me wince but did nothing to jolt him. I felt nothing under my fingertips—no pulse, no rising warmth. My other hand went to Ty's chest. The hole through the skin that peered down to his heart had filled with black oil. Unrippled black oil that showed no vibration. There was no heartbeat, no flutter. "Is...is this normal?" I'd been tranqued after the PVC battle and I hadn't stayed to watch Caius's transformation. "How long did it take Raven to come around?"

Nothing came through about Kendrick's possible feelings for her after the extended lip-lock I'd witnessed, or whether he'd meant what he said about us not being romantically involved. And I was glad. For the moment, those things could wait, especially while Harper was holding his breath for an answer beside me. "I found her when I went back to help clean up. It was a while later, but there are no hard and fast rules. Your ability is an enigma."

"So we just wait?" Harper's voice was hollow, but I was glad to see the color had returned to his skin after my almost lethal attack.

The sounds of battle grew increasingly louder, boots and paws pounding the ground just outside as beings leaped at one another.

"Dorian didn't come with us," Kendrick blurted. "I know the timing's shithouse, but I couldn't find him or Vanessa."

The distraction made it feel like invisible hands were around my neck and choking me. I gulped. "Marcus was using Dorian, but I don't know where he is." When I dropped the walls around the events that had brought me here, followed by what had happened later in this very room, Kendrick's jaw fell. I couldn't say it out loud, what Ty had done, not with Harper right beside me. "Vanessa's...dead."

Heavier thumps vibrated the floor beneath my feet and the surrounding walls, but I refocused on Ty. Cold and gray. No breath, no heartbeat. Only the decomposing scent of his oily blood. Nothing had changed.

"Amelia, I can't stay." Kendrick moved to the door, a burning need to take action rising inside of him. "I'll find Dorian and help win this war. With the wolves on our side, we won't lose." Wind began to spin around him as he clutched the glass doorknob. "Promise me something?"

After every sacrifice he'd made, I didn't hesitate. "Anything."

"When this battle is dust and we come out the other end, promise me you'll use that sharp end on yourself"—he nodded at the shiny stake on the carpet—"to make your heart beat again. No matter what happens here with Ty or out there. Promise me."

After all the death and destruction that was on my hands, I didn't deserve a fresh start. Especially if Ty's restore failed. But there was no time for arguing. No point to it either. "Okay."

Kendrick smiled, so much unsaid blazing in his determined gaze. "I'll see you out there when you're ready, soul mate."

"Be careful," was all I could get out as he unsheathed the dagger from his holster and slipped from the room.

I glanced down at Ty and returned my hands to their earlier positions at his neck and over the puddled hole in his chest. "Come on, Ty. Please."

With Raven, there had been a time lapse before her life returned, but with Caius, I hadn't waited to find out. Here and now, it had already been minutes, long forever-feeling minutes. And I needed to get out there, needed to help the wolves and the vampires…and Kendrick. I'd taken his blood. Not a lot of it, but because of his injuries and use of his wind ability, he was drained. I could feel it through the returning strength of our bond as he forged a path with his dagger through the damned on this level to reach the stairs. If anything happened to him out there, it would be my fault.

"You did the thing to save him, didn't you?" Harper looked like his world would end if his brother didn't wake up soon. At my nod he said, "Well, what if you do it again, will that help?"

I couldn't drown his last hope, but I couldn't affirm it, either. When I'd restored Raven and even Caius, I had been alive. Not transitioning into the thing I was now becoming. So was that ability now null and void? Lost to the life that had stopped my heart and was gradually killing my conscience?"

I didn't want to accept the possibility. Couldn't take it if this was now my reality. I could give a shit whether I could use the power on myself. And I prayed now to give up that chance if Ty would just come back.

My fingers at Ty's throat curled around his nape, squeezing as I stared down at him. "Wake up, dammit." I lowered my head to his chest, ear right over the hole in his heart. Nothing. My hope faltered and my sight turned red. It wasn't a sign of the transition returning with force, but instead came from the bloody tears that flooded my eyes.

It hadn't worked.

Accepting the horrible reality crushed me. My lungs ached even without breath as I shattered in two. Even with his body right beside me, I felt like we were miles apart. Like we had been this whole time, even minutes ago before my stake had plunged in deep. The loss of him again overwhelmed me. I saw his curiosity when we'd met, his intrigue and acceptance. I reached up to hold the amulet and lingered in the memory of his vulnerability at giving me his mother's necklace. All those seductive smiles, rough touches, his lips capturing mine... Oh, God. How could I stand another passing minute knowing they could only be memories now? That I could never experience them with him again? Already, I missed him with every fiber of my being.

Staring down at him, I ran gentle fingers along the contours of his face, through the satin of his black hair. The sight of every ridge and plane, and the feel of each strand committed to my memory. Held and captured for what would soon be a poor substitute for the real thing.

After everything I'd gone through to get to this point, I'd failed. And now someone was going to pay. My voice was deadpan as I sat up. "I'm sorry, Harper."

The boy lurched up to his feet, striding to the window as he wiped his cheeks dry. Pulling the blind's edge in, he stared out as the dim glow of fading twilight shone in from outside.

I lowered my head so that my face was beside Ty's. I brushed my cheek across his rough stubble and added that feeling to my memory bank. Then I hovered over him, closed my eyes, and pressed my lips to his. Our last kiss. A final and devastating good-bye. *I'm sorry I failed you.* The message was silent as red tears tracked down my cheeks and onto his. "I love you, Ty." With one last brush of my lips against his, I released his neck and drew away—

I froze in a half crouch, a scent striking up my nose and drilling into my brain. My fangs tingled and my mouth watered. The growing smell was pure and rich, but it was peppery, too. Harper was across the room. It wasn't coming from him, I realized as the rotting blood staining the air decreased and the other scent soared.

My wide eyes shot down, my tears melting away to clear my vision. The gray from Ty's face was fading, but those black veins that had forked up over his chest and neck when I'd staked him remained. I dropped to my knees and my hand pressed to his chest, feeling the ice thaw as his skin began to heat up.

Harper raced over, hitting the floor beside me. His golden eyes darted down to his brother then up. "What happened?"

A great thump popped beneath my palm as streaked black swelled out. A growing and erratic beat picked up as the sound of knitting flesh rose up. The hole through Ty's chest down to his heart was closing. His eyelids twitched, and my hands flew up to cup his face. My own heart gave out a single beat, aching as it stilled like it wanted to take flight. "*Ty...*"

Ty's eyes flung open, pupils black, whites flawless, and irises... glowing vibrant gold with chips of maroon. Love and vitality blazed from his stare and transformed every line on his scarred face. His lips parted. *"Amelia—"* His torso jacked upright, head tilted back as he sucked in a sudden dry breath. Tipping sideways he clawed the carpet, choking on the sudden rush of air to his lungs.

My hands stayed on him with Harper's, never leaving as he

fought his body's reaction to needing oxygen again. The retching and spluttering were the worst and best sounds I'd ever heard. Because even though Ty probably felt like he was coughing up a lung, he was moving, alive, and sort of breathing.

When the coughing died off, Ty rolled onto his back, gasping. A weak smile curved his lips as the unforgettable scent that belonged to him wafted up from his body.

"Ty." His name left my lips on a whisper, like I thought saying it too loud would somehow undo the revived life now coursing through him. "I…"

The tension in Ty's expression and body suddenly released and his eyes rolled back.

"What happened?" Harper cried as my panic peaked.

I rushed to check his vitals. His heartbeat was irregular—normal for a lycan—but strong and steady. His breathing was slow and deep, no longer quick and shallow. The loss of gray from his skin had returned that tan color to his complexion too, though it was paler than it had been before he'd died and now inked with black veins. I pulled up one eyelid and breathed a sigh of relief. Golden and slightly silver irises with darker chips of maroon. Ty was unconscious, but he was breathing and his heart was beating. My total relief was paramount. "Ty's alive. He's going to be okay."

As Harper sighed, the amulet began to sizzle against my chest, the silver casing and chain reacting against my skin like before. I whipped it off from around my neck and after a second's hesitation, I pressed the stone into Ty's palm. No reaction. No burning. His old lycan immunity was in operation. I'd returned his heart to life and now mine was the one cold and frozen.

"Now my heart in stone against yours," I said as I closed his fingers over the silver and lay his fist over his beating heart.

I slipped out of the room after taking the door key from Ty's back pocket and leaving it with Harper to secure the room. To keep them safe while Ty was unconscious and until the battle had run its course. Which, if I had anything to do with it, would be in our favor.

I hadn't risked everything and saved Ty only to have him recaptured and made into a soulless monster again.

I loathed leaving them behind, but the need to take action thrummed in my veins. The need to assist the cavalry who'd joined forces to save me and stop their common enemy.

And to distract the bloodlust swiftly rebuilding from my clenching gut.

On the third level the number of wolves, vamps, and damned had swelled, and so had the casualties. Between those still fighting, bodies lay wrecked across the soiled wood. Red blood leaked from them and mingled with what looked like black oil and coal turned to ash.

The potent smell and sight of those red puddles had my exposed fangs sliding out even further and puncturing my bottom lip. At tasting what leaked inside my own gaping mouth, I held back a bloodthirsty hiss. Finer particles of damned-fry floated in the air, catching in my throat as I tightened my fist around Kendrick's stake. With a shred of linen from the room I'd just left, the silver burn was kept at bay.

Over by the stairs, Mr. Malau—the biggest wolf I'd ever seen—chomped out the neck of a damned. His golden eyes registered me and I gave a nod. His canines bared, and even in wolf form, I didn't need a translator to convey what he needed to know.

I came his way as two damned appeared from behind a battling vampire. Determination creased the alpha's hairy muzzle and he leaped at the closest one. Caught around the waist, the damned face-planted the floor as I advanced on the second.

The damned stalled his strike when he seemed to recognize me and jerked to clear my path.

I didn't offer the same recognition and staked him through the heart.

With all the blood on brilliant display and soaking the stale air, I hadn't even thought to attempt a restore. And in this moment—when my impulse control was wearing thin—I didn't feel bad for missing the opportunity.

A damned rushed past me to the stairs then, and another two saw me, but shot around the balustrade to take on a wolf and two guards. None even attempted to challenge me…because Marcus had made it clear instant death would result if one even thought of injuring me.

To them it was safer to try their luck on anything else.

Without obstacle, I reached Mr. Malau and shot a quick glance back at the room I'd come from. "Ty's unconscious but he's alive. It worked. Harper's in there too, safe and whole."

The nudge of the massive wolf's muzzle against my hand was as good as any verbal thanks. I'd accomplished what I'd promised him I would all those months ago. I'd saved his son from a dark, soulless existence and brought him back to life.

I scanned the people I could see from this vantage point. The foyer was packed and the floor between levels was just as busy. More bodies and ash marked the way, some of the damned's victims twisted on the path down the stairs. But there was one important person I couldn't see. One that I couldn't feel, either. Kendrick was nowhere in sight, and our re-established bond was throwing up a brick wall.

With watered-down fear tingling over my skin, I jumped in front of Mr. Malau. A rushing damned diverted last-second and dove over the rail. "Where's Kendrick?"

Hesitation flashed in the huge wolf's big eyes, then he turned his muzzle to point down the body-littered stairs.

"Thanks." I picked a quick path down, my conscience working enough to keep me from treading on the dead. When I reached the second floor, I caught sight of a familiar face.

Uriel swung her sword, slicing into the side of a damned that wailed before lashing out. She repositioned the blade as the damned surged forward too fast to stop. The wavy-edged silver sliced straight through its chest, coming out black on the other side. A rough twist must have pierced its heart because the thing turned to sudden live ash.

As the body crumbled, I cranked an elbow out at a new one gunning for fresh victims. As it teetered, Uriel's sword came up and clipped the damned in the side of the head with a squirt of black.

"Good to see you alive," she said on a hoarse breath.

The attention of two more damned who'd just devoured a guard, saved me from having to lie about the 'alive' part. As they stalked for Uriel, I moved in a heartbeat and blocked the way.

The damned startled and their hands flew up as if in a show of non-threat.

I grabbed the arm of one and spun him around to where Uriel waited with her sword. At the same time, I struck out, my silver finding the other's cold, black heart. Its body fell and I spun back before the new puff of ash could coat my face. The aftermath of the one Uriel had just disposed of met me anyway, its sooty remains sticking to my skin.

My stake switched hands, sizzling with readiness to give my voltage a go. "Have you seen Kendrick?"

Another vampire around the other end of the horseshoe-shaped level was in need of serious help. Uriel began moving in their direction. "He went down—"

A damned appeared out of nowhere, spider-monkeying over the balustrade. It caught Uriel and knocked her down, chowing in with Pit Bull severity that had scarlet streams spraying in the air.

I sprang a split second after it did, but even as my stake drove in deep, I knew I was too late.

Uriel on her back was wide eyed and fish-mouthed.

The spark I'd tried to inflict was nothing more than a tingle as the concrete body between us disintegrated.

After using my power to bring Ty back, I was still out for the count on that front. And I didn't give a shit. The price of taking life was a bitch, and my conscience right now was like a dull cry at the very least.

Even as I stood up and left Uriel lying there, stained by black oil and ash, my remorse was little to none. Any control I still had was only keeping me from tapping any residual blood that filled her veins.

The damned part of me was reigniting on my insides, slowly taking over. But it wasn't in control yet. The one thing that kept my murderous side from turning on the vamps and wolves around me was the sliver of Kendrick's humanity that shone through.

But if anything happened to him? I'd be lost for good.

I hurdled the railing and landed dead center in the foyer on the scorched patch that now replaced the table I'd burned. Urgency smothered me as I scanned around. Wolves and vampires fought together against a common enemy. The battle was currently matched, more wolves and vampires to the number of damned who were stronger and faster. At the moment, the outcome could go either way. The feuding wolves and vampires took little notice of me as they kept up their attack. But the damned did. Before my sudden drop-in, their reckless assaults would have thrown themselves into where I now stood. Now they minded their advances, keeping well clear of me.

In my protected state, I spun. From what I could see, Kendrick wasn't here. A few faces I recognized from training back the Armaya. And Troy and Marika by the front door were sticking together in wolf form as they took down a pair of damned. Pure enjoyment highlighted Troy's wolf features while Marika caught sight of me and raised her muzzle.

I called out over the sound of tearing flesh, screams, and weapons hitting bone. "Ty's alive!" But I wasn't about to get into a friendly, battling side-by-side reunion.

There was no sign of Kendrick.

Without being able to connect through the bond, I couldn't hold back the morbid thought that he was one of the dead weights strewn about the green tiles. But as I squatted and spun, I saw he wasn't—I shot back upright, hand rushing to cover my mouth and nose. My studious gaze between battlers' legs had made the blood leaking out from the fallen look like a glossy invitation. One I was dying to accept.

Needing to move, it took everything I had to concentrate past the never-ending smell of blood, the sound of beating hearts, and the closeness of the bodies that held both. As I dodged through the battlers—my primal instinct to go ripper rising—the fighting tactic of the damned I weaved around changed. Now they shoved or pulled the vampires or wolves they were attacking as if trying to clear my—

An invisible force belted into me, even though not a single damned had. *Oh shit.* Kendrick had just been struck and I knew who by. Marcus. What he'd held back from the bond since leaving me surged through. His intent to take action...for me, for what turning

Ty had done to us all. And most of all, for his mother's cut-down life. The moment he'd left that third-floor room, he'd gone after him. There was no confusing his intent—he'd find vengeance in the death of the one who'd orchestrated all those heinous acts, or die trying.

I focused on our link, feeling the aches and stings that radiated over him. But that wasn't all. Dark, compacted walls and the smell of clay registered in my mind. I knew where they were.

Striking out at any damned I could reach, I forged my way with speed through everyone battling. Metaphorical hits to my head, gut, and back threatened to floor me, but I stumbled on. Past the central stairway landing, I found the cellar door and stairs and was down them in a flash. The door I'd hidden behind was open, and I shot through it as an invisible blow kicked out one of my knees. That clay smell owned the earthy tunnel I sped down, the temperature dropping the lower I got. Another smell dominated the air, the strong aroma of freshly spilled vampire blood.

Kendrick's.

I burst through the tunnel's end and found the cavern where I'd discovered Marcus—my twin—was leading the damned.

Across the vast and dark space, lit only by a single crackling fire pit, Kendrick was on his knees. His shirt, which had been torn and bloody from fighting Ty, was now gone. The red-stained shreds were scattered over the compacted dirt. Pink lines marked his chest where his earlier wounds had since closed up, but he was far from okay. New, more vicious lacerations covered his torso and his cargos were hanging in shreds, dark stains making them look black rather than blue.

My fangs tingled in my gums with desperate hunger, but I kept them leashed.

Marcus had his hand fisted in Kendrick's blood-streaked hair

457

and smiled my way as if glad I'd finally arrived. A few minor welts leaked crimson through to his white T-shirt and—not damaged but designed that way—torn jeans. He hauled Kendrick up by his hair and despite not needing to breathe, I gasped.

Kendrick's face was a black-and-blue mess, with one whole side puffy and a split in his forehead leaking a scarlet stream from his hairline down to his jaw.

"Marcus. Oh God, please stop." All the feelings that were numbing out with what I was becoming, flared back to life at seeing the state of my soul's mate. My fist cranked tighter around the shielded stake I clung to. I could fight; take on my twin with the intent of ending him for good. It'd kill me to do it, but for Kendrick I would. Only, with the distance between us, he'd see the decision and eliminate Kendrick from the equation before I even got a chance to move. So I had to pick a different route. The only one that might save Kendrick's life. A swap. My life for my best friend's. I'd join Marcus here and now. I'd turn damned too, if that's what it took.

Kendrick's voice rose with a croak, his lip splitting with desperate words. "Amelia, don't you dare give in to him. I'd rather die."

Ignoring his plea, I kept my eyes trained on Marcus. Kendrick could choose to lay down his life for me, but that didn't mean I had to accept. "Don't do this, Marcus. *Please*. I'll do whatever you want. Just don't kill him."

That same cruel smile that reminded me of what Marcus really was, what he'd been all along, and what I'd been too trusting and blind to see, made a gleaming appearance. "I'm not going to kill him."

"What?" I came closer, hand throbbing around the material-shielded stake I clung to.

Marcus's fangs lengthened through his lips. "You are. By completing the transition."

"Never."

Marcus jerked Kendrick closer, hand going around his throat and eyes locking on his like lasers. "Attack Amelia with *everything* you have left. Don't stop until she kills you. *With her bare fangs.*"

CHAPTER 36

*K*endrick came at me at a dead run. Lit by the orange glow from the blazing fire pit, his expression wasn't vacant but full of drive. The need to accomplish what he'd been compelled to do. But unlike when Ty had compelled me to kill my boyfriend, there were no loopholes here. Still I had to try.

"Kendrick, you don't have to—"

I ducked at the last second and Kendrick sailed past. A kick in his back made him stumble forward to his hands and knees. I winced, and not because I'd felt the kick through the bond. A wet tear announced the split of lacerations around his torso. They stung like cuts under water through the bond. But Kendrick didn't flinch, and then he was up again and in my face. Streaks of dirt stained his pants below the knees and his palms that reached for me.

I feigned left then clocked him in the jaw. "Shit. Kendrick, stop."

He hissed and spun back, elbow driving into my cheek.

Kendrick's stake flew from my grasp as I teetered, vision spinning as I righted myself. "Fight the compulsion," I rushed as my own internal war spiked. Being this close, the scent of his blood was so palpable I could taste him on my tongue. The transitioning part of me screamed to be freed. But I wouldn't give in. "If anyone can, it's you."

Nothing. No flicker. No recognition.

Just the cold concentration of someone deciding their next vicious move.

Kendrick's fist came out again, striking into my gut. I went to shove him away, but unlike me, he wasn't holding anything back. His hands cupped over my head and pushed down as he drove his knee up. The smell of dirt from his hands registered before pain exploded from my jaw to my skull. I dropped backward, fighting unconsciousness. But he didn't. He'd shut off his physical connection to me.

"Kendrick!" I blinked rapidly, trying to clear the stars from my vision. "I know you're in there. *Fight it.*"

Weight came down on top of me and Kendrick smashed his fist into my nose. Wet spurted up and into my eyes. The smell of my own blood mingled with the clay. If I didn't do something soon, Kendrick was going to kill me. I had no choice. I had to fight back.

And I had to lock out his pain.

With a cry, I released all restraint and my hands came up, knuckles driving into Kendrick's chest. He flew backward through the air and I leaped up, catching his shoulders before his feet touched the ground. Vans running, I shoved him back into the wall, the air belting from his lungs. My fangs lengthened to sharp and deadly spikes. Bodily need and want had the tips sending pulses up into my skull. Covered in blood and lacerations that seeped steadily, the scent was winning out over the shred of conscience I had left.

Just a taste. One long pull from that delicious pulsing vein up his neck.

Whatever happens...I forgive you.

Firelight highlighted Kendrick's unfading determination to fight as I struggled to keep him pinned. His back bounced off the wall, bucking as I fought to contain him. Those honest, unspoken words had traveled from deep inside his soul and through our bond. My dying heart was desperate to drum with fear and adrenaline as he kept up the fight. He had found a way to reach me. To show me he was still there.

Hidden but not gone.

My silent heart cracked, sending a hairline fracture through its middle. I faltered in my desire, my love for Kendrick overriding everything else.

"It's you or him, Amelia." Standing across the cavern, Marcus hadn't moved an inch. He'd remained to watch the show. To make sure what he'd put in motion played out. "Kill him, before he kills you. This end will be a kindness over the death I promise you he'll suffer otherwise."

"Never."

At my hissed words, the fight in Kendrick's body rebuilt with renewed raw force. He threw one arm up between us and clawed down my face, releasing blood like a stream into my eyes. Then he punched into my ribs as a punishing gust of wind belted into me. I propelled back but kept upright, clambering to clear the red from my eyes.

I heard Kendrick rush at me, and saw through patchy vision as Marcus booted the stake I'd lost across the compacted dirt. "Heads up!"

It rolled and wind bounced it up for Kendrick to catch right as he kicked into my stomach. My butt hit the dirt and I slammed back, head thwacking into the ground. I fought unconsciousness, hearing the sizzle from the naked silver in Kendrick's palm as his shadow lurched over me. Kneeling on top of me, his eyes were clouded. His hand shook like he was trying to restrain it. And losing. He thrust the silver tip straight at my heart.

Stop me!

My hands flung up with a non-lethal dose of lightning. The blue streak streamed into Kendrick's chest and sent him flying. He collided with the curved wall and fell like a stone.

Knocked out cold.

Marcus was there in a flash and lifted Kendrick by his neck with one hand. The other curled into a fist and belted into my best friend's face. "Wake up!"

Kendrick stirred, his eyes fluttering and head wobbly.

Scrambling upright, I rushed at them, then froze. The danger in Marcus's eyes promised to set something in motion that couldn't be changed. "Marcus, let him go." I took a cautious step forward. "You can't break us. And you can't force my hand. It's over."

Marcus flung Kendrick around in front of him so he faced me. His arm clamped over his chest to keep him upright. "Emotions are for the weak. And besides…it's the end of his shelf life."

Manic déjà vu flooded my mind's eye in a split second. Marcus had used that phrase about his aged father when we'd first met. The damned commander had spoken similar words in that emotionless tone to the Lord before chomping out his neck. And now… "Marcus, no—"

His free hand came around and hooked over Kendrick's jaw and snapped his head to the side.

A crack rang out with Kendrick's final words as I stared in frozen shock. *Ice freezes life.* The light vanished from his eyes and his body fell.

Dead.

Horror buried me like an avalanche, running from my choked-up throat down to my legs that were about to give out.

"Noooooo!"

I rushed forward and slid on my knees, gathering up Kendrick's floppy body so his head rested in the crook of my elbow. Crimson tears blurred my vision, but I didn't even attempt to wipe away the non-stop stream. Total disbelief stunned me into shock. This wasn't real. It couldn't be. But I could see too much detail through the teary blur as I stared down at his face. Lids open, mouth gaping, eyes vacant and soulless, head heavy as a boulder and neck kinked on an angle. "No, no, no." Keeping his head supported, I pressed my ear to his chest. Silence. No rise and fall of breath. "Kendrick, no."

Agonizing realization shattered my entire being. Broke me apart like I'd been hacked up into tiny disposable pieces. With rough movement, I shoved the bloody hair back from his forehead and lay my hand along his cheek as firelight danced across his exposed flesh. My tears suddenly dried up, letting me see the horrible truth with total, indisputable clarity. Something jagged pocked wickedly from the side of Kendrick's neck beneath the unbroken skin. His spine had been broken, severed and detached. Purple welts ran in diagonal lines across his skin, trauma from the deadly twist. Detached or not, this was as close to decapitation as it got. One of the ways to kill a damned. Except Kendrick wasn't damned. He was a living vampire. So much more fragile. There was no going back from this.

My own neck ached as if inflicted with the same damage. But it was only a trick of the mind. Because I couldn't feel his pain. Oh, God. A sob tore from my throat and I sucked in air I didn't need. The feel of being chained under mud imprisoned my lungs. "You can't leave me." With everything I had, I reached out through our bond. I needed to feel him, to get some response, any response. We were connected through life…and death. Forever bound by our souls. "Kendrick, *please*."

I glanced around as if his ghost would magically appear and saw Marcus. In the minutes of my total despair, he'd stayed to watch, remained silent and motionless. A spectator. There was no triumph in his expression, no regret or sorrow, either. Just indifference. From the guy who'd just murdered my best friend, my soul's mate…that was the *reaction?*

Fury lit up my insides like I'd just swallowed a fire torch. My now icy skin became hot as a poker. On the outside, I remained cool. I pressed my lips to Kendrick's forehead and lowered him gently to the earth. With slow movements, I pried the stake from my best friend's hand and rose to my feet. With one hand sizzling, they were both cranked so tight my nails sliced in and hit bone. A single word was spoken with a razor's edge, the malice of what was to come. *"Why?"*

I stepped closer and let the creature I was becoming off its leash. For what I had planned, I'd need to lose myself first. Let go of everything I had been, and become all I'd fought to keep at bay. The part of me that remained would save one last soul. But if I failed? The monster taking over would consume its first victim. Marcus couldn't be hurt by my power. But that didn't mean I couldn't burn away the damned part of him despite his claim. And afterward? They could put me down with the rest of the monsters. "Fucking tell me why!"

Marcus showed no fear. He made no move to prepare to take me down. "He was in our way, holding you back from what you really are."

His unedited words didn't shock me like they should have. Not now that I'd abandoned that last sliver of my self-control and given in to the monster prowling inside of me. Damned didn't dwell on

466

uncomfortable feelings and memories. They took control. They took action. They didn't care if their own flesh and blood had committed a crime. I wasn't one hundred percent there, but I wasn't far off. And for Kendrick? I would stop this monster who was my flesh and blood—one way or another.

In a flash, I pounced on Marcus and knocked him to the ground. "You're gonna beg for death." My fist plowed into his face and blood spurted up. Other hand burning, I drove the stake down—

Marcus's hands came up with a fireball to my chest and I went flying. He laughed as I bounced off the wall and landed on my feet, tank burnt and flashing my bra. The split in his face sewed shut as he stalked forward, a swift reversal of what I'd inflicted, but without the fists. Every unlit fire pit in the cavern exploded in flame, throwing shadows of his tall frame like star spikes around his feet as he walked. "Other half or not, you're no more a match for my power than Kendrick was. You're out of your league, Amelia. I thrive on pain."

"Good thing I'm not done yet."

I was in front of Marcus in a flash, fist driving up into his chin. His head cracked back and I plunged the stake in deep, letting my voltage channel through the silver. A direct hit, a bullseye to his beating heart with the full force of my lightning.

Except there was no glorious light. No waves of power pulsed out from our bodies. No burning sounded from the pointed silver protruding from his chest. It hadn't worked.

A cackle rose and Marcus's ribs vibrated as his head corrected itself. A smile lit his fanged mouth. He was laughing—staked dead center through the heart—and he was laughing. How the hell was he not dying in agony?

"I didn't lie, Amelia. I am what I am. Not even you can change that."

Throwing off my shock, I dug deep and sent every last wave into him, waiting for the phenomenon to take effect.

It didn't.

Instead, his body began to glow red hot, so boiling that my hand around the stake and the other on his shoulder began to fry. But it wasn't fire. It was much worse. "Yin to my Yang." Marcus clutched my arms above my elbows and held tight as I tried to break away. "You're like a battery pack, personalized for me. Your power feeds mine. Heaven's light. Hell's fire."

That red-hot burned brighter, the glow engulfing his entire body and spreading out. Fighting to break his hold, I screamed as it clawed up my arms. But his hands were silver cuffs and I was the prisoner. In a matter of seconds, the glow engulfed my body like an impenetrable cocoon as I stared into my twin's blood-red eyes. My mouth gaped, energy-zapped and unable to cry out. The firelight blinked off and on with the rise and fall of my lids.

Sudden footsteps rushed our way and fire exploded at the entry across the cavern. "Amelia!" The scream belonged to one person and one person alone. Ty. "You're outnumbered and trapped, Marcus. There's no way out for you."

I tried to call out to him, but I choked on what felt like acid down my throat.

"Let her go."

With the last fall of my eyelids everything faded, except for Marcus's voice. "My damned hybrid for your soul mate. Guess we're even...for now. Until we meet again, my sister."

CHAPTER 37

Sensations began to register against my chilled skin: cotton below and above, fine strands of hair across my face, stinging along the back of one of my hands, cushioning under my head, light like a spotlight through my closed lids and…heartbeats. With groggy grace, I clambered upright. My lids fluttered. Slitted light through a crack in the tall drapes streamed like a solar flare into my bedroom with a shock of pins to my retinas. I was back at the Armaya, safe and in one piece…

Sudden awareness attacked my body with a strike of torture spearing my chest. I was back at the Armaya in the same soiled clothes I'd been knocked out in. Away from the damned hotel. Away from Marcus and—Kendrick's dead body.

With agonizingly vivid detail the scene of his death whizzed through my subconscious. Kendrick stirred and Marcus clamped his forearm over his chest. In one swift move, he grabbed Kendrick's jaw and snapped his head sideways. Life vanished from Kendrick's eyes and then I was cradling him on the dirt. *"No, no, no."* Through bloody tears, I saw the jagged end of his severed spine poking at the side of his neck, the purple welts that ran in diagonal lines across his unbroken skin.

A horrible ache bloomed inside my chest as my eyes finally adjusted to the minimal but blinding light. Kendrick was gone, killed by my twin because he'd come to my rescue. Because I'd taken everything into my own hands and gone to save Ty. Because I'd been too weak to do it alone. I should have known Kendrick would never give up on me and let my life expire. I was his soul's mate, his best friend...had even been something more, too. His girlfriend. Without him there was no way I would have succeeded in restoring Ty.

For a split second I wondered where Ty was, and if he was okay. But I didn't deserve any relief, any respite at knowing I'd at least saved someone. Ty had lived. I'd heard his strong voice before losing consciousness. Kendrick had died in his place. Marcus may have inflicted the twist that broke his neck, but he was dead because of me.

I'd killed my best friend.

I doubled over on my bed as tears gathered and fell. Curling up sideways, the agony of his loss swept through me and fractured my silent heart. Giving in to the loss that overwhelmed my transitioning ability to shut emotions off, I wept.

Through the sobbing my lids opened and shut, opened and—

The mournful tears that rolled across my face and drenched my sheets suddenly dried. My hand went to my chest, palm pressing over my heart. My non-beating heart. The beats I had heard on waking weren't my own. With what I was becoming they couldn't be. My ears pricked, sharpening to pick up the source. It wasn't inside my suite, but right outside the main door. Four separate patterns belonging to four separate vampires. Four guards.

The muscle inside my own chest was still, not a beat or even a flutter. The rise and fall of my chest with breath was also missing... because I didn't need to breathe anymore. The stabbing through that motionless muscle shifted downward then as the distant beating hearts grew louder. In my head I imagined seeing into their chests as if opened for surgery, their hearts squeezing to deliver that fresh, live blood through their organs and arteries. As the pain resettled in my stomach, my mouth gaped and my fangs throbbed.

I rolled off the soft mattress and past the end post to crouch on all fours—and grimaced at the fleeting light bouncing from the lounge room into my eyes. The mini fridge set into the full-wall cabinet was throwing light like a killer laser. A beacon to distract and force my attention. I was around the white couch and coffee table in a flash, wrenching the door open to peer inside. Atop the clear, glass shelves were a few transparent bottles filled with blood.

Kendrick's blood.

The backups he'd stored there after I'd reverted from taking his vein. With slow and careful movement, I drew one bottle out, staring at it. My ears buzzed, smothering any other sounds and stalling my starvation. With his body cold and dead somewhere, this was all that kind of lived of Kendrick. Dead blood as it was called, but still red with life. Not ruddy brown and in the process of deterioration.

I licked my lips and the sound of heartbeats returned through the buzzing in my ears as my hunger spiked. There were only three options I could take. Let the damned that wanted full run of my body and mind loose and kill through full consumption. Restore myself— if I even could with what I was now becoming, and if my ability had recharged in my starved state. Or drink Kendrick's bottled blood. I untwisted the cap with shaking fingers, hating that I had to do this. That even with him dead, I was still using him. The blood slid cold down my gullet and I eased back on folded legs. The light but unmissable black wiry veins up my arms disappeared back into my skin. With a glance, I caught my reflection in the mirror siding the opening to the bedroom. My reddening pupils glowed vibrantly for a few beats, and then faded back to silver-blue.

A loud gurgle made me flinch as my gut churned around the dead blood. I gagged, feeling a wave rise up my esophagus that I choked back down. The dead blood may have hidden a few transitioning traits, but it hadn't been enough to cull my hunger. That fact was frighteningly clear as I imagined someone's gory slaughter at the strike of my fangs.

My focus slid to the foyer door that separated me from the guards, and I dropped the empty bottle. Like a lion on the prowl, I crept forward—

A sudden image of Kendrick's face flashed in my mind, spine jutting out and purple welts twisted sideways. I collapsed and curled my arms over my head, smacking my forehead into the stone. Once. Twice. Three times. Pain cracked through my skull, and the throbbing need that had saliva dripping from my mouth lessened.

When I dared to look up, the first thing I glimpsed was an out-of-place item beside my bed. One I hadn't noticed before. An almost empty blood bag was suspended from one of those metal hospital stands. The tube coming from the bag hung on the rug that spanned out from below my bed, a small red patch staining the carpet fibers. Stinging registered again and I noticed my hand as I sniffed. Taped to the top of one was the plastic valve the tube was meant to be attached to. I'd been on a blood drip…

With a snarl and nothing other than primal reaction, I was back in my bedroom. I struck out and snatched the bag off the metal pole and my fangs plunged through the tough plastic. The blood dregs were sucked dry with a double-handed squeeze.

What happened next froze me like a statue. But not on the inside.

My heart pattered with a severe ache as if in shock of being given sudden life. I stared down at the crumpled plastic in my hands. What the hell? With a sniff, I picked up a cocktail of scents that were undeniably blood, but not from the same source. Or even one species. As I puzzled over whose or what's blood I'd just swallowed, the irregular beat beneath my ribs faded to almost non-existence. The sound of the guards' hearts returned, but it was only a sound.

My hunger was sated.

For now.

WITH MY BLOODLUST on an unexplained leash, I kept my hand over my heart, feeling each beat that grew fainter and fainter. With a trialed gasp that made my lungs feel like overinflated balloons, the muscle went dormant again. I had to find who or where that blood had come from…

Striding to the door, a sudden internal tug stopped me. It felt like there were hands inside my body, grabbing at organs and pulling them forward to the main exit of this suite. I lunged through the foyer and swung the door wide open.

Unblocked by the separation of wood and stone, the blood of four guards assaulted my nose and made my fangs ache. With no breath passing through my nose or mouth, the potency that registered was shocking. But somehow it wasn't compelling enough in this moment to have to act on.

The four made no move, focusing only on the torn and dirtied jeans and tank I still wore from my disappearance. And I only just wondered now if they knew what I was slowly becoming? "Lady Bathory. Can we get you anything?"

Clearly unaware.

The *unseen* force tugged again and then again. As I looked to my waiting guards, suspicion dawned on me. *Kendrick.* Was he somehow reaching out from beyond the grave to me? What little hope still existed in my cold heart and fracturing soul came alive. If it was the last thing I did before plummeting into the far depths of hell, I needed to connect with him.

"My Lady?"

"Oh, no. I don't need anything from you. Just some...fresh air." Still affected but not made ravenous by the collective smell of their blood, I tunneled into each guard with my gaze. "Keep your distance."

Rushing out into the grand, glossy corridor, I followed that internal pull toward the arcing gilt stairs. In the quiet surroundings as I descended the smooth marble steps, I became acutely aware of the sound of my tailing guards' beating hearts. And my silent one. Picking up the pace, I tried to ignore the animalistic need to turn and pounce to stop the repetitive sound. My hands, tensed like an eagle's talons, buried in the pockets of my jeans and...found something. I pulled out—Ty's Zippo. I'd lost it after starting the bonfire to burn off my marks, which meant...Ty had put it in my pocket since Marcus had floored me. I began flicking the lid open and shut to cover their heartbeats and my missing one.

After clearing the wide landing, I passed the pews around the near length of the main hall and faced the double doors to the boardroom. Whatever was directing me was waiting in here. With my guards hanging back, I pushed down on the handles and shoved the heavy wood in...

If I could still breathe, I would have gasped. And almost did until my lungs seized in warning. The unlit boardroom with its long drapes drawn shut—that had to be replacements after Marcus's fiery ambush—wasn't empty. But it was free of the living. The thrashing figure across the room, chained with burning silver to massive anchors in the singed wall, was absolutely dead. Red pupils and gray pallor fitted with black veins that forked out like rotting tree roots. Long, pointed fangs snapped through cracking lips, starving for flesh.

It wasn't Kendrick. It was someone else I recognized well. The pulling sensation eased up then, turning into a dull link. Because I'd found the energy that had drawn me here. Uriel. And she wasn't just transitioning. She was one hundred percent damned. I'd seen her taken down at the hotel, dead-still and covered in oily black from fighting. She'd been infected, and now she was here. Which meant she'd completed the conversion and taken life.

In my state of transition I was somehow connected to her, drawn to her because of proximity. Which meant one life-changing thing. I could track the damned.

And Marcus.

New drive to seek vengeance lit with electricity in my veins.

When a presence appeared through the open doors behind me with the illumination of the wrought iron chandelier above the table, I spun. More heartbeats. More blood. My free hand came up, so badly wanting to plug my nose.

Lady Rasputin, in usual formal-gown attire, narrowed her eyes at me and my stained and torn clothes. "Awake, and in two days. Right where we need you."

I resumed the Zippo's click, click, open-shut.

Lord Strigon tipped his head and strode over the sooty debris of portrait remains to place a full decanter on the tray centering the table. "Time to get down to business, then."

More like time for my punishment. The consequence of taking off without permission. For being responsible for how many deaths?

And all while hiding the fact that I was dying, becoming the enemy they'd just fought to kill.

Remembering then that I wasn't breathing, I made a conscious effort to pass air in and out. Each draw made me want to cough and further highlighted the scent of their blood in the air. I kept up the act though, and backed up to the table. As the doors closed me in and the other two moved to their thrones, Uriel's thrashing settled down, a cold, calculated stare replacing the struggle as she seethed.

With all the self-control I could muster, I attempted to speak without letting my fangs fully out. "Why is Uriel chained here?"

Then I noticed the emptiness of the table's thrones as I slipped into my own. Lord Paole's was vacant, as was the Baldassare and Vladimir thrones. A fresh wave of pain struck my quiet heart, but I didn't ask about the last two. And I didn't let the watered-down emotions I felt show on the outside. I knew why they were empty. I clutched the arms of my throne to keep my ass seated, nails digging into the carved wood. "Where's Lord Paole?"

Lady Rasputin's stare intensified as she lowered in her throne. "Perished during Marcus's attack in this very room. The one you decided to disappear before without notice."

"Which Amelia sent warning about." Lord Strigon filled and dispensed three glasses. "We are *glad* you survived. We will never reinstate Caius to the throne. And until further notice, he can continue to rot in the cells." He turned his glass with edgy fingers. "The Seven are now three until a Paole successor is crowned. Uriel's the last of her line. We cannot afford to lose her, too."

With my hands shaking with poor restraint, I took hold of my filled glass. I knew why Uriel was here, and I wanted to help. But in this closed, draft-free room, that grinding was fast returning to my gut. My fangs punched into my mouth in anticipation and I picked up the glass. All eyes were on me, watching, studying. Breathe, stupid. In. Out. In. Out. I drained the glass quickly and refilled it. "You want me to restore her."

"Not only her." Lady Rasputin's fingers wave-tapped the marble, but her eyes didn't leave me, nor did the disdain at my appearance. "After your entirely reckless actions in the way you vacated the Armaya without your guards and all that transpired—good or bad— because of those very actions, a price must be paid."

"Although the ends have justified the means, a decision has been made," Lord Strigon added, tipping his glass and taking a sip. "A combat detail is being trained to kill, but any damned we capture will fall on you to be restored."

Lady Rasputin produced a cloth from the throne next to her and unwrapped a pure silver stake. Tipping it from the swatch of silk, it rolled over the marble and clinked as it tapped my glass. "Starting with Uriel. Now."

Not bothering to argue—because any penance was welcome—I refilled my crystal glass, raised it to my lips, and drained the contents. The last thing I needed was for my eyes to change color. It was already bad enough that my fangs would only retract half way.

Before either of them could dwell on that, I pocketed the Zippo and swooped up the stake. It sizzled as I leaped over the armrest of my throne, and my insides squirmed. But I kept up the in-out routine of unneeded air to my unimpressed lungs.

Facing Uriel, whose chains kept her arms and legs strung out like a star, I didn't wait for her to pick up on my lack of heartbeat. As a hiss raked from her throat, I lunged forward. A surge of voltage released as I stabbed the stake into Uriel's heart. Her body lit up like a flare and a second later she went limp. With her body suspended by chains, I slid the stake free and scrambled back on wobbly legs to my throne. Starving and with my sight red, I snatched the decanter from the table and chugged the whole thing.

Rasputin and Strigon didn't notice. They were in front of Uriel now and watching with wonderment as the black veins retreated from her flesh. A flutter of her beating heart made an appearance, and in less than thirty seconds her drooping head lifted. Her lids flung open with a rasping breath, revealing silver-blue irises that were flecked with maroon chips.

Lady Rasputin gasped. "You did it."

AFTER MINUTES of quiet inspection with Uriel in and out of consciousness and showing no signs of aggression, she was unshackled and carried off by guards to recover in her suite.

Which was exactly what I needed. A warm trickle now ran from my nose that I plugged with the silk swatch Lady Rasputin had left across the table. My fingers tapped around the empty decanter, wondering if smashing the crystal so I could lick the fragments free of scarlet residue would gain too much attention. With my brain throwing out a big fat, *yes, you idiot*, I started backing toward the exit as the others returned to their thrones.

"I see you're in need of recovery…and a cleanup." Lord Strigon said, stalling my retreat. "Though before you leave…"

Lady Rasputin clapped her hands and elevated her sharp voice. "Bring them in!"

The double doors opened and I stumbled back, shocked by their presence and pungent scent. I gaped at the three beings that entered in human form. Mr. Malau, Marika, and Troy. In spite of being on enemy ground, they didn't look on edge or prepared in any way to fight. No visible weapons were strapped to them. There was no sign of trembling to hint at a sudden shift into wolf form, either. *Oh shit.* This was bad, seriously freaking bad.

Despite the potent punch of their lingering blood, I put myself between them and the royals. "*I* included them in our business. *I* sent for them. Marcus had Ty and I had been working with them. It was all on me." I was trying to protect them, but as sick fantasies of crimson and tearing flesh entered my mind, I wondered if maybe they didn't need protecting from the RVC, after all. Maybe it was me. Still my mouth kept up the talk. "They didn't do anything wrong. *I did.*"

A hand came down on my bare shoulder, one that in the past would have been as cold as mine. Now that I was transitioning, it almost felt warm. I jerked away to see Strigon and hoped he hadn't noticed the icy touch. "They're not here under duress, Amelia. We invited them to return after the hotel invasion."

"What?" I realized I wasn't breathing again and resumed the in-out, trying not to make the normal bodily function look like a chore. Trying not to splutter as my lungs rejected oxygen with that overin-flated feeling, I took a needed step back. Then another. The collective smell was too much. The number of beating hearts—too much. "Why?"

"To make us an offer," Mr. Malau said, ears twitching as he glanced from my nose to my expanding and contracting chest...like he knew it was an act.

"We wish to offer the wolves a permanent truce." I looked to Strigon who, *thank God,* didn't seem to have noticed anything abnormal about me. "To join forces and work together in taking out the damned."

"As equals," Troy interjected, his voice as sharp as a blade and his face just as dead serious.

"Not slaves," Marika added. She sent me a closed-lip smile that was both somber and warm. "Working together, we kill every damned we find."

Mr. Malau let his canines slide free and his irises flashed gold. "Bar the few that are caught in the process."

"We two have already voted on this." Lady Rasputin stood up from behind the marble slab, looking like she wanted to leave now that the wolves were here. Like their very presence was a direct insult to her and her beliefs. "I am against the motion. So what say you, Lady Bathory?"

This vote, a vote to bring our two races together again as one— not as ruler and slave, but as equals—was in my hands. Hunger abandoned for a split second, I nodded. "Of course. Yes."

"Then we have an alliance." Mr. Malau stuck his hand out side-ways and waited for me to grasp it. The chandelier's light caught and reflected in his studying eyes as he waited.

The return took a few long seconds, my thoughts juggling with the act and if I could hold back from tugging him forward once I made contact. If I could refrain from turning from Jekyll to Hyde with the suddenly returning stabbing pain through my gut.

My hand shot out lightning fast, hoping for a quick release.

"Werewolves and vampires unite." Mr. Malau's eyes flared a brighter gold as he met mine. His voice lowered as I yanked my hand free. "Thank you, Amelia. Thank you for bringing back my sons."

CHAPTER 38

The second the meeting adjourned, I raced back up to my suite and shut the door behind me before my guards could even catch up. The quickest shower and change of my life did nothing to distract my hunger. And not a second later, I was in front of the bar fridge eyeing the last three bottles of blood. The easy option was to drink them to take the edge off, to make sure my eyes stayed silver-blue for just a little bit longer while I figured out what the freaking hell I was going to do. But then what? Kendrick's blood would be gone, just as gone as his life was.

I slumped back onto my butt and swung the fridge door shut. Movement outside my room announced the arrival of my guards along with the sound of their beating hearts. What I craved ran rich in each of their veins, on tap and ready for the taking. But would I be able to stop if I started? I'd mastered control before, but this was different. My entire body craved the *lifeblood* of a vampire, the last drop that came with their final breath.

I licked my lips and rolled onto my knees, fingers pried into the thick rug and ready to stalk my way over to a step I couldn't take back.

My hand flung up and sent a volt straight into my neck. The kind of pinch you needed to wake up in a dream. Only this was far from a dream. It was a nightmare...in the flesh. And I was the thing that skulked in the shadows. Still, the shock helped enough to slow my mind and clear my thoughts.

I needed space. I needed room to think.

Fast as lightning, I shot across the room to the window. Keeping to the lightening shadows as the sky brightened with the rising sun, my light-sensitive eyes stung then adjusted. But it wasn't working. Instead of the distance clearing my mind, it just increased my sense of starvation. Like fire up my throat, I felt like I was trapped in a desert, on the brink of dying if I didn't get a drop of fresh fluid into my mouth.

The sound of the door opening and shutting had me pivoting on the spot. "I don't need anyth—"

A woman bolted in from the foyer, expression of wrecked worry turning to pure relief as she wrapped her arms around me.

"Mom!" My hands came up like crowbars between us and I shoved her back. With quick steps, I didn't stop retreating until I smacked into the corner bookshelf beside the window. God, the smell of her blood was strong, the beat of her heart sending continual pulses of it at me. My mouth watered and I blinked as my eyes buzzed. Please don't turn red. Don't freaking turn red, dammit. "W-what are you doing here?"

Hurt flashed across her face as I went to a wing chair and clutched onto the backrest for dear life. My legs trembled with fatigue and restraint. Considering the look wasn't shock or fear, I guess my eyes had remained vampire-blue. But they wouldn't for much longer. "I've been waiting outside the castle since the team set out to bring you back. Since I found out both my children were missing… They wouldn't let me inside until you woke."

With our lack of interaction, our relationship was still far from okay. Bigger than that was her bombshell. "Dorian's still missing?" In spite of my fear for him, I couldn't keep this up. My long fangs throbbed, sending sharp jabs into my skull. The simmer of my gut turned into a roiling tidal wave. "Look, Mom, I can't do this right now…"

My excuse to make her leave and subconscious beginnings of a plan to locate Dorian dwindled, as an internal pull to what pumped from her heart and throughout her body grew. It escalated suddenly, becoming so strong that it almost had my bare feet sliding around the wing chair and across the stone. The invisible force was like a giant magnet, beckoning me, calling me to the source of what I needed most. The woman, my mother, standing just behind the couch became faceless with a slow blink of my eyes.

Unable to resist, I tracked the vein up her neck as I unhinged my hands from the wing chair. My bare feet moved over the stone, one foot first, then the other, until I was standing behind the massive L-shaped sectional and in front of my mom. Red glazed my vision and my stare locked on hers. *"Don't* make a sound."

Before she could even react, I yanked her arm out, and my fangs found that sweet, tender spot on her inner wrist. The blood wasn't pure, but it was vampire, and alive. It tasted like magic. Exactly what I needed…and what I'd kill for.

The lounge room faded from sight. Thought and understanding of the act I was committing abandoned me like the father I'd never had. Each pull was fast, making my head spin and my veins hum. As I drank deeper I turned, slinging an arm around the body before me to keep it upright as their legs became rubbery. It didn't matter that the race of their heart was starting to falter. It didn't even register whose body I was clinging to. As the splitting from my gums to my head receded and my stomach settled, there was only the fresh pull of drying-up blood.

Don't give in to the monster.

The unexpected words were internal, a thought from somewhere deep inside of me. An iota of conscience peeking through and shining a light on the horrific act I was close to completing.

In less than a minute, my mom—*my mom*—would be dead. Her killer would be me. Her own daughter.

With a tortured cry, I pried my fangs from her wrist and shuffled her onto the couch. The red from my sight was gone, culled by the blood I'd stolen. The blood I'd almost killed my own mom for. Because I was a monster, and only two things could change that.

With my vision red from fresh tears rather than bloodlust, I took my mom's hand and closed over the gouge across her wrist where my fangs had broken flesh. After giving her a bottle of Kendrick's blood—I wouldn't need it anymore anyway—I compelled her with my eyes. "Forget what I just did to you. Leave this place and never come back. Don't miss Dorian or me. Don't even think about us. Just…be happy. I love you, mom."

Helping her to her feet, the waterworks dried up. "Go now."

Mom said nothing, but she nodded her head. With slow steps she returned to the door, and I watched through the opening to the foyer as she slipped away. I wanted to feel bad for taking what she lived for away from her. But there wasn't enough emotion left to register past the knowledge that she'd be better off without me.

Everyone would.

With slow but unwavering steps, I went and sat on my bed. Glancing up, I saw my hoodie draped around the corner post. Someone had found and returned it? Pulling the Zippo from my jeans, I let myself think of Ty. I wondered how he was coping, if he remembered like Raven had all the heinous things he'd acted out while damned. The need to find him swelled inside me, to see his face again. But seeing the monster I was becoming would only amplify his grief. He'd been through enough because of me already.

I slid the bedside drawer open to put the lighter in, and another object made me pause. Ty's stake. He must have put it there himself.

And as if that wasn't a big screaming sign.

Stuck in transition, I was drawn to the damned. I had a way to track down Marcus. To stop him for good. But the state I was in made me a ticking time bomb waiting to detonate. Moral intentions or not, sooner or later I would lose control completely. I'd kill someone—becoming the very thing I was trying to rid our supernatural world of. Restoring myself—if I even could—would cure my need to kill, but it would also remove that link. Either way I'd lose. And I couldn't live with myself if I restored my conscience and the severity of my emotions—because Kendrick was dead, and nothing could bring him back.

I racked my brain for a third option, a silver lining to the dark cloud my existence had become, and came up blank.

So that was it.

I couldn't bear to cause anyone any more pain, and I couldn't keep my promise to Kendrick. There was no way I could be the hero everyone expected me to be. I was damaged and broken. My soul's mate gone and my own soul splintering. My heart was cold and dead, able to feel a mere fraction of what it could before. I knew that was true, because I was still standing, not racing out to find Ty or breaking down in hysterics at the loss of Kendrick. And while I could think rationally and unemotionally, I needed to take action.

As my hand gripped the silver stake, it gleamed with an intruding ray around the closed drapes as if excited to see the light of day. Fingertips sizzling, I rose up. With slow and purposeful steps through to the lounge, I met the clear glass of the terrace doors, squinting at the sting of sunlight. It was time to call it a day. Not by giving in and turning into the monster writhing inside of me, but by punching my timecard and ending my life.

Lifting the stake, I turned the tip on myself, lining it up over my heart. With an exaggerated blink, I felt my eyes buzz as I stared out at the gardens. The beautiful and pristine expanse of manicured hedges that wound in a labyrinth around various alcoves would be the last thing I saw.

With my free palm against the stake's butt end, I bared down with pressure to drive the silver home—

I froze as the tip bit into my flesh.

The leak of my blood bubbling as if being boiled from the silver hadn't gone unnoticed.

But that's not what kept my pushing hand from finishing me off.

Through the glass, sunlight was now rolling in a golden wave over the garden and...a guy. The golden rays coated his face and exposed arms in the muscle shirt he wore. He stared up at me, fear and pain resonating in his tan features. I let the stake fall from my burnt hands and it clanked down to the stone.

I blinked hard. And then again.

But my eyes weren't playing tricks on me. Not this time. Bathed in glorious sunlight was not the murderous damned I'd last seen him as.

My lips parted with his name. *"Ty."*

LEAVING the guards outside my door and unaware, I went out to the balcony and leaped over the railing. Ty had seen his stake poised over my heart. Did he think I'd been trying to restore myself? Not if he'd seen what I'd almost done to my mom.

I passed through the stone arch into the gardens, squinting at the glare coming off the sun. I felt somehow petrified and calmly ready. I was seconds away from seeing Ty in the flesh and up close. Alive and breathing. But would he be glad to see me, or was he here to stop the monster I was becoming? If so I'd stand there and take it. I'd even welcome it.

My bare-footed steps were soundless over the green blades of grass as I weaved around bends and curves. My hands didn't reach out to catch the leaves of draping trees, but remained clenched in fists.

In the time I'd spent away, the garden had grown and changed, the hint of leaves turning with the approach of fall. But none of that mattered. None of it really even registered.

What did was that strong and irregular beat that belonged to Ty's heart. His beating heart. And the scent of what could only be his blood. Both led me through the curving paths and past the trickling fountain.

I stopped short when I reached another opening. Inside was a weeping willow, its delicate leaves littering the grass with confetti. Sitting cross-legged in the dappled sunlight below the canopy was Ty. The scent of his blood was stronger, but after attacking my mom, I remained in control.

He glanced up with his eyes only, his head remaining still. The raw guilt in his golden gaze hit me like a stun gun. "I'm sorry. I shouldn't have left you—but they wouldn't let me stay in the castle until you'd voted on the wolf alliance. I should have fought harder."

If my heart could beat right now it would have been racing. Ty wasn't here to kill me, and seeing him across this alcove made me want to run and leap into his arms. To hold him close and breathe him in. Even if just for a moment.

But we weren't the same people anymore. We'd both changed.

Ty for the better. Me for the worse.

And even though my hunger wasn't raging, I couldn't give in just in case my thin control snapped. In the past I'd already hurt him enough. "I…" I didn't know what to say, couldn't find the words to start with.

Ty half shrugged and glanced down at his hand on his knee. "Tingles…now that I'm as much pure vampire as lycan. Guess I got what I wanted after all," he said, looking like he wished he'd never wanted that for himself in the first place. Like his wish to be on an even turf with Kendrick was to blame for so much that had come to pass.

I glanced up at the castle's moss-covered stone wall and at the terrace doors I'd seen Ty from. Of all the things I could have said to him, a lie rushed from my mouth. "I was going to restore myself."

When my head twisted back, I couldn't look him in the eye. I was too ashamed.

"No you weren't."

My head snapped up in surprise to see Ty's sad smile.

"You couldn't take what you did to your mom. You can't stand what I've done to you." Willow branches rustled as he got up and walked over. "But you can't give up. You can't stop the transition. I was one of them. I know. We feel each other. And with Kendrick… with him…*gone*, you need that link to find Marcus. To finish this once and for all. And you probably don't want it, but I'm offering to help." That sad smile took hold of his entire face with raw desperation. "I *need* to help."

I stepped back and shook my head. "Nothing can help me. Not even you."

It was Ty that looked up at my terrace doors then before returning his gold gaze to me. "I can help keep your cover. I can curb your hunger." He opened his mouth and pricked his finger with a single fang. Crimson welled and he held out the digit. "Let me show you."

I shook my head. After what I'd almost done to my mom, I couldn't be trusted with blood. Especially his. Even before the transition, my control with Ty had been challenged at best. He was my kryptonite. Now his vampiric side was level with his lycan one. And as a transitionee, I craved Pure Blood the most. "Ty, no."

As I went to step back further, Ty smudged the source over my bottom lip and my heel caught on an exposed tree root.

Catching his wrist to keep upright, my tongue forked out against my will and licked. Entranced by the taste, I pushed his finger into my mouth. My lids slid shut and I almost moaned.

Boom boom.

The beat took off in my chest and my eyes flung open as I all but threw his hand away. Resisting the desire to snatch the digit back up, I lifted and pressed a shaking palm over my heart. My *beating* heart. I whispered around elongating fangs. *"How?"*

Without fear or hesitation, Ty led me over to the willow's base and pulled me down beside him. "I was there when Marcus knocked you out. I tried to stop him, but he got away, and I was weak. I stumbled into that cavern and dropped by your side. There was no heartbeat. No breath. I thought you were dead." His whole face strained and he gulped as if swallowing a brick. "I was so desperate, I would have done anything. I fed you my blood. Your mouth and your throat worked as you swallowed…and then your heart started up. I thought maybe I hadn't turned you. That you had somehow remained a vampire—until your heart stopped again."

He glanced up at my terrace doors for the second time.

"That blood in the bag was mine. I didn't want the vampires to know you were transitioning until you'd woken up. I thought it would last long enough for them to let me back in to get to you. I hoped it would give you purpose to fight on and kill that asshole brother of yours. And before you start the *'I can't endanger you'* spiel, understand this…" Ty rolled his shoulders back with a crack, crack. "I'm not staying out of this. With the vamps and our wolves, I will stop him. The only question is, will you be there to help me?"

I'd seen that fierce determination before. There was no talking him out of this. And the only way to keep us both safe—or at least safer—was to join forces. This was the third option I'd been waiting for. A way to stay in transition without turning into a murderer. But something made me hesitate.

"You do want to find Marcus and end all of this? End him?" When I finally nodded, Ty sighed long and hard. "Then I guess you're stuck with me."

Stuck between a rock and the cliff-side of heaven and hell, I stared up at the sky. With my eyes watering, I prayed I wasn't making another wrong choice. "I guess so."

SECONDS SLIPPED into minutes as time passed after my agreement to Ty's offer. He stared at his outstretched legs on the grass, turmoil in his silvery golden gaze and tightness along his exposed chiseled arms. Like he had so much to say but had no clue where to start.

I kept quiet too, the beat of my heart still alive, but slowly fading.

After everything we'd been through, I didn't know what to say, either. I felt no anger at Ty for what he'd done to me while damned. None of that had been him, the real him. He'd died protecting me and my race against the damned. My own father had killed him. Then my twin had forced him to take a life to turn damned. If Ty had never been in that alley when he'd first seen me, hadn't been the one to stop me from killing that quarterback, he never would have gone through any of this. But I didn't know how to begin saying any of that to him. Didn't know how to start out the biggest *I'm sorry* of my life.

When Ty pulled a soft pack from his jeans and flicked one cigarette out, I remembered what I'd shoved into my hoodie before my leap over the balcony. Fishing my iPod and the Zippo free, I cracked open the lid as Ty started to tap the butt on the leg of his jeans. "Light?"

Ty met my questioning gaze and bit the butt between his teeth. Then he leaned in close, not breaking our intense eye contact as his body heat warmed me and my thumb flicked the roller. A deep draw in and then he leaned back against the bark. "I started after I stopped breathing. Made me feel normal, alive I guess...even for just a few minutes."

Lost for what to say, a slide of my thumb began playing music while my other hand got to work cracking the Zippo open and shut.

"I left it in your pocket when I put the stake in your drawer." Ty's words drifted out in puffs of smoke as he glanced sideways at the lighter. Sunlight caught the side of his head, making it look like his black hair had a golden shimmer. "Even if you didn't want to see me, I wanted you to at least know I was alive. That you had *fixed* me."

I paused my open-shut on the Zippo. "Why wouldn't I want to see you?"

A shrug and his ongoing silence with a fresh draw on the tobacco was his only response. Then the song *Start again* by Red started playing from my iPod's speaker.

Ty lifted his body on his arms and shifted a fraction closer to me on the grass. Warmth radiated from his tan and black-veined flesh as he neared. A lycan-hybrid, restored-damned heater. Ty reached into his other pocket then. What he pulled out caught the filtered sunlight and shone intensely red. His mother's amulet. "Found this in my hand when I came to."

He didn't look up, and I wondered if he thought I'd given it back as a statement. To say I didn't want him anymore. Nothing could be further from the truth. And I couldn't let the possible uncertainty stand. "I'm not immune to the silver anymore. But after I restored you…"

"I was."

With a deep sigh he tucked the stone back into the denim. Then he reached out, hand hovering for a moment, and then covering mine as he peered up into my eyes. Something heavy weighed behind his altered irises that now had an inner ring of blue and remaining chips of maroon. Like Marcus's and Raven's. But even as his lips parted, no sound came out. Long seconds went by and his eyes fell. His hand slipped away. He butted out the cig on an exposed tree root and began tugging at tufts of grass.

The severe emotion that battled in his expression and muscle-ticking body took me by surprise.

"I so badly want to ask if we can start again." He clenched his fists. I'd never seen him look so scared. "It kills me to be so close to you and somehow so far away. But I can't do it. I can't get past all the things that have happened. I just…can't."

My heartbeat stopped. Flat-out quit.

In its stillness, an ache took over, the muscle dying to drum. All my pinned-down emotions flared as I dared to look at him. Leaves danced and wind ruffled his hair as he retrieved another cigarette and started up the tapping on his leg. The old Ty, the one who owned my heart—beating or not—was right beside me. But he wasn't the same. He knew I'd been with Kendrick. He'd tasted Kendrick's blood when he drank from my vein. I winced at the memory of Kendrick dead in my arms. The next image of me taking his vein for the first time in the training room felt like I'd just been sliced in two —straight through my chest. Ty hadn't asked about the details yet. And I couldn't talk about it. Any of it. Not now. Not with him. I could barely stand to sit here, half-alive while my soul's mate was cold and still. I wondered now if his body was up in the Baldassare suite being prepped for a funeral.

So much had changed. Been broken, then fixed, and broken again. I wasn't the same, either. I never would be again. And Ty deserved so much better than me, someone who'd waited for him and not moved on and given up. There was no starting back from where we'd left off. Too much had happened. I couldn't forgive myself for my failures and betrayal any more than he could forgive me for them.

So here we were. Stuck. "I…I can't, either."

Ty tore his eyes away and stared up at the blinding sun as he reclined on his elbows. Despite the casual posture change, the muscles up his arms were tight and I heard the dry gulp of his throat as he swallowed.

"We're both damaged. Beyond repair. Kendrick's dead because of me."

"Amelia, that's not—"

A sudden burn like the bonfire I'd scarred my arm in had me crying out and cut off his argument. I shrank back against the willow and the cover of its draping branches.

Ty was right there with me, trying to look me over as I squirmed. "What's wrong? What happened?"

Filtered sun broke through as wind swayed the branches. The ray that caught on my collarbone burned like a hot poker, creating instant bubbles across my skin. I bit my lip to keep from crying out as a streaming ray sent a face-long welt from my forehead down to my chin. "What the hell is happening?"

"We need to get you inside." Ty whipped off his muscle shirt and held it up to shield my face. I huddled in close to him, hoodie-covered arms coming up to cover my chest. "You're becoming allergic to sunlight."

CHAPTER 39

*S*tanding before a massive, wall-length, gilt mirror above the vanity, I glared at my fogged-up reflection. With hot water flowing from the showerhead above the massive, claw-footed bath, the tiled room was filling up with the stuff. The steam was wet on my skin and heated up the oversized square room. Even through the fog, my mirror image disgusted me. The scars, the black veins that were hidden now that I'd emptied the glass in my hands, the brightening crimson glow that faded…I hated it all. Every visible or hidden trait was a memory I didn't want to live with. A reminder of every step I'd taken to get to this point. Of everything I'd lost, too.

Unable to stand the sight for a second longer, I dropped my clothes and hurdled into the bath's hot spray. The water burned, hot to a normal vampire, but scalding against my chilled skin. And I didn't turn down the temperature. I wanted to feel the sting. Not to dull the emotional agony that ran rampant through my frozen heart and soul, but to amplify it. I picked up the soap and began scrubbing, wishing the vanilla-scented block was sandpaper and not silky soft.

It was midday the next day. Dorian was still MIA.

And today was Kendrick's funeral.

The day he would be laid to rest…forever. Right now, his body was being tended to in preparation for the mournful event. And then I'd have my last minutes to say goodbye before Ty and I carried his casket down to the main hall. Knowing Ty would be there to help was both comforting and terrible at the same time. Ty was alive and Kendrick was dead. I didn't wish for him to be dead in Kendrick's place. Of course I didn't. But it felt so wrong that he was alive when Kendrick wasn't. Why did it have to be one or the other? I guess that was my living hell. Having one alive with the knowledge that the other would forever be gone…*because of me*.

When my body felt as raw as my heart and soul, I clambered from the bath and wrapped a towel around my body. I wished for the millionth time that it had been me. That both guys were alive and breathing and I was the cold and stiff one lying in my deathbed.

I faced the mirror again, only able to see the colored blur from my waist up to my head above the marble bench top. Clasping my hands together, I sent out a wishful prayer. "Take me. Please. For the love of—"

The bathroom door swung in without warning and Raven stomped in. Her pale face was flushed and her eyes were bloodshot. Tears created glistening tracks down her face, dripping down to the Burton hoodie she wore. Kendrick's. "He's dead because of you!" She clenched her fists in front of her like she wanted to throttle the life from me. "You may as well have snapped his neck yourself."

I jolted and clutched the towel tighter around me. I felt way too exposed, and not because I was dripping wet and naked beneath this towel. Raven's unedited words were right. There was no point denying it. And God, that smell coming off that hoodie was all him. How he'd smelled when he was alive. With a nod, I noticed the anger and despair across her face, and the tremors her legs created below white pants. Her emotional state made something else very clear. "You were in love with him."

Instead of looking shocked or guilty, she bared her teeth. "More than you ever were. Every day since they locked me down in those catacombs he visited me. Every. Single. Day." Steam swirled out with her words, then was sucked back in with a quick breath. "Unless he was away on one of your suicide missions. In over one hundred years I'd never met someone so genuine, so honest and caring." She stalked closer and got in my face. "He was falling for me, too."

Her vampire blood swelled in the hot room and I took a step back out of instinct. After emptying that glass of Ty's blood, my heart was animated and my bloodlust was simmering on the sidelines.

Not knowing any of that, Raven smiled as though she thought I were intimidated.

"I know he was," I said quietly. There was no point mentioning when I'd seen them kissing in the training room. I knew what had prompted that reaction. "When I walked in on you in Kendrick's room watching snowboarding races, I saw something there. Kendrick didn't admit it and I didn't want to believe it, but deep down I knew he had feelings for you."

"And you couldn't stand for him to want anyone else." She stalked closer to jab a finger at my chest. "So you lured him out there knowing he'd die to save you."

A quick retreat back had my legs hitting the side of the bath and forcing me to sit. It felt like I'd just been punched in the guts. "*What?* How can you even think that? I've known Kendrick all my

497

life. He was my best friend." My soul's mate and my boyfriend, I thought without saying. "I contacted him to warn him of Marcus's attack. I never told him where I was. I didn't want him to come for me."

"But you knew he would."

Raven came closer again, and I lifted a hand to cover my nose as my fangs began to ache. Leashed or not, what thrummed in her veins was alive and addictive. And I was the damned equivalent of a junkie that was forever on that downward spiral.

"A guy like that? He never would have given up on you."

"You think I don't know that?" I slid sideways on the bath and paced over to the marble vanity, keeping my back to her. In trying to protect everyone by going out on my own, I had done the exact opposite. And now Kendrick and Vanessa were dead. Dorian probably was, too. Silent crimson tears streaked down my face. "I never stop wishing that it had been me. That I could take his place. That—"

"You're dead."

The non-threatening tone of Raven's voice had me pivoting around to face her. She was looking from my towel-covered chest up to my mouth.

There was no fear in her voice or expression as she spoke. "It doesn't make sense, but...breath only passed your lips when you were speaking. You're not breathing. You're turning damned."

The beat of my heart had died down, not revived for long because Ty's blood had come from that glass rather than his vein. I let my tongue poke at the tips of my fangs in my mouth. Doing the in-out now would just highlight that I hadn't drawn a normal breath since she stormed in here. Tucking my towel into itself to keep it up, my hunger spiked. I curled my fingers around the edge of the vanity to hold myself back. "It happened before Ty came to my rescue.

Marcus tried to get me to complete the conversion…on Kendrick. I refused and…" Fresh tears welled and I sniffed them back. *"Marcus broke his freaking neck."*

Raven stared at me for a few moments, as if she were deciding if she believed me or not. Slowly the rage in her face morphed into sorrow. "He did love you…and trust you. And I'm not saying it's not your fault. It is. But I don't get it. How is your heart still beating?"

"Ty's blood. When he found me after Marcus fled, he tried to revive me with it." With a quick double beat my heart went dormant again. My hold on the vanity squeezed tighter. "The effects are short-lasting. Only his blood seems to work."

"Because he's restored." Raven's maroon-chipped eyes blazed. "Which means you can link to another damned. To that murdering asshole Marcus."

Facing the sink, I snatched the glass up and sucked down the dregs. It wasn't enough for more than a few beats, but it let me get what I needed to say out. "We're going after him. And…I'm going to kill him."

"Then I'm going, too." At my flat-out refusal, Raven smiled. But there was no warmth, just goading triumph. "I go—or the RVC gets a big fat surprise when I tell them what you are. What you're pretending not to be. A ticking time bomb they'll need to put down."

The single word from my mouth was sharp. "Fine." I placed the glass back down and made eye contact in the mirror. "But I'm not a babysitter. I won't miss a chance to finish this just to protect your ass."

Raven walked to the door and opened it wide. "That makes two of us."

∼

DRESSED in brilliant white and gold, I walked into the Baldassare suite, my gown as heavy as a mountain of stones. Every surface and counter was jam-packed with vases filled with colorful floral arrangements. The fragrant smell that filled the entire suite along with Ty's blood made me want to puke. I wasn't ready for this. To see his body lying there, breathless and still. I wasn't ready to say goodbye. How could I ever be? Today or in another four hundred-plus years, being here and seeing him…like that…

Oh, God. I couldn't do it—

Ty's calloused fingers grazed the side of my hand. "You can do it. You must."

Despite his strong, encouraging words, I heard his voice crack. He knew what this was doing to me, and it was torture. I could tell by the clench of his jaw, the way he gripped the cigarette pack in his black pants like a lifeline. The way he hadn't left my side since my run-in with Raven over an hour ago.

He squeezed my nape under my free-flowing hair and let his hand run down to the small of my back. "Go on. I'll be right here."

Since the wolf alliance, Ty had been allowed full access to the castle, so long as he remained under my strict observation. Which was laughable. In my current state, I was a much higher threat than Ty could ever be.

Without looking at him, I blinked hard at the coffin that was centered in the lounge room and supported on a metal stand. It was time to say…goodbye.

My heart galloped faster with every slow step, the muscle straining after being still and feeling like it wanted to go back to the quiet. This effect Ty's blood had on me seemed to reignite my conscience too. And all the heartbreaking feelings that went along with it.

One more step. Then another.

With shaking hands I rested my palms on the closed coffin lid. Images rose of how he'd looked the second before dying and as Marcus took hold and twisted. The blood, the bruises, that confusion as his lids fluttered open.

Oh God, oh God, oh freaking God.

I gripped the wood and levered it all the way open. Instant tears stung my eyes and choked up my throat. *"Kendrick."* Even though his motionless face was clean and he'd been dressed in a pristine suit, I still saw the blood that had splattered his face and the bruises from Marcus's fists...and my own. The top button of his shirt was undone—because the bone protruding sideways got in the way of buttoning it up. My chest constricted and I let out a soul-deep sob. Crimson sorrow streaked down my face and stained my gown. "I'm sorry. I'm fucking sorry."

At my side, Ty said nothing, but his hand went to my back and stayed there.

While I wept, I saw a movie reel of all the things Kendrick would never get to do. Of all the things he'd never do again. Smile, laugh, go snowboarding, run, hang out, hug me, show up with TVD, hold my hand, read my mind and share my thoughts, have a life with a girl who deserved him, grow old, have kids. Be the ruler he wanted to be for his mom and their line.

Tell me he loves me.

Words continued in my head, not to Kendrick, but to a higher power. *Bring him back, pleeease. I'll do anything. Take me instead. Just bring him the hell back.*

My silent pleas went unanswered while my tears kept on flowing. Staring down at the open coffin, time passed, endless and fleeting at the same time. Eventually my tears dried up, a tank running dry.

When I took a final wet sniff, a new scent other than Ty's blood and the existing flowers reached my nose. I rubbed my eyes and turned to catch a guy standing by the overflowing foyer table. "Dorian?" I rushed over and flung my arms around him. "My God. Are you okay? Where have you been?"

The blank stare on his face sent a chill through me. "Been?" He frowned, looking dazed and confused. "Nowhere. I mean...I don't know." Unfocused gazed lifting over my shoulder, he tipped his chin up. "Why's Ty here, and what's with the casket?"

I glanced back at the open deathbed and it felt like I'd been stabbed through the heart. Wincing as Ty took a few steps our way, I looked back at my brother. His response dumbfounded me, almost as much as the lack of surprise or shock in his features. Ty was here on vampire turf—breathing and with a heartbeat—not leading a horde of damned to attack. And we were in the Baldassare suite. There was only one Baldassare left who could be in that casket. "What is wrong with you?"

Ty was beside me then. The words out of his mouth were quick and to the point. "Marcus is the damned commander. He killed Kendrick."

Nothing. Not even a blink. A gasp. A step back. Nada.

"Vanessa's dead," I strained to say, desperate to see even a glimmer of reaction. Some recognition that he understood the words coming out of my mouth. "Did you hear me?"

"Oh, okay." He didn't meet my eyes but the slightest hint of a frown creased his face.

And I knew exactly why.

Ty's body tensed as if preparing to strike. "He's being compelled."

Unable to pin down that new scent that lingered in the air, my shoulders slumped. "By Marcus. He's still using him."

I stepped closer to my brother, wanting to break the spell he was under. Before I could try, his hand behind his back swung in front of him. "I need to deliver these to you."

The bunch of black calla lilies wrapped in crêpe paper explained the smell as he thrust them into my hands. The flower Caius used to give me when he visited before I'd known who he was, and the same one he'd left on my body after he thought he'd kill me.

"I gotta go now." Dorian retreated like a flash out the door and Ty went to chase after him.

"No, wait."

Ty growled, but walked back to stand before me as I plucked a note from the attached plastic stick. The choice of flower was a clear hint as to the sender. And it wasn't Caius. My heart almost stopped. And not from lack of restored-damned blood. I opened the small white envelope and removed the handwritten note.

"Oh…God."

Ty snatched the note from my hand. "From Marcus?"

I nodded—

"Amelia?" Raven poked her head in from the main door Dorian had fled through. Her gold gown shimmered, but not as much as her reddened eyes that threatened to release like a dam. "The funeral's ready to begin. I just—I need to say one last goodbye."

At my side, Ty took my hand and squeezed, not needing to say he'd back me up in this—all the way.

I glanced back through the opening to where Kendrick's body lay. "There's not going to be a funeral."

THANK YOU FOR READING!

Dear Reader,

Thank you for reading *Web of Lies (Blood Bound Series Book 3)*. If you enjoyed this book please turn to the last page an select a star rating, or if you have a moment to spare, you can leave a review. It doesn't have to be long—one or two sentences would be amazing. The more reviews a book has the more Amazon is willing to put it in front of potential readers. As an indie author, I don't have a big publishing company promoting my work, so every little bit helps and I'd love for my audience to be a part of it. I read every one of my reviews and completely appreciate the thoughts and opinions of all my readers.

http://bit.ly/reviewwol

Thank you, J.L. Myers

THANK YOU FOR READING!

Continue reading for a sneak peek at the final installment in the Blood Bound Series, *Born to Die*.

AMELIA'S STORY ENDS IN...

Born to Die - Blood Bound #4

*B*link. Blink.

The dark blindness behind my eyelids disappeared as my body took form.

Blink. Blink.

Wet tracks rolled down my face in a silent display of grief. Not because of anything happening in the here and now—I wasn't in either of those places. With vibrant green underfoot that spanned out into black nothingness, I knew this was a vision. One my mind and vampire spirit-gifted Sight had conjured. Here and now I was occupying my own body—in a future that had yet to play out. My hands were raised before me and shaking. Like I was saying goodbye to someone I couldn't touch.

And I was devastated.

With another blink, the vision warped.

Drip. Drip. Drip.

The sound came from an altar. Glossy blood had escaped a brimming chalice to drip from the altar's edges. I stood in front. Not alone. Marcus, my twin—my enemy—faced me in shitkickers and dirty jeans, his smile forced and morbid. The sight of him struck me as eerily familiar. I'd seen this. In a vision I had before learning Marcus was the damned commander.

Like before, his white shirt was unbuttoned, but the black alchemy symbol painted across his pale chest was instantly overshadowed. Beneath a blood-blooming tear in his shirt was a starburst of scarred and red-splotched skin.

I had staked him again? My damned-restoring ability had already failed to cull my twin's damned DNA once before. So why...?

The mindset change of my future self killed my burning curiosity. With no fear of the guy facing me, I was flooded with urgency while a deep sense of grief-stricken readiness almost floored me. "It's time."

Marcus joined our hands, trapping something between them. The look on his face was...compassionate? "You sure you're ready for this?"

My answer was displayed with a dance of blue sparks down my arms to our joined hands. "It's what we were born for."

Red joined the game, sparking from Marcus's chest to disappear beneath the white cotton. When the sparks reappeared from his long cuffs to meet our joined palms, our powers mingled, my blue lightning yin to his red lightning yang. Sources made for each other, destined to join—

With my fingers locked over my twin's knuckles, my body began to hum with power and heat.

The moment our voltage combined, the color changed to purple. Torture invaded my body at the same time as Marcus's—I could feel his pain somehow. Despite the strain across his angled features, his lips parted with a gurgle of blood to speak. But I couldn't make out the words as warmth dripped from my eyes, my nose…and my ears. Blood.

Unable to look away from Marcus's own bleeding eyes, I tried to speak. But the me who was witnessing the future unfold had no voice to question what we were doing or why. All I felt was the certainty that this was the only way, and…

Wait, was my heart beating?

No. It was racing. Impossible, as a vampire transitioning into a damned.

The sudden shift of power was as unmissable as it was unstoppable. Violet light split from our bodies, joining the surrounding black with a sonic boom.

One last blip and my heart stalled, freezing in my chest. My bones turned to liquid. My brain fritzed. All power and sensation fled my body.

As I fell, I felt no pain, no regret. This had been my choice. Somehow I knew that with total clarity as Marcus hit the grass beside me.

Get your copy now: http://bit.ly/bb4btd

CONNECT WITH J.L. MYERS

If you want to stay updated about my latest book releases and get
freebies or exclusive review offers, join my VIP list!
Visit : www.jlmyers.com and enter your email address. You can
unsubscribe at any time and your email will be kept 100% private.

Come check out my author page on Facebook. I'd love to hear
from you:
https://www.facebook.com/author.jlmyers

Come say hi on twitter or Connect with me on Goodreads!
https://twitter.com/authorjlmyers
https://www.goodreads.com/author/show/7178370.J_L_Myers

Don't miss my new releases. Follow me on Amazon & Bookbub
https://www.amazon.com/J.L.-Myers/e/B00DK4P0EO/
https://www.bookbub.com/authors/j-l-myers

MORE BOOKS BY J.L. MYERS

THE BLOOD BOUND SERIES

(New Adult Paranormal Romance)

What Lies Inside

Made By Design

Web Of Lies

Born To Die

~

OTHER BOOKS

Nerve Damage

(A Chilling Psychological Thriller)

~

FALLEN ANGEL SERIES

Ashes of Eden

Dawn of Reckoning

Breaking Lucifer

Cold-Blooded Fate

Falling Stars

Copyright © 2015 by J.L. Myers

The moral right of the author had been asserted.

This book is a work of fiction. Names, characters, places and events are either the product of the author's imagination or, if real, are used fictitiously. Any resemblance to actual people living or dead is purely coincidental.

All rights reserved

No part of this literary work may be reproduced, stored in a retrieval system, or transmitted, in any form or by any means, graphic, electronic or mechanical, including photocopying, taping and recording, without prior written permission from the author J.L. Myers.

Cover design by Digital Print Australia.
Cover art © 2015 J.L. Myers.

Visit the Website:
www.jlmyers.com

Paperback ISBN 978-0-9875653-7-2
E-Book ISBN 978-0-9875653-5-8

ABOUT THE AUTHOR

Jessica L Myers' vivid imagination and quiet demeanor as a child led her to the imaginary worlds of books. Even at a young age, her love for the supernatural was prevalent, with her first loved books being R.L. Stine's *Goosebumps* series. Following that she took an interest in other non-fantasy fiction, including Virginia C. Andrews series *Flowers in the Attic*.

In her teen years, Jessica spent many school hours writing poetry and dark short stories and took up sketching some of the terrifying things that came from the graphic night terrors she'd grown up with.

As an adult and after meeting the love of her life, Jessica got married and started a small construction business with her husband. With the birth of her son, Jessica suffered PPD and found escape in her books and their fantasy landscapes. It was during this time that her need to write flourished. In 2009 the decision was made and the first words to her YA novel *What Lies Inside* were written.

When Jessica isn't immersed in writing about extraordinary characters with dangerous and deadly obstacles to overcome, she likes to spend time with her two kids and husband, curl up with a good book, or watch anything and everything supernatural.

Contact J.L. directly:
www.jlmyers.com

 facebook.com/author.jlmyers

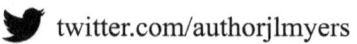 twitter.com/authorjlmyers

instagram.com/authorjlmyers